These Stained Glass Hearts

Sienna C. Jones

ISBN 978-0-6454522-0-4

Cover design by Miriam Schwardt.

To John and Glenda Schubert,
thank you.

To those who find themselves looking up at the moon and dreaming of a world beyond, may this world be one that you feel accepted, loved, and validated in.

'Even the Gods knew that their souls were one.'

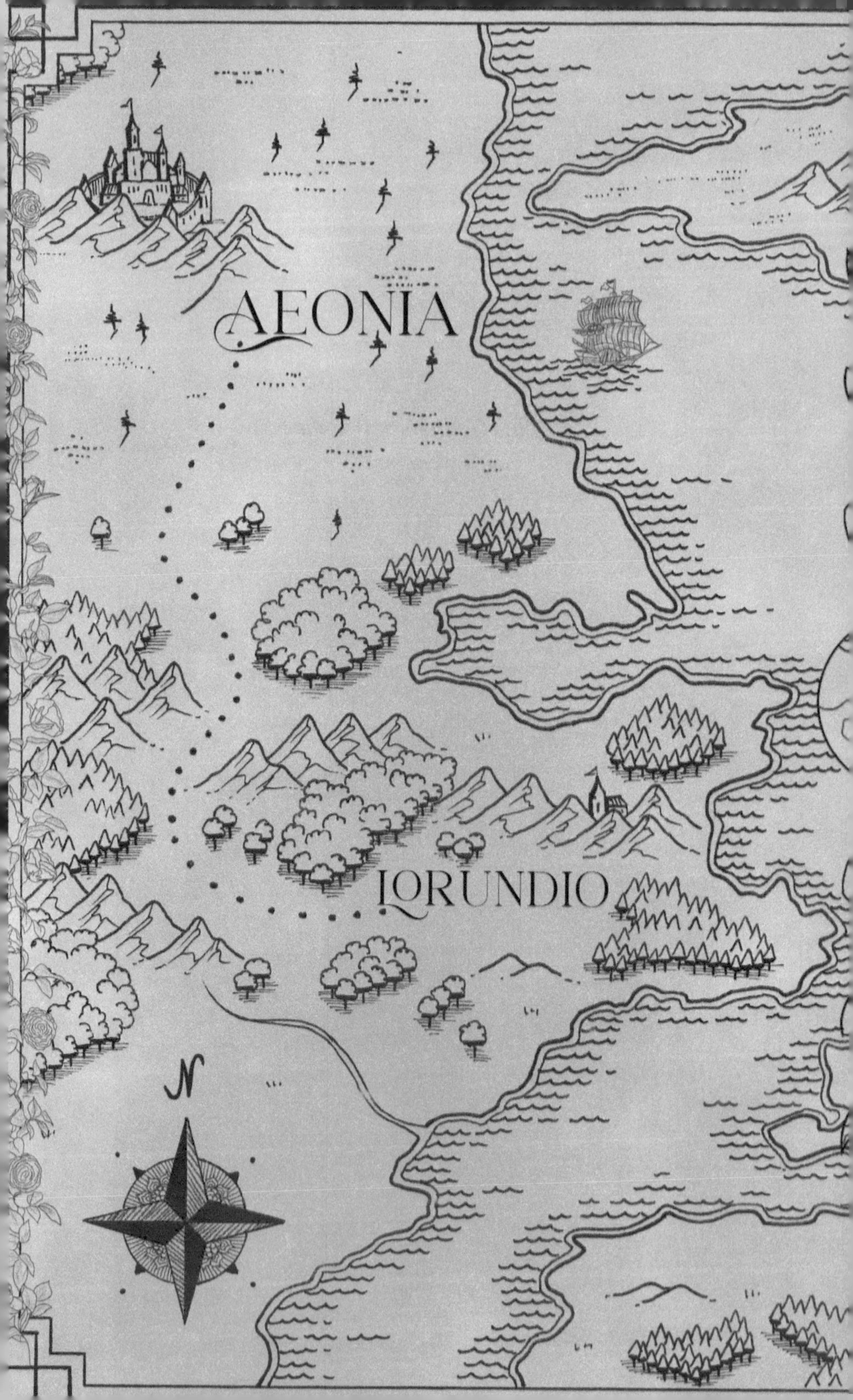
AEONIA
LORUNDIO
N

THE
ELEMENTAL
REALMS
SHINRIN

The Goddess of Sommsia

Holder of the Sommsia Realms

Fire, Sunlight, Warmth, Healing

The Goddess of Autumnia

Holder of the Autumnia Realms

Nature, Death, World-Warping, Change

The Goddess of Whyntiou

Holder of the Whyntiou Realms

Weather, Memory, Water, Storms

The Goddess of Flora

Holder of the Flora Realms

Rebirth, Renewal, Late Awakenings

Before we begin...

Following two souls who were destined to be one from the beginning, this tale studies the lives of Queen Althea Evangeline and King Kylen Noxwell.

Whilst the genuine story begins with our Queen awakening from a trance, the prologue may be confusing to you first-time readers. So, don't be afraid to revisit the prologue at a later time. Perhaps at the end of this book, at the beginning of the next... or even at the end of this entire story.

As then, with your knowledge of this history, the character's fates, and the fatalities along the way, you may gain a new sense of understanding of the God's intentions.

- W.N

PROLOGUE
THE TRANCE OF THE ELEMENTS

Death was crafted to appear as a delicacy when it consumed one's body and soul. It was whispered to caress the burdens of one's mortality away, and stitch the wounds forgotten long ago shut.

Perhaps that was why she didn't fear it now. Not as it took a mortal-like form, approaching her with a smile treading faintly across *his* twitching lips.

This darkness that danced around her was dreadfully deep. So inevitably deep and unyielding. It called to her like a whisper in the wind. Like a melody sung by the cruellest of creatures. However, there was almost something familiar to it… something like a distant memory. One that was lost but never truly forgotten. Because if it was forgotten, it wouldn't have found a way to come back, and that could have been so much worse.

Perhaps the lost Gods of the Whyntiou Realms were playing games with her. She always knew they were the Gods relating to the art of memory and emotion. Or perhaps, it was the Flora Realms infusing poison into the air through the glorious nature rumoured to bloom in this dying kingdom all those millions of years ago. *Amusing,* she had half the mind to sing, although it seemed as though her words were no longer under her control.

The girl's fingers dug into the scratched wood of the golden windowsill, feeling and mindlessly brushing away the golden ashes that coated her freckled skin. It was only when she felt a prick did she look down, automatically reaching for the splinter as she'd done so many times before.

It would've been just like all those other times if she hadn't noticed the slight difference in the bubble of blood to burst on her palm—the fact that it was lighter, less sticky, and stained the hem of her white dress red instead of black.

This isn't real, she found herself genuinely realising, and that forced her to take a breath and look around with her eyes darting in every possible direction.

The vision of her room at her father's palace, of the shadows standing tall before her, even the jagged sway in the distant creaking branches… none of it was real. She wasn't home, and the redness of her blood was enough evidence to turn her amusement into riveting anger. Oh, anger, anger, anger: what a cruel, maddening burden for a woman like her to hold.

A blurred hand appeared through the shadows before her, gracefully extending its half-formed palm that caught a shifting glisten of scarlet moonlight. The girl stared, however, as her mind was unable to make sense of what she was seeing. It dawned on her then that the last time she'd checked she was on her way to a kingdom destined to burn—and she had been preparing to become *the Queen*, *the bride*, the murderer of the man who unknowingly held the matches.

Putting her long-lived wit aside, the plan was that she was going to wed the enemy who'd managed to live up to all her father had said across the ages. All the loss, the agony, the pain… that was all his doing, and all would be just when her dagger slithers between his ribs the night she becomes his lawfully wedded bride.

By law, once the kingdom becomes hers, and her beloved husband's throne is nothing but ashes, it becomes her father's too —and he promised her so much more as a reward. *"Soon,"* he'd always whisper into the phantom of the night, *"this will all be over, and you will finally get to see the world I've crafted for you."* The world she'd only ever dreamt of.

Constantly through the recent weeks, she had to remind herself that it would be her walking away in the end, and he, the enemy, would be left to witness her grace, her beauty, as his heart slowed, and his breaths became nothing more than a distant memory.

He was a fool anyway.

A fool who tricked children, cursed nightmares, and stole the youth from innocents. Her father had told her that his kingdom was the most frightening of all, and after meeting him once and falling victim to his games, she no longer underestimated it.

Both then and now, he, the enemy, said that he was playing by the Gods accord; that if she for once believed in the Gods and their bullshit, she would understand him. But it was ridiculous. He was ridiculous. This entire plan was ridiculous—and she owed the child she once was to make his death hurt.

The Princess, taking a breath, extended her hand out past the windowsill, feeling as the curse came to life despite the trance her mind was trapped within. The dark, black, cloudy magick swarmed from her chest and found its way to her palms, mimicking the shadows of the man before her. Only, her curse was darker and thicker, like a gushing river, or a blazing fire. Whereas his was frail, angelic: timid before such power, and yet in awe of its beauty.

Watching her carefully, the shadows narrowed their distorted eyes on the intricate details of her swirling magick. Did it want to reach towards it, feel it, understand it…? If so, this girl knew that if it did just that whatever force it was reaching to her with would be shattered within half a second.

Perhaps maybe she should encourage it, it would certainly wake them both up.

Her magick was catastrophic, it was ungodly. It ached for the taste of blood, it yearned for the whispers of death. She shouldn't even call it magick; it was the curse of her father and the two he bargained it from—the two brothers, the two creators, who shook their heads at the rumours of greed.

No greed partook in the formation of this force, instead, it stemmed from the revenge she so easily understood.

It was bizarre, but she had a faint memory of meeting the infamous brothers once. Though as she stood in the darkness of the night, with the curtain rattling in the near distance, nothing was clear—not even her name, her role, or her purpose.

She was simply just existing.

With a tug, she allowed the cowering darkness to take shelter in the only thing that she could offer: her soul. And she watched as the blurred, unknown male dissolved into a twine of shadows that struck for her before she could even take the smallest of steps back.

The shadows seemed to fit with ease, leading her to question if she'd always been one with the cowering darkness of this world.

Instantly at his touch, the hairs on her arms stood on end, alerting her to the danger that for once wasn't *her*. *But who was he?* She found her lips whispering, though the lack of sound to startle this furious night told her that even here her voice meant nothing.

The girl expected to be scared, yet she could not bring herself to sheer away. It was almost exciting studying the shifting shadows of the male's face as the ghost of him haunted the passing wind. It was almost thrilling to watch his reaction as she flexed her fingers and felt her hidden darkness meet and dance through *his*.

But who was he? He couldn't be just a phantom—a mere

ghost born with the curse of taunting her. It had to be something far more cruel. It had to be someone far more treacherous than the shadows tracing her scars.

As far as she knew, he wasn't her father.

This shadow was a stranger, no matter how familiar it felt; and this stranger tugged her forward as her skin began to burn with the ash of history.

All at once, within a single fragment of time, Althea Evangeline felt the Elemental Markings, a system of magick so raw and untameable, slice through her skin. It formed a pattern engraving her flesh that now labelled her as one of *their* own. It labelled the magick she had no control of… no recollection of holding. The magick that her father craved to erase from the minds of all.

The shadow's hand tightened its hold on hers. Practically begging her to hear it: screaming at her to react in any other way. But she couldn't, she wouldn't. It was comforting, feeling someone, rather *something*, lose their mind because she was stronger than what they had intended. It offered her a break, a chance to catch her racing heart.

Why? It asked her. The whispers were full of such confusion that she couldn't help but grin deviously. *Oh, my princess. My sweet, sweet princess. Your existence has never been kind to you—has it? Oh no, no, no.*

If only she told this concerned soul just what her fate held for her now—how now everything and all that she knew was indefinite. She had the markings that her father wished to demolish. The markings she had killed so many for.

But why wasn't her mind racing—Why was her body not yet in shock?

If she was sane, she would be freaking out, and yet everything felt silent, soft, though cold? Was it the curse wishing for her to think and act wisely, or was it the Elemental Markings making a mockery at how delicate she seemed beneath its control?

Narrowing the shape of his eyes, he saw how the curse controlled her, how her father, without even realising it, was trying to keep her away from this new and foreign magick. They could feel it in the air—the way the curse was spiralling, wishing to attack. He pitied her, his mouth forming words of sorrow that silently caressed her burning ears.

Turning on her then, the darkness clouded her vision with its own quizzical magick as its hands clasped her lips shut. Everything began to fade around her, and yet she could see it all now. All the torturous magick that echoed through her lungs and the Realms beneath her. It was bright, it was colourful, and it scorched her flesh without any hesitation.

Althea should be afraid of what was coming; she should be doing everything in her power to get away from it. But she couldn't bring herself to. All she could do was merely go along with it, moving towards it without considering the consequences that waited for her in the *arms of her enemy.*

What enemy was that? She couldn't quite exactly figure that out—but she had a hint of an idea.

The darkness tried to show her something next, forcing her then shut eyes open: its fingers slipping beneath her eyelids as its nails wiped her tears.

A scene grasped at the darkness before her, a vision, and despite it being there this entire time, she'd never wanted to accept it. It had been hidden behind the shadows—it had been what *the shadows had been standing before*.

The girl that danced mirrored Althea's movements like a puppet, their features almost identical if it wasn't for the dark eyes and hair that she wore with a grin.

Catching onto the wind of the scene before her, the girl wore a long, black, lace dress that wounded her ankles with every touch. It mimicked the way her hair caught in the wind. *Even that hair…* It was so terrifyingly different from Althea's, and yet it was the same length with the same curls, *but it was black*, while Althea's was purely white.

Her skin looked paler compared to Althea's too; the soft, warm glow from her mother's youth was completely gone, wiped away and replaced with blood that dripped from the girl's fingertips. Blood traced every curve, every indent of her body, marking her as a piece of art that she knew her father would give to the highest bidder given the chance.

Watching Althea, her eyes told stories that were far too dark and twisted for any to hear. Yet, as Althea looked down at her own seemingly untouched body, purposely avoiding any sight of her new Markings, she felt as if she had a part in every one of them, like a pirouette in the ballet she dreamt of.

"Oh, my dear little dove, just look at where we are now?" the girl spoke, and yet no words left her smirking lips.

Glancing up, trying to identify the intent behind this illusion, her heartbeat filled her ears as she realised that she was now staring into a mirror holding a reflection of a girl that she no longer recognised. A girl who held ghastly features—mimicking the dead that Althea often stumbled upon. This mirror, however, only worked to send chills down Althea's spine, as there appeared to be crimson syrup seeping through every crack that bled beyond just the frame.

The reflection of Althea Evangeline grinned a malicious grin. One that caused all the air to be sucked from her lungs, forcing Althea's hands to quickly reach for her throat in panic. Only, all the fear that was brewing in the pits of her stomach intensified when her Markings came into sight, and she followed the scarred lines of her arm as it outlined so much more than just a crescent moon.

Flinching back, Althea met hands as scarred as the eleven seas. They brushed her shoulders, caressing her bones, and no matter how quick she was to turn around, already fighting her way out of his clasp, it was never enough time to escape the breath of her nightmares.

Kylen Noxwell stood there, the man who had left her begging for a second chance: the man who she was about to marry. Smiling down at her, with his same brown eyes and dimples that made perfect targets, Althea was thrown back in time. She was now twelve again, staring up at her father as he realised just what she had done—just what she had let Kylen Noxwell do.

Her eyes widened, her hands trembled. Althea stepped back swiftly, except Kylen was already gone, only the whispers of him and his existence remaining. Her head turned and her throat bobbed, and after a dreadful moment of her stomach turning *she too disappeared*—and she now understood what the Trance of the Elements was, and that it was just as maddening as they all claimed.

With a startled bump in the road, her eyes flew open, and instantly with a choked breath of relief, she took in the sights of the crowded carriage she'd been sleeping in. It was coated in florals and gold—though all was chipped and peeling, leaving flakes of it scattered across her clammy skin.

Wiping the cold sweat that had gathered on her brow, Althea ran both of her hands over her face. She scrunched her eyes, groaning at the headache that had formed sometime in the three hours or so she had been asleep. Nightmares like that had plagued her for a number of years now, but as she abruptly halted her actions, *and her eyes laid witness to the true, real Markings,* she realised that it wasn't just a damnable nightmare.

The forbidden Elemental Markings seemed to smile at her, and suddenly the world, the voices, all of it, went silent. Fear defied her every breath, taking over each beat of her heart as her father's voice took over her mind. *"I thought you were smart, child,"* he chastised her, each word thicker than the last. *"I thought you were pure."*

Althea had the Elemental Markings—the Markings that had been held by those she had watched tortured before her very eyes. She choked back on a sob as the realisation of the situation dawned heavily upon her shoulders, how now death was closer than ever before.

Not once when she tortured all those souls for her father had she ever thought that she would find herself in their position one day. She never would have guessed that she would become one of the criminals to be cursed with the Elemental Markings—What had she done to deserve such a punishment?

She had always followed every rule.

She had always kept hold of her bleeding tongue.

Althea was never one to let her own fear tear her down, but her mind was beyond reasoning. With every turn of the wheels, and every bump in this road, she was on her way to be wed—and yet she couldn't possibly go through with that now—Kylen would see right through her. He would tell her father of her treason and together they would kill her.

Ripping at her dress, so many questions filled her head. Her father didn't have such magick in his blood, so did that mean her mother had had it? *Did her father even know that her mother had had it?* Was that why he had put Althea through so many tests? Through so many examinations? How was he possibly going to react? She couldn't tell him. Althea already knew how he would react.

Her father was going to kill her, and Althea would see her mother far sooner than anticipated.

The Blessed

ONE
ALTHEA

Death was crafted to be seen as a delicacy when it consumed one's body and soul. It was deemed as one of the finest deceptive arts of them all. One so inevitably grand, that it had even the weakest of those scrambling to gather the last of their strength to impress whatever 'God' it was who decided who lived and who died.

The wind of the waters below sang out, filling the air with the screams of the dead as each wave caved over. Those sounds alone made the bile threaten to rise within her throat, filling her stomach with such anxiety that she debated whether or not the water would be a rather pleasant place to drown in. The whole concept of the ocean was so much more realistic now after seeing it with her own eyes. She wondered how many bodies actually hid within the tumbling surface.

Be quick, mother, be so very quick! Quick! Quick! Quick!

The girl ducked, looking up swiftly as four golden arrows shot above her head.

"Do not let her get away!" the guard dressed in Lorundio colours, maroon and gold, shouted as he aimed another arrow for her soul, wildly guessing that she was another one of the

Elemental's that Kylen Noxwell's Kingdom was known to have a large population of.

But she was a cursed, no matter the fact that she received the Elemental Markings just a few days after her nineteenth birthday.

Another shout was heard over her shoulder, and Althea looked, a gleam of death in her eyes as both wars of magick within her soul begged her to spare them some love. They, the army Kylen, her fiancé, had searching for her, had been on her tail all evening after watching her decapitate a man.

They should be praising her if anything, as this was the rare instance where her victims did in fact turn out to be rather *evil.*

He'd made an inappropriate comment to a young woman working in a bar, and as Althea stole a drink from a neighbouring table without any realising, she decided to play the role of a hero for once. Enough said. It was rather entertaining too.

Whispering their intended actions to her, her curse allowed her to know when it was suitable for her to act. When she should allow the darkness within her soul to shine. Of course, her new magick—the Markings that were sending her into insanity—attempted to overpower her, but the curse had control of nearly anything and everything. The imposing Elemental magick stood no chance.

The dark, quivering curse struck out, catching the arrow shot by one of the royal guards in mid-air, landing right in the middle of the wall of pure darkness that she held up with little to no effort. The man looked at her with astonished eyes, the air leaving his lungs as the questions swarmed his mind. He knew who she was now. He knew exactly who she was and *oh, how excited he was to tell his King.*

Her fiancé.

Althea grinned as her curled, white, frosty hair appeared from under the smeared dry blood. Watching with the purest satisfaction as the man began to scan her eyes for the symbolising blue that hid beneath the colour-changing magick. That was the power of the curse, because despite it having some control over her, she still wielded it to her advantage. Hiding the fact that she was the villain in a Kingdom full of heroes with just a click of her fingers.

"You—" before the words could fully leave his lips, her magick had already seeped into his lungs, prying his mouth open and forcing its way into his wild, malicious soul. His whole body spasmed and squirmed as he tried to free himself. However, her mind had already located the next of her victims, and he fell to his knees as the life drained out of him.

His companions appeared around the corner, their eyes quivering as they watched the magick retreat into her body. Passing back into her soul, entering through her palms and chest, and leaving nothing but a soulless skeleton of her victim behind.

"Hello there." Althea cooed.

How that sight had once made her soul hurt.

Because the curse was waltzing beneath her fingertips, Althea's eyes were covered by a darkness that many from her kingdom held against their free will: the blue hidden deep within. Her face lightened in colour, her cheeks hollowed, and her eye bags darkened. Her face began to form back into its natural state now that the magick was deep within her, leaving the guards to realise just whose gracious presence they were in.

Some began to retreat. Others… they dared to take a step closer. "By the orders of King Kylen Noxwell, we need to take you back to the Royal Palace at once." An apologetic and reluctant look passed over the guard's features, her face showing just how hesitant she was to speak to Althea at all.

Althea looked down at the body that was now at her feet, feeling the blood soak through to her toes. She swallowed, her eyes scraping over the blood that begged for her attention. The voices she had once learnt to tolerate filled her head. They used to only be heard when she was consuming any foul, untameable magick and passing it onto her father—but now they followed her around, *and the voices had changed too.*

The Elemental magick that was now slowly taking over her dark blood took charge. Their voices begged her to use their magick instead of the curse.

Use me, use me, use me, use me, use me, mother, please...

Something struck her from behind. Attempting to surprise her as if she hadn't been tracking his every movement this entire time. A pebble slipped from under his feet, and Althea began forming two daggers of cold magick that aimed for his throat. The guard jumped back, hitting the wall with a fierce grunt as he tried to escape the blade that missed him by a hairsbreadth. He turned on her once more, joined by another two of his fellow guards that Althea grinned at.

One grabbed quickly at her hair, and Althea laughed. She turned her daggers in her hands, feeling as the shadows extended each blade. The crime had already been committed the moment his body had come an inch within hers. If her father were here, the criminals would get something much, *much* worse than death. So, this, if anything, was a blessing. And a fair one too.

"You aren't going to give the information I seek," Althea exhaled, a small smile settling onto her lips despite how her body longed for air. "Therefore, I have to kill you, so you don't rattle on about my presence." Her hand shot forward, and her eyes closed. Preparing for the same process as every time before.

His head hung, the colour of his eyes fading as dark, black blood began to seep from them. Althea's hand wrapped around his heart, feeling as it ceased pumping that beautiful crimson blood. Her curse began to kill him from the inside out, his soul and emotions departing with it.

Althea remembered the first time she had been forced to do this. How her sobs had flooded through the room, and how her father didn't do a single thing to save her from this physical ache. He just watched, studying her and her heart.

Like so, whoever's magick she was capturing was forced to pass through her blood, locating where the curse hid. Then, when it was ready, it found her father's connecting soul, and it drained her energy as it passed through to him.

Now Althea no longer sobbed, she didn't so much as flinch. She became immune to the pain and how the curse controlled so many aspects of her. Althea stared ahead as the magick passed through her, listening to the beat of her heart as she counted to ten. Soon, this would all be worth it. Soon, she wouldn't dwell on the lives lost.

If she were to defy what this curse and her father asked of her, Althea would be left to drown through a great deal of pain. Her father communicated to her through the curse, ordering things upon her that she was left blinded towards. He would say that it was to make her powerful. To make her the strongest of them all. And was it truly so bad that Althea wanted to believe him? She was strong, and she was fearless, and she vowed to make Kylen's death hurt.

His magick moved through her, entering through to her soul slowly, and moving towards her father's, Kingdoms away.

A guard gained on her then, using this moment of vulnerability to send an arrow through the bottom of her stomach. She felt it, and yet she did not flinch. *She could not falter.*

Instead, she smiled as she turned her head. Narrowing her gaze on the male whose eyes were now full of fear.

Something she craved so profoundly.

"Oh, aren't you something?" Althea asked, the question pulling a laugh from her lungs. *"Truly something indeed."*

She leaned against the wall as her back arched, and her hand went straight for the arrow that pierced her ever so proudly. It didn't help that she could still feel the magick passing through her, it was as though there was a noose around her neck and no matter how hard she tried to breathe, she just simply couldn't.

An agonising moment later, which felt like an eternity and a half, it began to leave her at last; pushing for Althea's vision to clear. The sensation was foul; it was horrible, all of it. Feeling the newfound magick being ripped from her blood was never something she looked forward to.

Althea snapped the arrow in two, throwing one-half of it to the damp ground while leaving the rest of it in her stomach. She knew better now; *this was not her first production after all.*

Althea tried not to think; instead, she willed herself to focus on tracking the guard that was across from her. But her mind repeatedly asked her the same question. *What was her father going to think about her current situation?*

He must know by now; it had already been a week since she was meant to arrive at Kylen's doorstep. All wide-eyed and vulnerable. Willing to stoop so low and genuinely consider marrying the man she would rather gleefully kill. Her father had heard her whining; listening as all the complaints left her lips. And every time, he would remind her that in the end, she would be free, and she would be able to get the revenge that twelve-year-old Althea deserved.

He must have heard the news of his daughter's disappearance! It wasn't one that wasn't worth sharing.

Knowing him, Althea decided, he either didn't care, or he believed Althea to be capable enough to make the right decision, the right move.

Althea ran a hand over her face as her eyes finished clearing up from the curse. The feeling caused her to sway in her steps as she pushed herself up and off the mossy wall. The guard, initially mesmerised, went to move towards her now, however, with a deep breath and a heavy sneer, Althea began to run.

This was his fault.

Kylen Noxwell was somewhere within his fabulously foul castle, probably sipping his pompous wine while laughing at her weak attempts to slip through the cracks.

But these were no weak attempts.

And he was to blame for this all.

He would always be to blame.

The sea somewhere below began to thrash, the sounds counting every bone within her body.

Run Althea, RUN, RUN, RUN, RUN! The voices in her mind mocked her, a constant weight hanging over her head as she tried to muffle the voices of the Elemental Magick. *You need to flee these Realms. Run while you still can, Mother.*

With every step and every leap, the guards began to lose Althea. Relief instantly covered her quivering body as she collapsed into the dark wall at her side, and Althea groaned as her own blood splattered across her hand. She needed to hurry up and find Erwin, one of the creators of the curse, and flee from Kylen's maze of a Kingdom. This new magick—the Elemental magick, was weighing her down. She didn't know how to use it or how to tame it, and every time she went to do something, it leapt onto her, weaving its way into her every breath: eager for any touch she would spare it.

As it was, Erwin's lingering presence was fuelled by rumours. How was she to know if he was actually here or not?

Kylen was probably cackling by now—watching her through his many prying eyes.

Memories that she would do anything to forget slipped through her mind at the slightest mention of him. Slipping ever so graciously as if he was physically there, weighing them so easily over her head that she was left uncomfortable in her own itching skin.

She felt his hand on her cheek and his hands braiding her hair; his young voice deceiving her with lies of a future she would have given anything to hold.

Althea must have tripped. She must have allowed the blood dripping down her legs and the new magick within her lungs to distract her for a second too long. Because before she knew it, she was on the ground, rocks and sharp shards of glass slicing through the palms of her hands.

Today was really *not* her day.

Althea dragged herself to a darker side of the alleyway, leaning her powerful body gently against the damp crumbling walls.

She held her head back and up to the sky, narrowing her harsh gaze to the stars she'd always dreamt of seeing. Althea took a deep breath, wincing slightly. This was never the kind part, having an arrow through the skin that was not meant to be broken. Having glass upon glass through your hands as if they were tiny diamonds, preparing her for one of her father's many exploiting Balls.

Althea's hands shook as she tried to slowly pick out each rock and shard that covered her broken flesh, her eyes becoming a watery mess despite how used to the pain she was.

Sensing the soul before it came into view, her eyes darted up. Though this time it was the Elemental magick that alerted her to such a thing, with its magick far softer than the curse. Someone appeared before her, appearing through the shadows as if she had been there the entire time, waiting for the time to strike. Althea got ready to lunge in response. If this woman thought she was going down without a fight, how wrong she was.

Althea was weak, but she knew she was far more talented than the girl across from her. After all, this was her game, and it may not have been her kingdom, *but it soon would be*.

If she danced the right dance and made her father proud —*that was*.

In response to her flash of panic, the guard quickly held up her hands. "I'm not going to hurt you," a feminine voice whispered gently, "I promise."

Althea's eyes narrowed on the woman. A manic laugh bounced off her lips, filling the cold fresh air before her with a cloud-like smoke. She had heard that one before and was far too familiar with it. "Sure," Althea sneered. "Get lost; I can handle myself." Pain shot through her, but she moved swiftly, leaning over the gutter next to her and throwing up the dark black blood that was punishing the Elemental magick within her soul.

It mocked her, laughing at her. It teased her that it would tell her father all that she was keeping from him. This was the curse's punishment for sensing something so foul within her blood. This was her punishment for being a traitor, as it seethed. Her eyes fluttered as she looked towards the woman, and in the back of her mind the questions arose of why these Markings hadn't appeared on her nineteenth birthday but instead a few days after. It wasn't the time for such an issue, and yet the questions never left.

The woman moved quickly despite Althea's weak attempts to fight back, and she muttered things in a language she'd never heard before. Quickly, and without any hesitation, the woman's hand found the rest of the arrow, and she clasped it with a grunt. Althea's eyes widened in anticipation as her head shot up, panic racing through her soul before being replaced with the burning sensation of it being ripped out. Was the stranger infecting her with her Elemental magick? Was this some type of trick?

"*I'm sorry—I'm sorry*," the woman whispered repeatedly, soothing the Princess in her best attempt as she shuffled several steps back. Who was she to do such a thing? Did she think of her as weak? Vulnerable? Oh, Althea was prepared to show her that she was anything but—though, she did want this guard to realise sooner than later that Althea now had her sword, her belt, and the bag of gold that had hung on her hip.

"*You bitch—*" Althea spat through a breaking breath. "*Why would you—*"

Something was near. It wasn't clear at all, but it was there; she could taste it and feel it tingling in the air. The hairs on her arms and legs stood on end almost instantly, and in response, Althea looked towards the girl, the woman, the guard, who watched her with an expression she would come to remember until her end.

The woman had a strange scent to her. It tasted bitter, salty. Something warm like the sunshine that bore down on every Kingdom but hers'. Yet, all at once, it was also terrifying. It earned her Markings to begin to burn, and both their eyes dropped to take in such a peculiar sight.

Althea's lips twisted in agony as her nails dug into her Markings. She tried, with the strongest of attempts, to suffocate whatever was suddenly happening. But just as every time beforehand, the Gods laughed at her pleads, and her Markings erupted with a light so bright that almost the entire Kingdom awoke.

"Promise me." Lilith—the woman who looked nearly identical to Althea cried. She had the same long white hair and piercing blue eyes. "Promise me that you will watch over my home while I'm gone. They need a leader, and you know that you were destined to be a Queen." Tears streamed down her cheeks as her lips wobbled. Her eyes were red from the tears she shed, and she shook her head. But the other girl's expression was far too damning for her to hold. Lilith looked over the balcony's edge, squeezing her fists with such effort.

"You should not go," Sayah persisted, crossing her arms tightly across her chest as she stared the Queen down. "Your parents are dead, for goodness' sake! You are the only leader left of Harlia, and we need you," she begged, the desperation lining her voice. "You cannot go there! That man is a cruel creature, and he will kill you before you even make it home," her voice wavered, and so did Lilith's gaze. "You know this is true, so why aren't you listening to me? This is not the God's way. This is not my way—and I won't have it!"

Lilith shook her head. "You are being silly," she pushed. "He would never harm me or my people! There is good in him, I know it!" Her words felt like white lies, and even as Althea watched the scene before her she knew the woman was trying to hold onto anything. She was trying to make anything make sense.

"You say that about every single person you come across. And not once have you been right."

"I was right about you." She reached out, and her hands met her dear friend's face. She slowly cupped her cheeks, grazing her thumb across her cheekbones as though she was memorising her touch, her warmth. "I'm sorry." The glistening magick that Althea now knew began to ascend forward, reaching Sayah's lips before seeping through. Her own magick burned at that moment, and Althea looked down, finding twines of gold wrapped around her fingertips.

The pain radiated onto the Queen as she replaced her look of hurt with one much more painful. She whispered "I'm sorry," several times, though not once did she go to remove the spell. Althea watched, seeing the exact moments when the memories from this guard's mind slipped into the Queen's, and then into Althea's.

Sayah exhaled, and it was as though several tons were pulled from her shoulders as she smiled and nodded.

Lilith removed her hands, and Sayah immediately bowed. The look of lust wiped from her eyes. "Your Majesty," she said politely, almost like a greeting. "Would you like me to go get your bags?"

The *vision*, *memory*, and *dream*, that had been drowning Althea faded into the air she breathed; and Althea stared at the woman's hands before her, watching with a new, obvious fear as her wild magick slipped through her skin, over her stomach, and into her palms. "What did you do to me?" It felt as if their magick was infecting her mind because all the thoughts and memories that did not belong to her had already gone—and unlike the Trance of the Elements, she could not remember what her mind had just fought through.

The woman looked at Althea, meeting her worried stare.

There were words on the tip of her tongue, but as her throat bobbed, she forced them back.

The woman leaned forward slightly as she pulled the Princess up to her feet. Her dark hair fell over her shoulders, and the gold cuffs wrapped around every individual braid caught the shifting glisten of the moon as she scrunched her eyebrows in pity. She was beautiful, she held her emotions well, her narrow face looking as if she was fit for the role of Queen. She certainly fit the criteria that her fiancé had somewhere within his study.

"Why did you—" Althea gasped, her words strong.

The sounds of horrified shouting cut her off, and two shadowed daggers formed around her fingers. "You need to run, Your Majesty." Althea looked back at her with confused eyes. Her expression quizzical as she attempted to make sense of what type of exchange this was.

"Why—"

"I will lead them away, but please go. It isn't safe in these parts, especially for a woman as wanted as you are."

Althea stared at her as she took a few steps back, preparing herself to stage whatever it was that she was going to do. But she didn't get it, what was in it for this woman who watched her with kind eyes and dared to help her despite all?

Glancing towards where she was going to run, the many questions in her mind forced her to look back at the woman before her. She should kill her—she knew that. She needed to kill whoever knew who she was and where she was.

Yet her stare was so human and her smile was so terrifying that Althea wanted nothing more than to flee right now. It was amusing, Althea wouldn't mind getting to know more about this strange lady. She seemed… exciting?

"Thank you." The words left her lips before she could even think twice, and her expression must've encapsulated her shock at such words as the guard's smile widened.

She shouldn't thank these people. They were the ones who

killed her mother. Who killed *her*. But she did help her, and she knew who she was, which was surprising. "Thank you," Althea said again; her mind oblivious to the new memories that haunted the depths of her soul.

Who are you to thank her? The whispers of her mind asked.

I can thank whoever I want, she fought the urge to spit back.

The wary look on the guard's face was replaced by one that was unexpectedly warm. Her eyes catching the same shine of the dark moon, making them project the guard's true aura. "Of course, *Althea of Harlia.*"

Althea furrowed her brows as she danced off into the distance, the ring of those last three words echoing through the wind that followed her. Of Harlia… she hadn't heard that saying in a long time.

TWO
KYLEN

The blood washed off of his hands with ease, staining nothing but the ends of his white rolled-up sleeves with the darling redness of it. He remembered their screams… the way they made his bones clench as he forced himself to carry on. They'd known the answers of the Manikalo brother, and yet silence was all they exhaled.

Death was never something Kylen began with, but in times like these, he certainly finished with it.

Watching the water carry it away, a small sigh departed his lips as he felt the presence of the Captain of his Guards enter through the doors of his quarters, her very scent filtering through the air as if it was hers to claim.

Kylen opened his mouth to speak, the words on the tip of his tongue when she had already interrupted them with a wave of her magick. Silencing him.

"If what I said is 'that I didn't see Althea', then that means that I didn't see Althea." Sayah crossed her arms, challenging him. Typical of her, to read his mind before he got a chance to put up his shields.

Her magick wrapped around the sleeves of his arms, and

almost subconsciously, Sayah drained the blood from the new material that she had bought down at the market just a week ago. A time when everything had been easier.

Kylen rolled his eyes as he looked up from the now clean material to the siren laying back on his couch. "See…" he trailed on. "I would love to believe you and all, but I have also been told that you weren't with the rest of them when she got away. We hadn't known she was even in this Kingdom until last night, and then she was seen. In your territory, may I add, and you were missing." He hummed with a sigh. "I mean, I'm not making assumptions or anything, *but...*"

Sayah tutted as she listened, a smirk playing on her painted-red lips. She was being lazy, Kylen had half the will to point out. Her scales were scattered and yet last time he'd checked they weren't exactly bickering at the bottom of the sea. A risky game.

A game of death if she were anywhere else.

"It sounds to me, *kid*, that you are just trying to piece a bunch of things together that you know is nonsense. I'm a busy woman —in fact, I don't see you out and about when the sun is resting, so who said you have a right to argue with me about this?"

As the siren spoke, she flexed her blade beneath her finger-tips; and as always (no matter how many times Kylen asked her not to), she threw it towards the target that narrowly missed the King's head. He didn't bother to watch as the scoreboard automatically added another point beneath Sayah's name. As it was, his name deserved a wellness day.

With a scoff, and a mumble announcing his kingly duties, Kylen turned away from her and ran his hands over his face. "Fine," he gave in at last, earning a laugh of triumph from Sayah. "I am trying to add it all together because it just doesn't make sense!" he exclaimed. "Althea—my goddamn fiancé, is in my Kingdom, and she isn't with me." Sayah's face changed into one that challenged him; an eyebrow raised as she turned onto her stomach. "Don't get me wrong though, I get why she wouldn't want to marry me. I get it—I do. But that girl… Oh, she just needs to show up—*that's all I'm actually asking!* I need her to be before me. I need her to show me that she is alive, breathing, and *healthy*—and I need her to become Queen." Kylen paused, taking a breath. He'd known it all along that this would be tricky, but he'd hoped that the trickiness wouldn't begin until she was actually here, before him. "The training should've already begun, S. She should be almost ready to become the Queen—," he shook his head, and sometime between then and now, Sayah had reached for his hand and kissed his bruised knuckle. He'd found that in recent years, his infection made his bruises more prominent. Sayah said that it wasn't related, but Kylen knew it was, as time was never in his favour. "Time is running out—and even I cannot outrun it."

"Breathe."

"Oh breathing, what a luxury—except I cannot *breathe* because there isn't another Princess, Queen, Prince, King that's suitable anywhere—and even your bloody reading predicted that." Kylen spat, and even Sayah hadn't heard the word 'breathe' said in such a horrid way before. It was almost like it had been chewed, and then spat out by one of the creatures Kylen had sent Sayah after last spring.

"Kylen, we both knew that it was a long shot for Althea to actually come here. None of us believed it when she did accept the proposal in the first place… so can we really say that we are surprised?" Sayah rose, approaching the King who was still just a simple child in her immortal eyes.

"She wanted an out, so I gave her one."

"Several years too late."

Kylen pushed Sayah away; but not physically, never physically. Just as he did every time he was enraged. For now, he only felt anger, his magick ripping at his hands and begging to be allowed out. Darkness was taking over his skin, tracing over his fingers and running races through his veins. His hands turned black, the veins all throughout his skin beginning to seep with dark black blood. Kylen shrugged her hand off of him, turning away so that she would not see him like this.

He knew that if he got too close to anyone in physical form, he would hurt them. His magick would spiral out and feed on whoever's souls' there were, just to rot his own.

So, he chose to keep his space, pushing everyone away no matter how much he would come to regret it later. No matter how it would cause his lungs to ache with the curse that begged for his death.

Oh how he hated being infected.

"She should be mature by now," Kylen emphasised as he turned back towards her. "How old is she? Nineteen? *She is two years younger than me, right…?* Nonetheless, I have been acting like a true royal for years now." His words ran dry, and he swallowed the thickness that corrupted the back of his throat. Nails digging into his palms, he focussed on the wit that he lived for—the sarcasm that kept him young. However, no matter the situation, every time he was in a state as such, images he longed to forget haunted his mind. "Why isn't she acting like a Queen? I mean, I know she has a thing for glamorous entrances, but now is really not the time for that."

It wasn't even the memories of Althea the last time he'd seen her that plagued him now. It was something more than that—and the suffocating walls around him had him shaking his head as Sayah remained silent.

He could hear his brother's voice—his sister's squeals. He could hear his parents laughing for God's sake, and as Kylen looked over his shoulder he swore he was going to see them there, no matter how many years had passed.

He turned to the siren slowly. "I just need her to show up."

"She will in her own time—"

"And when will that be?"

The anger overcame him, and Kylen hit the marble wall

beside him to get the darkness out of his fingertips, watching as it seeped into the Realm beneath them: like tiny snakes slivering through the marble he'd helped his father build. Who knew what would happen to those around him if he was unable to withhold the darkness. "I'm going to go to Erwin. I'm going to go to him and ask him where the Hel she is and what she is looking for," he stated firmly.

The decision was made. There was no room for any debate, no matter whose input it may be.

The doors opened without his touch, widening so that they were nowhere near his cursed presence as he entered through. It was as if they too were afraid of the cursed magick that danced down his veins.

Sayah hurriedly followed him, shaking her head swiftly as if he could see through the back of his head, which in some sense he could. "No! Kylen, you mention a word to him, and something horrible will happen—I am sure of it. We have seen what he has done to his victims in the past, and none of it is nice—don't you think you owe her a few extra days—minutes? He wants her for reasons he has locked himself away from sharing. You cannot mention her!" Sayah exclaimed quickly, her anger radiating through the colour of her scales.

Kylen turned on his heel. "Well, she needs to be found! He has the magick to find her, so why don't we use it? Althea is meant to be here by now, already learning my way of life, and yet she is not. I am growing more ill as each day pasts; we both know I don't have long left." The pain in his voice was hidden by the restraint he held with everything in him. "So, we must take matters into our own hands."

"Kylen, Erwin's hands aren't our own," Sayah persisted, her voice strained with agony. "We need to give her time to come to us." He hated that she was right, but he had no choice. "Ky—"

☽

Erwin stood before them, leaning against the wall of his cell that they'd entered mere seconds ago. He was grinning, his eyes rolling back to whatever brains were meant to be there as he laughed, and laughed, and *laughed.* "You know this is actually quite hilarious!" he'd said a few minutes earlier before erupting into hysterics, laughing uncontrollably at whatever words the curse chanted in his poisoned mind. *"This is hilarious!"*

Sayah watched from the doorway, her piercing gaze burning through the back of Kylen's head once again. Her stare was so physical that he swore his head was alight, and Kylen had to play it off as he ensured that his hair was all in tact.

The King hadn't spoken a word yet. He had walked through with such intention that when he opened his mouth to speak, the words did not leave. As if his consciousness knew better than him. As if the Gods who loathed him did too. However, Kylen knew that Erwin knew. The way he had stared at the King with an expression that showed him waiting. Waiting for him to say something more so that Erwin could give the answers that he had kept hidden with such glee.

As he thought now, he presumed that it was some connection between the curse holders that alerted his prisoner to the fact that Althea was somewhere in his city. And, by extension, Kylen was here to find out just where she was.

"So…" Kylen began finally, with a click of his tongue. "Are you going to be of any help today?" he asked, turning the dark dagger across his fingertips. "If you even know what that means, that is. Hmm?"

Erwin leaned back, his chains clashing against the blood-covered wall as he attempted to slide down it, parts of his skin scraping off in the process. "Well, that depends," he said with a grin, blood dripping from his teeth. "Are you going to free me today? Or will that merely be another day?" Erwin questioned in return, scrunching his nose with a hiccup.

Sayah rolled her eyes at his antics, redirecting her gaze to the

King with a look that said it all. She hated this process; they had gotten nowhere with him, and it had been months. He knew the whereabouts of his brother, and yet he appeared far too insane to make any sense of that.

Kylen chuckled, not giving in to the boredom and frustration that stirred against his heart. "You know I can't do that," he said with a shake of his head. "I need to know where your brother is before I do anything of the sort. Do you really take me to be that stupid? I thought we were friends."

Erwin mumbled as he looked down at the puddle of blood that formed before him. "My brother is where my brother is. He travels with the sun and hides when it burns. It's a fun game, I must tell you. Oh! So fun! Fun~*fun!*"

Kylen watched the male, the question of his girl right on the tip of his tongue, begging to be let off of his lips. There was so much to be said about her, so much to revisit and think through. It wasn't delightful to think of her given the memories. But he didn't have much say in that matter at a time like this.

"I can see it, you know."

Kylen looked up from the puddle that he had turned his gaze to. "Pardon me?"

"I can see the questions that are running through your mind. I see it on your lips and in your eyes. She," he turned towards Sayah, "doesn't want you to speak of them, but who is she to tell a King what to do? Ask me. Go on, ask me!"

"She has more authority than you. I can tell you that much. Oh, and she's much wiser than either of us, so I think it's best to stick with her words." Kylen simply said with a shrug, pretending to be on her side this whole time. He could practically feel Sayah's eye roll. "I have questions, many of them. But I know that if I allow you to answer them in the ways that I want you to, then shit will go down that I can't be bothered to deal with." The truth of his words turned his stomach. Why did he have to be considerate, especially to a girl who tried to butcher his people?

"You can't be bothered, or you feel too weak nowadays?" Erwin dragged on the words, a taunt to his grinning stare. "You know… because of everything—"

"That's enough," Sayah interrupted with a sharpness to her tone. She never liked anyone speaking of his illness.

Erwin moved his eyes off Kylen, narrowing them on the siren as if he could see right through her. Erwin sighed, a dramatic, deep sigh that flickered blood across his chest. He moved his eyes once again, narrowing them on the King as he held his chin high. "You are both afraid that if I use my magick, it will drain the rest of your humanity away." The manic prisoner clapped his chained hands before him; blood splattered off them and against Kylen's now clenched jaw.

"You feel it *draining away*, your vibrant, dark skin that used to glow ever so brightly… but now it's fading. Every day you wake up and notice it's a shade or two greener and sicker than the day before. You try to cover it up with the makeup you stole from that woman and her girlfriend, but no matter how hard you try, it never works properly. Neither of them says anything… yet when you turn your back on them and look at me, I see the shared glances. They are worried, sceptical, watching you die! Who would want to watch you—you of all people die!" his lips pouted. "I see it all in your eyes, boy. I see it all. And I can also see through *Althea's*."

Kylen felt his whole body tense. He felt the burn of Sayah's eyes change to one of pity. A feeling he had avoided successfully for so long. Kylen turned on the prisoner, wielding his blade to Erwin's throat, nicking the first few layers of skin, and watching as blood trickled down. "Watch what you say to me," he snarled through a single breath.

"She's on the run, looking for something—*someone* who holds the answers she so desperately seeks."

"What is she looking for?" Kylen pushed, holding onto the sanity that is hardly ever seen in the old man.

Erwin shrugged blankly. "If she wished you to know, I think she would have shown up at your doorstep."

Oh, he was going to kill him, and it was going to truly make up for his miserable life.

He pictured the blade entering through his throat—and what relief and satisfaction that brought him. It was like a breath of much needed fresh air, the kind that made him breathe easy once again. One that took the curse from its hold around his lungs and left no consequence of any kind.

The King laughed, one forced and full of bitterness that he hoped wrapped around Erwin's twisted spine. "Well, looks like she's pulled all the smarter moves here. Because somehow, she, a nineteen-year-old Princess who's never left her castle, managed to still be untouched by the army that I have searching for her." The King paused, allowing it to soak into the air, into his cursed mind. "However, you, an immortal bastard with a quarter of a lifetime dedicated to training to hide from my wrath… managed to get caught within a day by that exact army."

Erwin stared at the King, unblinking. "She will die. You will die. That woman will die. Your family and everyone you have ever cared about will die! And if they are already dead, then they will be ripped from the afterlife and killed again!" blood splattered off his lips as he seethed those words he had been holding onto for far too long. "You think you are so lucky because you were cursed before you were even born, but your days are numbered, boy. They are numbered because the magick that has wielded its way from the curse is losing the war!"

Sayah stepped forward, and with the softest touch of magick, pulled the King back to her side. "Hate to break it to you, Erwin, but my family is already dead. You are a tad too late to the show." Kylen obliged Sayah's magick, leaving the ghosts of the dungeons behind and re-entering the world that was keeping

Althea Evangeline from him. Sayah, however, stayed. Her magick sent ripples and waves of such strength through the Realm as she reflected her agony onto Erwin. He had taken so much from her; it was all bound to catch up to him at some point.

The sounds of his cries and his cries alone followed Kylen as he fled the crime scene, and as he stalked his way through the darker parts of his castle, he could have sworn that his laugh was tangled up into the air too.

Kylen headed to his quarters. Making it to his bathroom without the smallest sound. Without the smallest breath. The moment the doors shut behind him, however, he ran to the basin, leaning over it before choking on the curse that he had been born with. His blood rose, leaving his lips and with each cough splattering against the mirror before him, covering it almost completely with the liquid that was turning darker every day.

The curse laughed at him, mocking his weakness as if it was a burden. He shivered beneath his skin, feeling as if Erwin's eyes were still on him, seeing him for everything he tried to hide. It was a feeling no one deserved. A sensation so disgusting that Kylen held onto himself as he lowered his shivering, ill body to the ground.

Kylen held his mouth up to the ceiling as he waited for this feeling to pass. He just needed to breathe. He just needed to breathe and find Althea, and then everything would be alright… *right?*

THREE
ALTHEA

"Tell me where he is," Althea spoke sweetly, putting on such a perfect smile that no drunken man could resist—no drunken man ever would. He had complied, of course, giving her an answer that was such complete nonsense that a second later, she had scolded herself for wasting her precious time.

More guards lurked in the streets. Not only Kylen's but a few of her father's too. Althea had only seen one, but she only had to see one of the cursed to know that more lingered in the shadows. Their eyes were dark; no white or colour to them, no matter under what lighting one gazed at them in.

They reeked of the curse that was filtered through their blood; she felt it in her palms, her soul. It wasn't inflicting any physical pain upon her, but the thought of it alone was enough to make her stare up at the newfound stars and wish for a beyond, a break.

It wasn't that she hated this magick; it was the magick that she partially controlled after all. However, it was a constant reminder that followed her around like a bad smell. One that constantly weighed over her shoulders, as if it too wanted her to fall victim to her father's trials. To her father's games.

The body before her stared up at the same stars. Wide eyes and dripping with the curse that Althea had sliced into his cruel soul. She had caught him hunting down young girls; girls who were no younger than her. She played him in return, and now his magick passed through her with a whisper. Althea kicked at his arm, moving it out of her way.

Her eyes stayed on her own hands, watching as the darkness found its home within her soul. Crawling into all of the crevasses and sending chills that rattled her bones.

Althea looked out and onto the street, lifting her arm up and rubbing the last tiny clean spot of fabric across her eyes. Guards passed her, and Althea waited. Waiting and watching as they walked away before she stepped out into the glistening moonlight. She listened for the noises that lurked in the shadows of the streets, waiting for the perfect moment for when she could leave.

The girl in disguise slipped down the streets of the night, her curse curling around her every step. The castle in the near distance radiated with a warm, uncomfortable glow that caught her eyes every so often; despite trying with all of her will to ignore it.

More deaths were occurring because of Althea. More guards were on alert and storming the streets just in search of her. They all believed the cold-blood killer to be spreading evil, when in reality, she was wiping it away.

None of them knew that it was her. They had simply begun to refer to her as the assassin of the night. The assassin, who was clearly working on Erwin's side as they shared the same magick, the same curse that was deemed as unfair in these lands.

The word of the wind was that Erwin, the man who was going to save her, was trapped inside the castle that she had avoided with all of her will. He was said to be there, hiding beneath the floors that the insufferable guests blindly waltzed upon.

With a sigh, Althea climbed up the side of the crafted walls, climbing her way up to the apartment's open window that she had been sneaking into the past few icy nights.

The bookshelf laid tilted against the nightstand that stood in pieces beside the empty bed. She hadn't bothered to move it. It felt wrong to touch what was not hers, like an ancient piece of history that should not be rewritten. She could live with sleeping in a home that did not belong to her, but touching and moving things around took it too far. As if she was the very one deeming them as forgotten, abandoned.

Althea looked at the pile of bloody clothes on the floor and picked a few of them up, putting them into the bag she had stolen earlier that horrid day. Her mind was elsewhere, off with the fairies, while wondering about how far she would have truly made it if her father's training hadn't been forced upon her. If she hadn't known how to kill. Would she be trapped in the enemy's castle, preparing to marry him after spending all these years apart? Or would she have already been killed? Left for dead because they all knew no soul in this Kingdom would help her, or so she had originally thought.

Althea climbed down the wall that she had climbed up minutes ago. Except this time, she didn't go all the way to the ground. Althea jumped to the rooftops beside her, landing silently while praying to the Goddesses above that she hadn't alerted any unwanted souls to her presence.

She made her way silently, running across rooftops to rooftops and climbing down the walls that laid just where she needed them to. Althea perched herself against a corner, blending into her friend that was the shadows as she fixated on the noises that had her by the throat. It was dead silent—almost too silent if she hadn't been aware of the current fear that everybody held.

Her feet dug into the soil as she reached the cliffside; having just jumped from the rooftops seconds ago, she had to make sure that no one had seen where she had landed. Althea turned her head, her eyes narrowing when she felt the tremors of the ground.

The tremors and the roars that she knew had to belong to Erwin.

She was going to find him, and in the process, she would destroy Kylen and his beloved castle. She would make him beg for mercy—she would make him beg the way she'd once begged him. Althea vowed that much.

Did Kylen view her as a fool? Did he think that she would not recognise the scent of *her* magick? Perhaps it was a trap, but then again, Kylen wasn't that intelligent.

Althea walked closer to the cliff edge, looking down to the entrance that she could feel but not see. If Althea had learned anything from her years of training this magick, it was that she should never trust it. It loved to deceive her. To trick… To mock… So, she stood there for a second longer, listening, feeling, scenting for anything that was out of the ordinary. But the entrance was there, she was certain. It was just hidden.

Don't dread what you know is already going to happen. The voices pried and Althea laughed. "That is awfully easy for you to say." But, she wondered just what they meant.

Althea pressed her hands into the dirt, ignoring the shivering that took control of her fingertips. Inevitably, she turned to the curse, however, the roots beneath her called for something else. The new Elemental magick in her bloodstream rejoiced, determined to rip from her bones and flourish beneath her touch.

Surprised wasn't the word she would use under circumstances such as these. Saying she was startled and flabbergasted was much better for her peace of mind. It was astounding how this Elemental magick answered the calls of her mind without even so much as a lift of a finger. She wasn't used to it—nor did she think she ever would be.

This was precisely why Althea was going to do everything in her power to get the newfound magick out of her system. It wasn't meant for her.

Althea wasn't sure what her new Elemental magick was going to do, but this certainly was not it. A large vine escaped from the Realms core. It reached for her, and as if she was under a spell, she leant towards it. The vibrant green vine wrapped around her arm and waist, sending her flying over the edge of the cliff before she could simply blink. While she wasn't sure whether she wanted to scream in fear for her life or not—Althea would not deny the way exhilaration clawed at her. A manic laugh erupted from her lungs as she flew down the cliff's edge, and she tried to replace her nerves with something far more professional. *Laughter.* Her hand tightened on it, but it assured her that all would be okay. All would be just.

No, no, no. Althea sneered at herself for allowing those thoughts to erupt from her mind. There was no way in the after-life that she was going to think that way, not after she had spent several years of her life undergoing tests to confirm that this magick was not going to flood through her blood when she turned of age. And of course, it didn't, but rather instead, a few days after. A few days after her father had already ordered the cursed maids to check every inch of skin for the Markings he loathed. She'd stood there, certain in herself. If only that girl got a glimpse of the one she was to become in the coming days.

Elementals were severely frowned upon, especially by those with common sense. They were the lowest ranking, the ranking below earthlings. Even though they were the offspring of the lost Gods, their magick was reckless and sought unnecessary blood-shed, causing the history of her family a great deal of pain. How could she possibly have that filth in her blood? She wouldn't even begin to deny the fact that she was a *traitor*.

If she had to pick one of the two lower rankings, she would've chosen to be an earthling… a witch, a wizard, a fae… at least they didn't have that bad of a reputation…

Even to be simply a human or a creature of the deep…

Anything would've been better—anything would've given her something more of a life.

Althea would not allow herself to stoop so low to keep them. She simply *couldn't*.

The vine abruptly stopped, and the dirt before Althea opened, creating a tunnel that her magick—the new Elemental magick threw her through. She stumbled into a roll as she hit the damp soil, her eyes wide as she flicked her head up and felt her hair fall back over her shoulders. "Oh, my Gods," she swore quietly under her breath and through a deep exhale. Her body reacted as if her natural *human* instincts were to be scared—but didn't the world realise that she was no longer human? That she had never been human? "That was certainly something," Althea murmured to herself. *Oh but you enjoyed it, did you not?*

Holding her two cursed daggers with clenched fists, Althea noticed the old cobblestone pathway that appeared beneath her feet. It must've been from the old mines, she noted as she took a step, glancing back over her shoulder as the walls of this tunnel began to shift. Althea may not be from this land, but she'd heard the stories of it.

The tug of Erwin's magick became stronger as she began to walk, so Althea kept going forward, swallowing back the giddiness that crept through her stomach with such delight.

This was it.

She would find Erwin, and he would take it away. He would fix her of this curse that was not *her curse* and rid her of the burden that was holding her prisoner. He was the only one who could help her. The only one who could rewrite this story.

The pathway came to an end as a wall of dirt and panels of wood met her eyes. She pressed a hand to it, displeased about the fact that she could feel the magick and yet could not see the source of it.

Use me. Use me. Use me. Oh mother, gracious mother, use me. This foreign magick screamed at her. Screaming with all its willpower to get her attention. Althea ignored it, suffocating the darling black Markings as she tightened the bandages around her wrist. *USE ME, USE ME, USE ME, USE ME, OR REGRET IT.*

Just as Althea was about to use her daggers to dig into the wall before her, a force of some type wrapped around her wrists. Her daggers disappeared, and instead, the palms of her hands connected with the cold wood. It only took a second, but only a second was needed, as instantly the entire wall blew up, screams of those on the other side nothing in comparison to the sudden ringing in her head. It reminded her of all those times she'd danced to the silence of her mind.

There were guards dead on the floor as the dust cleared, and their eyes were forever frozen as Althea held her hands to her chest. Choosing to look past whatever it was that just happened, Althea took a breath, then two, and she took a step forward.

She wasn't going to complain if this was all happening to her advantage. Althea narrowed her brows, her lips quirked to the side as she took in the sight before her. She didn't like being used—especially by magick. *But that certainly got the blood pumping.*

Eyes of some type were on her: eyes that were dark and malicious. Not to mention there was a murmur to the air that professed her treason, challenging her to run. Her hands flexed in circles, forming two more daggers that reflected the fire of the floating candles. While this magick was deemed as pure trouble, it caused her great ease to know that she could wield weapons with a simple breath. Althea held her chin high, looking down at the air before her with all of the courage that was purely adrenaline-based. She could do this. This was nothing.

The door to Erwin's cell opened with a creak, and Althea

pushed her magick out and into the room before her, searching for any possible unwanted prying eyes. Carefully, and with a grin that mimicked his own, Althea approached the old immortal male who hadn't looked her way yet. "Look at how you've grown," he spoke, followed by a cackle.

His voice was a tired thing, one that was so similar to her father's. It was almost as though he was here, his hands on her shoulders, his voice in her ear.

With his face bruised, and his left eye swollen, Erwin released a short breath before extending a hand forward, the air in the room crackling as every second passed. His eyes stayed trapped on hers as he raised his hand towards her wrist, and as she looked down, she swore that they began to burn. "And I see that you have changed for the worse. How unfortunate."

"That's why I am here," Althea replied rather too confidently, her smile wiping itself away as she stood before him. She held one of her daggers with her thumb and palm, using the rest of her fingers to clasp his chin so that he would focus all of his drained attention on her. "I need you to help me find your brother so that I can get rid of this monstrous mess. I, of course, would do it by myself, but that could lead to death, and I'm rather content with keeping my life."

At this point, she wondered if he knew that she was trying to remember all that she'd learnt about the Elemental Markings.

Erwin didn't answer her. Instead, he looked up to her as if he was admiring her in the foulest of ways. His eyes stripped off every item of security that she held so dearly close, and every instinct begged her to run.

Run mother, run mother, run! This is no saviour; he is a monster, one who will end us all.

"You won't get very far with that," a voice spoke out from behind her, one that she recognised with every emotion to plague her mind. Althea's fingers froze underneath Erwin's chin, her stomach dropping and her blood chilling. "I have been asking him to lead me to his brother for months now," the voice chuckled. "And just look at where we have gotten." The voice crept towards her, noting every bone in her still body and slicing between them until her lips trembled. "He must just simply adore my company."

"I doubt that."

Althea's stare wavered as she slowly turned around, bracing herself for the sight she had worked so hard to get rid of. The daggers in her hands extended out, taking the shapes of long swords, bloodthirsty ones.

Kylen Noxwell grinned at her, and she would almost dare to grin back if she hadn't been reliving every single memory that they shared. Anger layered upon hurt sparked a fire within her soul, and she wiped the blood that dripped with the sweat from her face.

This was what she had been waiting for—this was what all these years of waiting and praying to herself had led to. And she could only wait to feel the last few pumps of his heart beneath her fingers; how she longed for the taste of revenge.

Justice.

FOUR
KYLEN

"Hello, my beautiful, *glorious*, Althea," Kylen mused with a sly smirk, the ends of his lips curling from the very sight of her before him. It was true that her looks were powerful, but now that she had matured into them they were deadly; which just seemed to turn his heart for the worst. "Just look at how the Goddesses have brought us back together once again." Kylen watched as every word met its mark, as every word travelled to her soul and found shelter within her luxurious blood. He clapped his hands before him, holding them in a grand gesture before flipping them around, forming two daggers that imitated hers.

It was faint now, but he recalled the few times when he'd used his magick, and it had been exactly that. *His* magick. Sure, the curse had been there, after all, he was cursed. But when he was a boy it only played a small part. Whether that was through the form of a headache, or through his spells doing the opposite of what they were meant to do.

Now, his magick was basically gone. The curse had devoured it all. And every time Kylen did use 'his magick' it was the curse. He also knew the cost of his actions… what happens each time he dares to use the curse to his advantage.

The two of them stared at each other silently, tense, *waiting for something.* He looked over every visible feature on her body, noting how time had truly done him no justice because it had kept her out of his hands. Althea's eyes were the only visible thing underneath her hood, her darling rich blue eyes that swirled with a darkness he would never get used to. Kylen would recognise those eyes anywhere, and he would recognise that voice anywhere. After all, they followed him in his dreams.

Kylen raised his hands, showcasing that he was innocent and wasn't one to start a fight. *Not this fight, at least.* His thumbs held each dagger to the palms of his hands as he watched her carefully and admirably. The words were on his lips, but before he could so much as utter a single word, Althea lunged out. How could he say that he was surprised? He expected nothing less from his *Queen.*

Althea's daggers warped with her father's shadows. Magick swarmed from the palms of her hands and changed the shape of the weapons she wielded. The light to her eyes was gone—all the colour from within them was gone, and instead replaced with a dark-purply-black; the blue was now red, a darling, chilling red that he could surely get drunk on.

Her eyes were shining with a darkness that dripped from her soul, and it called to Kylen as he took several steps back from her. "Althea darling, let's talk about this—" Althea didn't listen, no. Instead, she used the curse. The same one that rotted his soul without the power of her knowledge. "Althea!"

Kylen tried to fight back against the trance, but he couldn't erase her from his mind. He could still see the child she once was. He could still feel the agony that rippled through his heart as he forced himself to leave her behind.

But then, her sword struck through the chains on the floor, releasing Erwin, and the sound of the enchanted metal hitting the blood-covered ground made his head shoot in that direction, his jaw already clenching.

"You—!" he stopped himself from swearing at the girl who he needed to be his bride, *cooling the cursed temper that threw daggers at her heart.*

"Did you say something?"

Kylen's head looked over to the girl who was running at him. Althea danced around him, her swords stroking his shoulders, causing dark, crimson blood to appear. Kylen winced, but he would not let himself react nor falter—despite how enticing it was to watch that proud smirk line her delicate lips. The King watched with wide eyes as she ducked below his strike, the dagger hardly holding any effect over her. Althea was completely unfazed by his attempt to fight back—and Kylen didn't quite know whether he should be ashamed or amazed.

This was brilliant; Althea, the same Althea that had been so childlike the last time they had met each other, was dancing with a blade in hand, never missing one of her famous steps.

"Althea—" He went to whisper, but she had already thrown a dagger for his eye, and it took everything in him to dodge that final strike.

Erwin rose to his feet, the look in his eyes so startling that Kylen instinctively held out a hand in Althea's direction, blocking her from Erwin's front.

She could look after herself. He was aware of that—he was, unfortunately, *more than aware than that*. But right now, given the situation that he found himself in, he didn't want to play any games. He could feel the curse squeezing his heart, the hold it had on him being far too deadly. Time was running out, and if she still wanted him dead by the time they were married, then he would gladly accept the wrath she dared to face upon him. But now was not any time for that. Now she had to be safe so that he could have a Queen.

He couldn't risk the life of the only leader his Kingdom

would have in the months to come. That was not an option to him, not one that he was at all willing to take.

His hand met with her wrist, and she flinched ever so violently that her sword quickly formed into a dagger just long enough so that she could swing it and slice her way out of his potential grip. But Kylen was quick, and he flinched back before she could do any real damage.

"Althea, I don't want to fight you," Kylen growled with such frustration; his eyes darting back towards where Erwin stood, stretching in his own skin. Kylen could sense what he was doing. He was trying to reignite his magick, *his curse*, and once it had fully bloomed, he was going to erupt. Kylen stalked around her, mirroring every action she presented herself with so that he would not be surprised when she launched into another attack. However, his eyes glanced between the two, swallowing the bitterness in his throat as he begged Sayah and Zaire to appear. "Let's work all of this out in the morning—"

Althea laughed. A laugh so un-queen like that he was sure his blood had dropped in temperature. "That's quite ironic, isn't it? That you don't want to fight anymore," she queried with narrowed eyes as she pressed her thumb against the blade, spiking some blood that would heighten her magick senses. "Because it seems you did want to fight back then, and they do say that I am still stuck in the past," she seethed through a daring grin.

Kylen began to move the same moment he felt the darkness from within him rise. He suppressed it. The panic in his head was screaming at him to kill her and be done with this. It seemed like his magick hadn't forgotten the past either, how unneeded that inevitably was. Kylen shook his head while reaching up to wipe away the blood that dripped from his nose. "How about this? We fight later and focus now?" he asked, referring to Erwin, who was channelling the magick of his soul, preparing *to kill them all.*

Althea advanced on him then, taking his moment of weakness to show him all that she had truly learned during these years apart, all of the anger that she held so close to her dark heart. How he would have once done anything to erase that burden.

Her magick wrapped around his legs, tripping him to the ground with a bone-crushing thud. He could barely breathe before she had found herself on top of him. Her darling eyes piercing right through the darkness of his.

Althea pressed her knee to his chest; her hair falling over her right shoulder and grazing the edge of his throat. Kylen reached up, wrapping the red, flaky curl of dried blood around his fingertips. A small action that had her gaze turning lethal.

Gods, she really was beautiful.

Her ice-cold dagger met with the flesh that covered his throat. The air that she breathed and used to her will just slightly brushing against his cold-cold dark skin. "Goodbye, Kylen," she whispered, a daring smile coating her lips.

The sight before him was confronting. He could see her; *he could truly see every part of her as a wave of deja-vu washed over him.* Her hood was gone, and it was revealing the girl he felt he saw for the last time just yesterday. "I must say, you do look rather gorgeous with red hair, although I still prefer the white," he purred in a feline-like voice, attempting to see that smile that had already been wiped from her lips.

Althea shook her head with a small chuckle as she pressed the tip of the dagger against his skin. Watching closely as she used his blood to create a piece of art that would be his death. Kylen didn't fight back. He didn't defy her. He was going to let her do this—he owed her that.

A grin swept across her lips as she glanced back up to his eyes, that very smile faltering as she caught his eyes already on hers. Watching her so intently that she pressed the blade harder, and Kylen swallowed to deceive his pain. How cruel could the Gods truly be? To make the girl of the man he loathed the most, so-so beautiful—and to bless him with marrying her, and then taking him away before he could truly enjoy the games she would play as Queen?

But the Gods know he didn't deserve her.

Not after he chose his Kingdom over her.

A crime like none other.

Kylen braced himself for death. He took a deep breath as he knew what her killing him would entail and what it would mean not only for him but also for their Kingdom.

Althea Evangeline would automatically become Queen whether she had committed the murder or not. That was the way royalty worked in this fucked up world. If she were to kill him, she would get his Kingdom and Realms—or if he were to kill her, he would gain half of her Kingdom and her Realm since she was one of two royals owning it.

Althea stopped abruptly, her glistening royal eyes growing wide with panic as the dagger that was clenched in her hands completely disappeared. Fading into nothing but air.

She choked, her mouth widening as she began to gasp. Such horrid sounds emerged from the depths of her chest that they physically pushed Kylen to freeze. Her hands began to tremble, sending tremors throughout the King's body that were not the result of his or her magick.

Kylen reached for her; however, something pulled her up and dragged her fighting body back as if she weighed nothing at all. Kylen watched the flash of movement that came from Erwin's hand appearing around Althea's now blood-stained and bruised throat.

How Kylen cursed the illusion of Erwin that was still playing repeatedly in the corner. Erwin had astral projected himself into the shadows, posing himself as still gathering strength before lunging to fight. However, he had been doing anything but that, and now he was seconds away from killing Kylen's Queen.

Althea's dark magick-infused nails clawed at Erwin's hands,

ripping the few areas of untouched skin that was left. Magick formed through his flesh, moving with no effort whatsoever that it seemed like the Dark Master had just woken up from a refreshing nap rather than a torturous one.

The dark magick that was not her own danced up her throat and across her cheeks, all before forcing its way through her gaping jaw.

Erwin was killing her. Erwin, the man who had such a similar magick to her father's, was killing *her*. The daughter of one of his most 'trusted' acquaintances.

Why? Had he truly lost the last of his mind?

There had to be some underlying reason that had not yet met the eye. A reason so terrible that he had turned on *her*—her of all people because of it. Kylen's eyes flashed across her body, searching, looking for the answer that filled his mind.

Kylen looked to the doorway as he quickly scrambled to his feet, ignoring the ache his lungs threw at him. Both Sayah and Zaire entered through the opening with electricity. Sayah's golden eyes widened as she took in the sight before her. Zaire didn't move *however*, even as Sayah summoned all of the magick within her, *they still didn't move.*

Kylen struck Erwin the moment Sayah's magick forced him to let the Princess go, his lungs struggling to keep him going as Erwin turned to him with a tilt of his head.

Althea dropped to the ground, landing on both a knee and a foot as she inhaled all of the air that she could physically clasp onto. Her breathing so struggled that she sounded to be drowning beneath the curse that had once been hers to control.

Kylen turned abruptly to Sayah. "Get her and go!" he exclaimed through gritted teeth, his magick reaching the ends of his fingertips, causing them to go black. "Get out of here and seal all the doors and exits shut. Understand?"

Sayah nodded quickly as she pulled Althea up, holding her securely despite the Princess' struggles to break free. "*Get off of me.*" She walked more than a few steps before Althea used all of her energy to push the siren away. Althea looked up, flipping her hair back before snarling, "*burn in Hel.*" It wasn't Sayah that her words were directed to, but rather them all.

The Princess found the floor once more, and she was there for no longer than a second before she began to run, her head flying up and her hair shining with something like fire. Sayah and Zaire were quick to follow her while Kylen turned his attention back to the man who grinned broadly at him, blood dripping off of his yellow-stained teeth.

Kylen matched his grin, however, his came off as more of a smirk.

"Kylen, my boy," he murmured as he circled him. "Now, no need to settle this like children," Erwin teased, raising his hands up as he felt the darkness spiral within his chest. The shadows wrapped around his hands, forming at his very call—preparing to kill the man who had almost killed his Queen.

Kylen looked down at his own hands, watching as what looked to appear as black paint began to spread across his fingertips. Stopping at the end of each finger and disappearing into the veins below, showing off what little of the curse he had learned to control. What little he had escaped from.

Erwin turned to escape, and Kylen instantly fought back, blocking off his path as the candles that lit up the room burned out around them, a newfound darkness advancing on them both. It was deathly dark in the dungeons now, and Kylen was quick to focus on his other senses. The shadows answered him instead of the old man, surprising them both while Kylen brought the shadows in and towards his soul from each corner. Perhaps it was the pleads that he sent the Gods, or perhaps it was the new magick he could sense. The magick that led him to believe that Althea had betrayed her very own father, just as he had done to her, during that time when the moon shone with darkness.

Kylen could hear the gasp of disbelief leave the older man's mouth, even as he held everything in him to fight back. The young King knew that if this fight were to last any longer, he would pass out; his magick was far too overwhelming.

So, Kylen acted quicker and not at all smarter.

He threw everything in him at the older male, watching as Erwin flew back through the darkness. He met the wall with such an impact that Kylen was sure he must have broken multiple bones. The curse radiated across Kylen's body. Scaling across every inch of skin, weaving through the hair on his body and extending from his fingertips beyond. This curse may be killing him, and it may have burdened his name before he was born, but Kylen had learnt a few things about it in his time. He never got the full, true story of how his name became burdened. All Kylen really knew was that his family had been punished and that his mother and father had been left with a curse deemed to kill their firstborn because of a war no one really spoke of.

Kylen had tried to ask Sayah about it to see if she could find anything more than what he already knew. But because of how secretive his family had kept it and how she had joined their lives when he was already born, neither of them knew anything. *"The time will come when you are old enough to know."* His mother had whispered so many times. If only she had known that she would be the one to die first.

The doctors didn't think he was going to make it during labour. They didn't think his heart was strong enough. *They knew nothing of the curse back then.*

The curse has always been a part of Kylen, and to him, it used to be his childhood friend that he would speak about in show and tell when he did have his schooling days. Everybody told him their own opinions about it—how he should try to rest and be calmer if he wanted a long life. But the curse had been fine then, it didn't feel like a true illness until he was around thirteen, and every step slowly began to feel heavier.

Kylen had told the world then, that the curse had finally freed his soul, but that was all a lie. The only reason he had said it was because he knew as a child King, he already had his age burdening his name, he didn't need this curse too.

And when the time came to meet Althea Evangeline, he didn't want her to think of him any differently for the illness he never had any control of.

Erwin snarled with such force; he knew the boy's situation, and yet he was left breathless, how that made Kylen grin with glee. "Getting old, are we?"

The chains which were still weaved with Sayah's florescent magick found Erwin's wrists and ankles, snapping back into place as if they had never been blown off. Wrapping around his skin and forcing the dark magick back into his veins.

A scream so loud and torturous echoed through the hollow air, pushing all of the rats to flee, not wanting to be there when the power overcame the old passed-deceased man. Kylen looked down at him as he rose to his feet. Eyeing the man that he had worked so hard to catch. "Why did you try to kill her?" the words left his lips with ease, the calculations in his head not adding up by any means. It didn't make sense. It made no sense as to why she would hold the Elemental Markings. "She's one of you. *Why the fuck* would you try to kill her?"

Erwin laughed, making the puddle of blood before him squirm. "She's not one of us anymore, *boy*," he spat like it was venom. "She has come of age, and now it's just wasted time until her father and the world come to know of it!" he exclaimed with such glee. "She's going to have armies come for her, all fighting over each other so that they can be the one to stab the rotten heart within the girl who shouldn't be breathing."

Kylen raised a brow, a hum of a laugh leaving his lips as he reached over to the old man, pressing one of the two blades to his throat. "We'll just see about that. Armies may come for her, but I think we both know that no army will be able to bring her to her knees."

The young King let him go with a hard push, listening as he fell back against the wall with a laugh that Kylen remembered hearing the night he found his family. He turned on his heel and fled the scene, staring ahead as he flooded into the halls, breathing for the first time in what felt like an eternity. "Just you wait!" Erwin yelled out, causing Kylen to flinch but not react, never react. He continued walking as he forced himself to ignore the male despite what he was preaching. "*Her* story is already written; *your story is already written, boy*!"

Kylen ignored him and finally came to a halt before looking around. Kylen swallowed the thick paste of blood that hung around his throat, trying not to flinch at the very bitterness of it.

He looked up, listening for what the wind, the shadows, and the mice had to offer. He waited, listening for any sound that could resemble the sweet breeze that was his Queen, in all of her glory.

Was it true? That was a question he desperately wanted to know an answer to.

Was what he was suspecting and Erwin preaching so confidently about true? Did Althea truly hold the one magick that her father would have her head for? He could already imagine it, his magick seeping into her and killing her—how he could put nothing past him.

How Kylen would do everything he could to ensure that the old cursed man didn't claim another life, especially not the one of his Queen.

He was so close to returning to his quarters to breathe again when he felt the walls tremble—and this time to his dismay and utmost shock, *it was because of his Queen.*

This time, he was left to face the wrath of Althea Evangeline with no distraction to save him.

FIVE
ALTHEA

The doors were locked. They were sealed and completely unbreakable, not budging no matter how hard she pushed. Althea turned towards the window, lifting it up swiftly before getting ready to jump out. However, her foot found the ledge when something stopped her—some sort of barrier that froze her in place.

Her heart raced within her ears, drowning out the vicious voices of her magick.

She was trapped.

Again.

"Althea, just breathe, honey, we aren't going to hurt you," the lady who she had seen the other night spoke. How hypocritical could she be? *How ignorant could she be?*

The lady appeared to be the Captain of Kylen's guards, the one who she had briefly heard of all those years ago—but it didn't make any sense to her, she was the captain of Kylen's guards, and yet she had still helped Althea…

Was that all just Kylen's doing too?

How idiotic Althea had been to leave her still standing. She could have at least wiped her mind of her presence. That would have at least saved her.

Althea's fists met with the invisible wall that kept her trapped within the nightmares that had already span a web for her to die in. She looked over her shoulder while her mind screamed. Althea stared at the two who looked at her, her face hiding all the pure emotions that she felt cracking her soul of wars.

Althea turned on her feet, raising her hands and feeling as both the different wars of magick within her fought for her use. “Let me go.” The words were like ice, slipping off her tongue with pure venom. “Let me go, or I swear to the Gods that I will kill you, and I will not falter. Not for one second,” she seethed through her clenched jaw, watching as Sayah attempted to step towards where she was positioned.

The creature behind the captain had bright orange shoulder-length hair, far too vibrant to be anything natural. They must be something of the mythically foul kind. Sharp pointy ears lined either side of their face, wrapping with a magick that had Althea sharpening her gaze on them. “We aren’t letting you go, Althea,” the fairy, Althea assumed, whispered with a snicker as they tilted their head, ignoring the fierce gaze Sayah shot them.

Sayah raised her hands in an act of innocence. “You know I can’t do that,” she whispered apologetically. Her features seemed soft; her dark golden eyes glistening with a sadness to them that seemed far too far for Althea to reach.

Not that she would want to, anyway. She didn’t need anyone feeling bad for her.

Althea snickered as magick wrapped over her skin, becoming a shield to protect her from her force. “Yes. *Yes*, you can,” she stated, “but you two are just too afraid to defy your little King.” The Markings on her wrist burned, sending fire through her core as she shifted in her position. “Let me go, or I will burn this castle and everyone in it to the ground.”

Run mother, run mother, run mother, run, run, run! If only her magick realised that she was trying to find any exit to flee through, but every one of them was wrapped with the same magick she could feel tormenting her.

How she would enjoy burning this palace to the ground.

"You have magick," Althea persisted, ignoring the alarming thoughts of being trapped once again ceasing through her heart.

"I do." Sayah didn't blink, and Althea stepped forward as magick wrapped around her hand like wires. "Why don't we play a game—"

"*Oh, but beloved*, all your games end with death, and I would much prefer if these two kept breathing," Kylen spoke as he appeared leaning in the doorway, Sayah's magick which had kept him hidden peeling away, revealing the very man she saw every brushstroke too. "As much as I do love your games, I am sure we can think of something else to do… perhaps a classic dinner?"

"You always have been such a bore," Althea snarled as she challenged him to approach her. Extending her blade out as both Sayah and Zaire stepped out of her way, how Althea dared to almost start laughing at their cowardness. "I tell you, you and I have so much to catch up on, Noxwell—" Althea lunged for him, but magick wrapped around her waist, and she was thrown back against the wall with such force, hitting it with such a thud that her magick shot out as if it was lightning. Pure, unbreakable lightning.

It sliced through the chains that held her back, and Kylen held up a hand as he approached Althea. "Leave us. *Thea* and I here, need to have a little chat," Kylen ordered, for once in a true ruler-like tone. Althea glared at him with a gaze that was deadly. How she hated that he was calling her the name he had praised her with when she had once dared to think that they were friends. The captain shared a glance with Althea before the creature at the captain's side grabbed at her hand, forcing her out. For someone who always held such character to his voice, his tone now was certainly dull. "What's your little secret, darling?"

"Which one? You will have to be more specific." Her eyes didn't waver, holding his as if she was staring into a dragon's eye, one she never wanted to see again. "I could tell you about the secrets I hold regarding this engagement, or perhaps the ones that hold your name with such power."

"And why would you tell me either?"

"Because you won't live long enough to whisper them to any other living soul."

Kylen looked to his feet as a smile spread across his lips. "I do rather like this confident Althea; it seems as if we haven't met." Althea held his stare with emotions, feeling as the air crackled under her very presence.

"Well, now you have, and *darling*," she mocked as if it was poison. "She has already dug your grave."

"I don't doubt it. Please be sure to visit it every day; I wouldn't want to fall lonely. But Althea, I really need to know where your Markings are, and specifically what Element you have fallen under." Kylen's words were arrows that aimed for her heart, seizing it before ripping it out of the cage which was her soul. She was meant to be the archer, so why was she now represented as the prey?

"I don't know what you are talking about," Althea whispered lustfully as she tilted her head to the side, a forced smirk appearing. She batted her eyes at him as if he was a fool, and in her world, he was.

"Now that I doubt." He stepped closer, and magick that was not hers to control forced her to stay frozen against the wall. She couldn't so much as lift a finger, let alone breathe. Instead, Althea was left to see Kylen truly for the first time in what felt like centuries as he approached her. "Where are they? Why aren't you blessing me with their presence?"

"They are anything but a blessing," Althea warned, with a bitterness to her words.

He looked to be a stranger in her eyes, so different, so intoxicatingly charming. Exactly like the type of man she had been warned about. One who would try to use his kingly looks as an excuse to cheat death, how she would be sure to not let that happen.

He had truly grown into his jaw, fitting his scars as if they were jewels. His dark eyes caught sight of the morning glow from the windows beyond, and Althea found that those irises no longer glowed with any trace of warmness to them.

Instead, *they held a darkness that was truly ironic*.

There was a scar on his jaw, alongside one that went over the bridge of his nose which she already knew of. She wondered which lucky mortal or immortal creature had been the one to strike him.

To bruise that charming yet *deceiving* skin.

"Considering that you have decided to grace us all with your presence, the Ball will still happen tonight. So, I advise you to get a move on with this and wash all that blood out; you know I am always one to compliment you. Still, I do but believe that the people of our Kingdom may react badly if they realise just whose blood you wear." Kylen spoke as he reached for her wrist, blind to the bandages that lay there.

"Why should they react any differently?" Althea queried as she focussed on the trail of Elemental magick she could feel and yet not see. *Break me free of whatever is holding me frozen*, she whispered to the blooming light within her mind; and for whatever reason, the Elemental magick decided to obey her. Althea broke free by electrifying the magick that held her down, a smirk curling at the ends of her lips to make it look as if that had been all of her doing. "I'm wearing the blood of those that deserved something far crueller than death."

"My darling, you murdered innocent people."

Althea's face wavered, and she moved out of his way, sliding against the wall before pivoting around him. "You do not know me anymore." She laughed under her breath. "These people were anything but innocent. They were child traffickers, murderers, abusers, et cetera." Her voice lingered through the air as she walked around Kylen. "I'm not like you, Kylen. I don't murder innocent people. I don't betray those that don't deserve to be pained in that way." She threw each word at him as if they were her personalised daggers, aiming for the target which was the centre of his soul.

"Yes, but I don't go and try to murder Kingdoms of innocent people, do I? Althea, let me see your Markings." Kylen persisted, earning a cruel laugh from Althea.

"No."

Kylen hung his head to his left, following her as her eyes darted to each possible exit of the room, of the castle. "Let me go, Kylen." With everything in her, she knew that she could kill him right here and right now, but that wouldn't solve her problem of breaking free. And even if she did manage to break free, Althea was meant to marry into his Kingdom's name. She could not kill him for it—*she needed to marry him first*. It didn't make sense to her; earning a Kingdom should be *earning a Kingdom*—there should not be a specific way to do it. But her father had been so clear, so dreadfully clear that she was to marry him to earn it: that a part of her was afraid of how he would react if she were to do anything else.

"I could protect you from your father, you do realise. No army of his could ever overthrow mine." The words Kylen spoke made Althea look to the ground as she walked towards one of the windows that she was yet to try.

"That's cute," she murmured.

"It's true. Agree to be my bride, and I will protect you from your father." She could feel his eyes burning into the back of her head as she tried to go beyond the window, but once again, a force field so strong met with her hands, and she seethed. "My father would kill you," Althea stated as she turned to him. "He would have your head, and I wouldn't stop him."

“I don’t need you to stop him—I just need you to marry me.”

“Do you honestly think that I am going to marry you? After everything you have put me through, after every war you have pulled me into? You have literally lived up to what the rumours have said of you. You have gone *mad*.” *No. Don’t, Althea. You need to marry him, remember? If you do not marry him, you won’t get the life your father speaks of.* The words of her mind scolded.

Kylen crossed his arms before him as he leaned against the wall. “Yes, I *madly* want you to be my bride,” he cooed, grinning to himself as if he thought he was genuinely smart. “That was meant to sound far more convincing; I apologise.” Kylen cleared his throat. Althea waited, brow raised. “You don’t have much of a choice, I’m afraid. Because I can go and tell your father about the little situation you have yourself in or—”

“You don’t have any proof that I am anything that you speak of,” Althea said convincingly.

Kylen raised a brow. “Erwin wouldn’t try to kill you without reason. And the one thing that could tick him off is that if you are now one of *us*—if you hold the magick of the Elementals.” He allowed those few words to pierce through the air before continuing on, every word that left his tongue forming into an arrow and piercing the archer into two. “But I’m not going to tell your father unless that’s my only option.”

“The Markings will be gone within the next few days. So even if I agree to sit here and be your pretty-little wife, it won’t last long.” *No. Don’t allow Erwin to erase us away. He is dangerous, and you need us, mother.*

“You’ll probably kill me before then anyway, so I’m not too afraid. But how exactly do you plan to rid yourself of this magick, dear?”

Althea tensed, how she hated every little nickname he threw at her. “That’s none of your concern—”

“Erwin won’t help you. He doesn’t believe in helping anyone

but himself. So, let me ask you again to accept your fate. Marry me, and I will protect you. Sayah can help you train this new magick—and if your father ever dares to show his face here, then you would have figured out already how to hide your Markings." He paused, and Althea looked down to the windowsill that she was currently trying to escape through, feeling as the weight that his words carried genuinely settled upon her heavy shoulders. "I can help you," he repeated, and Althea turned to him.

"Why do you need a Queen so badly?" she asked.

"I don't need a Queen; my Kingdom does."

Althea crossed her arms, damning her mind for genuinely considering this idiocy. If she did accept to become his Queen, she would not only gain his protection but access to Erwin—which led her to consider this idiotic idea with an actual intention for the first time.

She would be able to force Erwin to help her, and soon, these Markings would be gone—meaning she could still kill Kylen the night of their wedding and earn her father's blessing of freedom. "Where is it?" Kylen asked for what felt like the millionth time. If only he realised they were hidden under the bandages that were too hidden under the blood-soaked shirt that she had stolen the day before. "There is not much that a Princess of your type would hide, especially from a father who would give the world if he could. So, I can only presume it is the one thing that he would have your head for, the one thing that he would hate you for," he spoke, stating his reasons for his belief all over again, running her ears red.

"My father would not give the world to me," Althea declared. "So, I hardly think a little Marking is going to change anything under my circumstances. You, however, won't be so lucky." They both knew her words were straight lies, but she needed to believe them.

And he allowed her too.

"Where are they, my love?" he asked, persisting with the

same question that she wished to wipe from his mind. "Just show me what we are dealing with, and we can figure out a plan against your father."

Althea's heart dropped into her stomach, the very words causing her legs to feel as if they were about to give way any minute. "I don't know what you are talking about," she said far more evenly this time, hiding all the anxiety that bit at her throat. Kylen moved quickly towards her, his hand finding her waist and shoulder, stopping her from escaping his questions.

Althea looked up at him, sharpening her brows as he gazed down towards her. His breath reached the tip of her nose, threatening her with the minty smell of whatever mint he had previously had.

She felt this new magick warp around her skin, and she formed a dagger, one that aimed for the bottom of his stomach; the blade already pricking blood. Althea held her breath as his scent filled her senses, that same scent that brought her back to her cold bedroom floor all those years ago, how she had been laying there as he fled the scene of his crimes.

Althea cleared her throat, glancing up at Kylen as she pressed the blade to the bottom of his stomach. "Don't play this game with me, Althea. You think I am like one of your little townsmen. Someone under the wrath of your father's control, but that is just not it. Show it to me. I want to see what Elemental Realm you have fallen under." He spoke of it as if it was an achievement, something that she should be mockingly proud of.

Kylen had managed to find her wrist, all in a span of a second. He didn't seem to think it was there, or so she thought as he didn't do anything other than hold it firmly, waiting for her to take the initiative... but all she could do was smile.

For three long torturous seconds, she just stared at him, holding his gaze with all of the foreign and old magick that called to her like an army.

"Kylen, let her go," Sayah said quickly as she entered back

into the room, looking to the Princess as if this was her apology for locking her behind these walls. "She is stuck under your roof; that is enough torture for now. You do not need to put her through anything more." The captain had never genuinely left the two alone; *Althea knew that.* She could sense the captain's strange presence outside of the room, bickering with the other creature as she demanded to be allowed to stop this nonsense.

Kylen looked over his shoulder at her with an exaggerated, pissed-off sigh. "She is under my roof; therefore, I should know what type of magick she is going to be trying to kill me with," he said dryly. His gaze turned back on her, and as always, Althea held his stare. "If you can, go make sure that Althea has what she needs to get herself ready for tonight."

Sayah kept her stare on Althea, but she did not return it. Kylen scoffed as he seized Althea up and down, dragging his eyes over her every breath ever so slowly. "So, my love, where are the Markings?"

Althea tilted her head to the side, but before she could move her lips to speak, his hand had flinched away. His eyes fell to the crimson blood that coated his fingertips and how his eyes widened in horror.

"You're hurt," he stated as if it wasn't obvious enough. Erwin must have nicked the scar she had hiding there.

"I've gone through worse." A bitterness struck her words, one that met her mark of his lips perfectly. She focussed on the pain that began to haunt her—her ears adjusting to the softest murmurs of her mind to hear what was being screamed, chanted.

Gone, gone, gone, gone, gone. They are gone, and the horrible yet beautiful, tragic magick is going to get you next! Run! What they spoke made no sense, but then again, when did they ever speak with sanity?

"Show me where you are hurt," Kylen said, interrupting the thoughts that had brought Althea through Realms. He looked at her with wide eyes, the brown of them practically trembling.

"Did I hurt you—" The words were barely in the air before Kylen shook his head, dismissing his words as he cleared his throat. "*Show me your Markings, Althea.*"

Althea rolled her eyes with a scowl and pulled her arm from his grip before pulling up her sleeve; she kept her eyes locked with his as she undid the bandage. "You want to see them so badly?" she chastised in question. "Then here you are. Don't expect anything grand. The moment I get the chance, I will cut your tongue and slit your throat. I am only showing you this to shut you up as I can practically feel my headache forming." Althea heaved, slowly revealing the horrid Markings that coated her damaged skin. "They will be gone soon enough though; I vow to you that."

In the old language, people used to refer to the Markings as tattoos that could survive through wars. But tattoos were different. You had a say whether they appeared on your body. Even if you were drunk on the wine produced by the fae at the time of consent, you still had a say in the matter.

These… you had no say. From the time you gained your magick, they appeared, and when you lost your magick or ultimately died, they disappeared. Leaving your body worn and bruised, gasping for the air that had once been so controlled by the untamed magick.

Kylen raised a finger, his cold touch meeting with the unknown warmth that hid beneath her skin. He dragged a finger down the lines engraved on her wrist, his touch so soft yet so horrible. A tingling sensation lingering behind as his finger moved on.

Althea hadn't truly looked at her Markings yet. Sure, she had glanced at them in fear and looked away, panicking, but she hadn't seen them yet.

Extending from her right wrist down to around the middle of her arm laid a straight black line. In the middle of the line was a crescent moon, in alignment with the line. All the Elemental

Markings, she had realised, laid around it, dancing before her very face. On the right side of the line and above the crescent moon was a sun, a bright, vivid sun that sent lines of sun rays seeping across her skin. Underneath the sun and below the bottom of the crescent moon, there were detailed twines of wind, leaves, flowers, and other particles of nature being caught in the art that was the wind and extending across the rest of her flesh.

On the left and above the crescent moon was a large group of flowers, roses, lilies, et cetera. They would be seen as marvellous if they were anywhere else but on her skin, holding such detail and strength that the flowers truly were gorgeous in a general sense. Below the flowers and beneath the crescent moon, where Kylen now dragged his fingers across, laid one of the moon cycles, a waxing gibbous. One star to the left of it as if it meant anything. *As if it meant anything to the galaxy, it could have been. She* could have been.

Althea looked away, unable to face such horrors, *such death*, any longer.

He furrowed his brows, and she inched away, his hand flinching in response as if his movements were once again synced with hers. "When did they appear?" he asked, pure concern lining his tone.

"A few days after my birthday," Althea said through an exaggerated sigh. "Why does it matter? They aren't the usual Markings, I'm aware. But they will be gone soon, I assure you."

"I don't need your assurance." he exhaled. "Why does it matter?" Kylen imitated with a scoff that Althea was quite prepared to punch off of his lips. "I have never seen Markings like those anywhere—" she pulled her wrist away and shrugged her sleeve back down.

"So what?"

"Well, *do you* know anything about them?"

"No." There was no point in pretending she did. She never did claim to like any of that Elemental stuff. She had saved herself from learning it; after all, she did grow up hearing how wrong it was from the words her father seethed.

"It's okay," Kylen murmured more to himself than to her because she was fine, beyond fine. Her mind was at ease because now Erwin was within her reach, and she could access him at any time— "*You didn't kill Erwin, did you?*"

"No," Kylen said as he lifted his brown eyes from where they had been fixated on her arm.

Althea nodded. *Good*, she was rather pleased that he was alive because that meant that another part of her inevitable plan in her mind hadn't gone to shit. "*So*, how long do I have?"

Althea could feel the stare he had pictured upon her. It was one she recognised so easily, one she found herself trapped within. She blinked, begging herself to look away from the pain that skinned her alive. She should have accepted his deal of marriage when he offered it to her—now he knew the Markings she bore…

"Pardon me?" Kylen asked sceptically. "How long until what…?" the question presented itself evidentially, and yet he had no clue. Well, there was one thing that hadn't changed in all this time. "Did you hit your head or something, darling?" he moved his hand up to Althea's forehead, but she grabbed it swiftly.

Althea quietly fumed as she asked. "How long until you tell my father?"

Kylen didn't answer; instead, he just flexed out his fingers. "Evangeline," he started, using her surname as he had done numerous times all those years ago. Was it to belittle her? Or was it merely a taunt? He spoke factious, just as he always did; another thing that seemed to make her magick beg to taste his death.

"I won't tell your father," he said swiftly with a cock of his brow. Her heart leapt with something of shock, but Althea waited irritably; she knew something more was coming. It was on the edge of his nose, next to the few small scars that too were there. "I won't tell your father if you make this marriage work. You don't have to tolerate me for all I care, and by all means, make life more interesting… just be the Queen my people need." Kylen tutted, a sincerity to his voice that made Althea want to laugh—or perhaps cry, she wasn't sure. "You will present yourself as Queen and be a ruler—a good one to the few folks that you have left alive for us to rule."

Althea stood dumbstruck, her eyes slowly searching through the void that was his. "You still want to marry me—even after seeing the Markings?" Althea broke off, the confusion very much evident as she watched him carefully. She swallowed back the pain that she felt infecting her soul. He was so sincere about these people—how come he hadn't been like this to her when all she wanted was a place in his Kingdom. A home.

"Well, yes, I still need a Queen."

Breathe, just breathe, just breathe. Mother needs to breathe.

"Okay," the word was a bare whisper as it left her lips. "Show me to my room."

"Would you like me to help with your wound?" he asked as he began to walk in the direction she could only assume her room was in.

"No. I can handle myself." The disappointment in his eyes was truly ironic.

Her room was a mere minute away, not at all far, which was very kind considering the way her throat burned. She reached the doorway, but Kylen reached for the handle, stopping her from entering.

"So, you will be my Queen?" he asked, a million questions circling through his eyes.

Althea nodded slowly, hesitantly. She straightened her spine, releasing a cold breath as she tried to listen to the voices that spoke with sanity within her mind. Althea knew that she was one to hold onto grudges, to feel so incapable of allowing anybody else to feel at peace when she was hurting—but she needed to think about this clearly. If she married Kylen, she would not only abide by her father's orders and wishes, but she would also manage to gain unlimited access to Erwin.

And he could put her back into the position she was originally meant to be in.

A sigh—one that quivered along her spine, released itself into the world as she nodded again. "I will be. But next time, I expect a far grander proposal."

With that, Althea opened her door and walked inside. Not faltering for a second before shutting the door in his face. She leant against it, pressing her back against the cold wood before reaching a hand up to her mouth, muting the sobs that threatened to burst from the pits of her lungs. They were yet to erupt, but her heavy breaths told her that they were coming.

She didn't know what made her feel as if she was sitting in the cold of a new moon, but perhaps it had something to do with the part where Althea was never deemed worthy of Kylen's kindness.

How she hadn't deserved it.

How her efforts of her kind heart were overlooked because of the evil her father forced her through.

Or maybe it was that her father was going to kill her. That everything she had worked to regain had slipped from under her touch without any warning, and now she had nothing to hold onto to feel secure, to defend herself with.

Althea dropped her hand from her mouth as she looked up to the ceiling, blinking away the tears that slowly trailed down her cheeks.

She didn't want to marry him, but she didn't want to return home either—not in a state like this. Althea would have to marry him, and she figured that she should be pleased about the fact that she would get to kill him the night of their wedding because of her father's orders… but there was just so much to get through before that.

Why, oh why, did she have to gain the one thing her father would kill her for holding?

Why, oh why, did she have to see Kylen, the boy who she had ever only just wanted to be friends with, again?

SIX
KYLEN

Kylen was still unable to breathe. Althea had been in her room all morning after having Sayah silently heal her, and yet it did not feel like time had slipped by at all. One minute she looked like she was about to bring a thunderous storm down on them all, and the next, she was agreeing to the deal he had made up on the very spot, rushing away to her quarters where no sounds were heard as Kylen hesitated outside of her door.

How... charismatic?

It was clever, of course. Everything of his was well thought through. But he had been so prepared to continue with the threats and pleas that the chance of her accepting his deal was one that did not present itself well to him.

Kylen tapped his foot, tremors of the magick that was rotting his soul flooding across the enchanted floors around him. The door was shut in his face, blocking him out with whatever ridiculous magick she had cast upon it.

It was probably the one her father held such enormous control of and used to his own selfish needs, how Kylen would never understand how that was deemed as justice. Kylen knew that her father didn't particularly like magick—but that was in the sense of others. For himself, he believed magick (the curse) to be the solution to everything, which is most likely why his land floods with such death.

"Are you just going to stand there and gape?" Sayah asked from behind him.

He turned to her, feeling her warm magick flood around his legs, stopping the tremors that had the castle shaking beneath his fading wrath.

"What if she escaped?" Kylen asked. "I dare say that the Markings on her arms challenge yours." He had expected earlier to see a small sun or even a moon. There was a chance that she might have gained the Elemental magick of Autumnia or Flora, but for someone of her class, that was seemingly rare.

"She wouldn't have escaped," Sayah assured him as she guided him away with a push of her magick. She held a smile on her lips, her steps nearly silent compared to his; no doubt Althea was listening. "Come on, don't be a creep, don't crowd her—especially not at a time like this; she just needs time. We have other things we need to deal with."

The look on the siren's face caused him to fume silently, moving his stare away from hers. "You don't believe that the Markings I saw are true?" he questioned. "I saw them with my own eyes! And a King's eyes never lie."

Sayah tutted with a breezy laugh, giving Kylen Noxwell the only answer he needed. "It's not that I don't believe you; it's more so that I think that she has hidden her true Markings with a cloaking spell of some type or even a spell of illusions." She shrugged simply as she turned to dance her way down the halls, the curtains waving to her through the rhythm of the wind as she ever so graciously passed. Kylen followed just behind, enjoying watching her gracefulness.

"But she doesn't have that ability!" Kylen said. He held her gaze tightly, watching as her opposed demeanour changed to one softer.

"She may not have, but many people in the Kingdom do, whether they are out with it or not," she said, urging Kylen forward. "And I have been feeling strange around her. My scales pick up a sense with her, one that isn't too clear but most definitely there."

"I know." Kylen groaned as he looked towards the window he passed. "I know." He reached up to his face, brushing his hair back with a simple sigh as he averted his attention. "So, she definitely can't get out? It wouldn't make sense if she didn't truly have those Markings, then why was she so quick to accept my deal?" he asked, changing from one question to the next with such ease.

"I would hardly say that her answer came quickly," Sayah said as they entered the kitchens. "But that is true, knowing the type of person you have explained her to be, she would never accept something like this if she didn't have a motive." She sighed as she reached over to grab an apple. "But hey, now in your dying days, you can figure out just what her true motive is; that will certainly keep you busy."

Kylen rolled his eyes at her. "I will find time," he assured her through a short laugh. "For now, how is the Ball coming along?"

Sayah hummed as she placed her already half-eaten apple down. "Swimmingly," she answered. "The only problem is that half the guests are shaken up about all the murders and deaths that there have been. And well, the other half… *well,* they are dead. Curtesy to your lovely fiancé, of course." Despite talking about such horrors: a smile spread across her lips. How in her nature the siren felt. Admiring one for the death that they wear.

"I must admit, I never thought she could be so like her father. *I mean*, I knew they shared the same blood and all, but the last time I saw her, she was so… sunshine-like, so smiley." Kylen didn't want to think about his play in all of this, but of course, the siren had other plans.

Sayah held the young Kings' stare for a gratuitous second. "And do you think you may have had a say in the matter of the person she has become?"

"Me?" Kylen queried, waving it over in a matter of a second so that he would not drown in those thoughts. "Never. It's in her blood; it was destined to happen sometime, whether in this lifetime or the next."

A silence echoed between them. So, Kylen looked to Sayah warily, noting that she was trapped in a stare. "Do you think that I did happen to play a part in the person she now is?" To say he wanted an answer was an understatement. His mind was at a toll, both on different sides of a war, just like the position Althea and he was in.

His agitated tremors were noticeable by the siren, but as much as he wanted to care, he simply couldn't bring himself to. "And would you feel any different if I were to say, 'yes, I think you did play a part'?" Sayah asked. Kylen looked towards the window; towards the Kingdom *he had saved.* He could feel the vibrancy in the air, the way the music flowed through the sky as the people, the children, the animals all danced through the festivals of the Queen's safe arrival.

Sayah had entered his life in the most surprising way. When he was young, he had a friend. One that was sweet despite never once being able to speak to him. He spoke one of the old languages, a language that no one ever bothered to learn anymore, which Kylen had found out to his disgrace.

So, he made it his friend's birthday present, to be able to wish him 'happy birthday' in a language that he would understand. But before Kylen could share with him just what he had spent all those long hours learning, his friend, Raiugh, had died at war. Lost to the complete brutality of it. Leaving Kylen with this new language on his tongue, preparing to give a speech to honour the boy that he had never had the privilege of talking to.

He had damned himself for not acting sooner, quicker.

Kylen had been too slow.

Which was exactly why, from that moment on, he had been determined to learn every way of communication that there was, so that no matter who entered his life, he would be able to understand them, to make them feel comfortable in a place that he would make as secure as possible. His Kingdom was one that already spoke many languages. Kylen had learned that when his ancestors were the rulers of these lands and the population of this Kingdom was small, communication was quite difficult. Everyone tried to learn each other's language, or just enough so that they could ask how the family was or if they needed anything from the bakery... or just enough to say hello. Over time majority of his people learned more and more of the other languages. It was just the royals that were blindsided by this, as Kylen learned about with such confusion.

His mother had never had the luxury of royalty when she grew up. She lived in a small village up north, growing up alone with her father. Her father wasn't her biological father, but blood was never deemed family. He had pale skin and black hair, whereas she, his mother, had dark skin and black hair—making it very obvious that they weren't blood, as people liked to point out. The people of that village always mocked him for staying around as he'd had the opportunity to return to his extended family back in the east—but her father was happy there, and he never really liked that part of his family. He had made friends as well, friends who became uncle and aunt figures for his mother.

Kylen loved hearing those stories. Ones about Lisiany, who was apparently a half-witch and had the darkest red hair his mother had ever seen. About Kerti, who taught his mother that patience and honesty were the two keys to life. He had had dark skin too, but not as dark as his mother's, more so like the skin

Kylen bore, his mother had told him. Kylen had spent the first young years of his life hearing about it all, and through all the stories and memories, his mother made it clear that the only problem this world had was that it treated the people born into poor families with only a few specks of respect.

His mother had met his father when he went on a tour of the seas. He had stopped by her village for a small break where he went undercover just to find some peace for a few days. He had met his mother there, and from the moment they began speaking, both of them knew that their souls were one.

In the beginning, Kylen got to work quickly, going through the castle and asking every folk there to teach him the languages of their tongue, culture, and homes. And those who also wanted to learn, he invited along while his brothers did their jobs for them.

He noticed the way his castle, for the first time in so many years, *had bloomed with light*. The people beneath his castle—the people who kept this Kingdom running, *were finally able to communicate to him and how they had such glorious stories to share*.

And such *horrid* ones too.

They had been reluctant to share anything negative at first. They never wanted to come across as ungrateful or rude, fearing that the King might turn on them as every ruler seemed to be doing. But Kylen swore that he wasn't that man, that his parents had raised him to be better before they had passed and left the crown for a child. And eventually, with time, they believed it. One by one, Kylen sat and listened to the memories that had been suffocated beneath the new lifestyles that they had been forced to live.

He learnt how half of those working for this Kingdom had been ripped from their homes. Put on boats, ships, anything that would get them to other places to work. They didn't know if their families were alive or if their friends even remembered their names.

And that guilt had made Kylen furious.

But this wasn't about him; this was about them.

Which was how he met Sayah.

Kylen had formed an army of sirens, fairy's, goblins, creatures of all types. Anyone who would help him sneak into hidden lands and save those rotting beneath the patriarchy.

He snuck into forbidden lands, Kingdoms, lost cities. Using his excuse as a Privateer to find the families and lost ones of those that should have never been forced apart in the first place.

Death followed him as if he was on his way to the afterlife. The very scar across the bridge of his nose was an everlasting reminder of this time. The old King of the North, who was now dead, had found Kylen right as he was about to get on the ship with this Kingdoms' prisoners and flee. Kylen had forced the ship out of there with the last touch of his magick and then had faced the wrath of this King's anger with a blind eye.

The torture, both mental and physical, had lasted through the nights and days. Sayah must have realised that he never came home because she had practically burned the Kingdom to the ground looking for him. How he had grinned so lazily as he watched the siren tear the old man to shreds.

Nonetheless, Kylen continued his work and had only stopped going on those missions around a month or two ago because of the curse that was determined to tear his heart to shreds, leaving nothing but a pool of blood behind for him to drown in. It had gotten worse over the past few months, and Kylen had found that if he didn't get up at the same time every day, he wouldn't get up at all.

But rather drown in the heaviness that was his soul.

Sayah, being the heavenly saviour that she was, vowed to him that she would do his job for him, and he knew that she would live up to her word. She was an immortal siren, and he knew how she felt about bringing those who abused their power down to their knees.

The words of the whispers were that he was '*mad*', '*beyond mental*'; just because he didn't have slaves in his Kingdom, that he didn't have people living off of his streets, surviving on his scraps. No, he made sure all had a home, a job, something to keep them going. And if that made him mad, then so be it. He was quite fine with being recognised as the Mad King. They could call him the Insane King for all he cared, and Kylen would bow to the name.

His mother always said that the world was a cruel place, especially for those who grew up poorer; and that if Kylen wanted to be good, sweet, understanding and a powerful King, the best thing he could do was take time to understand what his people needed, what would help *them* survive. Kylen didn't just make his Kingdom as King; *they made it too.* He wanted to give them the best opportunity for life when he was gone.

However, it didn't really quite occur to Kylen just how much he had learnt until he was walking down his streets one long night. The day had been tiring, and his illness had decided to act upon him despite the several meetings he was forced to sit through. Normally, the calm and quiet of the night helped soothe this ache—little did Kylen know there were festivals roaming the streets. Parties that Kylen passed by slowly. He hadn't even been focussing on what words people spoke until he realised that he could understand basically everything. Maybe that was a part of the magick he had never learnt to explore, or perhaps it was just easy to learn something when he spent so much time fixated on it.

"No," he admitted in response to Sayah, gazing from the window back to the siren who turned to him with a scowl. Sayah held that same look on her face, which told him that she knew he was lying.

Within a breath, a sharp one—his fingers began to throb, a burn to them that brought a blanket of dread over his shoulders.

"*Kylen, Kylen, Kylen,* my Gods," Sayah mused, oblivious to the dark magick that was taking over the hands in his pockets.

He knew that she remembered the boy that he once was. She remembered the boy who used to be mistaken as her son even though his was at home keeping secrets from him.

Looking back on his childhood now, Kylen saw a boy who was oblivious. A boy who had rich skin not yet burdened by the illness that coated his lungs. His skin looked greener and paler than what it used to, his jaw was more defined and his eyebags were darker. Kylen remembered the glow that used to whisper beneath his skin; it was almost as if he too had hidden scales that appeared every now and then.

"Good," spoke the voice from nowhere but the air around them. "I have taught you well then." Sayah crossed her arms, her eyes narrowing on the air as Zaire's presence was scented.

"I would not say that you have taught him well at all," Sayah scolded. "If anything, you should be pushing him to keep his father's heart."

Zaire held up their hands as their body formed, and in the most inoffensive tone, they conceded to speak. "I am saving him from death. A virtue no one in his Kingdom holds anymore. Speaking of… does she look somewhat more presentable for tonight?" they trailed off with a scheme of something more in their eyes.

"Ask Kylen. He was the one hanging outside her door for the past four or five hours."

Zaire moved their gaze to him with a cocked brow.

"I was not hanging around her door," he assured them in a quick matter. "I was merely listening in to hear whether or not she was going to murder the last of us."

Zaire laughed with a venomous sound and Kylen's brows stayed annoyingly lost to the creases of his stressed forehead.

"Well, to be fair, I really don't care what you spend your time doing, just as long as it's not near me. Now, Erwin is out. He is unconscious, and every part of his body is trapped to the ground, so he shall not be disturbing the excitement of tonight."

"The Ball… right," Kylen whispered as he leant back against the table. "So many things could go wrong. Someone could die—someone could spot her Markings—someone could be killed—Hel, Althea could murder somebody—"

"I won't. It's not worth my energy." There it was, the presence he had suspected minutes earlier but did not say anything about in fear of scaring the almost wild beast away. She stood tall; her arms crossed across her lean, narrow body. "If I were trying to kill them all, I would not have spent the last lot of hours fixing myself up to your standards. Instead, I would have worked on gathering supplies and finding a location to where I could plant a successfully made bomb of magick."

Ah. Of course. One of her many infamous bombs. Kylen remembered all of her many inventions. The way she spoke of such things that he listened to for hours. It never quite made sense to him, but the weapons she dreamed of creating for the greater good always did seem to have some potential. *"No, you have to listen. You just fuel it up with a large breath of said magick as well as some fairies air and goblin aura and done. You wait."* He had never been sure on how she came up with all of those inventions, but he figured it had something to do with her many years of being trapped behind closed walls as well as the books full of such worlds that she spent her time reading.

Kylen screwed his brows together, shrugging sluggishly as he offered her an apple which she just glared at. "Interesting take, but alright." He lost her gaze—his peripheral vision, however, showed him that she had indeed listened to him and cleaned herself up, showing off her true beauty to the world.

Even from a young age, she had been beautiful. Her long hair and vibrant ocean eyes were richer than any had seen before.

Folks of all ages bid so much on just getting a glimpse of her; it was disgusting, revolting. It was a marvellous thing that her own father hadn't sold her off yet; she would go for millions, even if the millions were from his own money, in an attempt to save her from the life of what would have been slavery.

"Princess," Sayah said as she bowed out of modesty. "Is there anything I can get you to eat?" she asked over the muffled scoff from the fairy who had taken a more human-like form. Kylen noticed the way Althea suppressed her curiosity as the fairy changed. It was strange to even him the way Zaire had such control over their body. It was as if they were the God of themselves, and whatever they said miraculously happened. Kylen never found that it made sense to him, but he did learn over the years that it was better not to ask questions.

"No," Althea answered. "I am not hungry for anything you have to offer, and I would prefer to spend my time going around the grounds of this… castle," she snapped, taunting her thoughts to his ears which were already addicted to her voice.

"To plant your magick-filled bomb, I'm sure," Kylen pried with a grin that came across more of a smirk. "If you are tolerable tonight and do not show any threat to our people, then I will have Sayah lift her magick. I won't have you living like a prisoner. I don't want you to think I am anything like your father."

Althea didn't say anything; instead, she just slyly took in the large room in which they all were present. How the paintings across the walls truly did it justice.

There were new freckles on her cheeks, ones that might have appeared just days after he had left, or perhaps only recently. Her hair was no longer short; it was long and curly, with wild curls scraping across her backside like layered diamonds.

She was gorgeous when she was clean—and even when not, she was still beautiful. It was one of the many qualities she held so highly; it got her everything she wanted; a privilege Kylen did not have. Althea knew her beauty, and she weighed it like a true

Queen, something that had changed more finely over the past years.

It was her weapon of choice, one that he knew could bring armies to their knees.

However, he knew she was just as strong without it. She never needed anything—not even this newfound magick to be strong, nor the training her father had forced on her. Althea was simply strong because she was Althea, and she was the brightest star of them all.

Althea fussed about with the sleeve of her dress, doing it in such a subtle manner that Kylen's eyes sliding to her sleeves had shot her guard straight back up. She passed him a warning look as she raised her brow, a laugh on her tongue. She moved past him, passing Sayah's burning gaze, looking towards the fairy who had settled back into their original form.

Althea raised her hand, and darkness quickly shot out from it. Shadows that were ever so deep with darkness twirling throughout the air like twine. It grabbed the ruby red apple from the fruit bowl in the middle of the table, waltzing back to Althea's fine hand for her to take a bite.

Kylen watched, hypnotised by her movements, yet lost in the forest that was his mind. The other two jumped back before trying to hide their fear, but she saw it, he knew she did. The darkness used to affect her; she used to sheer away from it, visibly uncomfortable every time she was forced to use it. It would make her sick.

And despite smiling at Kylen every morning out of modesty, he could see the bags under her young eyes.

Now, it looked easy for her. She didn't bat an eye nor flinch, not how Kylen did.

She looked to him, a smile of pure feral glee coating her lips as she found the apple that she had plucked from the fruit bowl. Her face was covered once again with unspoken words, her eyes hiding the darkness that swirled around within. Althea turned;

her snow touched hair falling back over her shoulder as she shook her head slyly, ignoring the cat that slowly entered the room and leapt onto Kylen's lap, quickly falling into a deep slumber. "Let the games begin." Althea whispered as her voice danced down the hallway.

The question arose in his mind once more, even as he got himself dressed for the evening—even as he choked on the blood that was pure darkness; it was still there.

What had he caused her all those years ago?

A question that he was sure to drink away tonight.

SEVEN
ALTHEA

The apple's core turned to dust, coating the palm of her hand in what looked to be old, daring ashes. It matched the aesthetic of this castle in that particular way. Everything looked to be so old, so ancient. There was an aesthetic to it that made it have that feeling that you would see this type of scenery in a dream. It didn't look real; it looked like another figment of her very vivid imagination. One that she was not too keen on.

And it didn't help, of course, that the woman known as Sayah had a barrier up and around the outsides of the castle. One that just seemed to send a shimmering haze throughout it all. Bending the light to make everything seem so much more twisted—not real in any way.

Althea brushed her hands in the air before her, the dust fleeing into the air as if it had never been true. The dress that she had on fit her perfectly. It wasn't too revealing nor tight, and it seemed to be looser on all the areas that she hated to feel. Such as her throat, her stomach and now her right wrist covered in the Markings that she didn't understand. Althea closed her eyes as she ran a hand over her stomach, pushing the thoughts back and away as she opened them again, ignoring the burning pain the memories had around her throat. Why was he allowed to act as if he knew everything that there was to Althea when he knew nothing? Not anymore—not as she had once believed him too.

His death was going to be everything that she had ever dreamt of.

It was a beautiful dress, no doubt, one that highlighted her eyes the most since it was made of a royal blue material. *"I think the first thing that really caught my attention was your eyes," Kylen had admitted as he took another sip of her father's wine. He kept his eyes on Althea's as if he was lost in the seas of them. The way he spoke about them made her feel giddy inside, laughing purely to hide the nerves that bubbled within her stomach.*

How foolish and wrapped in the idea of validation that child had been.

It honestly made her laugh how a child had been clinging to this idea of love and friendship, romanticising any emotion within her life to try and make herself feel wanted.

Althea had been twelve then, and she had believed to be in love when what she really wanted was a friend. Someone who wouldn't hurt her.

That was why his death would be glorious, the voices reminded her. *He deserved nothing but pain and punishment, and oh, how amazing that would feel. To watch the blood drain from the heart we hold. To watch his eyes beg ours for mercy and how we will spit at them with venom.*

The breeze brushed against Althea's face as her eyes trailed over the waves of the seas below her. For so long, she had worked to forget all that Kylen had said to her over the duration of that one week. She worked every minute of every hour that followed those treacherous days on trying to use her curse to wipe her memories, but it wouldn't let her save herself by harming herself.

Why did it insist on punishing her for a crime she did not commit?

Althea shut the glass windows abruptly, blocking the smell of the sea from her senses. Perhaps it was a good thing that she hadn't erased it from her mind; because then, if she had, she wouldn't feel the satisfaction that Kylen's death was sure to bring.

The sunset here took longer than back home. And she had figured that it was because of the Realms that the Kingdom sat on. This Realm… *it sure was something.* It was positioned on the edge of the coldest season of them all, blessed alongside fire and the warmth of Sommsia, the Goddess of Summer, which the Realms of Sommsia were named after.

Two of the other four Goddesses had their play here: with Whyntiou, the Goddess of Winter. And Flora, the Goddess of Spring.

Lorundio was in the centre of it all, but nonetheless, the warmer weather held a great play over the days. Something she didn't think she could ever get used to.

The warmth died in the evenings, the cooler aspects settling in and reminding Althea of the only place she had ever known.

What would she do after her father gained control of these lands? Perhaps she could take a boat out and see the world and meet with the stars she had always dreamt of talking to. Althea wondered how her father would adjust in the near future here; would he be better at it than her? Or would he be worse? It was a silly thing to wonder when she already knew the answer would be that if he didn't like it, he would change it, forming it into another one of his ridiculous creations.

The sound of music swarmed down and along her veins, causing her magick to react in the utmost curious way. She turned her head and looked towards the doors at the end of the hallway that she passed, following the sounds that had her blood racing. This castle had a simple layout, one that made it so much easier to memorise when it came to planning her beloved's death.

The sun had officially set, and the stars were pirouetting. Lighting up the waves and depths of the sea with all of the colours that they glistened with. They made pictures she recognised from the mural her mother had once completed. How she wished she had gotten to the maids before they had already painted over half of it.

From what Althea had gathered from the whispers, was that her mother was always one to get lost in the meaning of the universe. Always wondering what more was out there. As if she was naturally drawn to it and now forever lost to it.

Althea figured her mother was where she had gotten her imagination from. She always did spend her nights on the roof of her old castle, staring up at the dark clouds and every once in a few months gaining a glimpse at the worlds beyond hers. How she had wished that someone would give her meaning. Give her a chance at something great.

Althea approached the large doors that separated her from the crowd on the other side. *How much of a crowd would there be?* The question that was filling her mind beyond Realms asked her. It was frightening to think about; even as she looked up with a thick swallow, her mind couldn't make out the answers she begged for.

The last time she had been in a room with real people was the first day of Kylen's trip to Aeonia. He had brought his guards, and they had filled the space; it had made the young girl so giddy to be walking into the room with such life. Such expressions.

Up until then, she had never seen a soul untouched by the curse; she had never seen a face that smiled back at her.

But now, Althea had killed many across the course of the few days that she had been hiding out in this Kingdom. They all had crossed her paths at the wrong time.

She didn't kill anyone innocent.

Althea wasn't that cruel.

Nonetheless, they were terrible creatures. If anything, Althea was a God for doing all that she did. They would die soon anyway; human lifespans weren't that long. Any basic creature would die not long after humans, but who would waste a lifetime loving them—loving anyone when you could gain freedom or the ability to see the world one has always dreamt of?

Althea pushed her hand out, feeling as the cold of the wood seeped through her bones, cleansing them of the deaths she held. Chilling the blood that swarmed her thoughts with evil. With darkness that spread across her shoulders like the plague. She closed her eyes and slowly counted each presence in the room beyond. People filled the space, but the gaps were evident. She furrowed her brows and explored their auras, noticing the difference her work made to their souls.

How some even dared to act freer than they had been previously.

Their auras were healing, and how that almost brought a smile to her lips.

"You waited for me. How utterly kind you are," Kylen's voice spoke, wiping the smile completely from her lips. She straightened her posture, looking over to the man who now appeared at her side with one of his charming smiles. He had correlated his outfit with hers, wearing a touch of blue across his figure and one shimmering blue earring in his left ear. She moved her gaze across him, narrowing her eyes slightly as she turned away, pure judgement in her stare that did not get under his skin as she had hoped.

"So, are we excited?" Kylen asked. "I don't know if you are aware of the rumours, but I throw amazing parties, especially afterparties—perhaps you will get a taste of that at the party after our wedding," he mused with a smile that looked more like an obnoxious smirk. He turned to face her, looking down at her with defined, furrowed eyes. “You look as beautiful as always; try not to frighten our guests with it… but then again, feel free to because life has been lacking some excitement lately.”

Althea looked at him through a sideways glance, but she didn’t answer him. She didn’t feel like she possibly could. His presence moved closer to her, and Althea looked away from the man who was about to whisper in her ear. “Try not to have too much fun tormenting our people. As amusing as it would be, we want them to like you, not fear you.”

“But a Queen can do so much with another’s fear.”

Kylen moved an inch back from her, an uncertain, almost amused look scraping across his features. Althea looked away, looking back to the doors that began to open.

This was it.

This was the moment that she had been dreading for so long.

The moment where she would be forced to greet the people that Kylen had chosen over her. The people that her father swore to kill. To torture.

Kylen reached for her hand as the first lot of eyes were seen. They all watched her, the beady whites to their eyes staring into hers as if they were in the position to judge. Althea rose her chin, her hair falling over her shoulders as she straightened her posture.

She heard the gasps, the murmurs, the whispers, and oh how the few doubts made her smile. Perhaps that was why she allowed his hand to find hers—that was until she looked to it, watching as his scars bent around her flesh. A feeling that had her distracted as Kylen gently pulled her to follow him into the crowd.

Everyone was *silent*.

The music was *silent*.

The only thing audible was her heartbeat, she was sure.

They were about to loathe her, scream at her, hate her, beg to taste her death. They were going to want her dead, and even if they couldn't physically do anything about it, their whispers and actions would. She wasn't afraid of them because she was not allowed the privilege to be so. Still, even as she squirmed in her shoes, there was no sheering away from the fact that she was fearful of what that wild unnameable magick could do—what it would do if it figured out that she held something of it.

She hadn't realised her fingers had dug into Kylen's until he gripped down gently on her hand, grounding her rapidly racing soul as they approached the two twin thrones. Her father's calls were rising, his excitement swarming through her Realm shattering blood. It was as if he was truly here and not on the other side of the Kingdoms.

Watching Althea's every step and waiting for her to stuff up.

Just as the people of this Kingdom were doing.

No. She was Althea Evangeline, and as she released the breath that held the weight over her shoulders, she shed herself of fear.

If anything, they should fear her.

She was unstoppable.

Sure, one may call her strong for the magick that she wields, for the disgusting Markings that were spread across her flesh, but she wasn't strong because of that. Althea had been strong her whole life. She was simply strong for surviving this long.

And she wasn't going to allow some dull mortals to question that worth.

"May I present to you, Kylen and Althea Noxwell," Sayah's voice echoed out.

You are his. You are his. You are hiiiiiiiissssssssss. It hissed, and Althea snatched her hand away from Kylen's as she sat down ever so graciously, looking towards the crowds with a sly smirk playing on her lips—if only they could feel the anxiety that crawled at her stomach.

"The King and the beautiful ever so gracious soon to be Queen of Lorundio."

Althea waited for the moon to fall, for the pin to drop, but then against all odds… people began to applaud her. Cheering and crying tears of joy because she had shown up unharmed, easing all the worries that all of these creatures shouldn't have been suffering.

That was Kylen's job.

Her mind had slipped from her clasp as she sat on her throne. Her head was far too deep into the voices to be brought back out so soon. ALTHEA NOXWELL… SOON TO BE QUEEN. She knew that by the stupid law of nonsense, she would be forced to take his name, even after death. But she never thought that she would hear it.

It never seemed to really occur to her.

She didn't think that she would make it this far.

A scarred, cold hand touched hers, and her eyes shot towards it. An icy sensation flooded through her blood, parting her magick in two as she looked up. It was like a touch of venom, something so horrible yet addicting. It was sickening, making her thoughts take a turn that was far worse than the previous ones.

Kylen's hand seemed to hide something more, a vibrating tremor of magick alerting Althea to such; almost as if the magick he held was responding to the magick she had—in the most obscure way.

Kylen looked at her with such worry and confusion that Althea held everything in her not to sneer in his face. The music began again, and people began to dance and laugh. The rhythm floated through her empty mind. "Enjoying the view?" she cooed as she moved her attention back onto *her* people.

How that made Althea squirm.

She sent another look over to him, finding his eyes still placed on hers; doubt shone heavily in them. Kylen raised a brow before he smiled, a smile that translated very clearly in her mind. Smile and show the world their Queen. So, she did just that, and how she had wished to capture Kylen's faltering expression before he turned away into one of her own personalised portraits. Althea grinned broadly. This was one of the very few good things that came from only ever being seen for your looks. People were deceived by you, and you could show them whatever you wanted them to see, and they wouldn't second guess it at any stage along the way.

Because you were simply beautiful, breath-taking, in all's mind. And it didn't matter whatsoever what knowledge you carry—*but mother is the wisest.* Knowledge held nowhere near enough power to help a woman survive in this miserable world.

"Please, enjoy your night," Althea said, holding her voice unwavering.

More applauds and cheers echoed out, and Althea's smile began to twist as they all turned to the food and music. People waltzed, they danced. Their eyes were so light in colour compared to those of her Kingdom who were infected with the curse.

She felt as her smile changed. Hypnotised by these free people and how they willingly responded to Kylen and now her. Her hand had somehow become interwoven with his again, but Althea pulled it away, looking up to him briefly before looking back towards the crowds of dancers.

He had chosen these people over her. *Don't forget it.*

"Seems like we lost you back there. Astra for your thoughts?" Kylen asked, flexing the golden coin he balanced between two of his fingers.

Althea scoffed at the man's antics as she rose. "As if any astra would be worth my thoughts," she snickered. "I'm getting a drink. Want one?'

Kylen nodded, a look of surprise to his lips as he grinned up at her, taken back by her sweet and wifely offer, "I mean, if you are offering, that would be wonderful, darling—"

"Well, you have legs. You can get it."

Kylen's lips parted in a gasp like laugh, and Althea grinned as she sighed; how she would miss tormenting him when his days came to an end. But she wouldn't deny herself of his death —she would never deny herself of his death. He was quick to fix his expression, of course, but she enjoyed it nonetheless while it lasted. His eyes turned down and a small expression of humour tinted his lips. "Exciting indeed," he whispered before quickly rising to his feet, his eyes falling into hers. "Please try not to get into too much trouble—remember what lies on the line."

"Your Queen," Althea replied with a feline-like voice. The tone like blades, all piercing beneath the layers of his heart that she wished to burn.

Althea made her way through the packed room, picking up a tall glass of bubbling faery liquor from a tray that passed her as she walked. She kept her eyes alert, a fake smile on her face that hid away the fact that she was listening to every conversation within the room, waiting to hear anything that could potentially be beneficial to her.

Whether that be related to herself in general, her father and Aeonia, or Erwin. Any one of those topics alarmed her, and she didn't exactly want people to realise just where she was weaving her way to.

Kylen spoke to his people, and every now and then, he looked over to her. His gaze found hers no matter where she happened to stand, finding her as if he had her steps memorised. He called her the full moon that made his new moon glow, believing that she was who made him glow. That no matter how far in a galaxy full of stars that she was, he would always find her. But she knew that those were lies. She had learnt that those were lies when she was far too young.

And that was why she wished to see his face the moment he realised that she was gone. That she had fled down the halls, finding her way to the dungeons that she knew great power lingered within.

EIGHT
KYLEN

Althea was gone. She had disappeared just over half an hour ago, and now she was missing. Kylen didn't want to fear for her safety. He didn't see any need to. He knew she was more than capable of looking after herself; in fact, he doubted that he would make any difference regarding her safety—but that wasn't what was causing his heart to race.

It was the eeriness in the air. The way the air crackled with an electricity that was hers and yet not. It was darker—crueller. The guests noticed it too. They turned their heads at the noises that he could hardly hear, and yet he felt every part of.

His heart began to ache with each beat. The curse warped around it and held him to the ground with cruel intentions.

"*Stay here*," Kylen had said to Sayah, already falling ill to the movement that his legs forced upon him.

He turned down the hallways, his eyes falling around every corner in fear that a body would meet with his gaze. Kylen followed the twines before him, the screams of the lost, the cursed, swarming his mind as he got deeper within the castle. Anxiety formed into a noose around his throat. He was never one to openly display his emotions or panic. Still, the expression of dread on his face preached otherwise.

"Althea?" his voice was so small. So dull. The fear was evident in the way the air crowded his lungs in fear of escaping, in fear of falling victim to the world's cruelty.

He reached the dungeon door that stared at him with a tilted grin, pleased that Kylen had subconsciously followed the twine of magick that it had sent him. Kylen took a step forward before halting. Noticing the slip in reality that bent with whatever illusion that was now concealing the doorway. "Erwin—" Kylen darted forward, feeling as the reality of every illusion within the castle gave way to the magick that once held such control over him.

The magick that once made him feel so alive.

How could he have been so oblivious? Of course, she wasn't going to stay put in a party when the man she needed to converse with was down below the very floorboards she stood upon.

He pushed the door open and sprinted down the steps, watching with narrowed eyes as the illusion faded. The dungeon doors were open. Wide-open. In the middle of the ordinary wood, the hidden door was *stained* with a dark black handprint. A handprint that could only match one other soul.

"Althea?" Kylen whispered, his voice seeping across the cobblestone floors like shadows.

Nothing answered him, and his worry for his Queen—*Althea*, grew stronger.

Blood splattered against the walls, and suddenly loud screams filled the air. Whatever happened had been evil. Had been so suffocating that the air he breathed was still suffering. Trapped with the evil spirits that murmured through the wind.

His feet slipped against the damp ground, sliding his way into the cracked cell that should've been locked.

"I swear to the Gods, Althea, if you—" Kylen paused. The words on his tongue halting.

The chains that had once held Erwin were gone, blown off the hinges and lay scattered across the blood-covered floor.

His heartbeat filled his ears, and Kylen should have focussed on that and the magick that surrounded the melting obsidian. Yet, his attention was caught on the girl who stood frozen with wide eyes a few steps away from him. "Althea—"

Kylen darted forward, reaching her side in a matter of seconds. He went to reach out to her to try and feel what spell it was that kept her frozen—but he could feel her magick already doing that for him; and how it was full of pure rage. Althea was powerful; he knew this—Erwin knew this. Erwin must have done something to her that even she could not prepare for. Kylen's thumb grazed across her cold skin, the very magick she had been running from biting at his flesh. It was both burning and ice-cold beneath his touch, a war that he knew would be fatal to be a part of. Althea had her eyes frozen open, and how her stare was one that was terrifying. What on the Realms had happened?

"She put up a good fight," a voice spoke through his mind. "It's a pity that this new magick wanted to protect her, wanted to conceal her from my touch. She would be dead by now if it hadn't trapped her in a bubble, and then we would have both been free from the burden that is her. I would have butchered her pretty little life the moment she came into view with the questions in her mind—but then she had disappeared. *Poof.*"

Kylen looked up and towards the darkness that slowly filled the other side of the room. The hairs on his arms rose, and he turned away from Althea as he felt her magick rising. He could feel the eruption brewing, and he knew that Kylen had to buy her time. "I'm not going to let you hurt her."

The curse laughed cruel sounds. *How you have walked in a full circle, boy.*

"Oh, but boy…" Erwin seethed, the words strangling his tongue. "Why are you buying her time? Her magick is mine to claim. *Her power is mine to claim.* I mean, look at her—she may act all strong and powerful, but she is nothing but pathetic. You want to know what I can do? I channelled not only my magick but hers and yours too and formed them into one strong line—and with that, I aimed it for her throat. But because Althea is so reluctant to use her new... *impurities*, it decided to save her by freezing her—knowing exactly that she was too stubborn to be allowed to do anything on her own."

"It's hers. It was given to her—"

"Why are you protecting her?" Erwin asked with a manic laugh. "Age has made you weak, dear friend. Don't think I have forgotten what you did to her in the past. Don't think that I don't remember the realisation swarming her mind. I may have been in the form of a crow then, but I could still feel her emotions. You broke her then; who's to say now won't be any different?"

"I am no longer in that position—she knows that I wouldn't do that to her. She understands that I did what I had to," Kylen replied quickly to the shadows as he focussed on forming a blade out of the curse that rotted his lungs.

"*But does she?*"

Kylen didn't have enough time on his hands. The shadows had already lunged for him, and all he could do was turn around and cover Althea, blocking her from the immense storm that was her curse. However, the moment his body went before hers, she gasped down a strangled breath. Althea finally blinked, already moving forward as if she was in the midst of a step. Such confusion took over her face as Kylen pushed her out of the way as the darkness lunged for them—but that didn't stop her from acting fast. His chest shuddered, and beloved air filled her cursed lungs as she pushed her hand forward, her own dark curse swarming out. Kylen looked away as the shadows in the shape of knives sliced through the skin on his back. He tried to mask his pain, not wanting Althea nor Erwin to see the way he feared the shadows' every move, every breath. But Althea had seen it all… and she didn't even blink.

The curse shot from her hand as if it wanted nothing more than to get away from her. It seeped from her skin like blood, shooting straight through the air to where it danced against Erwin's force. Althea must have sensed the strange sensation. Kylen could feel the rumble through the air as her head turned to her right wrist, watching as light upon light poured from where her Markings lay beneath. "Holy Hel—" Kylen breathed, and she looked at him swiftly.

Althea narrowed her eyes on him, blocking the harsh light swarming out of her Markings. She noticed the inch between them then, and he did too. While he almost had the audacity to snicker or say something to lighten the mood of sheer panic—Althea snarled. "Get the fuck off me—" her voice was rough, cracking as the words slipped from her chapped blue lips.

Kylen went to say something more when his eyes were brought back to the darkness that now shone with Althea's light too. Her expression lingered in his peripheral vision, how it held such hate, such muffled pain. Kylen tried to itch it away, but with each breath he took, the curse was bringing it back to him.

She had to know that he wouldn't do it again—that he wouldn't choose any soul over *hers*. Queen or no Queen. He had his past holding onto his ankles, and that drove him down, the regret and guilt in the shape of a noose around his neck at all times.

Kylen's whole body flinched as the shadows cut deeper into his flesh.

Althea had pushed herself up seconds ago, but now she pushed herself forward, gliding an inch before Kylen, where the darkness she controlled deemed her as their next victim. The shadows sliced her pale, ghostlike skin, but she did not react nor falter. Instead, she dipped her chin, lowering her gaze against it and forcing it back beneath her soul.

"Erwin," Althea seethed with such anger as she looked to Kylen, her own fierce gaze pausing as Kylen looked down to his blood-covered hands. He expected to see black blood, expecting for the curse to have already taken over the once seen purity of it. But that wasn't the case. His blood still held a touch of a crimson aspect to it, which made his heart severely heavy.

The curse must feel pity for him, something Kylen Noxwell didn't want nor need.

Althea reached forward, her fingers sliding over his as if it was an instinct. Kylen froze, the air halting in his lungs. His eyes connected with hers, but hers were focussed on doing two things at once: forcing Erwin away and whatever it was that Kylen was allowing her to do to him. *How her touch was so familiar and comforting in a time when comfort was a virtue.* Althea's brows furrowed, and she bit down on her bottom lip. She seemed to be listening to something screaming within her mind because slowly and yet ever so quickly, he could hear the murmurs of her magick too. It was chanting something in the old language of the Gods. Words that translated to 'heal him', but at the same time, another voice screamed 'drain him'. Whether she knew what she was doing or not was a mystery, but that didn't stop her. The light danced down her skin like snakes, weaving around each string before wrapping around her fingers and melting into his skin which she pressed her hand against.

Erwin's attempts at outshining Althea were loud, but silence took over the air once again as they both struggled to catch their breaths. Her chest heaved as she leaned forward within a moment of the voices silencing as well, Althea was quick to pull her hands away from his. "Get—" her words halted on her tongue as she noticed Kylen moving away, looking over his shoulder to the rips in his shirt.

His agony was gone, and now the pain was not the only thing on his mind. He noticed how his wounds were all healed. Not a single scar was left behind to mark Erwin's trail. Kylen looked to

Althea, his jaw gaping, his eyes astounded—yet her gaze was something far more terrifying. *She was frightened. And it wasn't because of the shadows.*

"Don't mind me leaving you two alone to drown in whatever this is," Erwin cooed from somewhere in the dark air. "I have some guests to meet, it has been a long time since I've eaten, and I do but have a craving for blood."

Silence breathed through them. Exhaling deeply as a scream erupted through the walls, catching onto each hair that scattered across Kylen's body and pulling him to stand. "What happened?" Kylen demanded, trying not to flinch at the steel of his voice.

He began to run, and she ran reluctantly at his side.

"Nothing," Althea stated as she went to flee the other way, but his hand caught hers before she could, and he watched as her whole body ran cold. "Nothing happened, Kylen, now let me be!"

"Well, that isn't true in the slightest," Kylen blurted as a hiccup of fear burned his throat. "I walk in here and find you… frozen in your own body—that certainly isn't nothing."

"I was—"

"I swear to the Gods, Althea, if you say some excuse, I will—"

"You will what?" Althea asked as another scream echoed through the air, one that made him flinch again. She, however, didn't bat a single eye. The ground shook and sweat bled across his forehead. "Nothing happened! And I mean that. I walked in there, and Erwin was gone. I barely had any time to react because the next thing I knew, you were before me tripping me to the ground—" she shuddered, two sharp blades appearing at her side.

Kylen looked away, looking back to the corridors that reeked of the curse.

"What the Hel happened? That creature you call Zaire said that Erwin was out—*unconsciously out*."

"Does it look like I know? I was merely trying to find you when I found your body instead. Couldn't you just wait one night? Now the people—"

"Oh, *Gods forbid anything happens to the people*," Althea rasped under her breath, a bitterness to her tone that had Kylen shivering against the memories.

"Althea—" he went to say, but then something went off, and Sayah's scream filled the air.

His heart plummeted into the depths of his stomach. Not Sayah. *Not fucking Sayah.*

People swarmed through the shadows before them; running towards their two leaders as tears and pain traced their faces. The halls they had been running down slowly filled with the darkness that Erwin was leaving behind, calling to the darkness that Kylen felt riveting within his lungs. Kylen looked to Althea as she took multiple steps back and away from the children who were reaching for her. She glanced up as a child took her hand, the children begging for her to take the 'bad man' away, leaving a stare of fear to line against her features. Kylen looked at her for a single second longer than he should have before disappearing into the fog of the dark.

"*Kylen!*" Althea's shriek was so familiar. So dreadfully familiar that he felt as if he had only just shut the wooden doors in her face.

If only he could have told her then.

If only he could have told her then just how sorry he was. That if he had said anything more back then, and her father had read her mind, then the world as they knew it would have burned, her included.

And he wouldn't let that happen, not now, not ever.

NINE
ALTHEA

The darkness was always so dreadfully twisted when you were the one trapped within it. When all you could see was pain and fear. It was even worse when that fear nipped at one's flesh, eager to taste the impure blood that roamed beneath. The child that she held to her waist clung to her neck. His little arms holding onto her flesh for dear *bloody* life.

Althea had never been in a position like this one before. She had never even seen a young child, *other than herself,* before.

His parents hadn't come for him yet; they had not appeared through the dark that lingered on the other side of the enchanted door. She sat still in a large room that had been one of the rooms far away from where Erwin had been. Althea would have liked to escape these walls altogether, but the darkness had infected Sayah's barrier, and now no one could escape this Palace. She didn't dare breathe too loudly, hoping that all who sat at her sides understood that they needed to be quiet.

The child had no idea who she was, what death she had brought, but that didn't matter, not now.

Everything seemed so little, *so small.*

Her heart hurt, and her lungs ached, but Althea wasn't going to let any harm come to this child. She couldn't bring herself to allow that to happen.

She and around twenty others had fled to this single room. One of the rooms that were there purely just for looks. Althea had slammed the doors shut, concealing them with a cursed magick that was sure to trap the evilness on the other side.

She leaned against the wall in the corner of the room as she felt the rumble of the floors. The child's tears stained her chest, but she didn't move him away. Instead, she held him tighter, resting her own head against the top of his. The guilt that she did not allow herself to feel took over every beat of her heart, a dark and twisted rhythm that Althea almost chose to listen to—all so she could hear what the voices of both sides of her magick were praising.

She had tried to speak to Erwin. She had needed to speak to Erwin. The sooner that she could shed herself of these Markings, the better it would be—but that plan of hers never involved hurting these people. The guilt seeped into the air she breathed, and Althea turned her gaze towards the window; these people had been so excited to have a Queen. They had been so excited to finally have another Royal to march these lands—*but couldn't they see that she was not their Queen?*

Not their true Queen, at least.

These Realms weren't Althea's to rule.

Her mind was trapped on Kylen—and every time she blinked, breathed, looked away, all she could see, feel, and taste was the position she had been in all those years ago. Waking up from nightmares every night, scared to move a single muscle in fear that her father would hear.

Time had been so cruel then.

And she had only been a child, no bigger than the child she held now.

The others all bared her small judgmental, soft, scared looks. They thought this was her grand scheme. The way she planned to go out. They mumbled about it, whispering to those beside them in anger. Were they really that blind? Did they really believe that she would be sitting here holding a child if this was part of her grand plan?

No. She would be up and dancing with a sword in her hand.

She couldn't do it. All of this waiting around.

Althea rose to her feet, and the child whimpered. She looked down to him, comfort being so unnatural for her that she offered it a very unsure smile. "It will be okay," she started with. "I'm going to go and find your parents." Althea turned to the man with three children, approaching him with a stern look on her lips. "Look after him; I'm going to go and—"

"How dare you leave us here when you have forced us through this!" the male from across the room bellowed in a strained, breaking voice. He was covered in blood, pure, crimson, mortal blood. "You are not the queen we want nor need!"

Althea felt her brows furrow, a chuckle leaving her lips as she cocked her head to the left. *Of course, they blame you*, the voices snarled. *You are deemed as the villain in their eyes. They will never forgive you for what your father has served them.*

"Well, that's unfortunate for you, isn't it?" Althea snarked as the child left her arms. "Please, enjoy your comfortable little spot right there, and I will go and see what is going on and if I can be of any use."

"Or perhaps you are fleeing!" the woman beside him exclaimed to Althea's dismay. She looked to the children watching her with wide eyes, reminding herself why she wasn't killing everybody right here.

Althea snickered dryly as she turned away, turning her wrist in a circle as she formed a dagger. "Don't tempt me, sweetheart."

The doors opened at her command and shut the moment she stepped out of them. Darkness filled the corridors, a fog so heavy that she felt each breath become heavier as she descended into it —but this would be far more challenging if she hadn't trained for this her whole life. Althea looked through it, focussing on her other senses to do her justice.

No sound was heard, but she could feel his presence, how it had appeared within the moment she left the enchanted room.

Where was Kylen?

She was going to be so pissed off if Erwin had killed him before she'd had a chance to.

"*Althea!*" the male who caused the hair on her arms to stand on end chanted, praising her name as if it was his to praise. "How I am so glad we are finally able to dance. I must admit that I was severely disappointed that your magick didn't allow us to do so earlier."

The old man with a wispy beard appeared before her, his face covered in crimson blood, and she watched as it dripped from his teeth as he smiled a wide grin, slipping down his chin and disappearing through the shadows beneath them. "Let's dance."

The words weren't an invite nor a question.

No, instead, he struck for her.

The shadows weaved around him as she dodged his every strike. The shadows screamed at her, begging for her to help them in anyway. Was he oblivious or just dumb? Erwin really believed to be on the higher ground here. But Althea could see his movements from miles away.

She called to the spirits, feeling as they weaved through her skin, attaching themselves to her soul that was battling its own war. "Why are you fighting me?" Erwin pried with a narrowing of his eyes. "Why are you protecting him—"

"*Protecting him?*" Althea barked through a laugh. "I am doing no such thing. I am protecting myself by satisfying the need to have your head on my wall after I force you to help me."

She moved around his presence, feeling where he was to move next by tracking the calls of his magick. "But you need me, girl—" he chanted, "You need me!"

Althea flinched beneath his tone, playing it off smoothly by ducking beneath his touch. "I may, but I only really need you for *that*. Then I'll find someone else. Perhaps your brother will be kinder—maybe even better looking?"

Erwin was not pleased with that. Not one bit. His skin crept with shadows. Seeping down the muscles of his arm before meeting with Althea's hands that she quickly held up. Her eyes widened at the fact that her magick—whatever one it may be, grabbed at the force of evil and turned it into… something less evil?

It sunk back beneath her skin, and Althea looked up to where Erwin observed her. "Poor little Althea," he cooed in a challenging tone.

Althea looked to his hands, watching as pictures slowly began to extend from them. The shadows bent, wielding into figures that she was hypnotised by. Althea took a step back but then a name—*her name*, filled her senses.

She looked over her shoulder, finding an image of herself, no older than twelve staring into the distance. Her heart faltered, and she took three steps back. The shadows showed her all that she needed to see, the pain, the horror, the emotions… *the beauty*. Althea, the oblivious child, stumbling over her quick steps as she reached for the doorway.

The shadows before the small girl looked back at her, taking the shape of Kylen—how she hadn't realised how much he had truly changed. He was so young then—so undoubtedly young and yet *so cruel*.

Kylen stared at the young Althea, watching as she begged him to stay, begging him to take her with him—to give her a chance. She pleaded that they could work all of this out, but he didn't listen; he didn't even look at her.

Althea stayed frozen as she watched the production. As she watched her pure heart break for the first time ever. She tried to reach for him, but Kylen held a hand out, and the young girl flew back. Being hit with a force that she was still unaware of to this day. Perhaps if her head were clear, if her mind were at ease, she would realise how dark the magick was. How it wasn't evil and yet not at all pure.

It was below evil.

It was hurting.

Althea watched as the young girl with a shattering heart hit the floors of her bedroom in Aeonia. She looked up to Kylen with wide eyes. Her lips curled as she refused to cry. She remembered that day as if it was yesterday. *As if it was this morning.* Althea had looked up at Kylen, noticing his shocked face and still had held onto the hope that begged him to turn around.

Kylen took a step back, the words on his lips dying. "I'm sorry."

I'm sorry. I'm sorry. I'm sorry. I'm sorry.

How those words held no effect over her now.

Her heart felt heavy, and she realised that the worst part out of it all was that she hadn't been mad at him for a long time. She was hurt, of course, but she didn't focus on that. Instead, she had blamed herself for not being a better friend.

That was the thing about her, one of her many weaknesses; she felt far too much.

Althea had thought from his perspective, making up every excuse under the sun to resonate why he had left her clinging to life—the life that she no longer wanted.

Althea turned away as she held onto herself, the tears burning her eyes once again. *No,* she wouldn't allow herself to cry. She was strong—she had moved past this and was now focussing on the bigger picture of freedom.

To see beyond the beyond.

"Do you see all that you went through?" Erwin asked as his cold hands traced lines over her shoulders. "He was so cruel to you. So unbelievably cruel. You didn't deserve that," he paused, and Althea tried to break free from his hold. However, his nails dug into her flesh and Althea was left to turn on him. She quickly formed a dagger that broke through the skin of his stomach. She felt his cold, greedy blood meet with her fingertips, how his blood burned her skin, causing her own blood to rise. He looked into her eyes, waiting to see her break, but instead she stayed watching him, slowly tilting her head to the right.

No pain radiated across his features, yet she could feel it in the way the air crackled and rumbled. Erwin leant forward, and Althea rose her chin, staring down at him despite being shorter than him.

"He was so cruel to you," Erwin repeated forcefully. "Allow me to help you—I can do so much worse to him than what you could ever do. LET ME GET OUR REVENGE. *OUR PEACE OF MIND,*" he bellowed; the last part making her shiver.

Althea had hoped that the impact to his stomach would have done something—hoping that perhaps he would have flinched or shown a little touch of humanity… but he did nothing. Instead, his hands moved up to her cheeks rapidly, pressing against her cheekbones to the point where a scream burned her lungs. But she would not let it out; she refused to.

Althea tried to flinch away and rasp herself out of his grip, but his hands only tightened on her painfully. "I'm not trying to save him—" Althea argued through a sneer, loathing herself for showing her weakness before the man who was sure to use it against her. "I would never try to save him—"

"Then why are you acting so weak?"

Althea stared into his grey eyes, desperately searching for some humanity to hold onto. But that humanity was long gone. "Weak? I am anything but weak." He held no more light within him. That light was burned when he watched his parents and sister burn. Althea knew the myths, the stories. Her father would tell her them before bed when she was a child.

Perhaps that might have been a way to get her to believe that he would protect her, to establish strength… *or perhaps it was for this moment now.*

When she was staring into the eyes of death.

She forced herself to chuckle despite the scream that was rumbling through her.

His grip tightened, her trembling bones threatening to break beneath his very touch. "If you think your little King will come and help you, then you should probably think again. That boy is long gone; he is past death." His words engraved scars into her shoulders. Althea refused to show the slightest touch of emotion; she wouldn't let him win. Not when she craved the taste of his blood.

Althea felt the magick within her soul rise. But it wasn't for the right reasons. For the reasons she hoped. It was answering Kylen's calls, leaving her soul hungry for the taste of blood. She can hear him calling for her through the abyss—his voice strained as Althea stared Erwin down.

Her feet twitched, and Erwin grinned. Her eyes, hands, and Markings all slowly beginning to glow beneath the bandages. She tried to push it down, begging the Gods she knew never answered—to answer her this once. Using the excuse that it wasn't for her, it was for the greater beyond. Those they cared for, those they *loved.* And for some reason, she wasn't included in that large population.

Althea's hands twitched, and she heard the first crack of her jaw. The pain was immense, flooding her features as her screams, power, all of the above sent the windows rattling.

She looked down to Erwin as he clasped her jaw ever so tightly and used his magick to hold her above him. His very magick wrapped around her skin as if it wasn't as cursed as it was. Althea looked down to him as her vision threatened to give way again. She was trying to think of every other way to get away from his grip that she had ignored the most obvious one.

Althea kicked him, hard, right in the groin. Erwin let out a shocked grunt, leaning forward so swiftly that he dropped her, finally releasing her jaw from the power that had turned her lips and chin black with blood.

"You pathetic bitch—" He rose his hand and Althea barely had a second to react before something wet and cold splattered on her. Althea opened her eyes and looked up to see a bloodied wrist mere inches away from her. Erwin shrieked and gripped his arm to his chest, the sound of his agony causing her magick—both sides of it, to freeze.

The hand landed at her side, and she was quick to kick it away. Breathing heavily, she looked up at Kylen who watched her with such concern. "Are you okay?" he rasped.

Althea rubbed her jaw as she looked up at him before casting her gaze over to Erwin, who stumbled back with his other hand clasping his blood-covered arm. Her face no longer ached as she quickly looked back to Kylen, and she could feel her magick melting through her bones and muscles, soothing the throbs that echoed through her head. "Of course I'm fine. When am I not fine?" she said through a single breath

Kylen didn't believe her; that much was obvious by the expression on his lips. However, he didn't get to act on that concern because Erwin's shadows had already shoved him back against the castle walls, sending the whole perimeter shaking.

"Kylen—" Althea gasped as she stumbled back, her eyes wide as Erwin's touch and breath filtered through her skin. "*Run!*" Kylen gasped with a single gasp before the curse was forced down his lungs, sending him choking. "Find S-sayah in the east wing and run!" his breaths were choked, struggling against the force which Erwin held against him.

Althea watched him as she took a step back, followed by another. She looked away, glancing to the floors that were slowly being seen through the fog of the shadows surrounding them, before looking back to the two males. Erwin had his face pressed against Kylen's, whispering cruel words in a language that she could never return. Kylen's face was turned up, looking to the ceiling as the veins along his throat filled with darkness. His throat bobbed, but never once did he look to be weak.

Her heart was at a toll. She wanted; *she pleaded* with the Gods to let her leave. To allow her the gift of running away to a happily ever after. That was all she ever wanted, *to be free*. And perhaps if she were to run now, she would get far enough to feel the seas, to see and feel sand as if she had known it her whole life. Perhaps if she were to run now, she would be able to keep her secrets with the moon and see everything it has been waiting to reveal to her all these years.

But that wasn't what she needed.

She—by whatever reasoning her mind was seething at her with, needed to help Kylen.

And she told herself it was purely because she *wanted* to kill him herself. *Is it that you want to? Or that you are being forced to?*

Kylen looked to her; stories, memories, and lifetimes haunting his mind; shimmering with a fear so bland that Althea could see and feel every inch of it. She had felt that fear the moment she had realised that he hadn't been lying. The moment where she realised that he was genuinely leaving her—and how his face had stained her shattering mind.

Use me, mother; let me wash away all of your sins.

I am a sin.

Let me wash you away then, bring some peace to your name. Perhaps then the other side will be kind.

I don't want to go to the other side. I want to go to the moon.

The moon will be there, and she is waiting with open arms and knives in her hands.

Althea looked down as Erwin's magick muffled Kylen's breaths. The sounds, noises, and whispers all excruciating to hear and sense. Piercing through the air as if it was his to take. Kylen looked towards Althea; his eyes full of flames despite the shadows taking over the whites of them. She wanted to turn and run to the hills before descending down them in freedom. But her heart was trapped, and she could hear her once pure heart whispering daring, heartfelt murmurs through her ears.

You know you are better than this. Be the Queen.

Althea took a breath, and then another.

She was a Queen, and no magick was going to make that any different. Althea began to approach Erwin, forming a blade in her hands as her magick finally began to respond. Words chanted throughout her mind, chanting words she wanted to torture. Althea ran through his shadows, dodging each blade that Erwin's shadows threw at her. They weren't physical, but they were real, and they had the power to rip her skin to shreds. She knew that if the blades pierced into her, she would not only be wounded, but the darkness within each blade would spread through her blood and rot her lungs and heart. It didn't matter that she was powerful with her own variant of the curse; Erwin was one of the two creators of it, and if he dared to lay a hand on her, Althea would be dead within minutes. She leapt up and dodged behind the two males, shoving her blade ever so quickly through the flesh that covered Erwin's throat as she forced his head back. "It has been fun challenging you, Erwin. I have always wondered what it would be like to claim your death. Your power."

I know I've asked you all of this before. But please, Gods, Goddesses, Saints, Heroes, Prophecies, anyone who will hear my cries, listen to me this once. People—your people, your beloved mortals, immortals, fairies, faery, sirens, goblins, all of the above lives' are at stake. I know you don't care for me, and I don't know what I did, but please help me help your people. I'm sorry for whatever it is that I did to you. Whether it was all the death my father brought or for simply being born. I am sorry for it all.

Black blood coated her hands as she pulled the blade out before he could grab it. Althea breathed, and Erwin turned to her, his eyes widening as he felt the new trickle within the air. Althea hadn't felt it yet, but she could sense it, almost as if it didn't belong to her.

She looked down, watching as her hands began to glow with the same brightness that she had so blatantly ignored before. It warmed her hands, a kindness that had her staring into it and wishing for a beyond. It didn't burn her, but it wasn't subtle. It warped across her fingers, seeping out and into the air as if she owned every inch of every land. Althea looked to Kylen, and she must have had that same child-like expression on her lips because all fear left his expression in a heartbeat. His eyes widened, taking Erwin's suffocating grip around his throat into account as he kicked him back. Using Althea's moment of distraction to free himself of the pain that *he was sure to meet on the other side.*

Althea wasn't helping him. She had to remind herself that. She was helping herself find a potential peace that awaited her on the other side. She looked back down to her hands before slowly raising them, feeling as the power, strength, and hope shone through her eyes and took over every sense that she held.

Her heart held onto the pain, feeling how each beat felt faultier than the last.

The Gods were going to help them.

But not her.

She was never worth it.

Her heart burned as Erwin lunged for her, a grin ripping onto her lips as if the pain her heart held had no effect over her. He could've hit her with such force, or perhaps by some miracle, he was held back. Either way, she didn't feel any pain nor any impact as she closed her eyes and drifted into the beyond. The Elemental magick within her soul took over the little magick of the curse she had been using. The force was so loud, so vigorous —it electrified the air. Althea kept her eyes shut. *You were never worth it.* Her heart burned with pain as she pushed those words away. She was worth it. She was. If she was not worth it for them, then she would be worth it for herself.

Althea owed herself that much.

She could hear her mother's words, how she whispered to her with such fear. Apologising repeatedly for the life that she was not going to be able to live.

She felt Kylen's eyes connect with hers. The pain in them was real, genuine. He felt guilty for leaving her behind, and he had every right to—*but her heart was so dreadfully tired of being pained.*

TEN
KYLEN

There had been death in his eyes just seconds ago. It had been so bitter, so foul, and so distasteful that Kylen had been prepared to shut his eyes while the darkness split the remainders of his soul into two. But then a light had shone, and it was a lighthouse steering him home. He had looked to Althea, and she had been so flustered.

A mix of shock, surprise, anguish, and every emotion under the sun shimmering across her golden features.

"Althea—" she had looked at him as if they were both still children, keeping secrets and sneaking through the castle at night. Playing games that were beyond any ordinary imagination. Their minds had been so large, so pure, and full of such unthinkable ideas that now were burned away. Staring at each other with such longing in an attempt to bring back the hope they had once both held.

Erwin lunged for her, but Kylen caught onto his soul. His magick may be severely weakened, but he didn't care. He still gave it everything he had, and he swore his heart had stopped for a minute or two.

Kylen's mind was running across fields, begging to catch up

to those that were still running. He wasn't going to allow the curse to take them too.

"You let me go, boy!" Erwin shrieked as the room began to glow with a glisten so bright.

Kylen couldn't respond; his heart, mind, and tongue were all too weak. Aching as his soul and the last purities of it washed away.

Erwin threw a ball of twisting, squirming shadows at him, and Kylen dodged them. Looking back over to where Althea continued to glow ever so brightly. He always knew she had some relationship with the moon, and now this just seemed to prove it.

She is the full moon, the voices of the curse that fed off of his soul chanted. *And you are the new moon. Whatever path she will light, you will always follow it.*

"You're going to have to kill me if you think I'm allowing you to get to her."

Kylen had no idea what she was doing. Why she was glowing with such light and seeping all of Erwin's failed darkness into her, but he could see that something was happening. And he owed her so much more than *time*.

Erwin's force connected with Kylen's shoulder, and he was pushed to his knees. Hitting the ground with such force that he prayed that *all* in his Kingdom had escaped this Castle that was about to fall. Kylen shot his gaze back up to Erwin, meeting the darkness shining there.

He pushed Kylen back and the walls above crumbled down, turning his dark hair lighter with plaster and bits of debris. Kylen tried not to let the pain overtake him, but every part of his body was overcome with the ache that strummed through his bones. He rolled on his side, wincing as his vision faded on him.

There was a ringing in his ears, bruises forming across his skin, blood dampening the clothes he had once prided himself in wearing.

He tried to push himself up, but the ground began to shake again. He narrowed his eyes through the darkness, the dust, looking towards the shining glow that Erwin's darkness was trying to overcome. Kylen looked up and then towards the cage she had created. Watching as her body forced her to stand before the door Erwin was trying to break into. He focussed on the sounds and noises that extended beyond the void. And he could hear a child's cry, mother's and father's soothing their crying children who shouldn't have been in this position in the first place.

Althea blinked, and the glow that showed through the seas of her eyes began to suppress, revealing the true blue to them. "Why are you protecting them?" Erwin questioned through a manic laugh, his eyes piercing through Althea's, whose lay unblinking. That one question was going to be the death of them all, and Kylen was prepared to pry it from his tongue so that he could never ask it again. "All they do is bring you pain—all they do is betray your little heart."

Kylen pushed himself with such force that he believed it was sending the ground shaking. He ran forward, forming through the little magick in his blood a large cloud of it. He smashed it into Erwin's face and how he wished he had gotten his expression framed. Erwin stumbled forward, snarling so deeply as he swerved over his shoulder. Laughs leaving his lips that had the air within Kylen's lungs tightening.

"Oh, come on, Erwin, don't tell me you don't want to dance?" Kylen asked as his chest heaved with heavy, ill breaths.

ELEVEN
ALTHEA

Her soul was screaming frightful words.

Help them. One voice would say.

Let them burn. The other voices would argue.

What did her soul want? She no longer knew.

All Althea could see and feel was the magick that protected her from the darkness that she had once feared with everything in her. She looked over her shoulder towards the changing lights that assured her that protecting these people was *everything* she wanted. But then the other voices stirred, and once again, her attention was on letting them burn.

Frustration burned within her mind, and Althea held onto her breath, tensing her brows as she looked towards her Markings. She didn't understand why *she*—out of all in her Kingdom, had received the Elemental Markings that her father loathed more than anything. Was this a lesson from the Gods or a more inevitable torture? It was ridiculous. What had she done? Althea felt the anger burn within her healing and yet cracking soul, and she released a breath that sent the construction around her shaking.

She needed to save those people; it was the *right* thing to do.

—But then she would be doing what Kylen had done to her all those years ago, potentially sacrificing her life in order to save Lorundio, the Kingdom she didn't want to save. *When did she ever put others first?*

She didn't want to look at it from his perspective because she had and was the one being affected. All those folks will continue with their life—*but not her*. She would either be wasting away six feet underground. Or she would be rotting in her father's cells, awaiting the punishment he was sure to bring her each day.

And she knew wholeheartedly what outcome would be worse.

There was a tug on the line before her, and before she could decide if she would run towards it or not, her head had fallen back, and her body was quick to follow. It felt like falling through the air, falling through clouds upon clouds.

Althea didn't scream nor wince.

This could've been death greeting her, but she didn't care.

All she cared about was hoping that it wouldn't be too painful.

Gods knew she had gone through too much.

She hit the floor hard, tensing and waiting for the pain; however, no more than a slight discomfort radiated throughout her body as she turned her head to the left. Looking over to the open window that filled the room that she was now laying in with a cold, icy breeze. She exhaled the air that caught in her lungs, turning her head to the right swiftly as the doors opened.

"*Kylen, please reconsider!*" Althea pleaded—the young and oblivious Althea pleaded, as she followed Kylen, who wore his hair far neater than how he did now; as well as a King-like-outfit that was far too large on him, presumably one of his fathers who was tragically lost to some gambling scheme; *they called it.*

"I can't," Kylen stated, and Althea—the true, mature Althea, could've sworn that she heard his voice break. "Althea, what is done is done. *Now*, wait here."

"Wait here for what?" the young girl argued as she continued following him, ignoring the rush of embarrassment that came from the tears flooding down her cheeks. "For you to leave me here as if you hadn't promised all that you did?"

"I'm sorry," Kylen breathed as he finally turned to face her, a knot in his brows. "I'm sorry for not delivering those promises to you, but unfortunately, things change, and I cannot stay here any longer," he replied, breathing the last few words as if they hadn't ruined all the hope that she had held onto.

"Kylen—" Althea quickly spat as she chased him forward. "Don't walk through that door! *Please!* I can help you—what do you need me to do? I heard you saying that you were leaving because I have already told you all that I can—but let me make you a deal. I will help you with anything you ask of me, if only you help me escape."

"I promised my people a promise I cannot break; *I'm sorry, Althea—I truly, truly am.*"

Kylen shook his head and continued walking away, and Althea, the true, real Queen, who felt far too much for such a small heart, turned away. Listening as the last parts of this vivid memory played on repeat in her mind.

See what he has done to you? What he has put you through? Remember those scars, those wounds? The way he had once drawn stars around them, comforting you from the horrors of your dreams all in order to deceive you? The blood you scraped from your sheets because you didn't want the maids to know that even your father saw you as a disgrace? Kylen did that to you.

Althea buried her head in her hands, and when she removed them, she found that she had returned to her sole body. And everything was happening so dreadfully fast.

Tears filled her eyes as she looked towards Kylen, seeing how time had changed him. How surreal all his features looked now that time had passed. He looked to her with pleads of guilt and understanding in his eyes. Emotions that were so foreign for her that she had to look away.

Erwin had stopped fighting, she had realised. He stood there, staring at his hands and watching as the shadows slowly drained away and out of his palms. Ascending towards Althea's soul, who too watched with such shock. "You—" he snarled as he ran towards her, pushing Althea's hollow soul into the wall behind her, allowing enough time for the barrier that kept him prisoner within her cage of magick to falter.

Althea looked towards him, a small wavering smirk curling at the ends of her lips as she watched her magick frighten him. It was truly a glorious sight to see the man who wasn't afraid of anything to be afraid of this.

Something that she held.

Althea shivered at the emotions that were overcoming her. She shouldn't be enjoying this magick, the way it made her skin thrum. She didn't want to enjoy any part of it. She wanted to loathe it and hate it. Althea felt the panic rise within her chest as Erwin stumbled away, his eyes wide as shadows slowly trailed through the air, wrapping and warping around the other. Kylen looked to Althea, and she felt his eyes on her. She felt the burn of his stare, the intensity of it.

Traitor, traitor, traitor, traitor, traitttttoooooorrrrr.

Her magick hissed at her with the cruellest word of them all. She was a traitor, and she could practically feel her magick beginning to eat her alive—*but she wouldn't stand for it.*

"Kylen!" Sayah's voice echoed through the air, and Althea looked over her shoulder. Sayah ran towards her, a fierce tone to her gaze. Scales began to line her skin like a suit of armour, appearing through the darkness and shimmering against the light that Althea held. "You're killing him!"

Sayah's sobs echoed through the air, her gaze flowing over Althea's shoulders and meeting with the blank expression of Kylen. He coughed once, then twice. Blood splattered across his chin, *and it was dark,* severely dark. Erwin's magick that was now within him must have done something, he must have done something, and she was now killing Kylen also—

Her heartbeat was getting too loud, silencing her from hearing the pleads Sayah held as she thrashed against the barrier. Kylen shook his head, but he fell to his knees. The light shining from Althea's chest faltered, and she looked to Sayah, who stood on the other side of Erwin.

Mother shouldn't have been distracted.

She watched as the dagger of dark magick left Erwin's palm, how parts of it fled to her soul, but the rest of it aimed for Kylen's heart. Althea held out her hand, reaching for him with no words in her mind other than one. "Kylen!" How that word made her heart turn with such stupidity.

All the magick from the prison Althea had kept them both trapped within shot for Kylen, catching the dark spear an inch before his chest and allowing Erwin the virtue of escaping.

Her heart tightened and sheer panic flashed upon her eyes as they widened. *He's going to disappear, he's going to run, he won't be at the end of your fingertips anymore, he's gone, he's gone, he's gone.* Althea looked towards Erwin as she exhaled deeply; the weight of the world waltzed upon her shoulders, dancing a dance that she no longer remembered the steps to. Sayah ran forward, and then Erwin and all of the shadows he controlled disappeared. Sayah froze in her steps, and Althea took two steps back, breathing heavily as she looked through the darkness, a plea in her eyes. "No—no!" She was about to send all of her cursed magick after him when an agony ripped through her bones, shooting through her body ever so quickly. Althea fell to her knees, the wind of her magick thrashing around her as if she was trapped in the eye of a hurricane. Her hands clasped over her ears; her skin feeling as if it was burning.

"Kylen—" Sayah gasped as she reached his side. "*We will get him again. We will—*" Kylen moved past Sayah with trembling steps. Blood had begun to drip from his eyes, but he didn't bother to wipe it as he reached Althea's frightened side.

He looked down at her as she fixated on her hands, watching with such fear as she tried with everything in her to contact the magick that she now no longer had any access to. "Althea?" Kylen whispered; his voice awfully hoarse.

Pieces were missing—pieces of her soul that allowed the Elemental magick to seek full coverage within her body. Pieces that she had never wanted to hold and yet had been forced to, and she had found comfort in them over time. The curse was never something she would ever want to admit to needing. But now that it was gone, and she knew that it was gone—her body felt bare, naked. Althea had been stripped of her security, and now she didn't know what to do. "Get away from me," she sneered, her tone like ice.

"What is it?" Kylen asked, his tone so soft compared to the ringing in her head.

Althea looked to him and then the creature over his shoulder. "My magick is gone."

"Your Markings are still there," Sayah whispered as she slowly approached, pointing to the rip in her dress that revealed the Markings to the world.

"I'm talking about the *curse*."

TWELVE
KYLEN

The castle was so quiet. *So empty.*

Even the spirits had fled.

The guards were sent to their homes and ordered to stay indoors with their families or friends; truly leaving the lonely King to suffer in this silence.

Kylen wandered down the hallways, looking out each window and watching as the rain that hadn't stopped pouring for the four days since the incident continued to fall.

He passed Althea's door, noting how the same silence kept him suffocating. She hadn't gotten out of bed since she had passed out and woken up in it. Sayah checked on her daily, bringing her every meal. But she hardly ate anything. She was too busy fighting the battles of life or death within her head. She feared that now she no longer held control of the cursed, venomous magick, she would die.

Kylen could hear her thinking it.

Other than that, Sayah was busy with Zaire, who he found out had also gotten severely hurt all those days ago. At first the panic had been near deadly, but now that he knew they were fine, he forced himself to breathe. To continue walking. Kylen approached their room now, silently opening the doors before shutting them behind him.

"Kylen, I don't need you to check on me every day; *I miss my silence*. With you and S, I hardly get any of it," Zaire spoke as Kylen came into view, approaching the same seat that he had been sitting on every day since.

"You know she's just worried about you," Kylen replied as he sat down, placing the books he held onto his lap.

"She has no reason to be worried."

Kylen averted his gaze. "You and I both know that that isn't true. She's worried that what happened to Khatri will happen to you. You know how she gets when she finds her emotions getting in the way."

"Okay, Kye," Zaire cooed as if their insides hadn't been butchered a few days earlier. "You are stretching a little bit far there."

"Oh, but I am not," Kylen replied rather quickly as he placed the glass of water beside their bed into their hands. "I see the way she looks at you, the way she relies on your approval for most things. You have brought the light back to her eyes; no need to be embarrassed."

"Sayah has sworn off falling for anyone, may I remind you," Zaire spoke as they shook their head, holding out their hand for the book he held instead. "What information do you have for me today? Anything fun? You have been awfully dull with all of this research."

"Nothing here has any information on Markings—*I mean*, we have basic books and texts and all, but nothing that specifies on Markings, especially multiple," he breathed through defeat. "But I did go into town today to see how everyone and everything was. I paid a visit to the families of those that died and the families that were affected, and after paying my condolences, I asked them if they could not speak of anything regarding Althea. Most said that they didn't know what I meant; others did. But that's not my point. I went to the library in town and found this. It's all in the language of the God's which I am still learning to read, speaking it is far easier may I add—but I know you are fluent so… *here*."

Zaire raised their brow at his rambles. "You want me to read this whole book just to help your girlfriend?"

"*No*—no. I just need you to look over it for any information. We know enough to know it's related to the Gods and specifically the magick of her mother's side. She was from Shinrin, which held a lot of myths?" the question and uncertainty to his tone brought amusement to their stare.

"Alright, only if you swear you will finally give me some space."

"I promise. Let me know when you are ready to tell me what you know," Kylen replied as he rose to his feet. "Do you want me to tell Sayah to give you space too?"

Zaire was quick to shake their head, and Kylen smiled slyly; a smug smirk lining his lips. "Never once did I think Sayah, *Sayah* of all people would be your type."

"And what is my type then?"

"I don't know," he shrugged as Zaire glanced up at him from their gaze on the pages, a challenge within their gaze. "I guess tall and frightening creatures who smile in the sight of death."

Zaire looked away and smiled, a very rare sight that he hadn't seen for years. It was only recently when he noticed the smile that they had shed towards Sayah for the first time. "So… Sayah? Just because she is all sweet and motherly to you, it doesn't mean she isn't just as deadly as what you describe. She is a siren, after all."

"Hmm?"

"She is tall, somewhat frightening, and most definitely gleams in the eyes of death."

Kylen chuckled under his breath. "*So, you do love her?*"

"I will always love Sayah, but she hasn't been able to love for so long, and I would never want to rush her."

Kylen watched Zaire, watching as they—*they* who never sheered away from death, pain, torture, any of it, sheered away from his gaze like a child. He could never say that to them because they would have his head, but they truly did look like a teenager in love.

He understood what they meant, and with Kylen's whole heart, he appreciated it. Sayah was the strongest person he knew. She had gone through more death in her life that it made him feel as if he shouldn't be hurting for what he went through, but she always told him to stop being so ridiculous. The deaths never stole her heart, *her human decency despite not even being human*.

Kylen remembered that first night after his non-biological brothers' deaths and how he had laid at her side, not speaking once as the night went on. She had silently wept the whole time, both the physical and mental pain catching up to her as they entered the first day where his brothers—*her friends and her lover wouldn't be alive in*. He remembered it all, and *oh,* how it made his heart tighten.

"I'll see you later, Kye," Zaire whispered through a sigh, and Kylen was carried off in the wind.

He crept down the same empty hallways, feeling as the cold memories swept across his shoulders. The night was turning cold, and the storms crept up on him. His steps began to fade as he reached Althea's door. Feeling as her silent breaths were heard, she hadn't moved, she didn't even seem to breathe, and he would have believed her to be dead if he couldn't hear her every heartbeat.

Althea had had the opportunity to break free and flee this Kingdom since the morning after Erwin's encounter. The barriers around the castle had fallen, except the ones around the perimeter were glistening. Yet, she could still get out if she wanted to; she was able to break free of them since the curse no longer burned through her lungs—but he figured that she was too frightened to do anything such.

Depression, mourning, sadness was like that.

And he, unfortunately, knew all about it.

Would this new magick lead her to death? He didn't want to think about it. All that he wanted to fixate on was finding something—anything that would help her get through this. Even if it were a spell, a ritual, a practice that would rid her of this Elemental magick, he would still help her. *He would always owe her that.*

THIRTEEN
ALTHEA

Her lungs felt empty. Her heartbeat was slow. Her gaze had been trapped on the window for days, days that felt like months. It didn't stop raining nor storming. She suspected the Gods were trying to make up for all of their wrongdoing, but then she knew it wasn't their doing but hers, because she could hear every new little murmur that erupted through her lungs.

And she could also feel *Kylen's lingering presence*.

He wanted to speak to her, to discuss whatever it was that was on his mind. But she couldn't even form words—perhaps the Gods had ripped her of that too.

It wasn't that she wanted to cry. It wasn't that she had given up on anything—it was simply that she had put everything on pause. Althea just needed to think of a *new plan*.

She held her hands above her, forming different weapons in her hands through the new magick that she wielded. The Elemental magick made each blade glisten with a light that contrasted against the dark aura each cursed blade had held. As well as that, she could feel the magick speak to her—it asked her what it could possibly do to help her with what she needed.

But Althea didn't know what she needed.

She was trying to plan something. *Something great.*

Perhaps she would sneak off in a fit and escape to the countryside, free of any burdens. Or perhaps she could murder them all just here and now; that didn't seem like such a horrible choice. Then she would be Queen, and she could be whatever Queen she liked—if she ignored the factor her father held over her.

Althea turned on her side, tucking her hands under the blankets as she moved her eyes back towards the murals of stars that scraped across the walls. There were three thousand and seventy-eight stars on this particular side, and on the side with the windows, there were two thousand and ninety-two.

The breaths in her lungs didn't get far. They didn't reach her lips, but instead freezing and burying away in the softness that was her sadness. She always did find a strange comfort in being sad; perhaps it was the understanding of finally realising what one was feeling.

It was a feeling that warped around her skin like smoke, smoke that appeared from the deepest and darkest cracks of her soul.

You just have to survive; you just have to breathe.

But how was one to breathe when their head was constantly underwater?

The door creaked open, and Althea could tell by the rhythm of their heart that Sayah had entered through the doorway. "Leave me be," Althea murmured through a long exhale.

She had been telling herself that this pain she was feeling was a lie. She was sure she didn't actually feel so weak now that she had been ripped of the magick she had used to rely on.

"Soon," Sayah replied in a proportionately as quiet tone. "I have brought you another tea. I will leave it by your bedside." Althea hardly listened to what the siren said, instead she watched as a white cat trotted by and through her open doorway; *a sway in her steps.*

The cat that Sayah watched with a fond, soft expression, jumped up and curled at Althea's side. Falling asleep within seconds and sending a melody of the cats purrs through the air. Her name was Chloe, she had learnt. Chloe the white cat that had laid at her side for hours on end over the past few days, *perhaps she would spare this felines life.*

She always did want a pet growing up.

Althea moved her eyes up, watching as the girl, who she suspected to be some type of sea creature, *siren* specifically, placed another mug of tea beside the five other full ones. "Would you like me to open your window and get some fresh air? I can put a spell over it to stop the rain?"

"No."

"Would you like to go and experiment with your new abilities? Perhaps if we give everything a stretch, you will feel better?"

"No."

"Well, I am going to open your window anyway. You need to be able to breathe again."

Althea didn't understand why this woman felt the need to act so motherly to her when she never once needed her mother. She never once needed someone to take care of her every move, *every breath.* It was foreign, *unnatural.*

It didn't take Sayah long to leave her to drown in her misery. In fact, if anything, it happened rather quickly. She scurried out of there like a little mouse, fleeing from Althea's eternal wrath, just as all the others did. A small smirk bloomed on the ends of her lips as she formed another blade in her hand.

That was all she could do. It came naturally to her as if this newfound magick wanted to soothe the ache left by the curse.

She turned over, laying on her back as she looked to the ceiling she had fixated on for days now. The wind from the open window howled, picking up every sense on her nose and laughing at her in pity. Her chest was fuelled with such agitation, every sense across her skin feeling like far too much for her to handle. Every breath felt like such effort, like such difficulty. Althea looked to the rain that poured outside, and with a quick sharp breath, she pushed herself up and off the bed. Her whole body felt sick, nauseous beyond measures that each step caused her mind to flow with difficulty.

She fell against the open window, reaching to shut it when the rain nicked her fingertips, and how *real* those small drops had felt. Her eyes were pulled up, and she looked towards the grey clouds, watching as they grumbled with the emotions she felt so clearly.

Althea took a breath, *and then two.*

Her feet found the edge of the windowsill, and with no hesitation, she began to descend down. Climbing and fleeing across rooftops came easy to Althea. After all, because of all the pretend attacks her father had set on her back home, she was more than skilled when it came from fleeing from places that she had no desire to hang around in.

However, Althea wasn't fleeing. Instead, her feet met the damp ground, and she felt the rain soak through her clothes, her hair. Althea looked up and towards the sky full of pain, watching as it wept down onto her. She squinted her eyes against it, and as she took a deep breath in, followed by a heavy exhale, she laid down. She was only a few metres away from the castle, but it didn't matter; Althea felt as if the Elemental magick was finally quietening.

Her grave was being dug through the earth, marking her death as one that all could claim. Althea laid down, and the rain danced across her skin, and for the first time in what felt like an eternity, she could finally breathe again.

Forgetting the burden that burned through her blood.

This was what she did after every time the world decided to

throw daggers at her. *She found the sky full of comfort, and she longed for it.*

The sky began to grow old, and darkness slowly overcame its brightness. Althea didn't turn; she didn't move. She merely laid there, waiting for the Gods to strike her with lightning, or perhaps they would send Erwin to finish her off.

A feeling radiated across her skin, and Althea exhaled heavily, feeling as the heaviness slowly flooded away. She would almost call herself to be at peace, but then a new presence was sensed from behind her, and she cursed herself for jinxing her death. *Why did she have to think such nonsense?* Althea formed a blade in her hand, preparing to strike when a voice halted her breaths.

"I can feel your worry from here," a voice that wasn't one that she was expecting spoke through the night. "You should come inside; you will catch a cold, my beloved."

"I don't need you to worry about me."

"But that's my job as your fiancé? *Don't tell me you are stripping me of that title?*"

Althea didn't look to Kylen as he slowly reached her side, sitting down as the rain continued to overthrow every ounce of warmth that she had once longed for. "Yes." She said, not returning his sarcasm.

"Well, that's too bad. I was rather enjoying chasing after your every need."

"Sounds pretty hypocritical considering you never once have actually cared about anything that has to do with me." His eyes were on hers, and yet she did not give in to the need to meet his stare.

"Oh, don't speak such lies," Kylen chastised with a chuckle. "Never once have I stopped caring for your needs." When Althea went to interrupt him, he spoke over her. "In fact, I am currently researching your needs. Since *you* haven't bothered yet to do so."

"And what exactly have you found out about my needs?" Althea pried, looking up at him with a glisten of unreadable emotions which shone brightly in her eyes. "That I love to get myself into problems because it is all so much more fun? That I—"

Kylen shrugged. "Nothing of any help yet—*but nonetheless*, I have found nothing alarming, so we can take that as a win." Althea shook her head as she looked back to the sky, feeling as if the rain blessed her once again. "*Noxwell*, just stop. You don't need to waste your pretty little breath on me."

An echo of silence filtered between them, and Kylen looked to her, noticing the crease she held in her brows. "Stop what?"

How she would enjoy watching him bleed out before her. She could imagine it all—and how joyous her days would feel from then on.

"Stop acting like you care about me—the *Althea* me. I understand that you need a Queen and all, but you are doing no good chasing me around and acting as if there is a part of you that needs me to be alright." Her words didn't make sense within her mind, but she didn't care. She had so much to say, and yet the world felt as if it wasn't giving her enough time.

"I do care about Althea, not just the Queen that comes with her title."

"No, you don't," she snickered. "That's like me slicing your throat and then saying, 'oh, I just adore you!'."

"Yes, I do." Kylen persisted quickly, turning her very own words on her.

She sat up and looked towards him fiercely. "Oh, I apologise. I didn't realise your way of showing love is through quite literally betraying a child?"

Kylen looked taken back as he took in the emotions that stirred beneath her eyes. "I was a child too." He whispered, and Althea rolled her eyes with a shake of her head.

"Why haven't you apologised for any of it?" her eyes

searched through the depths of his, and she cursed herself for allowing a glimpse of her emotions to show, to send the clouds rattling with a clap of thunder that was alarmingly heavy. "I never once did not have your back. Even when you did that stupid 'prank' with your brothers on my grounds—I still had your back and defended your name to my father!" Her voice broke, and Althea shook her head to erase away the memories of her tears. "I thought we were friends. I thought that I had finally met someone who was going to show me what my dreams whispered of."

Althea rose to her feet, and Kylen quickly followed. She cursed herself for allowing herself to sound so weak. So pathetic. She would not stand for it. "And yet you—" she spat as she pushed him back; his hand holding onto hers for a faltering second. "You never gave me a chance. I was a sweet, *kind*, young girl who would have done anything you asked of her, but instead, *you murdered her.*"

"Althea, please—"

"Please?" she barked with a laugh. "I was begging you to help me understand! I was begging you to help me understand what the fuck I had done to you? But I have learnt now that you are just as fucked in the head as the rumours say you to be. I haven't needed you to care for my needs for years, *Kylen*, don't expect me to need your help now."

Her voice must have triggered something within the cages of her Elemental magick because it decided to break free, and Kylen was thrown brutally back. He hit the ground with such severity that Althea could only gape, watching as he struggled to catch his breath.

The air left Althea's throat in a swift gasp as Kylen groaned in muffled pain, rolling back over to face her before reaching forward with a hand—a hand that was splattered in blood. "I'm fine. It's okay." His breaths were so mangled that she already knew that he was lying, and emotions she refused to fixate on stirred beneath her heart.

Althea took a step back, and Kylen shook his head again, a concerned, almost gentle look plastering over the pain on his face as he forced himself up, how she hated when mortals did that. “Darling, *really*, I have faced worst.”

His white shirt had already become somewhat clear from the rain, but the dark crimson blood took over it within a matter of a second. She had made him bleed, and it didn’t feel as glorious as she had expected it to.

Her mind was spinning as she turned on her heels, sliding through the mud with momentum. Her breaths were beyond reason as she began to run. “Althea!” Kylen yelled out, but she couldn’t bring herself to turn back to him. She was meant to kill him and grin over his dying body, yet this magick had just sent him flying back and had her eyes widening, filling with fear and panic as she ran to her death.

The rain tried to keep her back, the wind pushed—*begging* her to face the man who was letting her go, but her heart was simply too heavy, too full of *fear*.

FOURTEEN

KYLEN

He didn't know how long he was out there, allowing the rain to wash away his blood as if it were his sins, but it felt like a thousand eternities had formed into one. He could still see the vision of her running, the fear that had crossed her face when they saw the blood staining his shirt. *Again*, it had been a reminder of his humanity, but that wasn't what either of them needed at that moment.

Althea's words turned in his mind as he finally approached the castle again. Every little thing that she had screamed at him for, rotating until he found his own throat drying.

Sayah had been exiting Althea's room in panic when she saw him and the blood he carried. "What happened?" her voice was a rasp, and her steps halted.

Kylen shook his head, and Sayah already understood what he meant, nodding her head as if the weight of the last five minutes wasn't strangling them both. Zaire must have sensed the tightness of the air because they appeared too, and Sayah rushed over to help their forming body within a second.

"You mustn't use your abilities!" the siren hissed. "You are just going to exhaust yourself."

"Where is the girl?" Zaire asked, looking to Kylen, who dripped with the emotions of the skies and his own dark yet still fighting blood. Chloe brushed up against his legs, and he leaned down, slowly picking her up before holding her to his chest; hardly realising that her fur was too turning a dark red.

"Gone."

"But we need a Queen—"

"*I don't care about a fucking Queen!* I fucked up majorly, and now Althea is gone!" he ran a hand over his face, ignoring the exhaust his features held. "She didn't deserve this. To be once again brought into my life and then screwed over just like that."

Sayah ignored his burning panic, the way his rambles turned his words into spheres that aimed right for his already dying heart. "What did you learn?" she asked, looking towards Zaire.

Zaire shook their head, brushing it off as if their knowledge didn't send his already racing heart falling through Realms. "Why does it matter? She no longer wants our protection."

"Zaire—" Kylen and Sayah warned the Fairy in sync. "What did you learn?" he asked, and Zaire pulled their gaze towards him.

"Tonight's a full moon, is it not?" they replied in question, and when Sayah raised a brow, they continued on. "If Althea's Markings resemble something of the picture that Kylen drew for me, then her Markings are connected to the moon and Gods. And while I'm aware that all Markings do, hers connect more strongly because she has a touch of each one."

"Your point?" Kylen asked, earning a scowl from Zaire, who always hated his impatience.

"My point is that tonight is a full moon, and because she has all four of the Markings, she has access to open the gates to the afterlife. If Althea were here, I would advise you to keep her indoors and strengthen the barriers, but since she is not, then just let her go."

"Let her go?" Sayah gaped. "If Erwin gets his hands on her, then she is done for! Gods know what he could access using her magick."

"Is there anything else we should know?" Kylen asked as he looked at them. Althea was out there, *alone*, and he knew she could take care of herself, but this magick risked her life. It risked her falling victim to Erwin, which was something he would die to stop from happening. "Anything else that I should know before *I* go looking for her?" his hand was clamped down onto his wound, holding it together as the storms heightened outside.

"You aren't going looking for her." Zaire fumed. "It's dangerous."

"Like Hel I'm not."

FIFTEEN
ALTHEA

The markets were busy with people despite the rain. A buzz to them that she felt would never feel genuinely natural to her. Althea currently walked past the memorials of the people she remembered clearly killing, scoffing to herself about how blind these stupid, ignorant souls could be. The word was that they were *unnecessary deaths*. That they didn't deserve to die but rather live a wonderful, *true* life, growing old with their loved ones *that they so definitely did not abuse*. Althea disagreed with everything in her. Those people were anything but nice.

They tried to defy her as a person, as a human being—which turns out she never was one, but the respect you should treat one with shouldn't change because of their identity.

All these years, she had classified herself as human. All these years, she thought that the only magick about her was the curse that her father had gifted her when she was around five years old. Only to find out now that she was never human, she was an Elemental—and she had to think of what to do next.

She passed more memorials with a sneer and a roll of her eyes, holding her stolen cloak to her chest as she kept her eyes on the ground before her. It was useful to her now that she had already managed to memorise the basic layout of Kylen's Kingdom—not only for when it came to killing people and disposing of their bodies but for now when she fled the scene of her crimes.

How hypocritical in a certain way she sounded.

Althea had killed them because not only did they get in her way, but they also were a burden to the people around them. To the people that loved them. So as a matter of those facts, she got down and got her hands dirty so that she could help the world *as the kind-hearted girl that she was at heart.*

Oh mother, you are quite comedic.

If only that was what they had called her as she plucked their fingers from their hands.

All the people Althea had killed deserved it. They deserved nothing more than to rot in Hel. And she knew she would see them soon, no doubt that her father would get to her in that time. She hadn't fulfilled Kylen's request of staying within the walls. And now, not only he, but Erwin's running mouth too, was going to find her father and share the blessed news with him.

Did her father know about the magick she wielded? How she had avoided that question for so long. He would have to know by now—word travels fast, especially when it's the knowledge of something like this. Something so powerful that whoever learns of the news is automatically higher ranked than those blind to it.

She dreaded the days to come; he was sure to come here, to come and see if his daughter had betrayed him as Kylen had done to them both. It itched her mind to know that no matter how hard she would try to argue against it, he would never believe her. After all, once he had his mind set on something, that was it; she couldn't change it, no matter how wrong he was.

Althea stepped over the dead rat at her feet, her eyebrows raising as the cat she recognised from behind Kylen's walls appeared beside her, trotting along with not a care in the world. How she envied that feeling.

As she walked through this Kingdom with her head down, hugging the cloak she had stolen from some washing line to her body, she could not help but realise how different this Kingdom was. It may be raining and presenting itself as her Realm to her, but she knew that it was not. This was not her home—*she didn't have a home anymore.*

Althea looked back at the cat with a closed-lip smirk, trying to force her attitude to lighten up as she found the apartment she had been seeking shelter in. "Looks like your journey of following me has come to an end," she whispered, though her tone didn't sound as light-hearted as she wished it to be. "Scurry home, little one. The world is a dangerous place."

Althea turned back to the wall, already moving to climb her way up it. The wall was wet, threatening to crumble with every step, but there were enough hand and footholds to get her to the top before looking back down to the cat. "Go home;" she repeated, "it isn't safe in these parts." With one hand, she unhooked the broken window, pushing it up before swinging one leg through it.

Althea landed on the same wooden floor that she had first landed on in panic. Tears had been streaming down her cheeks that night, and she had been struggling even to take a single breath. The adrenaline that had kept her running through that Kingdom had disappeared within minutes, and she was left to face the daunting fact that she was on the run in a Kingdom she knew nothing about.

She shut the window behind her before pulling the blinds across. Her fingers trailed along the old, withered wood, and the Princess sighed. Despite the question being on her mind endlessly, she still had no clue what she was to do. Should she return to her Kingdom? —No, she couldn't do that; *she would end up dead*. And not to mention that she was almost certain that her father would have found out by now. He probably had a plan all structured out, preparing all the arrangements for her perfectly staged death—not that it mattered much about how perfect it was. No one would second guess His Majesty.

Althea couldn't stay here, though. This wasn't her home, nor would it ever be. She needed to hate these people; it would make their lives far easier. Perhaps in some aspects, she did loathe them; they supported a King who had deceived them all with his false kindness.

If only they had heard her screams, her sobs—then she was certain they would reconsider just how truly fond of him they were.

Althea sat on the edge of the bed, pulling her hair over her shoulder as she did every other time. She felt overridden with anxiety. She looked to the cracked frame beside the dresser, eyeing down the family that used to live huddled together here. She could feel their presence; it was like a drug that was deep within her veins, whispering words to her that she would constantly run from if only she were given the privilege.

She felt the curse—*her curse that had killed them*; its touch was like a distant memory. Searching through her blood for the void that had once held the curse she had clung onto like a lifeboat.

Althea looked towards the cracked mirror, catching her reflection as she began to part through her hair, pulling each section at a time to get the horrid knots that made her cringe in pain. Her eyes moved from the mirror to the floorboards, catching the pompous tremors that began to vibrate through the floors. She could spot those tremors anywhere, yet she was left to glance sceptically around.

There was no way he had found her, not already. If he had, she was going to riot; this was purely another unfair game of Kylen's.

She rose to her feet, calling to her magick at once. However, her cursed magick did not answer her, leaving her empty-handed as the realisation harshly confronted her. *It was gone; the magick that she loved and yet despised with every inch of her soul was gone and replaced with one she had no use for, one that would drag her to her death.*

How could she forget?

There was a noise behind her, and Althea whirled around, eyes wide, posture ready.

Who she was expecting to see was not there, instead replaced with another man, *one that made her heart drop* and the thunder in the skies halt.

"*Hel no.*"

Althea took a step back, glancing instantly to the window. She moved quickly, hoping with everything within her that he too, had lost his magick. Yet, as if the Gods were still persistent in punishing her, Erwin's magick lunged for her, wrapping around her waist before pulling her down. Althea hit the floor with such force that it sent tremors throughout the Kingdom.

She whipped her head back up, snarling in an attempt to mask her pure fear. *No*. She didn't need to be fearful; she never needed her magick to be strong before. Althea kicked her feet up, connecting with his abdomen, using his quick flash of shock mixed with agony to play with his sudden blind spot.

Erwin stumbled back, but he was quick to reposition himself. Althea swung to her knees, one hand pressed against the floorboards while the other was trying to search through this new magick; finding any link that would wield her a weapon.

The wind sent the glass rattling, and Althea grinned in its presence. Erwin darted towards her, his shadows already striking for her blood, but she dodged them in the nick of time. "I just want to talk," he said, blood flinging from his lips and decorating the floors before him.

Althea laughed a pure menace sounding melody. "That's not the first time I've heard that one," she replied. Althea pushed herself to her feet, pulling her sleeves up before holding her hands out before her. She did it in the act of protection, getting ready to shield herself from him, yet there was a glint of something more in his eyes. Something as horrifying as fear. She felt her magick rise then, and two daggers formed in her hands. Althea didn't waste a second; she had already sent them flying at him before she ducked for the window.

Althea was an inch away from the windowsill when his shadows wrapped around her throat. She was pulled back before she could react, hitting the floor with such a thud that she was sure she had been impaled, but *unfortunately*, that was not the case. Erwin gained on her, his blade extending out to the point where if she moved, her stomach would meet with the end of his sword, and that was a vulnerability that she did not need at this very moment.

Althea froze, staring down yet up at him with cold eyes. Her mind was racing, calculating a plan that she knew would work. Blood dripped, and Althea grinned, realising that both of her blades had met her mark. "*I must say*, despite no longer having your magick, you still present yourself with such fierce." Erwin cooed, a smug scent to his words.

Althea's stare didn't falter; she continued with staring him down, ignoring the feel of her father's eyes on her as she stared into the depth of his. "Well, they do say that I was born with it."

Erwin laughed. "They do." His eyes slowly dragged down, meeting the Markings that covered her wrist. "So, it's true…" he mumbled to himself in awe and a mix of panic. "Tell me, little great one, do these Markings bring you joy? Do you fantasize about the idea of finally being free? *Do you want them…?*"

"Do I want *what*?" Althea spat as the older male advanced on her, pinning her wrists back down with one hand; his nails dug into her skin and blood beaded through. "Do I want the offers you offer me? No, not in any world would I."

Erwin pressed the blade harder with his other hand. "That

was not what I was talking about." He nodded his head towards Althea's Markings, and abruptly a million new voices filled her head.

NO, NO, NO, NO, NO, NO, NO, NO. Run, flee, mother, you must escape! NO! NO! NO! NO! NO! NO! Run! Run! Run! Run!

They all screamed at her, all the different voices, and all the different souls that made up this strange and mystically warm magick; pleaded with her as if they were on their hands and knees begging her. "I don't have much say in the matter," Althea informed him with a clench of her jaw, restraining the fear that threatened to erupt within her. "I can't get rid of it even if I tried." The words like daggers straight to her heart.

"Oh, but that's a lie, and you know it." Erwin reached forward, his foul fingers just resting against her skin, and she could feel the age beneath them. Althea pushed herself back, earning a grin from Erwin. "Even Kylen tried to make you realise that, although his intentions were elsewhere..."

Althea narrowed her brows. "You were listening to our conversation?" she almost sounded offended, and Erwin tipped his head forward with a nod.

"I did." He tipped his head to the left, so human-like that if she were anyone else, they would think that he may truly be one. "Problem?" His eyes searched hers, searching for something that she did not reveal. He shook his head, erasing whatever it was that made the darkest of the dark shadows swirl throughout his eyes. "Let's get back to the point."

"There's a point to this?" Althea snarked in reply, and he narrowed his eyes.

"Yes, as I've said before, I can help you get rid of your magick. It's easy, you know." He paused before abruptly turning, and Althea inched further away. "If anyone can help you get rid of something like this, it's me. You do realise that, don't you?"

Althea glanced down.

"So, you do have some common sense in you?" he pried in a

questioning, dull tone. "Well, good, it's about time." He looked down, tapping the broken watch on his wrist. "We must go. We must complete this sooner than later as your dear fiancé has just left the building we need to enter."

"I'm not going with you," Althea stated through a laugh that hid her true fear.

"Oh, but you will," Erwin said. "I have caught all of the messengers who were racing back to tell your father about what they had seen. They are locked in my room, and if you help me help you, then I will wipe all of their memories on your behalf, little-little beauty."

Althea watched him, trying to figure out if what he was saying was the truth or not. Her body froze as he disappeared, and her heart sunk deeper as his hands clasped onto the sides of her head, his nails digging into her skin.

A vision appeared before her, and sure enough, she saw a room full of prisoners, all of which were bruised and bloody. The females looked far worse than the men and the bile within her throat stirred. Althea stepped out of his clasp and took multiple quick steps back towards the window.

"So you will help me get rid of it?" Althea asked, her voice so small as she pulled on her sleeves. Perhaps if the day had risen and other options warmed the palms of her hands, she would be able to kill him right here and right now. But time wasn't on her side, and she was almost positively sure that her father would have her head the moment he found out.

"Yes."

☽

"I'm not doing this anymore," Althea stated as she glanced towards Erwin, allowing the gut feelings and emotions to speak on her behalf. "I believe that I can do this some other way."

LIES, LIES, HORRIBLE LIES. YOU MUST NOT LIE, MOTHER.

Her eyes glanced around to the doorways, her mind spinning beyond reason. She wouldn't admit it aloud, but she was searching for Kylen. He had to be here; this was his castle after all, and they were in the ballroom, close to his quarters. Why on the Realms name was the castle so bare? Why was it so empty? People had to be here, guards of some type at least. Why weren't they here?

"You've already made up your mind, Althea. I can feel it in your heart."

"Well, that's obviously wrong."

He looked to her; his vision furrowed on her in a warning. "I don't think it is."

I just need a dagger. A dagger, a knife, a sword. Anything. Please. This cannot be good on your behalf—so let me defend myself, please!

Erwin tilted his head as he approached her. Althea instantly began to walk back; however, whatever barrier he was keeping her enclosed in snapped into place, not allowing her to flee anymore. He pulled his blade from his belt, and she watched with such guilt as the shadows from his soul waltzed upon it. He pulled her wrist up, and Althea whimpered, her eyes burning with tears as the blade slipped beneath her skin. Cutting open a long line that went straight through her Markings, revealing dark crimson blood in its wake.

How she had expected her blood to still be infected with the curse.

His grip tightened, and she quickly pulled away, her chest heaving as she tried not to let herself panic—she wouldn't be able to escape if she was panicking. "Finish reading," he instructed, his tone leaving no room for questioning.

He left the circle he concealed her in, and Althea hesitated; her eyes burned through the gaping wound that throbbed on her wrist. It ached, *it throbbed*, blood dripped down and puddled at her feet, and Althea was reminded of the dream she had felt trapped within all those nights ago. She felt Erwin's magick push her forward, his blade against her back.

This was going to be fine; it was going to be good. It was all going to work out, and tomorrow she would wake up with no Markings, *no horrible magick whatsoever*.

Well, that was what she was telling herself.

The voices in her mind *begged to differ*.

How could you be so stupid? You know what he is doing; you have realised it now. The moment you became re-trapped behind these castle walls under Erwin's magick, you realised it. He is going to steal your magick and kill you in the process.

SIXTEEN
KYLEN

"Chloe! My Gods, did you follow us? It isn't safe." Kylen tilted his head as he looked down at the white cat, who watched him with laughing eyes. "You don't just sneak up on people—especially when a psychotic serial killer is on the loose!" he whispered aggravatedly, brushing a hand through his hair as his eyes darted in every direction.

Sayah hit his arm lightly as she walked past him, furrowing her gaze against the harsh wind that pushed them back towards the castle they were escaping from.

Kylen reached down, picking up the cat as he peered over his shoulder. Confirming that no one was following them. He looked back to the siren at his side, his eyes full of concern and fear, with a touch of worry. The cat moved within his arms, distracting him from the bites of anxiety that stirred within there. Chloe would not stop; it was like she wanted to go back the way they had just come. "I think Chloe wants to go home—"

"*—You should go home.*" Zaire's voice spoke as their body was yet to appear. "In fact, you should probably get a move on with going home because we have some visitors that are making my restraint questionable."

Kylen placed the cat down and watched as she instantly began to run away. Disappearing down the pathway to his castle. "What do you mean?" Concern laced the colour of his soul. It was an uneasy type of feeling, one that used to threaten him when he stepped onto his ship.

Zaire disappeared and reappeared behind him, their small yet deathly strong hands pushing Kylen forward. "It means that my castle is about to get blown up because of whatever Althea is doing behind closed doors with Erwin," they sneered. "And I recently got something that I would prefer not to lose."

Sayah appeared at his side instantly; her face drained of emotion. "They are at the castle—*he has her already?"* she asked, and Zaire nodded. "We need to go now!"

"That's what I've been saying!" Zaire argued as they all began to run. "Have you not been listening?" No voice answered theirs as they ran in silence. Zaire disappeared again, and all Kylen could hear was his *own voice*.

His voice was so rude, so cruel. Talking about Althea as if she wasn't a person. It told him to leave her be, to allow death to conquer her as that was her fate—*but he*, for whatever reason, was determined to rewrite her ending.

Althea would probably be dead the moment they got there, he knew that, but he refused to accept it. Althea did not deserve to die. He had put her through Hel and back, but he knew more than anyone that she did not deserve this. She acted as if he didn't remember her wide smile or her giddy laugh, but he did. And he loathed himself for taking it away.

He was going to kill Erwin. Even if it got himself killed, at least then, she would be able to reign in peace if that was what she chose to do.

☽

He could feel her new magick; it was alive—*she was alive.* He released the breath his lungs held from him. Such an incredible frequency ringing through his own soul as he crept closer. His steps were near-silent compared to her heart-wrenching screams.

Kylen kept his eyes shut, pushing away the uneasiness that came from hearing her pleads pierce through his heart. He needed to focus on saving her. Kylen looked up and over to Sayah, watching and silently begging for Zaire's orders of when to strike to come sooner than later.

He could hear the screams of her magick. It was all Althea; she was begging, crying, pleading, asking him with all of the courage she had left to stop, *to leave her alone.*

Erwin was ignoring her—or perhaps she was answering the Dark Master, just in a silent way. He could hear her rushed breaths; he could hear how truly panicked she was.

It was a sound like no other, one that made his gut twist and turn in such agony.

He didn't understand why he felt as if he was the one being tortured, but perhaps it was his guilt. All he knew was that his soul felt as if it was on fire, a torture far more painful than the curse itself.

Kylen turned to Sayah and found her eyes peering through the wood that stood between them and her. The magick flickered off in her eyes, and she looked at him, concern radiating off every part of her body. He raised a trembling hand of restraint before turning away. It was physically choking him to wait. He wanted to go in there and murder Erwin—he wanted to do anything that would gift her with the prize of peace.

"*Please!*" Althea screamed; her cries sent tremors along the floorboards, aiming right for the target of his soul. Before him, the wooden doors shook, and Kylen dared to step closer, but Sayah's hand stopped him from moving any further. "We need to wait for Zaire." She mouthed, and from her expression, he could see that she understood what this restraint was doing to him.

He was mad, frustrated, infuriated—yet he could not stay mad at her. He understood where this need was coming from. She needed these Markings gone, and Erwin had presumably deceived her, just as Kylen had done all those years ago.

Within a second, Sayah's eyes lit up with the magick of Zaire, and she nodded.

It was time, and he was not going to restrain himself any longer.

He heard the muffled gag of Erwin, and so he pushed the doors forward, running through them as quick as ever. The room was blindingly bright and Kylen expected Althea to be somewhere in the midst of it all. "Althea!" He steered away, looking to where Erwin now stood on the outskirts, the magick from Althea's soul still travelling to his despite being on the ground with Zaire on top of him.

It was like a twine of pure gold, the string of it reaching from one soul to the other, and he could see the physical darkness sinking into it.

Zaire kneeled over him, their long spear of green vines piercing through the shadows of his chest. It wasn't enough to kill him right in that very second, but it was enough to keep him down for a few more trembling seconds. "Find her!"

The man had been so fixated on draining the life from Althea that he hadn't suspected or sensed their presence. Kylen ran forward, wasting no more time as he instinctively headed into the eye of the dragon. The magick that belonged to her soul began to falter as it remained filling the air; the darkness that was seeping into it predictively butchering Althea's soul of light, pure magick. "Althea?"

His steps halted as he met with a barrier of some type—it didn't hurt; in fact, he didn't feel anything other than a firm wall before him, so this magick wasn't out to kill him. It was a barrier that wasn't visible to see through. It held a shimmering haze to it instead, but it too held the rhythm of Althea's heartbeat, a sound that was panicked and yet pissed off. Kylen stepped forward and through the barrier, feeling as it opened for him for whatever reason.

The voices came swarming at him, blaming him for what he had put the girl through just because he needed a Queen. Didn't they understand that he knew that it was all his fault? But everything seemed to be his fault these days because if he didn't have a Queen, his Kingdom would die. But if he did, Althea would have to see him again, and that brought a pain to her heart that he wished to erase.

The sight before him caused his heart to stop, dropping to the bottom of his stomach as his steps quickened and he ran through the blood.

Althea laid unconscious before the blood-covered table. Her hair was glowing around her, stealing the last of the air from his darkened lungs. His eyes went to her wrist, seizing with such guilt as he saw the long wound that scraped there, splitting her delicate Markings in half. "Althea?" he whispered, his voice barely audible compared to the sounds of his panic.

Death, death, death, death, death, death, death, death.

She looked as if she was a fallen angel—forever burdened with the curse that was out for her. She looked like a gift from the Gods, one that was carved especially for him. That's what made it so painful because even when he was fourteen and she was twelve, *he knew that they could have been friends*—beautiful true friends where he could gift her with the world's presents. They could have both ran away and explored the world, just as he had promised her. They would go from island to island, from village to village. Althea wanted to see it all, and Kylen had felt so giddy when he promised her that she would.

Kylen begged for any answer that would leave her lips. He needed any answer that would let him know that she was okay and that he hadn't gotten her killed. "Althea, please—" His cold, scarred hands scraped across her cheeks, guiding her to open her eyes and bless him with the seas that thrashed beneath them. "*Open your damn eyes*."

Her skin was like ice, her vibrant, exhilarated magick throbbing beneath. His hand made it to her pulse, and Kylen instantly felt as if he was going to be sick.

Nothing responded to his calls of magick; nothing responded to the calls he begged for.

Althea was dead.

Kylen had failed—but then he felt the illusion her magick was deceiving him with. *Of course*, he thought. *Althea would never genuinely allow Erwin to be the one to kill her. If she were going to die, she would probably go out in a blaze of glory.* Kylen forced himself to breathe, although that seemed awfully difficult when he was looking down at a girl who inevitably looked to be dead.

Althea's twelve-year-old eyes stayed focussed on the couple in the distance, watching as the male stood before his wife's deceased body just minutes after it got lowered from the rope she had hung on. "How can he just stand there?" she asked as her eyes stayed captivated on the two. "That isn't fair to her—if anything were to happen to me, I would want someone to hold me. I would want someone to stroke my hair because that is the least anybody could do. They would need to tell me that I will be alright, even if they are watching the life drain from my eyes. I want to be told that everything is going to work out."

Kylen slowly and very carefully held Althea to his chest, his hands slowly running down her face as he tucked the blood-stained hair behind her ear. He had done this to her—he had put her through all of this misery because he was selfish and needed her to be his Queen, without even considering the position that she was in. Even if she was not dead but merely deceiving the world into believing that she was a dead girl—he still felt the guilt claw at him for putting her in this position. He cursed himself repeatedly for putting her through such pain when she was only a child, and now he cursed himself for this. How much of a coward could he be? Surely, if he just had spoken to her and gotten her to understand, she would have realised that he never wanted to be the bad guy. He never wanted to be the one on the other side of the blade as it pierced its way through her ethereal carved heart.

He stared down at her, wishing for a world where they could have gotten everything they dreamt of.

Freedom.

He wouldn't lie. When he had figured out that she was the one determined by the Gods to be his wife from one of Sayah's readings, he had been *excited*, because then the last of his days wouldn't be wasted away. He would spend them bickering and arguing with the girl he used to boast about marrying, despite how young they had been. She would make the last of his ill and wicked days entertaining with the prideful and judgmental personality she carried.

There would not have been a dull day because he would either be dodging the end of the blades she threw at him or doing all in his power to make her ready for his people—whom he didn't even want to think about anymore.

Kylen clenched his jaw as he rocked her back and forth. His spare hand rose in the midst of the air and reached towards the twine of magick that Erwin was stealing from within her ice-covered chest. Kylen grabbed at it, his fingers clasping around it before infecting it with his own blood-infused magick. Kylen felt the impact of it, and he felt himself choke on the agony it threw at him. He looked up, away from the girl in his arms, his lips quivering as he forced whatever magick that he had, to defend this light that was her magick.

Kylen had done what he'd had to in the past, and if he had to do it again, he would. He would do it ten times over, and each one of those times, he would do everything in his power to find another way around it. To get the same response and answers; but not have her—Althea Evangeline hurt in the process of it.

"*Kylen,*" a voice that he knew from long ago whispered and his heart for the tenth time today threatened to stop. "*Kylen.*"

Kylen looked up, his eyes wide and glowing with Althea's power that surged through him. His eyes searched for the presence that he felt ever so clearly as he held the girl protectively tighter. He felt the presence over his shoulder, a presence that should not be there, *so heavenly light yet so awfully dark*. There were millions of tiny whispers that followed the presence as if the other souls who rotted in the depths of the afterlife too wanted nothing more than to escape.

His eyes met with one of his three nonbiological brothers, widening in not only shock but fear as the man knelt before him. Emotions took over his soul as his eyes searched through his brothers, such confusion in them that the room began to feel as if it was spinning.

"Kylen," Khatri whispered gently. "I need your help, brother."

SEVENTEEN
ALTHEA

The pain throbbed throughout her soul and along her bones; an ecstasy—one that felt so good and yet so excruciatingly horrible. One that she would want to spend every day of her life running from, *if she could.*

She didn't remember what had happened—Althea physically couldn't. It hurt her mind to even think about it, which just seemed to piss her off even more.

One minute she was looking at Erwin, her teeth bared and hand raising. The next, death had greeted her as if she was just an old friend, a smile appearing on his beautifully carved lips as he swept her off her feet for a kiss, and how familiar those lips were to Kylen's.

There were options before her. Ones that stood at arm's length and yet did not falter under her heavy gaze. How was she to choose? It seemed almost impossible, and that led the breath to freeze within her lungs. The first was cold, and almost immediately, she sheered away from that option. The second one was softer, so she gave it a second chance. It was not the easier option, but it held a type of security one could only yearn for. That feeling only expanded when Althea stepped into the light, holding onto the hands that welcomed her before 'forming' a blade and demanding to know where the Hel she was.

Almost immediately, Erwin's anger rocketed through her, but she didn't mind. He had tricked her—even after she had promised herself to be smarter. This was her revenge. Going off the rails that he had lined up perfectly before her.

Not to mention her revenge of making them believe she was dead. *Oh, how she wished to see Erwin's expression when he had realised that she was anything but.*

Althea felt the sunshine brush against the edge of her cheeks, and she opened her eyes, blinding herself with the glorious light that dared to sneak up on her. "Hello, little bird," her mother whispered as she knelt before her, a glistening smile appearing on her once mourned face.

Althea's brows furrowed. "Mother?" she whispered, the confusion evident. She reached for her mother, all the emotions she had been pushing aside now striking within her, aiming right for her heart which deceived her with such wicked lies. Althea quickly pulled her hands back, her eyes wide.

"Oh, look at how you've grown." Her voice was sickly sweet, and Althea swore that she could feel the deja-vu wash over her like a bucket of cold water. Her mother's hand met with her own, and she rose to her feet, never—not even for a second dragging her eyes away from the woman that stood before her.

This could not be real—her mother was dead.

Was Althea truly dead?

She heard a bird's call, and finally, she broke her eyes away. Moving her attention to the view that they stood so proudly before. She raised her free hand up, feeling as the sunshine felt real and warm against her fingertips. "I died, didn't I?" There was a sudden understanding to that question, one that turned the pure air in her lungs to stone.

Her mother looked at her with a saddened expression before exhaling. "I'm afraid you did not, dear."

Althea turned her gaze quickly on her mother, "I didn't?" she choked. A self-satisfied smirk curled on her lips, and she nodded twice, ignoring the look her mother shed her. "Well, good. Do they believe that I did? That I genuinely died?" She asked, averting her attention from her mother, who was waiting for her to react to her presence in some—*any way*.

But Althea couldn't. She didn't even want to look at her mother, let alone feel the emotions that came with doing so.

"Yes." Her mother, Lilith, stated. "They cannot hear, feel, or sense your heartbeat because of the spell your magick cast."

"You know, I expected something grander, something more… *exhilarating*. That's probably why I am not dead yet. I would much prefer to die at the ends of a God than Erwin, don't you think that sounds far more fun?" she asked, briefly skimming her eyes over her mother—and before the dead women could answer, Althea asked, "does Kylen know?"

"Yes. He just found your body."

Althea grimaced, nodding. "Does he believe me to be dead? I bet he's over the moon about it if he does," she mused aloud, ignoring the awkward gaze that was set upon her by her mother, who she did not want to see. "I bet he is so thrilled that now he's physically out of options which means he doesn't have to be stuck with marrying me—perhaps he will dump my body somewhere and when I wake up I will be free of him and my father—because no doubt Kylen would admit to killing me to him."

Her mother sighed, and Althea slowly returned her intense stare. "Well, actually, there are two things. One: the illusion opened to Kylen, so now he knows you're not actually dead. And two: you have seven minutes until you *are* dead."

It felt as if the air began to burn her throat, as if the hold it had on her was far too tight to cope. Althea didn't care about the first bit—Kylen somehow bending her magick to his advantage no longer seemed like a concern to her. "I am going to be dead in seven minutes?" she whispered, her voice awfully hesitant.

Her mother reached forward, tucking a strand of hair behind Althea's ear, which caused her to straighten up slightly. "Yes, but you know you still have the option of fighting?"

Althea turned, and her eyes met the nearly identical ones to hers. "What do you mean?"

"I mean, you can fight for your life. That is an option but only one that can be taken now," her mother exhaled with a smile, "and if you do that, then I will help you. But if you choose to find peace… well then, sweetheart, I will help you with that too."

Althea turned away, sheltering her face from anyone's view. This was a new opportunity. Did she deserve to find peace? Probably not. But she wasn't even finished with life yet. There were so many things that were left incomplete, so many stars that she never got to see.

Althea sighed a heavy, heart-straining sigh, feeling as her stomach twisted with knots of the unknown. "If you want to fight, then you need to fight now. You have seven minutes until you are officially dead, seven minutes where you can fight for the life you —" her mother said, distracting the voices before Althea cut her off.

"But I don't know if I want to fight," Althea admitted, cutting her mother off. "There's nothing left for me there. I didn't help Erwin in any way, which means the news is going to reach my father—which means there is nothing left for me there. I have no home, no Kingdom, no people, no one." She breathed through quivering, weak breaths. "I—I just don't think that there is anything worth fighting for." The way the words left her lips with such ease had her heart straining, her life trembling.

No, not the right attitude, mother. You need to fight. Fight, fight, fight.

Her mother nodded, understanding with that same sickening expression that burned through her distant memories. "But just think about how glorious of an entrance it would be for you to come back from the dead and to claim Erwin's life as your own?" her mother offered with a soft smile.

Althea reached back for her hair before pulling it over her shoulder, ignoring just how truly enticing that sounded. "Is this the afterlife?" Althea asked with a quivering breath. Of course, she didn't really remember her mother, but a part of Althea had always yearned for the figure that she had read about for so long. She was jealous when her father had told her that other children had mothers; and that Althea had been disobedient or naughty, which caused hers to be taken away. She had always wanted that love, that attention, and not once did she ever think it was fair that she didn't get it.

"No."

Then where was she?

Althea turned her eyes back to her mother at once, her confusion evident. "Then how are you here?"

"I am a figment of your imagination." Althea rolled her eyes with a shake of her head, however her mother continued. "Because you aren't officially dead, you are still trapped in your mind. You are seeing the version of me that you used to imagine as a child. You used to picture me as someone who was patient, kind, sweet, honourable," her mother explained. "And so here I am."

"I never imagined you to be anything of the sort," Althea replied defensively. "I pictured you as a coward because you are. You chose the easy way out of a marriage that you wanted nothing more to do with."

Her mother looked pained at the words as if she truly were real. "If I'd had the choice, then I would have never left you."

Althea laughed with a shake of her head. "So, this is a safe haven of my imagination?" Althea asked with a scoff. "How cute." Her eyes skimmed over the buildings and houses that glistened with sunlight that did not burn.

"This may be all your imagination, but this is what the Kingdom where you are from looks like."

"It's far brighter than Aeonia," she mused, remembering the place that she never truly belonged in. Shinrin was the lands that got ruled out by the wars, it was the Kingdom that her blood was from despite the world claiming for her to be Harlian.

Growing up Althea never had access to the world, but she would never forget that one maid who managed to break free of the curse—the one that began to scream at her for abandoning the Harlian throne. Althea had just watched of course, taken back because Harlia was a place of myths, a place her father had once read to her about in the folkloric fairy tales.

"It is," her mother eagerly agreed. "But after the war stormed through it, things began to look different. So, if you do make it back and go there, you will see that this isn't exactly what it looks like anymore." Lilith leaned forward and fixed the blue mesh collar around Althea's throat, a small smile on her lips. "So, what will it be?"

Althea tucked the curls behind her ears, doing anything at all to keep herself distracted. "I—"

"*She will fight,*" Kylen—*Kylen* stated as he appeared through the doorway behind them. "That is her decision, she will fight to get out of this beautiful yet wretched place of death."

Althea's expression changed drastically as she turned her shocked expression from him to her mother. "Okay, now I definitely know that this is nothing to do with my doing; because there is no way that I would have summoned him here!"

Kylen smiled one of his mischievous grins as he approached her. "Oh darling, don't lie to yourself." He stopped approaching her as his smile faltered, his hands dropping to his sides. He cleared his throat and turned to Lilith. "I would say it's an honour to meet you, but in all honesty, it's not exactly an honour, and I'm not too fond of you. Thea, sweetheart, you need to fight."

The expression on Althea's face changed from one of amusement to one of disgust. "Quit calling me that," Althea begged as she turned to him, her expression aching.

"What?" Kylen asked. "Sweetheart or Thea?"

"*Sweetheart*, *darling*—I am not your anything!" Althea spat, holding her chin high so that she could look at him down her nose.

"Oh, please," Kylen sighed. "You are meant to be my sweetheart, *my alive and healthy* wife," he cooed rather quickly as if it was a race to get it off the tip of his tongue. "And yet you are being truly idiotic, may I add."

"Kylen, I am just about dead," Althea stated bluntly. "If anything, you are a widower."

"I am not a widower," Kylen quickly snapped back as if he didn't have a care in the world. "You are right here, are you not?" he questioned with a cock of his brow. "I am looking right at you."

Althea crossed her arms as she turned her full attention to him. "I am. But I would rather that I'm not because if I were at peace, then I wouldn't be put to the task of staring at your—"

"Two minutes."

Althea turned on her feet, eyes wide. "What?" she gaped.

"Two minutes until you are officially dead, brain dead, all dead." her mother informed her. "If you want to start fighting, then you must do it now, Althea."

Althea looked to Kylen, finding his expression equally as weary. "What?" he whispered. He turned his stare to hers, finding her eyes now shut, squeezing ever so tightly as she wished all of this just to be a bad dream. How was she to make this decision? If this was basically what death was, then it wasn't too bad—but that didn't take away the factor that there was still somewhat of a life to live.

"Althea, you have to wake up," Kylen pleaded as his cold, scarred hands found her arms. He sounded so desperate that a part of her wanted to laugh and die out of pure revenge. Her body stilled and she looked at him with a hesitant expression. She felt his thumbs draw circles across the material covering her arms—and yet she could not bring herself to sheer out of his touch. "You have to wake up, and you most definitely have to fight. If not for me, then for your Kingdom, for all the new people who are so thrilled to have you as their Queen."

Her lips trembled, and she looked away; her eyes moving to the view that felt so familiar yet so new to her. She would not allow herself to cry before him nor be vulnerable. Not anymore. "I don't want to—*your people don't even like me.*"

"Oh please, they most definitely do. So what, one person had a problem with you the other night? The rest adore you." Kylen's hands reached for hers once more, except this time they halted mid-air, his fingers balling into fists. "Please," he whispered. "There are things *beyond your understanding factoring into this*, but I need you to realise that I need you to be my wife, I need you to be my Queen, and I need you to take what's mine and make it yours," he pleaded. "Darling—*Althea*, just *please, fight.*"

Althea watched him, her head held high despite the shivers that circled down her spine.

"—You did it! Did I tell you that?" he questioned before answering himself. "You brought back three people from the dead. Your power—*it is incredible*, truly the most powerful I have ever seen. Think of everything that you can learn to do with it; think of everything that you can achieve and gain for yourself with it?" The words floated through the air as his hands slowly met with hers. Now she truly knew that he had lost his mind because there was no way Kylen would willingly stack this many compliments upon her shoulders if he had no reason to—or perhaps he would; he always did seem a little over the top. "Leave it up to the Gods then," he offered. "You have around a minute left to fight, so why don't you leave it up to the Gods? If you fight and make it, then you *fight and make it*. But if you don't… then well, you will find your peace; wherever that may be."

The words surged through her like a blade, and Althea closed her eyes, trying to drown out the panic that echoed through her head. She counted to ten in her mind, focusing on the soft smell of vanilla that flooded through her senses sweetly. Her hands ran over her eyes slowly, trying to wipe away the stress crawling at her skin. It was so evident, so physically there that she could feel it pulling at every strand of hair that covered her head.

Althea opened her eyes, and instantly, everything completely and utterly stopped. Time as she knew it became another illusion that she was lost too. "Kylen?" she whispered, the words leaving her tongue with her own touch of desperation, a tone she never liked to hold. Her eyes unknowingly searched for the brown that she knew hid within his, waiting on the edge of her toes for it to appear.

He was nowhere to be seen, and neither was her mother. Althea was alone. She was left to make a decision—one that she did not want to make.

Althea turned to the Kingdom before her, feeling as the wind of her magick swept her hair back over her shoulders. She took a deep breath as she began to watch the world around her slowly fade into dust.

I want to fight. I know it's late, and the decision's rushed—and I'm not entirely sure if it's the right one to make considering all, but I want to fight.

The decision was right before her, so clear to her faltering blue eyes. But it wasn't the fact that it wasn't visible; it was that she just didn't want to accept it. Her life was left unfinished, and a part of her knew that—Kylen knew that. And for whatever wondrous reason: that made Kylen appear before her in her subconscious.

Nothing happened, and Althea bit her lip, fumbling nervously with the ends of her hair as she looked around.

"*Please.*" Again, nothing happened, and no one answered. They ignored her calls and instead left her standing there like a complete coward, facing the wrath of the decisions she regrettably made.

Her heart was in her head as she looked over her shoulders, towards the doorway her beloved enemy had appeared through what felt like minutes ago. Now he was not there, and yet she could still feel his voice wrapping its way around her spine.

"Step up." It wasn't her words that spoke to her, but they were ones she was willing to listen to because even in the face of death, she wouldn't play the role that the world had in line for her.

Althea held her hands out as she stepped up and onto the top of the railing.

The wind began to stir, creating knots that pulled her hair in a warning. She took a few deep breaths, her eyes wavering slightly as she took in the height beneath her. She was used to jumping from such heights, but now that she didn't have the support of her magick, it seemed far more daunting.

Althea looked around, her lips pursed. "This is my mind, my soul," she stated to comfort herself, yet the words just hollowly floated through her head, not making any sense to the brain that was near death. Her eyes began to shut, and not because she wanted them to, but instead, because they felt heavy, like it was a burden to keep them open.

The cold rain clasped her wet, drenched hair to her back, slicking it along the sides of her face that it felt as if snakes were there. Her grip on Kylen tightened, and he looked down at her. "Pull me up!" she screamed, the panic practically dripping with each droplet of rain.

Kylen's hand began to loosen, and she shook her head. She saw it there; it was as visible as ever; the betrayal. Something seemed to flicker in him, and his grip tightened on hers, already in the motion of pulling her up. Forgetting whatever troubles had had led him into those thoughts.

Althea felt the ledge become comfortable beneath her, and she squirmed her way into his arms, throwing her own over his shoulders, embracing him with her sobs; how a day later, she would be left looking back onto that moment and realising what that hesitation was.

"You caught me."

"I—I did."

It was so surreal how memories displayed themselves as if they had occurred yesterday, when really, they had occurred when she had been twelve. There was still humanity in that girl. She hadn't yet gone through the torture that physically and mentally marked her body.

Althea's feet slipped from under her as her eyes fell closed again, and this time the air didn't go to catch her as she fell. This time no one was going to grab her hand to save her from the distance; this time, no fear echoed through her soul as her body fell through the Realms.

She was just falling, entering through the different Realms until death decided to greet her.

"*No,*" she didn't speak the words, and yet they sounded to be from her lungs.

Althea opened her eyes and found herself standing on a bridge, the world around her still evolving into the shape that the Gods demanded it presents itself with.

Through the shadows before her, a figure appeared, and this time she was no version of her mind. Her mother grinned at her through tears, already in the process of running towards her daughter. Althea froze, barely registering the fact that this woman was real and that she was before her.

"Oh, my sweet Allie," her true mother cried. "My baby—my sweet little bird." She pulled her hands back, finding Althea's cheeks. "You cannot be here; it is not time for you, nor will it be for a long time."

Althea stared at the woman before her, her lips slightly parted and quivering as she took a step back, out of her mother's embrace. "I'm dead?" Althea questioned again, her brows furrowing with such horror. "I actually died? But I asked to fight; *I wanted to fight.*"

"No. You did not die. The Gods just want you to stay here with them." Lilith shook her head. Her mother's hands reached for Althea's face, and for a moment, the Realms around her began to break.

Althea's eyes widened as she looked back to her mother, finding now that two spirits of different colours were on either side of her. On her left, there was a figure of pinkish and another of yellow. On her right, there was one of blue and another of orange. They were very faint, pastel, transparent colours. Hardly visible, and yet they had already stained her memories.

Althea blinked, and just like that, they were already gone. Her attention was instantly brought back to her mother's arms which were both flooding with colour. Twines of it were beginning to swirl around them, looping around her bones just to reach Althea's cheeks.

"What are you doing?" Althea whispered as she felt the magick surge into her soul.

"I know this is new for you, and I am so terribly sorry that I am not and will not be there to coach you through it, but Althea, you need to defy the Gods, and you need to live. You need to defy your father as well and get back everything he took from me. You were born for the greater good, and now you are the chance of survival," her mother cried. "This isn't a fairy-tale, and you aren't the hero of this story," she whispered as her thumbs traced over Althea's cheeks. "But you don't want to be the hero; they never make it out alive. You simply need to be the hope.

Things are going to become scary; they will make you want to scream, and the best thing you can do is scream."

Her mother's legs began to disappear; her whole body gradually fading away as the lights around them began to soften. Her stare was soft as if she was trying not to scare the girl despite the horror that was echoing throughout her head.

Althea reached forward, her hands clasping onto her mother's arms. "Stop it, please," she begged as her voice faltered.

"I—I don't want this; I'm going to go back, and my father is going to kill me—I have betrayed him with the magick that belongs to you."

NO. Mother, you cannot change your mind. You cannot change your mind! Althea shook her head to silence the voices targeting her within, but they kept screaming. *No mother, what are you confused about? Why don't you want to return?*

What is there for me back in life? Althea asked with such desperation. *Yes. I know my life is not over and that I 'have so much to live for'. But my mother is here. And as much as I loathe her for what she did and what she put me through—I may get a chance at peace.*

Oh, don't be ridiculous! You want to live. Stop being so stubborn.

"You haven't betrayed anyone, my sweet girl. Your father—don't worry about him. You are stronger and far wiser. Use your brain and imagination, and you will get out of this alive."

"What will happen to you?" Althea whispered, her voice breaking as she watched her mother, who she always denied loving, give her life in the afterlife up for Althea's.

"I will be fine," she promised as she wiped away her daughters' tears. "I will be with you, in your heart. But I won't be on the other side waiting for you anymore, and I know that was never one of the reasons why you wanted to find peace, but just keep that in mind."

"You're erasing yourself?" This was mad—she couldn't possibly allow her to go through with it.

Her mother smiled sadly, her face one so alike Altheas that it was like looking into a mirror. She had skin that was tanned, white hair and blue eyes nearly identical to hers, and that smile—that smile was one she saw in dreams.

Althea never loved her mother; if anything, she hated her. She hated her for leaving her in this world with no support or comfort. But now, against all odds, she was leaping forward, throwing her arms over the shoulders of the woman who was giving the world for her.

"I don't want you to do this," Althea cried, her grip tightening and fingers digging into the woman before her. "Please don't give up your life here for me."

Her mother pulled back as her hands on her daughter's face began to fade. "I have no life here," she spoke gently. "Follow the moon, and she will guide you home. As for your magick, nothing about it makes you disgusting, weak, or anything of the sort. You are strong. —And Sayah will tell you everything. She doesn't remember it, but as the time comes, she will."

She pressed her lips to Althea's forehead before the last of her fingers found the girl's shoulders. The lights began to burn as Althea was pushed back; a cry ever so loud erupted from her lungs as her mother completely disappeared.

Her own heartbeat, the real and less anxious one, began to echo through her ears. She felt like she was drowning, like there was water all around her, and that no matter how hard she tried to swim, it just kept pulling her down.

Something around Althea changed, and she instantly gasped, breathing down all of the cold air as the bright lights forced her eyes to shut. Tears dampened her cheeks, and she blinked the rest away, instantly looking for her mother.

Scarred hands met her instead, holding her cheeks in the same place as her mother had been mere seconds ago. Althea opened her eyes, and through squinting against the sudden bright room, she saw Kylen, his expression damned. He was looking at Sayah, shouting at her to do something.

Sayah replied with something that must have had something to do with her because Kylen's eyes snapped back to her—and oh how they widened. In fear? Shock? Anger? She didn't know, but either way, his grip tightened as a sob erupted in her lungs. He pulled her chest to his, and she didn't fight him; her tears were already staining his shirt.

"Althea?" Sayah spoke as she pushed past Kylen, falling to her knees beside her—and almost instantly Althea let Kylen go, realising just exactly what she was doing.

"Where's Erwin—no, *where's my mother?*"

EIGHTEEN

KYLEN

"Where is he?" Althea demanded as she rose to her shaking feet, ignoring the fact that she had asked for her mother a second ago. Her eyes desperately searched through the room for the man who had disappeared minutes ago, and yet none had the heart to tell her that they had lost him because they were all fixated on her and the three males who were now staring at them with wide eyes. "*I need to stop him before he leaves—I need to make sure he doesn't get out.*"

"Althea…" Sayah whispered, her voice near silent.

"*No*, where is he?" Althea asked as she pushed past them both, her steps immediately faltering as she noticed the three men who were strangers to her standing at the edge of the room. She recognised them; he could see that. When she had brought them back, she must have somehow met them—or perhaps she remembered briefly meeting them all those years ago.

Atticus tipped his head, bowing to the Queen that they were just now meeting properly. The other two, Khatri and Uzziah, joined him, all in sync, going down to their left knee.

"Where is he?" Althea continued to ask as she looked back at the siren to his right. "I can't let him go—where is he?"

"Althea, sweet girl, you just healed your soul; you need to rest."

Althea turned away from the siren, instantly giving up on her the moment she realised that she wasn't going to give her the answers that she wanted. "I didn't heal myself; my mother did." Her lips trembled as she spoke, but she ignored the faltering.

Out of all in this room, his Queen made her way to him, her face covered in pure distraught despite trying to hold it with such strength. "Where is he?" she repeated the words like venom on her tongue. Althea looked at him as if she knew he would not be able to lie to her. Her eyes stayed connected with his and for a moment too long he held her stare, a short sigh leaving his lungs as he reached for her.

"Gone," Kylen stated, answering her straight up and ignoring how raw his voice sounded. "We couldn't stop him in time; we tried to focus on saving you," he continued, not stopping despite the crushing look that dripped from her face. "I'm sorry if that wasn't what you wanted."

Althea stared at him like a deer in the eye of an arrow, her eyes wide and lips slowly parting, like the Gods were purposely slowing down the news from entering her brain. "That can't be…" her voice trailed off, her eyes glued to the brown of his. She was searching, looking for the lies he was best known for keeping. She exhaled a deep heavy sigh just a second before her chest began shaking, sending tremors along the scratched floorboards beneath her, causing Kylen to feel the exact pain that she was feeling. Althea stepped back, taking two single steps before turning to the doorway. She rushed out of the room ever so quickly that Kylen, *for a breath of a moment*, considered following her.

Sayah turned to him, her expression tight as she fully turned around, facing the eyes of the three men Kylen hadn't seen in years. His heart was tight, crawling with a dread that held him back from the men that watched him.

Khatri stared at Sayah, his expression just as it was yesterday. Uzziah and Atticus had been talking and looking at Zaire a moment ago, but now they looked at him, and he felt as if he had just lost them all over again.

He couldn't do this now. He couldn't admit that they had been gone for years when really, for them, it had been five seconds. "Kylen—" Atticus said his name, but he had already started moving. He followed Althea's scent, the rich scent of her magick; even without it, he could hear her panicked breaths of restraint. She was trying so hard not to break that the sobs were practically there, just a step away from the tears. She reached her quarters, and the moment she got there, the door slammed behind her, and Kylen knew that she had not done that physically.

Her magick was already acting in favour of her, answering the calls she did not realise she was making.

"Althea…" Kylen spoke as he reached her door, the concern there despite him wanting nothing of the sort. His hand laid flat against the cold wind, his eyes on his feet as his brows furrowed. "Listen, I don't know what type of shit you are going through, but just let me in." The door was locked in his hands, rattling in response to his constant attempts.

"Leave me alone—I don't want to see you or anyone, Kylen!" Althea shrieked, and this time he could hear her sobs, loud and clear.

Something seemed to change, like a flicker of a fire, and the door was no longer magickally shut, it flung open, and the sounds of her panicked breaths were replaced by one large bang. Kylen pushed the door wide as he ran through; his eyes instantly meeting with Althea's tired ones from where she knelt on the floor. "You need to rest," Kylen advised as he reached her side, already holding his hand at her back to help her rise. She made no such movements, so he went with the easy way. "Sorry, beloved," he breathed through a light and unamused chuckle as he picked her up bridal style.

She looked up at him with eyes of exhaustion. She looked tired, severely tired. She had a look to her that told stories of a thousand lifestyles, stories that were far too tiring to hear, and yet if she began to tell him of them, he would listen.

Althea pushed at his chest in a weak attempt to fight back, but other than that, she did not try anything more, and Kylen knew that she was far too tired even for that. "Yeah, yeah." he breathed, dismissing her in the kindest way he could. Althea cleared her throat before asking, "my mother?" he wasn't sure what exactly it was that she was asking, and yet he answered with a small nod. "I saw her."

Her glamorous bed came into view, and Kylen leant down, trying with all of the sanity left within him not to flinch as her hair grazed the scarred skin of his hands. He looked down at her, and his eyes widened; panic flooding through him as he realised that her eyes were shut, her whole face relaxed. His hand shot to her throat, searching for the pulse on her now almost glowing skin.

"How is she?" Sayah asked from somewhere behind him.

"Has a pulse," he answered.

Kylen ran a hand over his face, landing on his nose, where he sighed.

"Of course she has a pulse. Not only did she deceive Erwin into believing that she was dead but she managed to come back to our reality after something held her back. I'm not sure what it was but I could sense it." Sayah said, her voice falling low as she inhaled. "They—"

"I know, but I don't want to know because if I do know *—then I need to think*," Kylen rambled as he turned to face her. "I get it, the boys are back, my brothers are back… but Sayah, you know how exhausting that was to go into Althea's mind? I think I genuinely just drained four weeks off the month I have left because now I feel as if I'm going to die." He had begun to walk by her side, exiting Althea's chambers before entering the ghost-filled hallway.

He envied the state he was in weeks ago. The state where he did not feel quite as ill nor nauseous. Now Kylen felt sicker by the day, and it wasn't until Sayah's reading of the Gods intention of who he was to marry did he realise that they already had a date of his death ingrained in their minds. From the beginning of last month, his health had begun to go downhill, and now Kylen truly felt as if death was a door away.

"You're still sick?"

Kylen turned and found Uzziah staring at him amongst the three others, his bright red hair standing out severely against his ghost-like pale skin. "Yes—of course I am, because while you were off dying, I was off wasting my life!" Kylen yelled as he kicked at the rug on the floor. They didn't deserve to be scolded, but the curse was screaming at his emotions.

"Well, I don't particularly recommend doing either because, quite frankly, I didn't even realise that I had died," Atticus said with a slight shrug of his shoulders, his eyes noticeably avoiding his.

Kylen stared at his brothers, his face blank. *They were here.* They were standing there before him with the oddest of expressions. His hand found the buttons of his jacket, and he began to fiddle, forcing the darkness at his fingertips to disappear once more. "You're here," Kylen murmured, the utter disbelief in his voice as evident as day. He pleaded his voice not to break, but he was too exhausted, and it ended up doing just that, *breaking*.

"We are." Khatri nodded before his face softened. "I'm *so* sorry, brother." His accent was thick, just as it had been the day he left. Kylen walked towards them, shaking his head as a small laugh of disbelief left his lips.

The three approached him, leaving Zaire's side as they went

to embrace the man who had gone through Hel and back several thousand times.

"You're back," he repeated, sounding so childlike that he just wanted to laugh more. This felt so surreal, so strange to be standing before the three men he had felt die. It was like a dream, like the many he wished to never wake up from. And yet, as he did laugh, all he could feel was guilt. Agony.

They all pulled back, and Kylen's eyes grazed across the three of them, looking for any damage, any injuries that may take them from him once again. Khatri flashed him a charming smile, his teeth so white compared to his dark skin. Atticus laughed, wiping away the tears that Kylen knew he felt so confused about. He looked like the same childlike puppy he had met when he was six, and he sounded the same too. For him, mere minutes had passed, but for Kylen—he didn't even want to think about it. Kylen reached up and ruffled Atty's brown mousy hair as he met those eyes that looked near-identical to his, a glisten to them, one that reminded him of the pure parts of his childhood.

They were back, his brothers were back, and now he had to explain to them just how he had managed to find a stage further down than rock bottom.

☽

Uzziah sipped at his wine in the famous glass that had sat untouched for years. "Shit," he stated bluntly, his brows furrowed as if he was searching throughout all the Realms for something more to say.

"I know." Kylen agreed. "We are in deep and inevitable shit." He looked at Sayah, who stood in the doorway, her stare so glassy as she stared at the man who was once her fiancé. "And once news gets to her father," Kylen continued, "then another war will most likely break out."

"So, excuse me if this is a dumb question, but if Althea is now the source of our problems, then why don't we get rid of her? Hand her back to her father so that he can deal with her, and we don't have to fight a war that's not ours to fight?" Uzziah questioned as if it had been a question in his mind all along.

"How are you able to suggest that about the woman who just brought us back from the dead?" Khatri asked, dumbfounded. "She brought us back here, and I think that means that we are now in her favour."

It was subtle, but Kylen noticed how the sly smile crept across Sayah's lips as she listened in.

"I'm with Zye," Zaire stated as they smiled at their biological brother. "Good for her, she brought you three back, but she didn't mean to. If anything, she was probably trying to kill you three to get back at Kylen."

Kylen watched them speak, feeling as the strange sensation of déjà vu washed over him so effectively. They were back, and they were real—and they were talking to him. They were right before him, and yet he could not wrap his head around it. It felt far too surreal, like that sensation alone was following him in his every step. He wanted to run from it, but when he did, it only sped up, beckoning him with the voices he dreaded most. Kylen was digging his own grave, and he didn't know what to think of it.

"No," Kylen spoke, answering rather the voices in his mind. "I am the one forcing her to be my wife. So I think the littlest I can do is protect her from her father. Plus, I think I owe it to her after everything."

"You think?" Sayah questioned as she approached them all. "No offence Kye, I know you had the best intentions and all, but you put that girl through Hel and back. *We all did.*" She looked to Zaire before raising a brow. "I think the least we can do is offer her our protection."

"Whatever," Zaire responded with a flick of their wrist. "If she gets in the way of anything or even dares to lay a hand on anyone, then I will see things get treated differently."

Kylen cocked a brow. "Z, I don't remember upgrading you to the role of King or Queen?" he attempted to bring humour to his voice, but it was as flat as the seas he had once travelled across.

"Yes, well, I don't need a title. If I see something that needs to change, I will take action into my own hands," Zaire stated matter-of-factly.

Kylen rolled his eyes and rose to his feet, brushing his hands on his clothes before him as he did his very best to ignore the anxiety that clawed at his bones. "We better prepare for the worst then. Sayah, I want you to upgrade security everywhere and more so on the grounds. Zaire, I want you and Zye to go look through the Kingdom for any message on the King's whereabouts. Atticus… do what you do best and try to befriend Althea; I don't think my company will do her any good." The real reason was there, and it was as alive as ever, dancing across his scorched spirits and imitating the King and friend he had once been.

Sayah laughed, a small chuckle ever so light and dry bouncing off her lips and flowing straight to Khatri and Zaire, who he dared to say watched her with lust.

Sayah turned, moving to disappear through the exit when Khatri rose too.

"Khatri—" Kylen began before he was waved off.

"I'm busy," Khatri replied within a moment. Before Kylen could beg to differ, he was off and out the door, following Sayah's tail. It was such a familiar thing to do that Kylen was left staring for a second, feeling the nostalgic tidal waves crash within him as he cleared his throat.

"Alright." Kylen looked to the last of his friends, his family. "Let's prepare for war."

He exited the room, turning to the left instead of the right as Sayah and Khatri had done. He approached his room, keeping his posture straight and his lungs empty until the door shut. He could barely hold it; his stomach churned; he was sure he was going to be sick—it was far too consuming.

Kylen barely made it to the bin before blood began to erupt from his lungs. He fell to his knees, the coughing fit so harsh upon his weak body that he genuinely thought he had just instructed his last ever orders.

He didn't know when night had turned to day or when day had turned to night, but he just knew that the life faded out of him quicker than he would have liked, and before he knew it, he was waking up in a puddle of his own blood.

Looking like a bloody crime scene from the streets of Aeonia, the Kingdom he would do anything to stay away from.

NINETEEN
ALTHEA

The light flashed against her features, bringing warmth to the dead of her skin. Althea opened her eyes and immediately wished she hadn't. Her body didn't ache, nor were there any signs of headaches flooding through her crowded head. She simply stared at the roof, the thoughts so daunting and loud that standing on the edge of her balcony that overlooked the edge of the cliff didn't seem like such a harsh idea.

She felt the presence at the end of her bed, the other soul, the other mind, the other girl, but she just couldn't bring herself to move. *Her father was going to find out.* The people had gotten out—Erwin had gotten away. Althea was going to die. She was going to die again, and now her mother no longer existed in any of the Realms.

Sayah slowly moved over to her silently, and without saying a word, she sat on the bed next to her, already in the motion of running a hand through Althea's ratted hair. "I'm sorry," she whispered. Althea didn't care to answer; she couldn't. The words were burning her throat, the flames so alive that she swore she could feel where they danced. Sayah kept running her hands through Althea's hair, and she rolled the other way, moving her stare onto the blue sky she used to dream of seeing as a little girl.

The world was too harsh, too bright. The whole concept of it was far too daunting, so Althea closed her eyes once more, allowing the exhaustion from her lungs to take over.

It was like that for hours—or days… she didn't know which was which anymore. She only got out of bed to have the occasional shower and use the bathroom. But no matter how many times she scrubbed underneath the warm water, the Markings would not fade away.

Althea sat at the end of her bed, watching as the rain fell outside, crafting patterns of such beauty across the windows of her quarters. The doors opened abruptly, and Althea didn't bother looking his way; she had sensed his soul approaching her room from a mile away, one of the new horrendous benefits of this magick. "Oh! You're awake—I didn't think you would be."

Kylen ran a hand over the back of his neck. "So, how are you feeling?" he asked, almost as if he was encouraging her to speak, to say anything that would prevent him from drowning in this silence.

She didn't answer him; instead, she simply stared ahead, going through the memories of her past in her mind, desperately trying to stay in this coma of depression. It was a soothing feeling of being sad, and yet it was horrible. Still, something about the quietness of it brushed a hand over her face, urging her that it was okay never to want to get up again.

Kylen sat somewhere on the bed behind her, and she glanced over her shoulder, noting the meter he kept from her. "We are still trying to track down Erwin," he admitted with a sigh. "He has gone completely off the grid. As for the folks he was keeping hostage, well, we have managed to find a few of them—" he paused, and Althea heard the sharp intake of reality. "But it is predicted that the news has already reached Aeonia and that we should be expecting a visit from the King within the next few weeks."

"How do you do it?" Althea questioned, her voice dry and raspy even as she cleared her throat from the pain. "My father will be coming here, and you aren't even batting an eye."

"Not true," Kylen responded instantly, his eyes curving over her every breath. "I have just found that wine does wonders in circumstances like these." Althea looked down, and Kylen went silent; the room's atmosphere got heavy. "Would you like some wine?" Kylen offered awkwardly, his gaze still on her. "You know I own the best wine; *alcohol overall*, in all of the lands."

"No."

Kylen rose slowly. "So, are you just going to let this define you or what? Because quite frankly, who cares if your father knows?" he asked. "Sure, he will probably want to kill you, but that man wants to kill everyone. You will be fine, just train with Sayah, and before you know it, you will be Queen. Don't play dumb, Althea; you know that even without magick, you can bring any army to its knees. This magick will merely heighten that, and you've been meaning to find someone who will be a good match, have you not?"

Althea turned to him, her eyes meeting the brown of his; her mind trying with all of the scraps of the strength within her to ignore the scars and bruises that her father had been the cause of. No matter how painful that was to swallow away. "All I'm saying is that you have to trust me. I will protect you—"

"And I'm meant to believe you?" Althea asked through a bitter laugh. One that sent the room crackling. "I'm meant to believe that *you*, the man who ruined everything I had gained, will genuinely protect me from the man who now wants to kill me?" Althea laughed as she rose to her feet. "Do you know what happened the moment my father found me in my room? Do you know what he did to me for the weeks that followed your betrayal? I know I had been young and reckless, but part of me had trusted you, a part of me thought I was—*I was in love with you!*" Althea yelled. "I was still a child, young and in love with the thought of being in love—*being wanted*, and then you came around and crushed it all. You say my father is the cause for all these years of war, but really, it was you. Because you took a perfectly happy young girl and crushed her heart right in the palm of your hand, leaving nothing but bruises."

Kylen stared at her, his face taken back, his eyes rounded down as if the words were repeating right before him. He didn't say anything. He just nodded while clenching his jaw, admitting defeat. He turned on his feet, and Althea watched through blurry, tear-filled eyes. "Okay." He mumbled.

"Don't walk away from me!" she yelled as she stalked after him. "I am not finished with you!"

Kylen turned back around, his calm eyes once again meeting with Althea's hurt ones. The door opened behind him, and Atticus became visible; Althea hadn't formally met him yet, but Sayah had spoken of him, and his features were quite easy to recognise.

Althea pushed Kylen back, her quivering hands meeting with his chest, holding her an inch away from him. "Should I —" she heard Atticus ask, the hesitation clear. Good. She wanted him to be hesitant; she wanted him to be afraid. The more they were afraid, the better. Althea wanted everyone to be afraid because them being afraid was far easier than them being kind.

"No," Kylen answered. "Leave and shut the door behind you." Atticus obeyed, and Althea pushed Kylen again. He was holding himself back, not wanting to inflict any more pain on the girl he had already ruined. That wasn't what she wanted. She wanted him to fight so that they would be evenly matched once again.

"Fight back!" Althea seethed. "Fight back! *Just fight back!*" Tears rolled down her cheeks, and as she hit Kylen with everything in her, and she saw the pain that wasn't physical float around within him.

"I'm not going to fight you, Althea. Do what you must, but I'm not going to lay a hand against you. You were once seen as the daughter of my enemy, but now I'm not so shallow-minded, can't you see? I am sorry for what happened in the past, and I am sorry for what the situation is that you are currently caught in, but I brought you here; I am making you, my Queen. *You almost died! For fuck's sake!* I was left to hold nothing but your lifeless body. Do what you must to me, but I am not going to hurt you, not again, not anymore." Althea hit him again, and this time his hand caught her wrist; his fingers slowly flexing over her trembling hand.

She looked at him, her brows furrowed, her lips quivering. She wanted him to fight her; she wanted him to treat her as if she was his enemy once more. She hated him; with everything in her, she wished he had never come back into her life, so why were his words swarming throughout her soul.

Althea stopped trying. She stopped trying to fight him. She sighed a deep, heart-breaking sigh before allowing the sobs to break free. She moved her other hand up to cover her face, looking down so that he could not see the weakness that now coated her features like a virus.

She was waiting for him to push her away; she was waiting for him to reject her in any way, shape, or form. He used to comfort her when she cried; he used to hold her and stroke her hair, but then things had changed, and he was no longer the sweet, charming prince that had swept her off of her feet in a matter of days. Althea sheered away, going to walk back to her bed, when the hand around hers pulled her back.

Althea followed the movement, falling victim to the spells Kylen's actions held over her. She wasn't aware yet of what had happened, nor was she aware that Kylen's arms were around her. Everything just felt so natural. It just clicked.

Her head was pressed against Kylen's chest, and despite the fact, she could already hear his heartbeat loud and clear, feeling the warmth from his chest while listening still stabilised her. Grounding her as her wicked yet glorious magick unknowingly began to glow through the lines of her Markings.

Kylen looked down, and she felt his scarred hands gently clasp her wrist.

Althea pushed herself back an instant later; these feelings, these emotions, it felt all too familiar. Like she was once again playing herself into Kylen's game, a game she had promised herself not to get involved in again. She pulled her body back and hissed in a low voice, "Get out—*please*."

Kylen's hand weakened on her wrist, and his dark brown eyes met hers. They seemed to search hers, looking for an answer she could not give. Althea turned away, and as she reached the edge of her bed, she heard Kylen finally leave. He was silent, not wanting to disturb her more than he already had.

Althea sat down before burying her hands in her face, not moving the slightest even as Chloe, the white cat, made her presence very clear. She just stayed there, not wanting to move, not wanting to accept the new ways of this world, of her life. Minutes turned into long hours, and she barely moved, feeling so clearly as her muscles began to cramp, as her whole body began to stiffen. She looked up and over to the moon that was directly in line with the glass doors that led to one of the balconies.

She stayed there, dust collecting on her as if she was a doll with pinned-up hair.

She remembered some of what her mother had said, but not all. It was in pieces, trying to make sense in her mind, like a dream, despite the pain it was so heavily inflicting upon her. Lilith, her mother, had told her to follow the moon, but to where? Everything was in line with the moon; that was the one thing about every Realm and Kingdom; the moon always shone above, bringing some light into the darkness.

Althea rose to her feet, her head turning to exit her chambers as she began to walk towards the doors. The castle was near silent as she stalked her way through it. *No one was alive;* no one was awake. Other than the cat that was on her tail. Althea looked over her shoulder and the cat tilted her head under her gaze. Althea smiled weakly at Chloe, watching as the cat followed her, never leaving her alone for a second as it too was afraid of what she might do if she were to be alone.

The ballroom presented itself before Althea had the chance to turn away. She stood there, her heart racing through her ears as her eyes grazed over the empty room. She had only been in this Kingdom for two weeks or so, and yet she had lived through memories in this room that would never leave her.

Althea took a step inside, and finally, the cat stopped following her. It stood in the doorway, slowly sitting as it waited for the future Queen to do whatever it was that she was doing.

Her feet found the middle of the room and she slowly dropped down to her knees. Althea's hands laid flat before her, and she closed her eyes, listening to what the words in her head told her to do. Listening as the voices began to change into the tone of her *mother's*.

"What are you doing?"

Althea jumped as she heard the words leave an unknown males' lips. She looked over her shoulder, finding the same male that had tried to save Kylen from the pain Althea was so ready to swarm him with.

"I didn't mean to scare you!" Atticus quickly added. "I'm sorry if I scared you, Your Highness. *I just couldn't sleep, and I heard a noise.* I didn't want anything else to happen to you or Kylen or anyone, so I went to investigate—" his voice sounded unsure as he fiddled with his hands before him. "And then I found you, and yeah… *I am sorry.*" He looked down as he finished anxiously rambling, avoiding her confused gaze.

"Don't be sorry," Althea whispered as she tucked her hair

behind her ears. "You can't sleep?" she asked, looking over the boy who seemed beyond terrified.

While she did enjoy watching the male who looked no older nor younger than Kylen squirm, she did not particularly have the energy at this very moment to go on with it.

He shook his head. *How fortunate he was.* If Althea fell asleep, that meant her dreams and nightmares would meet her, chasing her to the ends of the Realms, all in order to torment her. "We haven't officially met yet. I'm Althea."

"I met you when we were younger and when you saved me," Atticus said as he approached her, offering her his hand. Althea looked to it before looking back up at him with clear judgmental uncertainty. Usually, the people her father brought to her or had over at the Castle for important dinners avoided shaking her hand; they believed that she was too dangerous. They thought that if she was to make any contact with their souls that she would butcher them.

Perhaps she would've if she'd had the chance.

It wasn't that their souls were clear, the curse was still there… it just wasn't as loud.

But now, she felt dangerous for reasons that were beyond the curse. She felt dangerous because of the Elemental magick that sent delicate whispers through her bones. Althea reached for his hand and slowly shook it before looking away, ignoring how that very memory had her heart racing, sweat seeping. "I don't have any recollection of that," she lied. Althea did remember that. She remembered parts at least—just not enough to know what to do now.

Atticus rubbed the back of his neck awkwardly. "Right, sorry about that."

Althea looked back at him, and despite only a second or two passing, she felt as if hours had flooded by and out of her grip. She studied the way he avoided her gaze. Anxious to even make any contact with her. *Was she really that daunting? What was he doing here being a servant for Kylen?*

"I'm sorry you died," he blurted in a childlike fashion and finally met her estranged stare.

Althea didn't know how to react, so she simply laughed, looking back down to where her hands were extended out and focusing on seeing if she could feel any hiding magick that would dare to shield itself within the small pipes beneath the castle. She could feel everything within these walls. She could feel the castle and who made it, those who were now asleep in it, et cetera. Althea followed the way the pipes curved, feeling as water from the seas flowed through them. A benefit of this magick she presumed.

"What are you doing?"

"Trying to relive any moment that flowed through the air of this room, I'm trying to make sense of it all so I can plan accordingly," Althea told him, casting another look to where he slowly hesitated to sit beside her.

"Why would you want to go through it all again? I saw your face after it all, and tell me if I'm wrong, but that expression didn't look like one of glee."

"Because," Althea paused as her throat tightened and her voice threatened to quiver, "I need to make sense of what my mother said; I need to figure out everything and just… none of it makes sense. And if I can't make sense of it all, then I must face the fact that my father will turn against me."

Atticus nodded, trying to understand despite not being able to. "Right. Do—do you want me to wait it out with you?"

She didn't want to say yes, nor did she want to say no. Althea had no right to be mean—*she didn't hold the strength to at this point*. "I don't care." There, an answer that was easy. Atticus sat down slowly, crossing his long legs and looking rather lanky as he looked awkwardly around.

He opened his mouth; however, his lips abruptly fell shut as he questioned his being. "Do—" Althea looked over to him, "do you *love* him?"

Althea almost choked on the air she breathed. "Pardon?"

"Do you love him? Kylen?"

The name, the way it was said—the memories it brought. How she already felt as if her skin was turning on her. How her brows furrowed with a twitch as she tried to shrug off the anxiety that nipped at her. Althea tilted her head, her lips tensing.

Was that really how he was going to start off this conversation? "No. I have no reason to."

She could feel Atticus watching her for a moment; she looked back at him challengingly. He looked as if he held such knowledge in those judgmental eyes. "Marriage should be about love. Why are you marrying him?"

"Because he needs a Queen, and I want to gain more power. Marriage isn't about love anymore; it has never been." Was there a potential reality, Realm, or universe out there where she would be in love in a marriage? Her heart had always been so full, begging to have a touch of any love the Gods would spare her.

But despite all the passages she wrote in her books, all the annotations that she left in her novels, wondering about who would be the one to claim her heart for their own—*love had never been kind to her.*

Love was cruel.

It was so cruel.

And she had been in love once, or so she thought; but that love was grabbed from her clasp before she could react. *Before she could scream.*

Now, she didn't think there was any Realm out there where she would be gifted the kiss of love. Her spirits had been crushed long ago.

"Have you ever been in love?"

Atticus looked up to her, and he smiled, a genuine smile that had a part of her heart faltering. His heart, however, reminiscing on a memory that she could have only dreamt of being a part of. "I have been. But you cannot tell Kylen this as to this day he does not know."

Althea couldn't help but smile slyly, feeling as breathing became somewhat easy again; it was not fully easy, but sharing a secret with one of Kylen's closest friends seemed rather somewhat enticing. "You have my word."

"*Arle,*" he spoke the name as if it was the only name in the world, as if it was the only name to ever matter to him. "We met a few years back… well, a few years before I died. He is my age and his family was one of the rich and wealthier ones of this Kingdom, but his parents were cruel people. He did all that he could to protect his younger brother, and one day we got a report from their parents saying they had run away or been kidnapped. I went out to the job, found the two of them and took the minute to understand why they had run. Arle had bruises all over him, and I knew it wasn't from some kidnapper. I allowed them to go; they had a friend's house with parents who adored them. Every week onwards, I would stop by, and slowly, we became closer. I knew the first time he spoke to me that there was something more there. Something I would fight for." Atticus smiled as he laid back on the hardwood, and Althea watched, her eyes glued to the smile that was so vibrant. "He allowed me to love him without ever asking for anything in return. It was simply a bond that we were both wrapped in. Arle never pressured me into anything. He was as sweet as they could be, an angel in the shape of an outcast sent from above." He turned his head, and his gaze locked with hers. "I don't know what happened to him, though, and to be honest with you, Your Majesty—Althea, I'm too afraid to ask. I guess a few years ago for me is really a century ago." His smile wavered, and he turned to the glass roof.

"You're afraid that he died or moved on with his life?"

"Dead, cursed, et cetera. If he has moved on, then I won't hold that against him, just as long as he's happy." Atticus smiled, and Althea looked away. She grimaced, trying to shake off the emotions this talk was bringing on. She hated all this touchy-feely shit. “You should try to find someone or something to love. It makes everything feel lighter, easier.”

Mother did love someone once, but oh how she was murdered.

“I’ll love myself. At least that way I can never let myself down.” Althea closed her eyes again, focussing on the sounds that crept through the floorboards. “And anyways, love is weakness; *you died* because you were weak.”

“You died too,” he rebutted.

“Not quite,” she sighed. “I almost did, but I would’ve died because of the love Kylen holds for you. I died because your three lives drained the life out of me. I was not weak; I was just led blindly into a situation I was too lenient and desperate in. Now I have learnt my lesson, and I am left to try and gather myself from the scraps, so if you could please just give me some peace and quiet—"

Althea didn’t look up; she just listened to the sounds of him gathering himself to his feet, his presence slowly leaving the room, allowing for the emptiness to dive right into her scorched soul once more. “I hope you do find something to love.” His voice spoke, replacing the sensations of his soul. “It’s a lot easier to get through life when you have someone to fight for.” She watched him now, her eyes burning wounds through his back.

“I did love many once. I was full of such love that I had been blind to the ways of this world. I will not be blind anymore.” Althea turned back to the floorboards beneath her, her eyes already glassed with tears. Her fingers were trembling, the floors beneath her trembling with the tremors of her magick. Althea sighed, a weak, vulnerable sigh of defeat. Nothing answered her; nothing would talk to her.

There was a sound of a breath, and instantly, Althea’s magick got ready to attack. “I told you to leave me be!” No one and nothing answered her other than the feeling of warmth flooding over her shoulders. Althea leant into it, her heart rate already in the process of slowing down. The tremors across the floor stopped and the glass above no longer threatened to break.

"Hello, sweet girl," Sayah whispered as she sat at the girl's side, her arms already wrapping around her. "I already tried. I tried to search for anything that would help you, anything that would make this all less daunting, so please don't waste your strength on this."

"Did you find anything?" She hated how desperate her voice sounded, how it sounded to be ready to weep at any given second.

"No," Sayah admitted sadly. "But that's not going to change anything. Althea, you almost died. You are still very weak, whether you admit it or not. You need to train; the magick will get out just as it did then. It looks for loopholes, so when you are showing or hiding emotions, it will get out that way. If you train with me, then it will stop, and by the time your father gets here, you will be a master at disguising it!" This all sounded like a speech, one that Althea was not too keen on from any perspective. "And it may also jog your memory of what your mother said; you do remember bits and pieces, yes?" Althea nodded, and Sayah squeezed her shoulder. "That's what I thought."

"I remember that she mentioned you." To that, Sayah's expression dropped. And her gaze most evidently averted away. "*What do you know?*" Althea asked immediately.

"Let's get you off the floor and back to your chambers, shall we?" Sayah spoke as she pulled the girl to her feet, already in the process of moving even as Althea went to disagree.

"*No,* tell me what you know," she pushed. "I have every right in all of the Realms to know."

Sayah let Althea go as she stumbled a few steps back. She went to catch her, but Althea had already caught herself. "I used to be a maid for your mother. Back at Shinrin, I mean, I never willingly went to Aeonia; I never followed her there as a few others did." Althea felt a stab of pain interlace its way through her heart. "*I never was close to her, though!* Which was why I never told you, *honey.* I was going to tell you sooner or later, but the opportunity never came."

"You knew my mother?" Althea asked, dumbfounded as the broken words that her mother spoke presented themselves to her. Loud and clear.

"I did; she looked exactly like you. The same sun-kissed skin and all," Sayah admitted with a smile. She crossed her arms before her, her gaze lost in thought. "When I saw you for the first time a few years ago, I immediately knew who you were because of those eyes."

"Is that why you called me 'Althea of Harlia' when we first met? Because of my features—that was what the people called my mother was it not?" Althea asked and Sayah nodded.

"I called you that because that's what my people call those with features like yours—not to mention that I could scent the strange magick you kept hidden. Harlia is a mythical place that has been locked away for years, and well it just came to my tongue."

"My—*my mother's gone,*" Althea whispered. "She gave up the rest of her soul to save me, and I don't understand how she was able to do that—and I don't understand why it is hurting so badly."

"I know. I felt the moment her magick interlaced with yours. I'm not sure either, but I will be by your side every step of the way; we will learn together." Sayah paused as she took a step forward. "We will figure this out."

There was a pause, and then Althea asked a question that left Sayah surprised. "Did you train her?" The question earned an expression of almost pity from the woman. But it wasn't pity directed to Althea, but rather herself. Like she missed something for reasons she was unaware of.

"No, I don't think I did. I might have, but I genuinely cannot remember."

"And you want to train me?" Althea asked. She didn't know why she was leaning towards accepting the offer; it seemed like a trick beyond reasons. Like it was a puzzle that she wasn't a fit piece for. Her mind was at the beginning of a maze, and if she went one way, then there was the chance of discovering what her mother said, *what her mother knew.* She mentioned something of being one with her, so perhaps if she had her mother's magick too, then there was a chance at getting rid of it altogether. But if she went the other way, would she be led into the darkness? Or would she be led out of it?

"I would be honoured to, Your Majesty. I, of course, will go at any rate you are willing to go. Even if it is merrily learning how to ground yourself, then let that be it. Or if you are willing to learn more about it than we can go at that speed too—it is really whatever you are comfortable with—"

"*Okay,*" Althea spoke, interrupting the words that were swarming at her with disapproval.

THE MOURNERS

TWENTY
KYLEN

The words were mean, harsh. They made Kylen squirm under his sheets, clasping the pillow harder over his ears as if that would be the blessing that would block the voices that laughed at him within his mind. The curse was horrible, it was horrendous, it was there, and it was mean. It laughed at him as if he was a sport they were actively engaged in. One that they wanted to watch for centuries.

Kylen opened his eyes, and this time he found the sun had begun to rise. Perfect. Good. He could pretend that he had a busy day to attend to, and if someone (Sayah) didn't believe him, then he could state all the reasons why he must be proactive.

Such as 1. Althea might be getting hunted. 2. Althea has magick that could potentially kill them all, but he wasn't sure yet, so he must do research. Or 3. Althea needs a lot of comfort and support. Which he did not feel in the mood to give her, so he would hand that task onto the siren, as he did with basically everything.

Kylen made his way to the kitchen, finding it empty as he had suspected. He reached the brewing coffee and thanked the

Gods that it was ready, just at the right temperature. He didn't think in the slightest he could make it if it wasn't.

Kylen grabbed a mug, one that had been handcrafted by his biological little sister centuries ago. He sipped at the warmth, waiting to feel that calmness enter his body that he so desperately longed for. However, it never showed, and he left his now clean cup back in his spot before turning to his rounds.

He started by acting King-like, deciding to act the part for the little time he would be it, going out into the fresh air with some hope that the cool crisp morning air would do his lungs some justice.

Kylen felt the wind brush his face; he closed his eyes, welcoming it. He reached the first guard, one of the ones who had returned from home yesterday, eager to be of any help. Rowan bowed. "No need for that." Kylen grinned at the man who was one of Sayah's most trusted. "Any update for me? Whether that be about my Queen, her father, the curse, the Kingdom, anything really?"

The guard sighed as he held his sword tightly. He took a step forward, making sure that his whole body was inside of the invisible barrier that brought death to outsiders. "Regarding Her Majesty, we have no update on her father or her. The only thing we know is that the word has gotten out within the Kingdom that she has turned on her father. People celebrate that because… *well…* no one is quite fond of him. Regarding the curse, it has appeared that more outbreaks have appeared throughout Hendrix and Leminair."

"They are far yet too close. Make sure that any contact with those towns is dealt with."

Rowan nodded. "It's a good thing that it cannot spread in a contagious type of way. But I have already spoken to Captain, and she has ordered three new guards to be stationed at every entry of the Kingdom. If they see any carriers, word will get to you immediately."

"Good, thank you. The Kingdom sees your work, and you are appreciated, my friend." Kylen looked around before turning back to him. "Tell me, how are the kids? What is it three now?"

Rowan grinned before rubbing the back of his neck. "Yep, they are good, very good. They are up at the safe house now. My wife and her mother were at the ball, and after everything that happened, I knew it would be better for them to be safe elsewhere."

"That's good," Kylen responded as he patted the man's back. "Well, I better continue on; see you at sunset." With that, Kylen made it to the next guard. She didn't have much to say, just the same as what Rowan had said. Kylen reached the doors of his castle once again, and he sighed as he entered through them. The air had done nothing, and if anything, he was left feeling worse than before. His lungs felt tighter, smaller.

Kylen hadn't been watching where he had been going and before he knew what had happened, his body met with another. Instantly as fear struck his soul into two, Kylen reached out to catch the girl he had pushed back with such force.

Althea stood there, her movements already in the process of tying back her hair in a long ponytail. "Watch it," she grumbled, barely casting him a second glance.

"Good morning to you too," he greeted with one of his many charming smiles. "How did you sleep?"

Something flickered in her gaze, and she turned away, going to walk back down the way that she had come. She kept her head high and her shoulders straight, her posture like a dagger ready for blood. "Fine."

"That's excellent," Kylen quickly remarked as he sped up to her side. This was exactly what he needed, the adrenaline from talking to the girl that didn't seem too fond of him. "I'm glad to see that you are up and out of bed and feeling better, I presume. What are your plans for the day, my love? How about we get something to eat—"

Althea scowled at the nickname, and Kylen grinned. "I have plans, but they most certainly don't rotate around you." She had her usual spark back, her usual sass that kept him feeling young and healthy.

"Very well. It will please you to know that I have no news or intel to tell you regarding your magick or your father," he said, glancing down at her with a click of his tongue, "I, however, am even more pleased to tell you that you are now the glorious talk of the town."

Althea stopped at that, her gaze hesitant with worry as she turned to him. "I expect that I should be as I am quite wonderful—but what do *you* mean by that?"

"Relax, I merely mean that the Kingdom loves you. They believe that you have turned against your father and that you have joined the dark and glorious side."

Althea looked away, her face deathly pale. "And this is good news, how?" she demanded. "I hardly see this as anything but bad news. *It is horrible*. I don't want them to think anything of the sort!" she fumed as she fiddled with the layers of her outfit.

"Well, it's good news because you didn't have to do anything to make them like you and thank the Gods for that because you do not have very good people skills," Kylen noted as he continued to stride forward, guiding her to follow him.

Althea crossed her arms, standing still in her spot as she refused to follow behind. Kylen came to a standstill; his head tilted to the side as he looked her over. "Have you been sleeping alright? You look a little—*ill*." There was something there, something that he could see so clearly yet not at all.

"I did just physically visit my mother, so I doubt I will be looking my finest."

"You still look beautiful and all. It just looks like..." he let the words fill the air that suffocated his lungs with such delight. His eyes stayed perched on hers, watching as she did everything in her power to avoid his gaze. He wondered that if she was to look at him would she see it? Would she finally see the eternal illness that had somehow interwoven its way through his magick, wrapping its way around his heart with such force that it completely shattered, and just now, all these years later, he was putting the last few pieces together? He knew there was no point in still trying after all these years, but he didn't want to let the curse gain even more than what it already had. He didn't want to give up because the moment he did, he was basically accepting *his death.*

"There you are!" Sayah announced with a clap of her hands. "I was wondering where you had gotten off to. Ready to start your first training session?"

Kylen's eyes furrowed at that, and he turned swiftly back around to the girl who was to be his wife. (Another thing he was about to spend his time preparing for). "You agreed to train?" The disbelief in his voice made him want to snicker; it was never something he imagined Althea agreeing to.

"Yes," she answered with nothing else. Giving him a singular word to work with, how sweet of her. She forced a flash of a smile to coat her lips before turning away—a smile that was one of pure mockery and yet earnt one from his own lips.

"Did Sayah put you under a spell or something?" he questioned. "Because I know that you would not have agreed to that willingly." She finished tying her hair back and crossed her arms, waiting for him to finally allow her to answer.

"And you know me so well, do you?" Althea asked in response. She turned to Sayah and said, "let's go."

"Very well." Sayah looped her arm through the girl's and began to guide her down one of the hallways that Kylen knew led them down to the training rooms.

He watched, his vision beginning to blur as his hand slowly met with the wall. He stood like that for several seconds, cursing the horrid magick that wanted to make such a disgrace of him. Althea disappeared around the corner by Sayah's side, and he took a breath, grounding himself to the ground he felt was about to give way.

"Kylen," Zaire's voice demanded. In a panic, he turned around and found that the fairy's upper half was the only thing showing, the rest of their body still hidden away by the power of magick. Their expression froze for a split second, their magick reaching out to figure out what had caused the ends of his fingertips to turn black. Kylen held up his hand, the little magick that answered his calls forcing theirs away.

"What?" he asked. "Got anything?"

"Yes, actually I do. But it is not to be spoken in an area like this; come down with me." As Zaire spoke, the rest of their body disappeared, their magick twirling its way like twine through the air, beckoning the young King to follow. Kylen obeyed, of course, denying that the ends of his fingers still looked to be dipped in a harsh dark black paint. He felt it seep back into his skin, entering through his veins in such a quick manner that for a second there, he thought he was going to faint.

He followed the twine of green magick, his lips perched as he tried to figure out what it could be that was so demanding of his attention. He wanted it to be something to do with the King, something that would ease the stress that coated Althea's face like his curse.

He reached the doorway that opened the stairs to the underground rooms. One was the training rooms that Althea and Sayah currently trained in, their souls alight and burning with an energy Kylen had once been warned to stay away from. And the other was the room where he could sense Khatri, Uzziah, and Zaire in. Out of all their souls, Zaire's and Khatris were the most concerning. Zaire being a fairy meant that everything they did was unpredictable, and their magick thrived through that.

Having come from the same islands Sayah did all those centuries ago meant that Khatri still had some of the origin magick of the sea streaming through his blood. Of course, he preferred to use his weapons, but that didn't mean he was less powerful. Kylen knew that the Markings of the Sommsia Realms were on his lower back, as back when they had first met, they'd had an argument, and one thing led to another and before he knew it, he had caught sight of the glowing Markings. Uzziah opened the door before them both, a tight-lipped smile that told Kylen he was in for a wild ride.

Uzziah, being a half biological sibling to Zaire, meant that he was half-fairy, half-human. He didn't have as much unpredictable magick, but he was still deadly nonetheless. You could scent the Autumnia magick within him; it was vibrant and screaming across the floorboards.

Kylen approached the chair at the edge of the room and he leaned against it, crossing his arms across his leather jacket. "So, what news do we have?" Kylen asked as his eyes danced from each creature to the next. "Let me guess," he began as he took in Khatri's weary look. "Something to do with the King?"

He hadn't spent much time with either one of his brothers, but that was because he couldn't bring himself to. It felt as if, at any given moment, someone could take them away again, *and that was one of the things that Kylen feared the most.*

Khatri sighed. "You guessed right," he admitted as he ran a hand through his short, braided hair. "We have intel that the King no longer resides in his castle, that he had gotten out in the midst of the night."

"Do you think that as soon as he heard the rumours of Althea, he left?"

"Yes," Uzziah answered for him. "We believe that the news got to him through a wave of magick, and now he knows he is wasting no time to see if it is true." He paused, looking at his brother with a look that made them look away. "But we could be wrong; he may still be inside, just not visible to any eyes."

"From what Zaire has told me," Khatri spoke, "that Kingdom is basically a walking graveyard. It is a miracle, if anything, that

Althea is still breathing after having lived her whole life there. So really, we don't know what is true and what is not. Perhaps he wants us to believe that he is on his way, to spread fear down our spines. Whatever intel we receive would have to have come from his lips because there is no other walking soul in that Kingdom who has the ability to speak freely in any way."

Kylen kept quiet. This was not what he wanted to hear by any means. How was he to tell the girl who was meant to be under his protection that her father was *most likely on his way to kill her?*

"I know that we have already increased security; so, you," Kylen said as he nodded to Khatri, "and Sayah put an extra barrier around the entire Kingdom, as well as the perimeter. I know that it may drain you, so feel free to do it over the course of the next twenty-four hours. I—*I don't want either of you dying.*"

Not again.

Khatri nodded. "Of course." He paused and his vision met with Kylen's, and instantly the young King knew what his eyes spoke of. *He was scared*—Sayah had been avoiding him, and so had Zaire. Kylen felt bad, but how was he meant to say anything that would stir his heart to peace? It had felt like yesterday for him, that Sayah was in love with him, dancing at the ball he cursed himself for throwing, but really for her, *it had been years,* and she had been forced to move on with life.

"I will talk to her," Kylen said.

"Thank you," Khatri muttered and with that, Kylen turned to the siblings. "You two, please go into town and the outskirts and see what the word is. He wouldn't have arrived yet, but the news of him may have reached the people. His carriage isn't one that's recognisable, but the scent of him is."

Zaire and Uzziah nodded. "Would you like me to talk to Atticus about coming into the Kingdom with us? He has been awfully eager to go back."

Kylen hesitated, and from the corner of his eye, he could see that Zaire hesitated too. The last time they had gone into the heart of the Kingdom, they had been faced with death, leaving the news to travel to them through the wind. He had never seen Sayah that distraught, *that broken*. It was still a sight that made his memories daunting. It was a sight that left him feeling as if the word was going to break from his very touch. He knew that day he had lost his three brothers, the three men that meant more to him than any else in this retched world, but he had bigger issues to worry about, like trying to keep Sayah and Zaire alive.

Those two had been by his side through it all. And to them, he owed everything.

Kylen nodded hesitantly. "Be careful. We don't want any more…"

Death.

He didn't have to say the word because they knew. They knew what was terrible that no one dared to say the word. They knew what was so terrible because it was like its very own curse flowing through the air. Kylen wondered if Althea knew whose magick it had been to kill his brothers, to kill the men she so unwillingly brought back from the dead. Her father's magick was so terrible, the magick that he had stolen from all the generations out there. It was still unknown by the world who helped Erwin create the curse, but Kylen was going to find out. He was like Althea regarding that; one of the many little things that they had in common, he wanted to figure it out so he could put an end to it. He wanted to gather those who created the curse so that he could find a loophole, one that would end this misery that he refused to show. He had his hands in his pockets, but he knew the veins there were black. He knew the curse was working its magick in all of his misery.

Zaire looked away from their brother, a look on their face that he remembered all too well. One that looked to capture the first fall of snow, longing for something they would never be able to put into words. A sensation that he knew he related with.

"Of course," Khatri said. "Later, could we all catch up?" he asked, and Kylen felt the need to agree. "I know we have things to do and all, but so much has changed, and well, I would like to know all about it."

Kylen approached his brother. "Of course." Their hands linked, and he pulled the male towards him into a hug, his other hand already in the motion of patting his back.

"I will see you all later, for now; don't get yourself killed, *please*." He wanted to stay and talk to them all for hours on end —but his heart felt to be faltering, and with each breath he was reminded of their deaths; of the pain that had sought comfort within his bones.

Kylen turned down the narrow hallway, Khatri at his tail. It was lit by candlelight; fire controlled by the burning magick of Sayah's blood. They had only gone out once, back on that fatal night that none would forget.

The door opened, and immediately, Kylen's brows shot up. Althea ducked under Sayah's arms as the siren pulled out a flaming sword of fire, aiming it to strike at the girl. Althea copied her movements, and to her apparent disbelief, she pulled out her own sword, except this one was different. Her sword was gold; light radiating from it. It had four crystals aligned with the centre of it. One pink, one orange, one yellow, and one blue. They reflected the fire in her eyes, and Kylen dared to say that he saw Althea grin.

"See," Sayah purred in a feline-like voice. "I told you it would come naturally to you in a fight."

Althea laughed as she ran her other hand through her hair, pushing the front pieces back and off her face. Kylen watched with a blank expression—almost daring to ask her to laugh again so that he could get a glimpse of the girl that had followed him in his nightmares for so many years. "Yes, I guess you did." She held the sword before her, her eyes glistening with admiration. "This is nothing like what I've used before," she mused aloud. Althea must have scented Kylen's soul because she turned, and her gaze became fuelled with fury once again.

"Khatri—" Sayah blurted; but Kylen had already accidentally cut her off.

"I always knew you were full of wonders, *my love*. But this; this would have to be by far my new favourite thing that you have surprised me with—honestly, I can't even say that I am surprised."

TWENTY-ONE
ALTHEA

Kylen spoke words that she wanted to throw up. He spoke with such ease about *her* that she could not help but imagine plunging this miraculous sword of such magick through his heart. *How delicious that would be.*

She could feel the magick; it was settling, soothing. Like a melody a mother would sing to their sick child. It was sweet, soft, but no matter how settling it was, it would never be able to stop the gruesome thoughts that echoed through her soul. "Well, if you are taking Sayah away, then I need a teacher," she stated as a matter of fact. "Care to fight?" she questioned, with a sly grin of her own. "I mean, I know that you have little magick, closer to none. But I think this will really help me settle in with my new magick."

She was making a mockery. Out of not only him but her magick too, because no matter what she did, she knew that it would never feel natural, it would never be one with her. Althea swung the sword around and through the air, testing the weight of it as she watched him with a tilt of her head.

Kylen hesitated, but she could see the sly grin of his own

pushing the edge of his lips. “Alright, but I must say I won’t go easy on you.”

Althea shrugged, her sword reflecting the light of her soul in the process. It was a challenging light, one that pushed colours into her vision that she did not know the meaning of. “I wouldn’t expect you to.”

She stepped back, and Kylen stepped onto the floor outlined in white. He reached behind him, grabbing at the air. For some unthinkable reason, she had doubted that his magick was going to respond because she could sense the little that he had, and she knew that it was extremely weak. It was *weak* and *afraid*.

Kylen pulled up an all-black sword, one that glowed with red, *one that seemed too like the weapons back in Aeonia*, the palace that no longer felt like a *home* to her.

He lunged for her, his sword flying where her body had been just a second ago. She ducked back, using her years of training for not only battle but ballet to her own advantage. Her back bent, arching so that she could dodge his efforts. Her head flew back, and her braid slipped against the floors before she was back on her feet, *death in her eyes*.

Kylen watched; his sword placed before him as a spark began to shine within the darkness of his eyes. “I see that you have some hidden abilities there.”

“You’ve always known about them; I showed you the last time. But you were just too blinded by your own plans to take notice.” Althea started for him again with her own sword, the tip of her blade just nudging the skin on his chin. He stepped back quickly, and with a loud crash, the two blades powered by magick met. She took a deep breath, the emotions in her eyes changing so rapidly to one of rage.

Her sword danced against his, and it was as if they were waltzing. She went low, and he went high. Her back meeting with his, and again, she waltzed by his side. Gaining some distance on the young King before turning back to face him. Her feet slid against the floor as a newfound ribbon of crimson magick extended out from her hands, wrapping its way along her blade. She was letting the voices take control of her actions; she was allowing them to do as they pleased just as long as she wasn't the one to get hurt.

Please, mother, please, let us taste death, let us taste that beautiful magick.

Despite no longer having the darkness within her soul, she still had memories of it. The voices lingered around like a bad smell so that she would never truly be blessed to rid herself of that burden that was the curse.

Kylen had sensed that, and she knew that he knew. For every strike, she lunged out to him: he was able to waltz his way away. His free hand located hers, begging for it to follow him into the darkness. But she wouldn't, *not again.*

"I could have helped you, you know," she stated as her sword skimmed the edge of the leather jacket coating his arm, it threatened to break, but it didn't, and Althea was determined to get it too. Her sleeve danced up, and from the corner of her eye, she could see the black ink that coated her wrist. "If only you had given me a chance, then I could have helped you. I was willing to do anything to go see the world, so when you came into my life, I was willing to risk it all." She breathed harshly with each droplet of sweat, resuming the conversation that they always seemed to leave unfinished.

Kylen went to say something, but she was already speaking again, not wanting to be cut off from the words flowing with such ease. "I would have told you everything you needed to know if only you were genuine about breaking me free. You may want me to take up the role of your loving wife, but I will never forgive you. Not for the heartbreak you put a child through."

Althea plunged her sword through his abdomen. She knew it hadn't physically gone through because of the cursed horrendous magick that ran through her blood; the Elemental magick prevented him from death as if it could read into the small part of her that was still a child. The child who did not wish death upon him. But she played it off. How desperately she had wanted it to go through made her want to laugh, she had been so desperate to get revenge that she hadn't noticed the magick that was set into place, turning the sword from a physical item to one of the imagination.

Kylen fell back from the force of her strike, and unwillingly she fell too. Her knee pressed against his chest, and she looked down at him. Her gaze was one of burning, one that she wished would drip with real flames. "Althea," he whispered. Why did he do that? Why did he always whisper her name as if it was a plea? One that would never be his to beg.

Althea shook her head; the exhaust was evident. "Forget it," she sneered, the fire slowly dying in the sea of blue. "I don't know what heart I ever saw in you."

Her braid fell over her shoulder, resting against the side of Kylen's throat. He swallowed, his eyes calm and yet his magick burned with such force that she could feel how desperately it wanted to kill her. Her eyes searched his, waiting for the answers she had waited lifetimes for.

"I am sorry—"

Those three words. Those damn three words that she wanted to drown within.

Althea raised a brow as she stood up, pressing onto his chest once more before rising to her feet. She laughed. "Of course you are." Kylen pushed himself up as he followed her, his hand already going for hers. The way his face looked so hurt yet so fierce aggravated her, and Althea wanted nothing more than to look away.

Typical Kylen, thinking he can do anything to anyone and not face the consequences. She turned on her heels before abruptly turning back. "You know I kept tabs on you through the years." Althea tutted ever so casually. "I knew just about everything that happened, and yet I could never gather why you did what you did to me. Nothing added up to why? *Why Kylen?* Why did you trick a child into telling you all her father's plans while promising for a future that you knew you would never, not for a second, consider giving her? Why would you lock a child in a room while she screamed for you, while she screamed for you to *forgive her?* Because despite it all, despite you being the one in the wrong, I still thought I had been the problem."

Kylen didn't look to be breathing. His face was lost, his expression dammed. Althea dropped her sword, and she didn't have to look to know that it had disintegrated because of the loss of contact. "I knew about the time you lost your brothers; did you know that? I knew about the time your Kingdom held a mass for them, all mourning the three sacred lives that apparently meant more than mine," Althea continued, her expression and tone acting as if she didn't care in the slightest. "Oh, and don't you worry, you didn't leave half of me still standing. There was still half of me that was ready to fight for myself, but my father worked in favour of you. The moment he found out, he didn't waste his time looking for you—see, even while you had betrayed me, I had still worked in your favour. He spent those few fatal hours breaking the half that was still standing, not stopping until there was nothing left. And now look at me; you say that you know me, and yet you have no idea who I am. Not anymore."

"I never wanted it to come to that," he spoke it so genuinely that it almost didn't sound like a lie, but she was no longer that stupid. "I wished there had been another way I truly do, but I was not in the position to bet so freely. War was right at the ends of our fingers. I had to act quick."

"You don't wish," Althea seethed, her magick physically restraining her from inflicting any pain upon the man who she wanted nothing more than to kill. "Do not say that you wish that you hadn't done what you did because you and I both know that that is not true in any shape or way."

Kylen dropped his sword too, and this time she watched as the darkness seeped from within it. Filling the air until there was nothing left. "Don't say that," Althea repeated. "Do not say that you wish there was another way when I know you would do it all in a heartbeat again. You think you are some miraculous King for giving your Kingdom to a Queen like me, but you are nothing of the sort. You are a traitor, a coward—"

"I would do it all again if I had to."

Her expression dropped and Althea dragged her eyes back to his.

She knew it. She knew that he would; because he had never hesitated throughout the whole process of it. Althea had waited; she had waited so patiently to see a change of heart, but it never came. And even as she waited for months to pass, *she still could never find it.*

"I would do it all again if I had to," he repeated. "But each time, I would always look for a loophole." Althea opened her mouth, the snarky words on the tip of her tongue, ready to strike their target. "No, let me speak. Throughout it all, I was begging the Gods to present me with a loophole, another option that would leave you out of it. *Do you think I didn't realise what I did to you?* I do, and I see it now clearly more than ever. You may be your father's daughter, the same father who has taken everything away from me, but you were also your own person." Kylen ran a hand through his hair, clearly stressing himself out over the memories of it all. "Sayah and I—we did *everything* we could to leave you out of it. Trust me; we truly tried everything we possibly could think of!"

"Then why didn't it work?" Althea sneered through a laugh. "I saw your face when you left that room; I saw it well and clearly." Her voice was calm, deathly calm.

"Well, whatever you saw was clearly a twist of your mind!"

Kylen exclaimed. He moved towards her. "Please, Althea, I know you do not trust me... but try for this marriage—"

Althea raised her chin, her lips quivering before she bit down on them, doing everything she could to stop the true pain from erupting. "I don't want this marriage to work."

She turned around, heading towards the door that Sayah had initially brought her through. "You should be grateful that I'm even still here," she mused aloud as her hand found the door handle. "I could be long gone by now, and yet I am still gracing you with my presence. I really am handling the role of Queen well, aren't I?"

The darling of her eyes met with his, and he watched, stepping forward while his hand slightly rose. Still, she cut his actions off by opening the door, stepping out of it, before shutting it in his face.

☽

Althea's face was strained of colour. Her heart stammered within her chest as if it was trying to break free. She stared at Zaire; her eyes dimmed with colour because she could not physically grasp the news that she was hearing. Of course, she predicted it and all. *Still, hearing confirmation of her worst nightmares was a far worse feeling than she would have ever imagined.*

"He's on his way?" Althea asked, her voice faint.

Zaire grinned as their eyes scraped over the room. "Yes," they cooed. "He's on his way to get you."

Atticus nudged Zaire uncomfortably. "Stop it." Zaire's smile only increased as they heard the words leave Atticus's mouth. "We won't let him reach you, I promise."

"Your promise is worth nothing." Althea began to fidget, her hands moving from her hair to her face. It couldn't be true—*she knew it was true,* but she begged it not to be. Her stomach felt as if tiny little spiders were crawling from the depths of it. The weight on her shoulders only seemed to amplify a little more as each second passed by.

"You watch your tone, pretty lady," Zaire warned. "Kylen may be offering his protection to you now, but it can be taken away just like that." A glisten of green magick shone in their eyes and Althea looked away.

She put her head in her hands, trying to massage away the headache that she could feel forming. "Why didn't Kylen tell me this?" she questioned as she looked up. "If he knew since this morning, then why didn't he tell me himself?" The heartbreak on her tongue was mean, cruel to her even.

"Why would he tell you?" Zaire laughed as they tipped their head. "You have done nothing but be an inconvenience since you arrived here," they sighed, their breaths long. "I keep telling him to have some fun with it, but he seems *quite pitiful towards you.*"

Althea scowled. "Get out." She looked toward the exit of her room, and Atticus immediately nodded. "Sorry for bothering you, Your Highness. Will you be joining us for supper?"

Althea shook her head. Out of all of them, Atticus seemed the most tolerable. He had a personality to him that made her —*HER*, feel kind of sorry for him. "No, I won't; thank—*thank you.*" And not to mention that the poor boy believed in love. *He believed in love, and now he was suffering for the price of it.*

"Oh, look at who's being sweet now," Zaire mocked with a roll of their eyes.

Atticus pushed Zaire along, forcing them out of the room. He turned back to Althea, his expression certainly uncertain. "Sorry again for bothering you."

With that, he shut the door, concealing Althea into her room once again. She rose, already on her feet and on her way to the shower. The warm water met with her skin, and she closed her eyes, slowly leaning her forehead against the marbled tiles. She had to think of a plan; she had to think of something that would work, *something that would get her out of this mess.*

She could still go with the original plan of claiming Kylen's life for her own, but she didn't believe that that would still fit.

The moment Althea exited her bathroom, she couldn't help but stare at her bed—her eyes dragged to it as if it physically held such force over her. It seemed so large, so cold, like a pit of torture that was going to swallow her whole. Althea laid down, her head slowly meeting with the soft pillows. "I'm going to die." She mumbled, the exhaust coating her voice. *Would life always be like this? Would things always happen, or was this just the height of all her troubles?* Ever since she could remember, bad things followed her around like she was some statue. She could never catch a break, and to top it all off, her spine wrapping with the twine of her Elemental magick really pushed her off of the edge. It was a feeling ever so horrible, one that kept her dreams spiralling.

There was something there, a feeling so real yet so morbid. It was there, yet she could not see it through the darkness. It would not present itself to her.

Althea took a step back, and a yelp escaped from her lungs as she felt something brush against her leg. It felt eery, slimy, like the curse she knew far too well. Althea's eyes widened, and she looked over her shoulder, her eyes searching for the room she had just been in.

There was a breath, a deep cold breath that smelt of poison. A hand clasped the base of her throat, one so scarred yet nothing like Kylen's physical scars. She turned back, already gasping for much needed air that she knew was full of the curse. It floated through the air like a gas ready to burn alight.

Althea's face dropped, her heart stopping within her chest as she recognised that same face there. She felt so small, so tiny, like no one could see who she really was. "Hello, Althea." her father snarled.

"Let me go," she whispered, except her voice was barely audible, barely meeting his ears.

"No can do, honey." His grip tightened, and she was lifted off her feet. He threw her down, her heart meeting with the blood-covered floor that she found herself lying on. Tears streamed down Althea's cheeks as she pushed herself up, her arms threatening to break from beneath her.

Her father presented himself there, his eyes full of such glee that she could see them dripping with the curse. A figure moved from behind him, but he was still too far to see. "You know I refused to hear the news when they told me. I told them they were all lies; I even devoured their souls on your behalf."

She looked down at her hands; that was what it was, the blood of the souls he had just claimed. Althea hated it. She always hated this part; it made her want to scream and fight back with all the strength he had given her over the years. But throughout the story of her life, she had learnt that it was far easier to stay quiet. "No—no—no—no—"

If you stayed quiet, then you wouldn't get hurt.

"Once I had confirmation that it was true, then I couldn't wait to see you. If what they said was true about the magick you possess, then I couldn't wait to taste yours." He paused, cocking his head to the side with a skin curling grin. "Of course, I can't help but thank your dear old lover boy here."

The figure in the back stepped forward, his face forming through the darkness, reflecting a warm light that came from a light source she was unaware of. The world, the voices, all of it went silent as her lips curled and her tears fell. She looked to Kylen as her heart broke into a million pieces; shattering beneath her very hold.

"Kylen..." there was a plead on her lips, one that sounded as if she was ready to fall to her knees and beg. His eyes met hers, and that brown was no longer so soft. "Kylen—" she repeated.

How could you? She wanted to scream. How could you do this to me? How could you put me in this position again?

He took three more steps forward before he was aligned with her and she began shaking her head. Pushing herself back as sobs broke free from her lips. He knelt before her, his hand gently cupping her bruised, throbbing cheek. Blood dripped from her forehead, and he wiped it away with his thumb. "Oh darling, I'm sorry, but I couldn't protect you from this one." He laughed, his laugh bouncing off of the walls and sending arrows right back into her faltering heart.

His other hand found her other cheek, and before she could register what had happened, her neck had been snapped, the screams of her lungs slowly dying in the process.

TWENTY-TWO
KYLEN

Kylen's favourite place to walk at night was the castle. It was so quiet, so still, as if all the pain and worries were being preserved so future historians could look back at it as a lesson. Everything was quiet, including the venom that threatened his lungs.

That was until he heard the whispers moving down a hallway he had purposely avoided. His eyes went to it, finding her door at the very end. He looked down, finding the wooden planks before him as he focussed on whatever sounds he could hear.

There was something there, a cry, *a sob*. She was talking to herself, pleading with someone he could not sense. It was still very faint since her room was one of the many in her chambers. But as he stepped closer and closer, the cries became more evident.

Before he could realise it, he had pushed her door open, pulling out a sword made of the curse that was rotting his lungs as he prepared himself for the worse. "*Kylen!*" she said his name as if he was the enemy. As if he was the one pushing this unknown torture onto her restless soul.

Kylen ran through her chambers, pushing her bedroom door

open a moment later. His eyes searched for hers through the darkness, finding her struggling through the layers of sheets on her bed. Her breaths were rushed, her magick flying through the air, swarming in circles as if they were the birds of the dessert ready to feast on her rotting flesh.

Kylen expected himself to be afraid; he waited for the little magick to fade. However, that didn't happen, and instead, he was pushing his way through it, hardly flinching as the sharp shards of her glass-like magick nicked at his skin. "Althea!"

The sounds of her cries weighed heavily on his shoulders, like a physical reminder of all that he had done to her. He wanted to give her a better reason, to tell her that it was the only option. But truth be told, he could have taken that second option that had presented itself that last morning. He could have married her right there and then. *Sure*, they were both still kids, but he knew he could love her. Her heart was so full, so addictive. He found himself searching for any news that regarded Althea Evangeline. *Sure*, the news of her father made him want to die, but he would always risk asking, "what about my—what about Althea?" He knew full well that he no longer claimed any ownership over that title, but he felt guilty. *Guilt that ate at his soul just as the curse had been doing all along.*

Her hands flew, trying to fight off whatever invisible monsters that did not meet his eye. "*Althea—Althea—Althea—Althea!*" Every time he spoke, it was as if he was increasing her level of pain. She sobbed and sobbed, choking on the fresh air around her.

"Wake up!"

Her whole body jolted, her eyes flying open. The fear in her eyes met with Kylen's, and immediately, he sighed with relief. There was no curse to them, no evil that wasn't herself. "You're okay," he tried to soothe, but she was too shocked to acknowledge it.

"Kylen?" she whispered, a sound of pure disbelief filling the air. Her eyes were dancing over his face, his features. She reached up, her hands moving from his chest to his face. Kylen stiffened; he didn't know what to expect. *Should he expect the worst? Was she going to snap his neck and have him done for? Was she going to push him down and pull out a dagger of some type?*

Her soft hands met with his cheeks, and instantly, she was up, sobbing ever so hard as she threw her arms over his shoulders. Whatever she had seen had truly messed her up because she was clinging to Kylen as if death would occur if she let go. He froze for a moment, but it took no longer than a second for his arms to hold onto her as she sobbed into his neck.

"You're okay," he repeated. Kylen reached a hand up to the back of her head, running his fingers through her delicate curls. She was covered in a sweat that Kylen knew was dripping with her old magick. He hadn't realised it yet, but the magick that had cut up his arms and shoulders was gone; it had entered back into her soul; waiting for the next time it would be called to protect her.

Her breaths were still rushed, but slowly as he increased his hold on her, she began to soothe. She was trying to stop herself from showing any more emotion; he knew that. It was what she always did, even as a child.

"It was just a bad dream," he confirmed for her quietly, in a tone that he made sure wouldn't spook her. "Everything is okay here. You are safe; you are alright. Your father isn't here. *He can't hurt you.*"

Althea pulled back, ghosts haunting her vision. "It wasn't just my father." her voice lacked any tone, any enthusiasm or bitterness that he wasn't aware he cherished. "It was *you* as well." Althea sat back, pulling her knees to her chest. "You were the one to tell my father, you—"

She couldn't get the words out, and he understood why. He reached a hand forward, but he saw the way she studied it scarily, the way her shoulders dropped because of the tension added just by his mere movements. He dropped his hand, allowing her to make the first move.

Althea sniffled before looking away. She closed her eyes, and Kylen could see how the exhaust and dreams were getting to her. "I wouldn't do that," he admitted gently. "I know I can be a bit much sometimes, and I have made stupid decisions before, but I would never tell your father anything like that—Hel, I wouldn't even speak to him in general." He tried to get her to smile; he tried to bring back some light to that darling face.

"I'm fine," she said in a tone that told him anything but. "I'm just tired."

"*I know*." Her eyes dripped with a sadness that he would do anything to get rid of. He didn't know exactly what he had put her through, but he knew enough to know that it was bad, that no heartfelt child should ever go through what she did.

Kylen rose to his feet, straightening out his shirt as he looked back down at her. "Would you like me to get you some water or anything?"

Althea's eyes followed him, watching his every movement as if she was afraid he might try something. There was something she wanted to say, something she wanted to ask. But he knew that look, the one that made her feel weak if she were to ask such questions. "What is it?" his tone was near quiet, a soft and calm quiver that beckoned her to continue.

"Stay with me." It didn't come out as a question, but he knew from the expression on her face that it was one. "Stay with me?" she said again, this time the question there, the uncertainty too.

The question caught Kylen off guard. Had he truly heard what he had thought he had? Did she just ask that? Just earlier today, she had tried to kill him, and now she wanted him to sleep in her bed.

"It's alright if that's too much or if you are uncomfortable—I would never want to make you uncomfortable—well, I do, but not in that type of way, more so in the way of... *physically inflicting pain upon you?*" she glanced up at him sceptically. "That was stupid of me to ask; I'm sorry. Please just forget I said anything—"

"Oh, be quiet for once." Those words brought back a glisten in her eyes, and immediately, he applauded himself internally. "If you weren't going to ask, I would have; you aren't the only one haunted by bad dreams." As he spoke, he walked over to the other side of the bed, hands moving to his hips as he looked down at her. He watched as a small appreciative, yet surprised smile found her lips. "Now, do you want me to keep my trousers and shirt on? Or can I take off my shirt and just leave my boxes on—you see, *it's merely for comfort.*"

Althea tucked her strands of loose hair behind both of her ears. "You can take your shirt and uh—" her cheeks flushed, and her eyes noticeably avoided his. "Your trousers too. Just don't you dare try anything, Kylen, because I swear to the Gods," she reached down beside her bed, and to his amazement, she held up one of *his* daggers, "I will kill you."

"Oh, I have no doubt about that, darling. I wouldn't expect anything less." Kylen replied. He moved to the buttons of his shirt, slowly undoing each one before dropping the shirt to the floor. Althea's eyes slyly moved to his body. She tried not to look, but he could see how her curiosity took over. He wasn't going to comment on it, of course, but he felt her stare slowly trace down his abdomen.

He moved to his pants and instantly, her head shot the other way. She laid back, her head meeting with her pillow as her hand slid the dagger back to wherever she had pulled it from.

He placed his trousers on top of his shirt before moving to the bed. He lifted the blankets she had layered over herself, and slowly he met with the sheet that had her infectious scent. Whatever perfume she had been using, the one that caused him to recognise her in an instance, was covering it, and for once, it didn't make him feel queasy.

Althea turned her head, slowly looking him over before looking back at the roof. She closed her eyes, but almost a second later, they were open again. If anything, he expected that he might be the problem, but he noticed the way she didn't so much as react to his movement.

A single tear trailed down the side of her face, and instinctively, Kylen reached up, his fingers already in the process of brushing the pain away. *Would she be okay when death claimed him? Would she survive being Queen?* He rarely saw her walls down, her state of vulnerability. As much as it was terrifying, it was also heart breaking because he couldn't help but feel the guilt of his decisions weighing heavily upon him. Althea closed her eyes to his touch before moving the other way.

She shrugged in a way that carried his hand with her. Kylen didn't have to be the smartest creature in the world to know what this meant; he just did. He moved with her, his body slowly fitting hers. He wrapped an arm around her, and even if she would always deny that this ever happened, he was still grateful that he could be of some comfort.

Althea was quiet. She didn't talk, nor did she want to. So, he didn't pressure her to. Instead, they just listened to the silence that was their breaths. One was heavy, full of panic. The other was loose, painful, so full of the curse that it sounded so shallow.

He heard the moment she fell asleep because her breaths evened out, the Gods allowing some peace of mind now that he was here.

Kylen leant forward slightly, his nose brushing with the famous white hair. He closed his eyes too, soaking in the scent he could spend his life getting drunk on. He pressed his lips to her head before sleep washed over him too.

And for once, his nightmares weren't full of pain.

☽

The scent of her filled his senses with such ease that, for the first time in a while, he didn't wake in a sweat that caused so much pain to the curse. Kylen turned, his whole body freezing slightly as he felt the waist of a tinier figure. Kylen opened his eyes, and through a narrowed gaze, he could see the outline of Althea's face.

How could someone look so angelic while sleeping? Her features were relaxed, her cheeks slightly flushed and her eyes puffy from the tears.

Kylen closed his eyes again, his hand leaving the bare of her waist. It felt wrong to hold her while she was asleep, wrong to touch her whatsoever. He didn't deserve to be graced by her presence by any means. He was the infectious curse that was going to be the death of her. At least when he was younger, he never had to see her unconscious—*aching* body. Now he had, and that image wasn't leaving his mind any time soon.

He ran his hands over his eyes, trying to brush the eeriness away that haunted his features. He didn't want to leave; he didn't want to get up. But he knew he should, for multiple reasons.

The first being that he could seek some good news to ease the pain that was drowning Althea. He wanted to know whether the King was truly on his way or not. He wanted to know if he should prepare for the worst or if he should already pay for a graveyard dedicated to them.

Secondly, he didn't want to put Althea in the uncomfortable position of waking up by his side, waking up by the side of the man who was ready to go hunt down her father, all so he could be the one to push a dagger through his broken heart. He knew that last night was the worst of it all, it was the height, and she was crumbling beneath it. Now that time had been gentle and allowed her to sleep with little stirs; she would be different. Her defensive walls will be back up, and her attitude will be skyrocketing.

Kylen moved his feet off of the bed, and Althea stirred due to the dip in the mattress. She didn't awaken, though. Instead, she tucked her hair behind her ears before placing her hands back under the pillow. He watched her, his lips slightly parting as he tried not to crumble beneath her very presence. The bags from under her eyes were gone, and he even dared to say that the hollowness of her cheeks had worn off too. Kylen's heart thrummed as he took a breath. His emotions were all over the place and full of such confusion because he just did not understand why Althea had allowed him to sleep at her side. Did she trust him? That was good. He wanted her to trust him—but was it wise of her? He had never thought about this factor before as it didn't present itself as likely to him, but if Althea was coming around to him and slowly forgiving him, then her heart was going to be crushed all over again when he died.

This was a mess. This whole plan was a tragic mess. She didn't deserve to receive the burden of becoming Queen.

Kylen slipped his trousers back on before moving to the buttons of his shirt. He looked towards the window, seeing the small crack in the curtains sending a wave of sunshine over to highlight her features. He approached there first, brushing the curtains over so that she could sleep peacefully for a little longer. Kylen didn't bare her another look as he exited her quarters; instead, he just looked around as he fled, looking to see if she had rearranged anything and made it home.

Neither appeared themselves to him, and Kylen sighed. He reached the doors before opening them silently, slipping through the crack a moment later and not leaving a trace of his presence behind. He loved the castle at night; that was no lie. But as he walked down the halls of this old castle, he couldn't help but admire the way the sun bounced off everything.

It was as if his very own ancestors had seen this and decided to place everything perfectly so that when Kylen debated whether his Kingdom was good or not, he just had to go for a walk down the halls.

Kylen passed Sayah's doors before going to enter them. His steps haltered, however, because to his great surprise he could hear another voice, one that he recognised clearly. Kylen cleared his throat before knocking. He heard the rush on the other side and couldn't help but smile to himself, despite the pain that appeared itself to him that would hurt his dear brother.

Zaire opened Sayah's doors and grinned mischievously, a look on their face that he didn't want to know about. "She will be with you in one moment."

"Interrupting something, am I?" Kylen questioned with a cock of his brows.

"Perhaps—" Zaire answered.

At the same time, Sayah yelled from somewhere behind them, "Zaire!"

Kylen laughed; a light laugh that he hadn't shed in a long time. "Right. Well, tell S I am going out. I will be back sometime later."

Before Zaire could barge their way through him with questions, he had already walked off. Turning to the next hallway down and heading towards the hidden doors that held a straight pathway to his Kingdom.

Thankfully the King's quarters were on the way there so he managed to grab new clothes and his leather jacket.

The sunshine managed to bring some warmth to his cold feeling skin, and for a glimpse of a second, he swore he could see the skin he used to hold with so much love—because it reminded him of his mother.

The walk into the Kingdom was light, easy, with only one hill that he had tracked countless times. It shouldn't even be considered a hill, more so a light bump in the pathway, acting as if there was a creature beneath the surface who had died in the process of erupting its way through his Realm.

Sounds of people filled his features as he arrived on one of the narrow pathways. Kylen took a deep breath in; this was what he liked. The sound of chatter, laughter, children speaking with so much joy as if the world was weightless. He lived for moments like these, and what really topped it off was that the people knew him. They knew who their King was, and despite vowing on their lives to protect him, they treated him as an old friend.

Kylen grinned at the old lady that passed him, remembering when he walked to the flower-stand across the road with his father and talked to her when he was just a small boy. How the man who still to this day worked there begged for him not to waste his precious royal money on something like flowers, but Kylen and his father insisted. Then the next week, when they had heard the news that some cursed person from Aeonia had stupidly wrecked his stand, Kylen, his father, his biological little brother and sister—whose deaths he no longer liked to speak about, had all gone into town and physically helped rebuild it.

He didn't understand why his mother hadn't come, but then the next week, *she was dead. His father was dead. His sister was dead. His brother was dead. They were all dead*, and Kylen was left kneeling at their graves as he held his father's heavy and blood-stained crown in his hand.

He hadn't been ready to accept the crown, and yet his people had helped him through it; and they all understood why he needed that break on the sea so desperately. "Good morning, Your Highness. How are you today?"

Kylen smiled at the child who was using such formal mannerisms with him. "I am good, thank you, how about yourself, young lady?" he asked with a charming grin.

The girl giggled before turning to her brother. "William!" she exclaimed, snapping her fingers in his direction to steer him away from the stand of chocolates he so eagerly hung around by.

Kylen reached into his pocket, grabbing a coin before nodding to the boy. His other hand held up two fingers, and the boy grabbed two chocolates before approaching his sister. Kylen flipped the coin to the stand owner before looking down at the children. "Thank you, Mr King, sir."

Kylen felt the ends of his lips tug up at that, and he nodded. "Of course. Now you two be good to each other, okay?" They acted so much like his siblings, Elara and Huntio, that Kylen felt uneasy for a good two seconds. He kept on his way, however, turning to the direction of the Kingdom that he knew would hold some news if any part would.

He needed to find something good; he needed to find something that would give him what he wanted. *So please, to the four Goddesses out there, bless him with his. He forgives you for cursing him; just please give him this pleasure. This won't help him, but instead, Althea.*

TWENTY-THREE

ALTHEA

She fixated on the empty half of the bed beside her. *It couldn't be real*. Surely this was all a wild dream that she had unfortunately lived through. She begged whatever God that was said to be out there to tell her that Kylen didn't come to her rescue last night. She didn't want to be rescued, nor did she want him—*him* of everyone to come to her side. She wasn't weak, nor should she fall victim to Kylen's ways, so why had she?

The towel on her head held up her heavy soaked waves of hair, trying to hold some of the heaviness that still hung so intently over her shoulders. Althea had tried to have a shower to distract herself, and yet it felt like she had fallen and that she was still falling. Nothing felt real. It all felt surreal. But while saying that, there was one true thing she denied accepting; *her night had been without terrors.*

She had woken up feeling the 'best' she ever had.

Sounds of doors opening beckoned her head to turn to the doorway, watching with great relief as Sayah entered through. "Good late morning," Sayah cheerfully greeted. Her steps came to a stop a moment later, with a strange look appearing on her face. "I see Kylen came to visit you."

"How do you know?" Althea practically spat in shock, feeling her face turn red with embarrassment.

"I can sense his magick Althea, and it's very evident over there," she spoke as she waved her hand in the direction of the bed. "But don't you worry, my lips are sealed."

"*We didn't do anything,* I swear *—on the Gods name.*" Althea defensively stated. "Not like I would do anything with him. I was just—" she didn't know quite how to word it because she didn't want to admit to having nightmares.

She didn't want these people to think she was still a child.

"Oh, don't worry, I understand," Sayah merely replied with a shrug of her shoulders. "If you had done anything, then I would be able to sense that too, and I can't, which you know…" she clapped her hands before her, changing the very awkward subject. "Once you are up and ready, I would like to take you into town to get breakfast."

Althea looked at her with a blank expression. "Into… town?" she paused, her eyes glancing sceptically across the siren's face. "You want to take me into the Kingdom?" she asked it as if it was rare for a Queen to travel into their Kingdom, but truthfully, it was for her.

"Yep. And once we do that, we can continue with today's training," Sayah mused with an excited grin.

To say Althea wasn't a touch enticed was a lie. She had wanted to see the Kingdom properly, and Sayah probably was the best out of everyone here to show her.

"Alright." Althea agreed. She looked to the siren, who was dressed in the richest reds and oranges. She caught the glisten of surprise, highlighting her features the moment Althea agreed.

"Beautiful!" Sayah cheerfully cheered as she pulled one of her box braids over her shoulder, wrapping it around her fingers. "Once you get ready, follow my magick… this will be your first lesson of the day!" she exclaimed and a rare smile coated Althea's lips.

☽

Following Sayah's magick had been a lot easier than she had originally presumed; it presented itself well and clearly to her. Like it knew just how troubling it was to think about. Althea had been internally freaking out about it that when she first stepped out of her quarters, she had hesitated over her own instincts, leading her to walk the wrong way at first; before the magick pushed her the other way.

"If you don't mind me asking," Althea began with a sly glance towards Sayah, who was facing the sun that shone ever so brightly above. "You are a siren, are you not? I presumed on my first few days here that Zaire was a fairy, but I never learnt what you were, not really at least—so there is a small part of me that could be wrong. What's Kylen also? Is he human? I never wanted to engage in unnecessary conversation with him."

"*I am* a siren," Sayah answered the girl with a click of her tongue. "Which is why you may see my aura more physically clear than others, and when I'm lazy, you can see my scales too. Kylen, on the other hand… really isn't any specific type of creature—but you could somewhat classify him as human. His bloodline just has always had magick in it that he believes was gifted to him by the witches. Zaire is a fairy, yes. So is Uzziah, except he, being a half-brother to Zaire, is half fairy-half human. While Kylen refers to the three males as his brothers, they aren't biological. More so adoptive—but not actually adoptive. So, Uzziah's magick is the same as Zaire's, but his abilities are limited. Atticus can control the Realms; he was gifted with the magick of Autumnia, and so now he can wield nature to his pleasure." Sayah paused as she slyly turned back to the castle, her eyes searching for someone who she did not want to see.

"Khatri is from the same islands I am from, which is how we know each other." A heavy breath escaped from her lungs, and Althea felt her own tighten. She had sensed it the moment she quite physically came back from the 'dead'. It was there, the chemistry, *hurt—pain* between them as if it was a physical rope.

"We don't need to talk about him if you don't want to," Althea said as casually as she could.

Sayah turned back to Althea and smiled. "I appreciate that, but I will need to one day, and you and I are going to be working together for quite a while, so I might as well." Sayah breathed before holding her hands before her. "Khatri isn't exactly a siren as he was born from one of the other tribes. However, his magick and abilities to mine are the same—all except the fact that he cannot wield a tail nor scales and yet he is still a siren."

Althea nodded, understanding to the best she could. "Do you have any idea what I am? What my magick is from?" She wanted to know, with everything in her heart, she wanted to know. But it was daunting, *so incredibly daunting*.

"I have an idea."

That was not the answer she had predicted. "You do?" Her words were barely audible, yet Sayah caught on. The siren nodded, and Althea turned back to the path before her, her mind spinning in absolute circles. *Did she want to know what she was?* It would help her know what to do to get rid of her Markings and perhaps hide them if her father was really on his way here. "What am I?"

"I believe your magick was a gift from the Goddesses themselves. Whether it had been a direct gift to your mother, her parents, or the generations before that, I'm unaware. Either way, I believe that you have the gift of the Gods, which explains why you basically defied them and death."

Althea held her breath, and when Sayah had finished speaking, she let that breath go, exhaling the air that made her want to ask more questions yet forced her mouth shut at the same time.

"Is that why my Markings are different?" Althea asked, "why Erwin wants me dead? Because I was a supposed opponent?"

Sayah nodded. "Yes. Your Markings are different because you have a touch of everything. I have the Marking of Sommsia, a small little wave as well as a wind symbol on the bottom of my right foot, and when I transform, it appears between my breasts. Zaire has the Marking of Autumnia behind their left ear; however, they keep theirs covered with magick, as for a long time fairies were being hunted for their wicked ways."

"And Kylen? Does he have a Marking or anything that symbolises it…" Althea asked, already internally guessing what Marking he may have.

"Despite not fitting into any of the Realms, he does have a Marking. All the magick in the land comes from the Gods, fitting into one of the four regions also known as Realms, so when Kylen turned nineteen, he got his Marking. It is one on the middle of his back. But because he is also royalty, he has that intertwined with it. His Marking is a sword that goes down his spine, wrapped with vines that ultimately represent the Flora Realms." Sayah explained, and Althea could see that she was trying her hardest to make it as simple as she could. "And I believe that is why you also have a line and a crescent moon through yours."

The outskirts of the Kingdom presented themselves through the line of trees, and Althea felt a twist of nerves. The last time she had been here, she had been blindly led into a trick by Erwin, and the time before, she had been on the run from Kylen's guards.

They entered through the trees in silence, and all throughout the journey to the small café Althea stood close to Sayah. She knew people recognised her, after all, she was their expected Queen. A male bowed, and a woman greeted them. It was strange, walking around like this and having people recognise her. If she had been allowed to do this back home, no one would have recognised her because no one had a free brain to think. Although she had never had to worry about that because her father didn't allow her out, he had said it was a dangerous world, when really it now seems that he was the danger this whole time. *He was the curse that she feared.*

Althea looked around at the people watching her, watching as they all gazed at her wondrously. This was basically her first formal public appearance out in public. No wonder why they gazed so star struck at her.

There was a tug on the ruffled blue dress she wore; it was like Sayah's, the same design except in blue. Althea looked down at the little boy who stood there. The corners of his mouth were covered in chocolate, and his sister gazed from behind.

Althea leant down, feeling a natural smile highlight her lips. "Hello," she greeted in a soft tone. Everyone was watching, but she didn't care. This little boy wanted to give her a present.

"This is for you." He extended out a blue flower that matched her dress. "It's blue. M-my sister ssss-said blue is your favourite c-c-colour." Althea watched him stutter over his words, noticing how his leg bounced repeatedly.

Althea took the flower he extended to her slowly, not wanting to rush him. "Thank you; it's beautiful." She brought the flower up to her ear and placed it there.

Sayah placed a hand on her shoulder, and she rose back up. "Ready? I'm starving."

Althea nodded. "Of course," Her smile stayed on her lips and she turned back to the children and waved goodbye—her chest feeling lighter as she continued on.

They reached the small café moments later, and they climbed the stairs up to the seating area, taking a table near the edge of the balcony. Althea allowed Sayah to order for her, watching in great awe as she knew what to do. She couldn't help but stare; everything was so different from how things were at home.

Everything just didn't sit right with her, which left her feeling out of place more than anything else.

"I wish I could tell you more about your Markings because then you might feel less stressed out about it all. But I don't know anything more. *I am researching*, however."

Althea looked around anxiously. "Aren't you afraid someone might hear us?" she asked as she looked back at the siren with a small voice.

"No," Sayah answered. "My magick is wrapped around us, so whatever we say is only audible to us. Do you have any questions about anything? Anything you want to get to know and understand or just know about?"

Althea was quiet for a moment, considering whether she should ask this next question. "You don't have to answer this, but how did Atticus, Uzziah and Khatri die?"

Sayah's face grew weary, and Althea cursed herself for asking such a thing. "They died from a variant of the curse. It was meant to be me who died, except I was sick that night, throwing up after I—" she cleared her throat and Althea opened her mouth to speak. "I had received news that I was with child." Althea could already see where this was going and how the voices in her head slowly silenced one another. "Khatri was with me when I learned of the intel that there was a particular outburst. He, being himself, decided to take charge and ordered Atticus and Uzziah to follow with him. He wasn't aware of my condition, but he knew that I was sick. I waited seven hours as the Ball went on, waiting to hear any news of what had happened to them. In fact, my scream and outburst of magick were what stopped that party. The curse got to them, and their souls couldn't handle it, but I didn't just lose those three that night, I also lost my baby." Sayah explained. Her expression was calm, gentle, and Althea could see the shadows beneath her eyes.

Althea listened, her heart twisting in pain for this woman that she now somewhat knew. "I know something of what you were feeling—not about the loss of your child, but about the loss of losing someone you love." Althea admitted as her eyes strayed away. She wasn't sure why she was sharing this, but it just naturally left her tongue, like it was finally time to talk about it.

The air seemed to tighten but she took a breath, a strong, deep breath. "I lost a girl that I loved because of my own doing. She's not technically dead, but her soul is, and what is someone without their soul? I guess I just wanted to tell you, considering I now know something about you."

Sayah reached forward and met Althea's hand, a small comforting expression lining her lips. "Thank you for sharing that with me. It's not something that's easy to talk about."

Althea nodded as she watched the girl—the girl who seemed to have a heart that was kind to hers.

Both heads turned, and instantly, the two pairs of eyes lit up as they saw the delicious pastries approaching them. *"Are you ready to have your first taste of real food?"*

Althea looked back to Sayah. "I guess I am." She could sense the barrier of Sayah's magick slowly fall, revealing them and their words to the real world.

TWENTY-FOUR
KYLEN

There was a familiar soul, one that he could sense somewhere before him. Kylen held up his sword, feeling and listening for any sign of struggle. Whoever they were with was masked, their magick shielding them for Kylen's little senses.

He followed it, his eyes shooting like arrows around. It was close, just down this path a little further, and he should see the great threat.

His brows furrowed as the first figure came into view. His eyes spotted the white hair first, watching as she sat cross-legged by the water. Something appeared from behind her, and Kylen watched as Sayah joyously appeared. "Again!"

Althea looked up to her with *a smile*, a smile that pulled the air from his rotting lungs, *a smile that was so natural that Kylen couldn't help but feel a rage of jealousy spike through him.* Why wasn't he being smiled at like that? Was he still such a bad person in her mind—*of course he was; who was he kidding?*

Althea held up her hands before her, her fingers slowly moving in a seemingly random pattern, forming a ball of light that shone through them. Althea turned back to the water, her hands slowly extending out, her palms facing away. She raised her hands, and slowly the whole lake began to rise, not any of the land but rather the water and creatures within.

Kylen moved around, moving his position so that he could see her face. Her features were highlighted by the hidden magick that flowed so easily through the palms of her hands. He had not asked Sayah yet about what she could be because... *well, he hadn't had time,* and he was afraid of what the truth may bring.

Sayah must have sensed him a while back because she didn't so much as flinch as he appeared in view. Instead, she met his eyes, a grin on her lips that turned back to the water before her.

"Look!" Althea exclaimed with an amusement that brought a melody of a tune to his lips. "Look—can you see? Please do not tell me that I am hallucinating it—"

Sayah laughed, but it wasn't she who answered.

"No, beloved, you are not hallucinating."

The water dropped before her, so harsh and so quickly that it rebounded back onto Althea, coating her whole figure with lake water. Sayah closed her eyes as the water brushed onto her, unfazed as her clothes clung to her skin. Kylen however, jumped back, rushing away from the tsunami.

Althea gasped before turning to him, her features lethal. "I—"

It took four seconds, four seconds for reality to set itself upon Althea, and then she ticked. She rose to her feet, her hands shaking away the lake water that now covered her. Her hair was drenched, the curls of it sticking to her like glue. Her clothes would be transparent if she hadn't been wearing so many layers. "Kylen Noxwell." she demanded before holding out her hand. "You son of a—*give me your jacket at once*."

"If you wanted to see me naked, love, you could've just asked," Kylen mused lightly, trying to float a joke through the air. Althea stared at him in response, and from behind Althea,

Sayah tilted her head with a brow raised, urging him to give her his jacket. "Okay—okay, I'm sorry."

He shrugged off his leather jacket before turning around. He heard as Althea got to work, and just moments later, she was pushing soaking, cold clothes into his hand. His eyes went to her legs, the curiosity about what she was wearing there taking over. Althea still wore the bottom dress of her undergarments, a long silk skirt that just reached her ankles. She held her hands in the pockets of his long leather jacket, and Kylen couldn't help but grin as his mind wandered.

"You are a complete jackass!" Althea swore. "Who are you to spy on us?"

"I wasn't spying," Kylen retorted. "I was merely seeing if you were in danger since I could sense your magick and all." He followed Althea in a hurry, hardly realising until the last minute that Sayah had been approached by three of her guards.

He looked over his shoulder at her before looking back at Althea, watching as she stormed away, cursing numerous foul words under her breath.

"Follow her," Sayah said before disappearing through the trees. His eyes flowing with her. *What was wrong—?*

He wasted no time in doing so however. Kylen caught up to his fiancé within seconds, watching as she looked up to him with such horror. "This is why I don't do water or any of the sort!"

"Yes, well, you are just fussy. Water, in general, is beautiful. Have you ever gone sailing? On a ship? Oh, I tell you that it's the most beautiful feeling; perhaps I will get to show you in another lifetime." There was something like mourning to his voice, but he doubted Althea could hear it since she was too busy scolding his actions.

"*The sea is gross.* I hate water. I hate any form of large masses of it. It's horrifying." Her sentences were short and sharp, a terrible bite to each one.

"That's right," Kylen laughed. "You do not know how to swim."

"Why would I need to know how to swim?" Althea asked defensively fast. "I am a Queen, not a pirate like you." The castle came into view, and Althea's steps only quickened. Her hair was starting to dry, shooting back up as if it were a crown.

"Privateer, actually. Oh, I may have spent a few years at sea and all, but I am still King. Learning to swim is a very practical thing. It can keep you alive if you were to ever fall in," he said as a matter of fact. "Perhaps I could teach you?"

Althea laughed drily. "I am never going to be in a position where I might drown. I am not that stupid nor idiotic." She sent him a side-eyed glance.

"You aren't stupid if you fall in the water, love. I have fallen in many times, during battle and for fun. It is quite enticing may I tell you."

"You may not."

Silence echoed between them like a rock, so physical and hard that Kylen searched for ways to get around it. It seemed that Althea was too, because as she walked with her head held high, her eyes dancing all over the place. Her lips tightly pursed.

"Did you sleep well?" Kylen offered, a hand moving up to the back of his head. "Do you want to talk about anything regarding last night? Or would you prefer that I not speak a word of it?"

Althea kept quiet for a minute or two that his thoughts began to echo. "I slept well." The words caused a swarm of butterfly-like creatures to waltz about his stomach. "Surprisingly," she moved her hand up to the hair sticking to her shoulder. "I thought it would be the opposite if I'm being honest." She glanced up at him, meeting the eyes that were already on her.

"That's good." Kylen offered as a response. "I'm glad that I could ease some of your worries."

Althea tucked the hair she was fumbling with behind her ear.

"As for the second question you asked, I would prefer you not to speak to anyone about it because then you are saving me from the hassle of having to cut off their tongues."

"Why do you believe that showing emotions makes you weak?"

Althea looked at him; her face flickering with unreadable emotions. "Being weak in a Kingdom of ghosts is like being the villain in a Kingdom of so-called heroes. No matter how hard you try or even speak to justify your reasons, no one will ever hear you. Because they have this mindset that what you are is wrong. You aren't acting wrong; you are wrong. My father taught me that being weak is allowing the enemy a front row entry to your heart, and we all know how that turns out."

"Being weak shows that you have a heart. It shows that you aren't as cruel as any rumours may say." Kylen struck back in response. He knew he was partially—mostly to blame for the way of her thinking, and Gods knows that her father probably used him as a reasoning to think like that, but he wanted her to see from his point of view, no matter how dangerous it may be.

"Having a heart on its own is weak. You mustn't show the heart you possess if you want to survive, that's how I've learnt to survive and I've only almost died once."

"You used to have a heart," Kylen objected as he looked away, noting that the steps to the castle were mere metres away.

"I did." Althea replied before her eyes dragged over to his. She tilted her head, her gaze locking onto his. "And just how stupid I had been, look at where it had gotten me. Absolute Hel."

She walked up the steps, lifting her skirt up so that it, being soaking wet, wouldn't pick up any unwanted mud, no matter how eager she probably was to wreck the castle before her. Kylen followed her inside, watching as she walked in the direction he did not. "I still think you should learn how to swim," he suggested loudly as he turned back towards her.

"Oh, shove off."

Kylen lightly grinned to himself before starting his way to Sayah's quarters, the questions already burning through his mind, ready to be spoken. He was worrying. *He was freaking out.* He pleaded that Althea's father wasn't the reason Sayah had been taken away so quickly. He silently begged anyone listening that he would not have to see that villainous face.

TWENTY-FIVE
ALTHEA

The emptiness of her room crawled at her skin like the curse she had once had. She held her knees to her chest, her gaze on the window as she beckoned the sun to rise sooner. It had only turned to night around half an hour ago, but that wasn't good enough. She needed it to be over now. She could not live through another night of terrors… presuming that they would occur now that she was alone.

Perhaps Althea was wrong, perhaps they wouldn't, and she was just being dramatic as she always was. She slowly leant back, laying on top of the blankets so that she wouldn't feel so trapped like the previous night. Her eyes shut, and she focussed on the sound of her breaths. She took a deep breath in, another breath out. Her name was Althea Evangeline; she should not be afraid. But she was, she was deeply afraid, and that stirred her dreams in the wrong direction.

"Look at you, in bed with the enemy." The words woke her up, her heart jumping from within her chest as she quickly scrambled out of the sheets, out of Kylen's grasp.

Her eyes searched through the darkness, meeting with the owner of it. "I expected more from you, Althea; I truly, truly did." His words were bitter, sharp; she swore that she could see thick heavy blood dripping off them.

Her hand slid down, shaking her King at her side and begging for him to wake. He didn't so much as move. Althea noticed then that she could not hear his breaths—his heart. She turned her head, and her eyes flew wide as venom crawled at her throat.

Kylen's throat was slit, dark black blood dripping from it. It was a fresh wound because the bed was only just dampening, which meant that he had been alive a few minutes ago, and she hadn't been able to save him. "No!" she screamed, turning on her knees before clasping her hands to his throat. "Wake up! Wake up! Wake up!"

Her whole body jolted as she began to gasp for the cold, cruel air which hung haunted dreams over her. Mocking her in all her misery because the Gods that she had so-called been blessed by enjoyed her agony.

Althea gasped for air, her whole body visibly shaking that she almost mistook it for the curse. Her heart raced, and despite clasping her hands over her ears, it didn't drown it out. If anything, it amplified it.

The door handle moved, and Althea sprang into action, her hand already clasping the dagger at her side before moving to strike. She aimed it in his direction, watching with wide, bug-like eyes as Kylen presented himself to her, and this time he wasn't covered in his own blood.

She stared at him, her dagger wavering slightly in the air as she took in his figure, searching for the wound that she knew was somewhere there. He approached the bed, and she pushed her dagger further toward him. "Stay back," she begged through a broken voice. "S*tay back.*"

"Althea," Kylen warned. "It's me."

"I don't know *who you are*," she whispered, her voice quivering to the point where it was barely audible. The wind mocked her, running down her spine with such joy before twirling back around it on its journey upwards. It pulled at her, forcing her to straighten up.

Althea wanted to cry. She wanted to hop in the shower and cry because that was the one place where you could drown your tears. She said that she hated water but truthfully, using it to her advantage was something she had learnt to do when she was only young.

"Yes, you do," Kylen whispered gently in a tone that she knew was not meant to scare her. "I am the man who you loathe. I am the man who turned you into the woman you are today. I am the monster that came into your life and flipped it for the worst when I could've saved you from this misery. *...And worst of all, I am the charming delight you will be marrying.*"

Althea's lips wobbled, and slowly, the dagger dropped to the bedding before her. She held a hand up and over her eyes, sheltering her tears from him. "I'm sorry I know this is probably the last thing you want to deal with," she said while choking on a cry. "I'm fine, really, I am fine." Kylen looked at her with such concern that Althea felt as if she was a child again.

She forced her tears back before wiping any evidence of them away. Althea looked up at him, her eyes redder than the burning sun that was hiding.

Kylen slowly moved forward, his hand meeting with her damp, bruised cheeks, running his thumb over the trails that the tears had left. "You don't have to say anything, and I will not speak a word of it to any, but nod if you would like me to stay the night by your side. I will not think any different of you. I know that you are still that strong pain in my ass who could burn the world if she felt like it. But I know that even the strongest of souls need time to gather themselves up. They need time to regroup, reinvent themselves so that they can come out stronger." He paused, allowing those words to settle upon her. "That's exactly what you are doing, my love." He spoke so gently that Althea had dug her nails into her thigh, testing whether this was a dream or not. And to her great surprise, *it was not.*

There was no hesitation there, no matter how much she would curse herself the next day; Althea didn't hesitate. Instead, she nodded, her eyes dripping with two singular tears which escaped from the war within them. Trying to flee from the pain that this very man had put her through.

Kylen moved instantly, shrugging off the clothes as he had done the night before. He laid in her bed, and she followed, slowly climbing beneath the covers. She watched him with such curiosity that she almost looked concerned.

He set his head on the pillow, mimicking her actions. His eyes stayed locked on hers, reaching forward once again when he saw another tear fall. She closed her eyes to that, taking a deep breath and opening them back up when she exhaled.

Althea expected to see something out of a nightmare when she opened them; she expected to see something so fierce and dangerous that she was sure to scream; however, when she opened her eyes, she saw Kylen, the same Kylen that used to lay by her side telling her stories. They weren't allowed to sleep in the same bed back then, but he would always sneak in, telling her stories of the world beyond.

Her favourite ones were about his days at sea. He had arrived back from his six months or so journey the day before they met, and it was said a week after everything happened, he descended upon them again. Althea had been so jealous, so incredibly jealous that this cruel man who she was still so desperate to see again got to travel the world he so wrongly abused.

"How are you feeling?" Kylen asked. "Would you like me to get you water or anything?"

Althea shook her head, feeling as the exhaust from her dreams suffocated her from the inside out. "No, I already have a glass. *I came prepared,*" she drily yet humorously said with a tight-lipped smile. "I feel… like I'm drowning," she said as an answer, looking to him in hope that he somewhat understood. "It's like there is this wave that follows my every step. And every time I reach the surface and finally feel at ease to the point where sleep might be kind—it crashes back down on top of me."

Kylen nodded. Surprisingly, he understood.

She sighed a deep heavy sigh. "They will be gone soon; I am praying so."

"You don't pray."

Althea hadn't realised that she had closed her eyes before she opened them, a sly grin appearing on her lips as she laughed gently. Trying not to rock the ache within her chest. "There's no need to call me out like that."

"Oh, I don't mean to. They haven't done anything for us, I used to pray to them all the time, but I guess you could say that I lost my faith in anything like that." Althea knew briefly what Kylen's life had put him through; it was one of the reasons earlier on why she didn't allow herself to cry or feel bad for herself. How was she to feel so broken and sad if he had gone through so much worse?

"You and me both." Althea yawned, a heavyweight only increasing its hold on her as she exhaled again. She stared at the bed before her, the bedding that kept the two apart.

"Sleep," Kylen whispered. "Sleep, and we can talk in the morning; it will be better in the morning."

She laughed dryly in response. "I know it won't ever be better. I will just have to grow up and face it. But it seems a little too daunting to face tonight." Althea whispered. "All is well that ends well, but my story doesn't end well. Nothing ever works out."

Kylen listened, doing all that she could possibly ask for. "You don't need to grow up; you just need to remember that you aren't alone to face them anymore—" he cut himself off, sighing subtly. "You have Sayah, Zaire, my brothers."

But not you. Not the one my soul longs for.

Althea closed her eyes, pulling the blankets up and closer to her. "We have all the time in the world to speak, considering the odds. We don't have to rush anything." She knew that was partially true and partially a lie. They didn't have all the time in the world, nor did they want to. They were both running from different monsters that led them straight to the other. As if even the Gods knew that they were destined for one another. *Even the Gods knew that their souls were one.*

☽

Althea felt the magick before she could register. Like an old, haunted soul revisiting her, leaving the feeling of suffocation along the bones of her spine. It was a feeling so absurd and so horrid that she wanted nothing more than to believe that it was a dream.

She looked to the empty spot in the bed, just now realising the impact Kylen's body had on it. Her eyes grazed over the neat blankets, moving back to her hands. Althea did not hold the magick that she could feel, sense, taste so strongly, but it was still somewhere there.

Slowly, Althea rose from her spot on the bed, slipping on her robe before moving to the doorway; she pulled out one of Kylen's swords that she had stolen the day before, in case of the rare chance that what her mind, body and soul was screaming at her was true.

Althea's shaking fingers found the door handle, and she held her breath. She slowly began to turn it, unlocking the door Kylen had presumably locked when he had left, however long ago that may be. The sun was still down; it was pitch black outside. The moon wasn't even on display because even she was afraid of what her gracious presence might have to see.

The door opened, and her grip on the sword dared to let go as she took in the familiar face. This wasn't like a scene in her dreams; no, this was real life. And Althea did not let the view of her father before her shake her down. No, she kept her chin high, a sly mastered smirk on her lips as her eyes danced across his foul face. This was real life, and it was taking everything in Althea not to cower under his very stare.

TWENTY-SIX

KYLEN

He stared at Sayah and Zaire from across the table. His eyes were full of such confused anger that he truly did not know what to think or feel. They were quiet now, having just discussed the King's whereabouts turning silent the moment they all sensed that magick that each one of them knew a little too well.

Kylen himself sensed the other magick then. The faltering magick that wanted to laugh at him, the faltering magick that also wanted to scream and cry.

The door opened from behind, and as he turned, he saw from the corner of his eyes Sayah's magick swiftly sending the papers and maps that covered the table into her quarters. Disappearing just like that, because she too could sense the *pain* and *agony* on the other side of the door.

"I hope I'm not interrupting anything. *That would be just tragic*." The words echoed through the room before the King he loathed with everything in him appeared in view. *There he was.* There was the man they had worked so hard on fending off.

First, it had been the news of the seven dead guards, then it had been the news of the dead wildlife on the outskirts of the

Kingdom, then most tragically, they hadn't received any other word, so they gathered here—and how Kylen wished he had awoken Althea.

"Hello to you all. I trust everything is *reasonably* well."

Kylen met the man's eyes, and he felt his chest heave. He did not want to stare at him—he did not want to relive the memories that hid behind those cruel eyes, and yet he couldn't find the power within him to turn away. *It was as if he could physically hear the cries and screams of his parents as the curse slaughtered them all.* The King stepped further into the room, and Kylen's chest tightened as his eyes laid sight on the cowering girl behind the other King. He watched as Althea's eyes met with his, the worry in hers burning holes through his. She was untouched, alive—*not dead yet*, and that brought a sense of relief into his blood.

"What are you doing here? I wasn't expecting you for another week," Kylen asked, his tone awfully flat.

"Well, I did say I was going to come and visit in one month, did I not? Don't tell me you forgot?" He turned to Althea; his expression dark. "You didn't forget, did you dear?" he asked in a rumbling tone that pushed her spine to straighten.

"No, father." Her voice was so quiet, so dull. Her eyes were on his, and he saw the mask climb up. As if it was more evident with this magick, *he could see it*. It was so terribly strange seeing her this way, seeing her whole demeanour changed.

"Good." The King of Aeonia turned back to Kylen. "You know it would be very irresponsible of me if I left my daughter for any longer than this in a Kingdom that we cannot trust."

Althea looked to her feet, her strands of long wavy hair falling over her shoulder. She looked just about ready to admit defeat. He knew she had gone through these scenarios many times already, through her dreams, thoughts, and nightmares. She had already lived through this one-to-many times, and Kylen could see how ready she was to give in.

If he were in her position, he would too, *but it was Althea he was thinking about.*

"I apologise for my sudden arrival. You see, I heard news that I could not allow to be true." As he spoke, he turned on Althea far too quickly for her to react. He grabbed at her wrist, the panic leaving her body as her eyes widened and lips parted in a gasp. Her breaths quickened as his grip on her wrist only tightened. "Get—" Kylen could sense her magick, and, yet to all their amazement, the Markings were not there. And considering Althea's expression, she hadn't expected that outcome either.

"*Get your fucking filthy hands off of her*," Kylen growled, the walls trembling from his sudden outburst, and his body already moving forwards.

The King obeyed, dropping her wrist as crimson red blood appeared in the spots where his nails had pierced her darling skin. Althea's expression had changed from one of shock to emptiness—*past anger*. She stared down at her arm, watching as the blood dripped down, creating trails that no one would ever dare to venture down. "Please prepare a room for me," the King spoke in a tone that invited them to know that he was not asking but rather convinced in his delusions instead.

"How long will you be staying?" Sayah asked in the most even tone she could gather.

"That's none of your business, now, is it, *girl?* Prepare me a room next to my daughters. I do not want her alone in a place like this; I do not want her alone with anyone like you," he said, directing the last part exactly at the siren because of the magick he could sense in her blood. The King didn't care that she was a girl or that she was from the north; he only cared that she had magick that defied his.

Sayah nodded, signalling slyly for Zaire and Uzziah to follow. Rage filled Kylen's head and he had to hold onto everything within him to suppress the darkness.

"Now you can go back to bed, boy," he said to Kylen.

"There's still time for sleep, and you will need it for tomorrow. I want a complete rundown of everything that has happened since she has gotten here." The King looked to Althea. "Goodnight, dear. Sleep well." Every word that left his mouth was like a complete violation on her behalf.

The King turned around, walking past Althea's frozen figure, completely ignoring the ghostly pale mask her face had turned into. He disappeared, leaving her in a room full of people she most likely didn't want to speak or interact with. *Leaving Kylen in a room that was feeling surprisingly small despite how truly large it was.*

His foul, disgusting presence was gone, his magick was gone, but Kylen had not yet sighed with great relief as the tension drained off his lungs because his attention was purely fixated on *her*. His brown eyes stayed on her as Althea dragged her eyes off the floor.

Althea turned down the same hallway her father had just disappeared through, her own magick hollow and empty, begging Kylen to save it from this torturous pain.

His eyes softened, and yet the anger burned in his stomach. He turned to Khatri and Atticus; his face weary. "We are not letting him win this one," he mouthed, knowing full well that the foul magick of the curse was listening in. His eyes wanted to soften; they begged to be of some comfort to Althea. But he was once again too focussed on something that was steering the ship in the other direction.

Kylen turned back to Khatri and Atticus; his eyes full of orders that he could not give aloud. He didn't have to speak the words because *they knew*. He didn't have to say a single thing because *they already knew*. None of them would be able to win this war. Of course, all of them would fight with everything in them, but other than that, they had no real abilities that would be able to fend off Althea's father.

Althea perhaps would be able to stand a chance, but considering how she had just frozen under the spotlight of her father, he knew that it would be more than just abilities needed when going up against someone and something like that.

☽

The morning had risen, and yet none of them had slept. They were all too frightened, too scared. They were on the edge of their seats, and it was only a matter of time until Kylen's tipped. Leaving him to drown in the sea that he had been born into.

He wondered if his parents ever knew things would come to this. He wondered what his parents may do if they were still living, *breathing*. Would they be proud of him for everything he did to keep this Kingdom breathing? Or would they be mad? Would they be cross because *of what his Kingdom cost?*

Kylen tapped his feet rapidly, the rhythm matching with the beat of his heart. The King of Aeonia was in the throne room, sitting upon his throne *as if he owned it,* when Kylen knew that he would rather go through a tragic, torturous, slow death than let that be true.

Althea stood in the same room as Kylen instead of the one her father stood in, finding comfort in the small space that was protected by Sayah's magick. He watched as the siren approached her, bringing a warm cup of herbal tea that he knew held a calming melody. One that Althea seemed to need to get drunk on, given the circumstances.

Althea looked to the siren, her face blank. It was so strange looking at her because no matter how intently he stared, he could not recognise the girl from the night before. He could not recognise the girl who had weakly smiled at him under the sheets that he had clung to.

"So that's it?" Zaire asked, breaking the silence Kylen had unknowingly led them into as if it was darkness. "We just don't have a plan?" They wanted to laugh—and they did. A laugh of not only enjoyment but bitterness. “Are you stupid? Are you mental? Why would you let him break us down like this?”

“Zaire, don't say that,” Sayah responded with a cross of her arms. “Have some respect. We are not currently in the position to be making a plan. This is all we can do.” Her eyes sent a look over to Althea; noting how her expression looked over each face.

“We are doing nothing!” Uzziah exclaimed on behalf of his sibling—earning their swift gazes. “We are just sitting like bait, waiting for the fish to catch the line.” He looked to Althea, already moving his arm and hand up in a motion of a fish catching a line before pointing to her; causing Kylen to scoff.

“No,” Kylen said before Uzziah got the chance to say anything more. “*Put your finger down.*”

“Don’t tell him to put his finger down!” Zaire exclaimed. “I am with him on this one. We should hand her over and leave her to be done with. Then we get to go back to living our *glorious life*, and she won’t be a pain in our ass anymore—”

“Zaire, shut your mouth!” Sayah snapped so harshly that it immediately shut them all up. It was shocking to hear the normally calm siren lose control, even for a second.

Kylen looked to Althea, finding that even she was slightly shocked at the outburst.

“Rude,” Zaire mumbled. “A simple sigh would have done just fine.” They stated.

“I’m not going to let you get rid of me that easily, Zaire,” Althea spoke, breaking her silence. And what a relief it was to hear her sweet voice.

“Oh, so she’s talking to me now?” Zaire questioned. “Funny because before, you seemed not to want anything to do with me!” They exclaimed and Kylen sighed at their antics.

“You aren’t worth my time. You aren’t of any use to me.” Her face was still so blank that Kylen felt the fear radiate off the others like warmth seeping from the sun. “None of you are, but Sayah and perhaps Kylen. At least they can offer me something

—and I don't have to feel bad for that," she tutted. "Because in the end, we will all end up dead, and I would have just achieved more than you in this lifetime."

"So that's your plan?" Khatri asked in a genuine tone. "You plan to just… *die?"*

She hadn't said those words, and yet Khatri had read between the lines and understood.

"Well, I plan to do what I can to survive, and it seems this," Althea said before moving a hand to hover over her chest, acting as if it was her soul; her *magick*, "doesn't want me to die either so I am going to see where that leads me."

"Are you honestly surprised if she wants to die?" Zaire laughed. "Have you seen the way she cowered under her father last night? She was terrified; with a father figure like that, death would be a virtue. For once, I agree with her."

Althea stared at Zaire, her expression unbothered.

"Zaire, stop that now," Kylen warned in a tone that told them it was better not to argue. "I'm with Thea on this one. As I've said, we can't form a plan because his moves are unpredictable, but what we can do is attend his Ball tonight and show him that everything is normal. What we can do is help Althea keep her cover as a normal girl for as long as he's here."

Something changed in her face, and he looked towards the Princess; watching as she looked towards the door as if she was physically scared of what may be hidden on the other side.

TWENTY-SEVEN
ALTHEA

Althea stared at the people who had willingly come to a Ball that would result in their death. She stared at them with such judgement because how could they be so stupid to willingly walk into a place that was being controlled by the enemy.

She hadn't spoken to her father again; Gods knew she probably wouldn't be able to even if she tried. The words wouldn't come; they would stand her up, leaving her to falter under the laughs of her Elemental magick and her father.

Althea stood by her father's side, feeling as Kylen's hand slowly found hers behind the many layers of her dress. She felt his scarred hand, his calloused palm. The way his magick was barely there beneath his cold skin, and yet hers synced with it automatically.

Kylen squeezed her hand, and yet she could not bring herself to react. Her mask was fitting perfectly, a cold blank stare to her face that hid away just how scared she truly was.

She didn't want them to judge her because of how she was acting in front of her own father. She didn't want them to see her as weak because she could feel death calling at her from the gates. Althea knew what they would do, and she knew they would be excited—over the moon when they realised that she was ready to get on her knees and scream.

And that feeling only increased when she noticed the two guards of her fathers standing beside a girl *she knew* all too awfully well.

The air froze in her lungs and almost immediately she felt her body beginning to give way.

Eloise stood in the middle of them all, and Althea waited, feeling as her heart froze within the cage of her chest. *She so desperately waited for the darkness to appear*—to relieve her of the agony of seeing an uncursed girl who looked so much like her first love. She waited to see the curse appear from within her pure and outgoing soul because if she didn't have the curse, then that meant that *her Eloise* was truly here, alive and breathing.

Althea's grip tightened on Kylen's, her nails digging into the treasured flesh that scraped his hands. He didn't react, however; he took her pain as if he could see right through her and her situation.

The guards and Eloise bowed before Althea, a recognisable and unrecognisable look on her perfectly pink cheeks. "Congratulations on your engagement," Eloise spoke on the others' behalf, knowing full well that even if they tried, they would not be able to get a word out of their controlled and poisoned mouths.

"Thank you," Kylen responded in a tone that sounded sincere, yet Althea knew was also sceptical. "Go enjoy your night."

That was the last of the congratulations, and now she needed a drink more than ever. "I'm going to get a drink," she said in a tone that her father should not have been able to hear and yet did.

"Kylen get us drinks, boy; I want to have a word with my daughter." Her father interrupted, tapping to the throne at his side, *Kylen's throne.*

Althea obeyed, knowing full well that she did not have the energy right now to argue or defy him. She sat down, crossing her leg over the other as her eyes glanced hesitantly at him before looking away. She took a deep sigh like breath, feeling as her voice threatened to break when she released it. "Did you like my present?" her father asked, earning his daughter's blue-eyed gaze to go to him.

"What present?" she asked, hoping with her whole heart that he did not mean what she knew full well that he did.

"You always loved her; I saw it in your eyes. So, I thought, why not give her another chance at life as a gift to you." He was quiet for a few moments, allowing her eyes to travel back to the girl who made her heart ache.

The first time Althea had realised she had been in love with her only childhood friend was when she was thirteen, still a child compared to the brutality of the world. "She gets to live this life, you know; a life of freedom and purity, *if only you tell me the truth...*" she waited for it, feeling it approach quicker and quicker with every beat of her heart. "Tell me, sweetheart, is what they say true? Have you gained the evil magick that your *mother* once possessed?"

So father, father, father, truly did know.

"No," she protested. *Had it always been this easy to lie to one's father?* She didn't know, but the guilt flooded her with such ease either way. Althea looked down at her black dress, watching as her fingers picked at the lace that itched at her sides.

"Are you lying to me?"

Are you? She wanted to ask. *Are you lying to me about my mother, about her magick, about what she possessed?* Those questions swarmed through her mind, nipping at her flesh and daring her to say something more. But she had always been far too afraid, scared that if she were to say something, she would lose all that she had, which was hardly anything anymore.

She remembered the moments that defined her relationship

with her father so clearly. Not only were some experiences horrible, but some were also so foul that bile threatened to escape from her throat each time she remembered them. Yet then there were the ones that made her weep, the few good moments that had her remembering the messed-up childhood he had lived through. She remembered him sneaking into her room on her sixth birthday, bringing her all the snacks and treats she had requested that previous night. They spoke for hours, talking about things that were strange to reflect on now.

It all seemed like a generous fever dream as if none of it had ever been real.

Because after everything that had happened, after she had led Kylen to victory and her father to the ground, everything had changed. "No." How easily the lie slipped off her tongue again… it was like a drug, finding its own joy in her rotting and decaying body.

"Good."

Althea's eyes moved up quickly as she watched the invisible yet visible magick fade around them. Trapping her in a bubble where his words would only meet her ears. She looked towards him, her gaze faltering. She wanted to hate him, she wanted to loathe the man with everything in her… but her heart always felt so heavy when she remembered the relationship that they shared when she was young.

Why did time make him hate her? Was she really such a bad person for just growing up?

"Because Althea, if I find out that you are lying to me, it's not going to be good. I have worked for years, guaranteeing that you aren't *cursed* with the magick your mother was—doing all that I can to give you a good future, a good life. I put you through every test under the moon to ensure that you would live a long and healthy life," the King ranted, his black eyes meeting with her frightened yet masked ones. "If I find out that you do have this magick, then you know I'm going to have to take the high road here. I will save you; I will help you, I will—"

"Enough!" Althea exclaimed through a breaking whisper. "I do not have the magick, so just let me go and interact with the guests!" Her heart stammered in her ears. Awaiting with such fear as her father's eyes took their damn time dragging over hers.

The King pursed his lips, and Althea shuddered under his gaze. "Very well. *Eloise?*" he purred in a feline-like voice—and every bone within Althea's now frozen body threatened to break.

"Yes, your highness?" she appeared in less than a second before them, her dark red hair so real that Althea debated whether or not she should reach out to touch it.

She pushed herself back in her seat, her eyes glancing around for Kylen. *Where was he? Why was he leaving her in a situation like this? Did Zaire convince him to leave her to die? Did they leave her to be captured by the clammy hands of death that belonged to her father?* If they had, she had mere seconds to run. She didn't have a destination in mind, and she knew she would probably be dead after no more than two steps. But she needed to escape from his grip, *from his reach.*

"Why don't you take Althea for a walk? Why don't you two catch up?" he asked, offering her to play a game she did not want to play.

"Of course." Eloise bowed before Althea, already offering Althea her arm, and despite not wanting to make contact with the figure who looked so like the girl she missed more than anyone in the entire of the Realms; she knew that if she didn't play to his game, she could potentially risk the deaths of all of these people in this room. *Gods how she hated sounding like Kylen.* But it wasn't even that that stopped her; it was the fear that these people would be forced down the same path she was being pushed down.

Althea rose, feeling as her tall narrow heels shook the floor beneath her.

Eloise wore a thin dress, one that meant she could feel the skin beneath it. Althea's fingers wrapped around her arm, her whole body stiffening as she felt the warmth there. This was real. *She was real. And she was there.* Althea looked at her as they walked through the doors. Her face was so soft, so perplexed that it confused even her; she didn't understand what she was seeing. What game she was now playing herself into. Each breath that Eloise took felt like an illusion in itself. Each shudder that escaped her lungs sent Althea back into her nightmares, the ones that forced her to remember the days when she lost the dear girl.

The doors opened before them, and Althea looked away from her scared stare at Eloise, moving it over her shoulder and to the crowd that didn't even seem to pay her a second glance. *Where was Kylen? How come he wasn't here?* Althea waited for him to present himself; she waited to see the face that she had loathed and yet blindly loved for so long.

Why oh why was love like that? Only appearing in the times when it's the last thing you need and then ignoring you when you do go searching for it.

Eloise's steps quickened, and Althea brought her view back to where they were heading, watching sceptically as the kitchen appeared before them quicker than she could register.

Eloise moved fast around her, pushing her back and against the counter so that she could prepare Althea for something that she did not want. Laughter threatened at her lips like a cool wave of pure poison. This wasn't her, *from the simplest thing she knew*. Eloise was horrible in the kitchen; if anything, she loathed it more than anything. Cooking was never her strong suit, but while stating that, she never allowed Althea to eat anything that wasn't tested by her.

"Don't look at me like that," Eloise said, breaking the silence that kept her trapped in a cage.

"Like what?" Althea asked, having to clear her throat to get the very words out.

"Like you've seen a ghost." There was something about how she said it that seemed so familiar, *so her*. But no, this wasn't her; Althea couldn't allow herself to think that it was her when it very clearly wasn't. She glanced up at her, her gold crystallising eyes meeting with hers.

"Where's Kylen? Did my father do something with him so you could sweep me away?"

"I don't know," Eloise claimed with a click of her tongue. "And why would you care if your father has done something with him? Wasn't this whole plan rotating around you killing the guy after you two were wed?" She spoke it with such ease that Althea had to take a sip at the glass of water before her; she had to do anything in her power to get rid of that feeling of bile rising within her throat as well as the little anxiety critters that were crawling their way across her skin before piercing through her beloved Markings.

Eloise harshly dropped a plate of fruit in front of her before pausing to take a better look at her. "*Oh*," she sighed, a mumble of a sob leaving her lips. "Oh, I'm so sorry." she buried her head in her hands and with no warning, she began to sob. "I'm so sorry for everything I put you through, Allie. I'm so sorry for it all." She looked up, and her eyes looked so true to both herself and Althea.

Althea watched the girl before her, watching as Eloise begged for her hand, striking for it so slowly as if she could predict the fact that she was going to pull it away. "*Stop that,*" Althea pleaded, her voice holding back all the pain it threatened to roar with. "Stop pretending that you are someone you are not. It's not doing you any favours and especially not *myself*."

"*Y-you still see the curse in me?*" Eloise questioned, the eeriness of her being terrified of that idea slicing its way into Althea's trembling skin. "It felt so strange to have it removed from my soul. It was like the piece that I always hated the most was being torn away." She shuddered, moving her bone like fingers up and over to each elbow to hold. "How was I missing the piece that took control of my life? That was putting me through torture? I felt ridiculous, but even more so, I felt empty. Unbelievably empty." Eloise's eyes moved off the bench and up to Althea's, clasping the vulnerability shining there and crushing it with a force so that she could barely breathe.

"I then began to demand that your father tell me where you had been sent off to. I thought it had been only mere minutes… I guess you can say I was pretty star-shocked when I found out that it had been years." Eloise paused, and Althea held her breath, demanding that the words didn't sink into her mind as they pleaded with her to. "I found out that he had sent you to marry Kylen and… I knew how much you hurt when he betrayed you, *so I begged him to kill him himself*, but he denied. He said that he needed to speak to you first, *that there may be something there that none of us knew about.*"

Althea felt the insides of her twist and turn as the words finally weighed upon her.

She knows; they all do. They can see through you like you are a ghost. You are one to them.

They see right through me.

They see right through me.

You are a ghost that is so inevitably lonely that no one will be there to remember your name when your father tears you to shreds. They know what you are hiding. Your magick may be trying to keep you safe... but just how long will that go on for? You know that there is no source powerful enough to shield anything away from your fathers' prying eyes. What he wants will find him, even if it is death that hands it over to him.

"He was so concerned when he spoke about it," Eloise went on. "He was afraid on your behalf and on the world's behalf." Eloise sighed a heavy sigh. "This newfound magick he speaks of could seriously hurt people. It could hurt them in ways that weren't ever intended."

Althea shook her head. "I would stop myself from hurting anyone; I'm not him." The words left her before she could fully think about what they meant. She had never viewed her father as the enemy before. How could she when that was the only being she ever knew?

There were times when her love for him faltered, times when she had a glimpse into the true being he was. For instance, it was when he stole the soul of the one true love she ever had. The one soul who had never made her question herself in the slightest. Althea loathed herself for forgiving him for that easily. She had still been feeling the urge to dig for his approval after everything that had happened, *all because she had betrayed him in her own way by running her mouth.*

"I know that, *of course I know that.* Althea, I am worried; I don't want this magick to kill you."

"Don't do that!" Althea yelled as she slammed her hands down onto the countertop, revealing the true temper that crawled at her fingertips. "Don't act like you are my Eloise when you are just a creation of his bad doing." Althea clenched her fists, begging the darkness of her magick to cool down so that she wouldn't be in the position of revealing herself in front of someone who she swore she was sensing the curse in.

"*Althea, please*—I know that you are in a confronting position right now, but—"

"No! There are no buts!" Althea exclaimed through a manic laugh, ignoring as the glass before her flew back from the force of the magick in her words. Althea tried to suppress the sudden fear that Eloise had seen inside her new magick, but thankfully she could tell from Eloise's expression that she figured it was still the curse that had things flying everywhere. "*You can't possibly grasp onto the idea of my position.* I want to believe that it's you; *I so desperately do.* But Eloise—if you truly are *my Eloise*, I am looking into the eyes of a girl who I watched die. Who I watched drop dead to the ice-cold floor without a soul."

She raised a hand to her forehead, stammering with her words. “That did fucked up things to me! That put me through things you could never possibly imagine. So please, just shut up and let me think!”

Althea squeezed the palms of her hands at her temples, her breaths quick and rushed as she tried to think. “Althea, we don’t have time to think you could be killing yourself! You—”

“*You aren't her.*” The words left her lips like a plea to the Gods, begging for them to erase her from this world before things got out of hand—which they had already gotten.

“I—*pardon?*”

Althea shook her head, her lips quivering as she begged the Gods with her screams. “You aren’t her. Eloise, she—she always helped me breathe. Whenever I got stressed or came close to panicking, she would help me take a minute. Her hands would move to my shoulders so she wouldn’t bring too much stimulation to my cheeks as she would usually go to hold, and she would help me take a few breaths. No matter the circumstance, she would help me breathe. *She would just help me.*”

Tears began to roll down Althea’s cheeks as she looked up, watching as the darkness of Eloise’s soul flashed right before her eyes swirling within the frozen warmth of her. “Please,” the redhead whispered. “Please, Althea, this is my only chance at gaining a physical body. I just need a chance at freedom, don’t you understand?” she—the spirit of darkness that had taken hold of Eloises body spoke as she walked around to her, her arms already moving to the point where Althea felt too frozen in time to move away.

Althea listened to the girl beg, her pleas hitting the centre of her heart as if it was an arrow striking for the kill.

Althea felt the girl sob in the crook of her neck, and she froze, turning away as she did not want to be the one who had to do this. “Whoever you are, *go,*” she argued, trying with all of her willpower to push some strength into her voice. But it didn’t work; her voice sounded as flat as a child's cry when she knew her father didn't quite care if she had scraped her knee. "*You want your chance at freedom, so GO!*"

"*No*—no!" Eloise exclaimed. "Please, don't do this. Please let me love you, let me stay here—please protect me as you hadn't been able to before." She pulled back, her face meeting with Althea's crumbling one. "Please! I—" Eloise felt it then, the overriding darkness that had appeared through her very tears, turning them black with blood. Her tears stopped, her expression flattened, and Althea even dared to say that a smirk came to Eloise's chapped charred lips.

Althea looked at Eloise, her eyes searching through the gold of hers and watching with great horror as the darkness began to resurface. "Oh, and to think you might have genuinely believed that I was whole and safe." Eloise—the spirits who decided to give up chuckled, a hum to it that made the candles controlled by the magick above flicker. "How sorry I am…" *she knew it was all a sick joke; she just knew it.*

Althea pushed herself back, meeting with the sharp corner of the bench as she tried to escape from her grasp. "Don't try to run, Althea. I know that you are hiding something, and I know that I want it." Eloise—no, *the spirits of the curse* grinned at her, left-over tears of darkness spilling from the spells of her eyes. "I saw it in your eyes when you lied; I felt it in your soul when you tried to make a mockery of me. I felt it. It was there, and oh, how clear it was!" Eloise laughed as her hands rose from where she had them placed.

Her father must have lent her a little more of the curse than usual because now she could wield it and only those with hearts of inevitable gold had that ability.

Darkness swam in circles around the palms of her hands. Althea pushed herself back, her eyes desperately searching for a way to go around this because no matter how dark of a soul the Gods had given her, she couldn't kill her. *She still loved her.*

She still so deeply cared for the girl before her that she knew no matter what reality she was in, she would not be able to sanely plunge a dagger through her dead heart. Althea just wouldn't be able to. This was the same girl who had stuck by her side through it all. The same girl who had defied her father on multiple occasions just to bring a smile to Althea's lips.

Eloise's soul had been the gold twine that had held hers together, and now that twine was on fire. Leaving tears to burn Althea's eyes despite how hard she tried to hold them back, it was as if her pain was endless, circling back to strike her each time she built herself up.

Althea looked to Eloise, watching as she took a step forward.

She could do this. It was easy. Simply another death.

She was Althea Evangeline, for Gods' sake. She was her father's trained assassin who never flinched away when taking a life. She had managed to successfully sneak through a Kingdom deemed the safest across all Realms.

She was a God. *In some malicious sense.*

Althea was her own God, so why was this sacrifice so difficult?

She took a breath, then two, then another.

Eloise struck upon her, already moving to kill and devour her magick, when she felt the surge of her own magick rise. Time seemed to slow down, and Althea knew she was presented with a choice. She could let her kill her and be done with this life that the curse found joy in torturing… Or she could let her magick kill Eloise, a soul who was already dead and yet lived on through Althea's dreams.

Her hands moved without *her* permission.

Her magick surged without *her* permission.

Althea didn't know what she was doing, but she still listened to what her magick instructed her to do. The cries erupting as she watched the realisation dawn in those golden eyes. How it made Althea's gut drop, leaving her in the worst position possible.

It twirled, bringing magick to her chest that only her ears could hear. It was as beautiful as a melody sung by only the darkest and cruellest of sirens. Her magick wanted to listen to it; her magick wanted her to listen and take it in. Althea's magick didn't give her a say in whether she should listen to it or not. It just forced her to.

Her shaking hands clasped either side of Eloise's face, her thumbs moving to the girls' temples that were already dripping with the blood she summoned. Dark, rich magick dripped from her fingertips, spiralling out as if it was on a mission and she was merely its carrier. "*I'm sorry, I'm sorry, I'm sorry, I'm sorry.*" Her words were rushed. Stooping so low to beg for forgiveness from one of her next victims.

Althea couldn't breathe properly. Each breath choked her, punishing her for the sins she had never once dwelled upon.

The magick asked her to be pure; it asked her to be magick of the light, of the soul, but she was in too much pain to make it anything but villainous. Althea wanted to force herself to suffer; she deserved this pain because she was causing the girl she loved throughout all to scream under her force.

"I'll forever love you—I'll forever love you—please forgive —" Her words faded into a sob she choked on. One so painful that she felt her very soul shattering.

Tears streamed down her inflamed cheeks as she looked at Eloise, feeling as all the waves merely washed over her head. Breezing through her hair and moving on to the next lifetime. How Althea hoped that that one would be kind to her.

Althea sobbed such horrible sounds, whimpers of pure pain escaping her lips as she watched Eloise's eyes roll back. It was such a horrible sight, watching the life of darkness drain from those who had already lost it all. *Those who were already gone.* "Please forgive me—*please forgive me*," Althea rasped, sounding so pathetic just because she had emotions; the words were hardly clear because of how wrapped in her cries they were.

Eloise's power surrounded her before bursting through the colours of her eyes, and she screamed, a loud horrible scream that immediately sent her spine straightening. Her magick wrapped its way around her hands in the most unusual way. It was so like the magick she used to own, except this one was so much more foul, poisonous, and clearer than ever. It spread throughout her blood like a wildfire, and the worst of all was that it felt good.

It felt glorious.

Tears dripped into the puddle at her feet, one that Althea wished she could drown in.

Althea felt the pain surge at her fingertips as Eloise dug her nails into Althea's bleeding skin in an attempt to get the magick away. However, the princess kept her grip strong, her fingers wavering slightly as she begged herself not to hold this memory within her mind.

"Traitor," Eloise whispered as her legs gave way, as her heart finally faltered. It was that word that sent Althea's hands flying back to her very own chest. The word that pushed her lips to break apart in a shocked sob and her eyes to widen with revelation.

Althea had killed her.

She had actually killed her.

TWENTY-EIGHT

KYLEN

Kylen was on his way running down the halls in search of Althea when he found something far more daunting. She had appeared through a doorway, in a rush to leave the kitchen and whatever it withheld that caused her hands to shake ever so rapidly. Althea held them before her chest, her grip deathly tight as her crimson-stained eyes echoed with stories that he was pulled towards.

But it wasn't that that worried him; it was the way that she hadn't even noticed him approaching her, that she hadn't even sensed his presence when he came within a few steps of her.

His hands found her shoulders, and Althea instantly snapped out of her trance, jumping back with a whimper of a yelp as her darling eyes of pain found his, concerning him immediately. "What is it—*are you hurt?*"

Althea looked at him, and he could see the way she pushed her pain back, the way she completely shut off. Althea wanted to cry; she wanted to sob. He could see all of that. It was as clear as day, glistening off her quivering features. Her mouth moved, and she went to speak, but the words wouldn't come out. He realised the words wouldn't leave her tongue, keeping her from being weak and allowing the pain to show. Even as Kylen nodded, encouraging her to continue, Althea just stood there, her lips parting before falling shut.

Anger towards whatever had caused her to act like this struck through him. Althea shook her head, words failing her and instead she continued walking in the direction he had been going. Her gaze swiftly went to the doorway that looked to frighten her. He walked at her side, figuring that silence was the best option as she stared at it with such intent. A thousand thoughts screamed behind those eyes, and yet he could not hear any of them. They passed the doorway, and Kylen saw it then. He saw the girl, her eyes plastered on the roof as tears of darkness puddled at her side. All of which mixed with the blood that he could see dripping from her mouth. Whatever Althea had to do wasn't nice, and now she was left to stare at it and relive the actions he knew stole a piece of her pure heart.

Her hands found her mouth, and she gasped through a sob, breaking Kylen's heart in such a strange way all over again.

This girl was a trained killer, and yet something about seeing this girl truly dead set her off. He knew that look in her eyes; he had felt it himself many years ago when he had found the bodies of his family. It hadn't been their kind of love, not the one you share so intimately, but it had been the love for his family that had sent him to the ground screaming.

Althea held her hands before her, cries erupting from her lips as her eyes scraped over the sight. Kylen looked at her, watching as her weak stance threatened to break from below. He moved towards her quickly, his figure already going to hold her. Her cries filled the hall, and Kylen's chest tightened. He didn't know what had happened, but he knew that he wished she hadn't been the one to do that. Kylen wished there had been another way, any other way so that he could take the burden from her hands.

A part of him had held a grudge against her for so long, a grudge that made his guilt easier to live through. But now, as he held a girl who sobbed into his chest, he knew that that grudge had been a lie. A big, horrible lie. She was just born into the wrong family. Born and raised to be something that he had truly been the one to set off. Kylen had turned her into this monster in his mind because he hadn't wanted to accept the truth. *He was the villain*. He was the one who had murdered an innocent young girl and turned her into what she should never have had to be.

Kylen resented the magick that had swarmed for shelter through her blood. Loathing it for taking away his family and cursing him before he even took his first breath. However, now that it was gone, he was just beginning to realise the effects of his mistakes.

"Oh, Gods—" Althea sobbed, her words barely making sense and yet slicing through his heart with such precision. "What have I done? What have I done?"

She tried to push herself out of Kylen's arms so that he could see the monster he had created, but he refused to do anything but hold her. "I've got you," he whispered, watching as the words floated through her as if he was just a ghost.

"What have I done?" her words were broken pieces to a puzzle, one that he knew would never be whole. "Breathe," Kylen instructed, watching as the words began to choke her. She couldn't breathe; *it was killing her*—her own magick was killing her. She was killing herself for something she'd had to do.

Althea began to gasp. First gasping through sobs and now gasping for air. She needed a distraction, one large, beautiful distraction that would push the air back into her lungs.

Kylen went to do something that he probably wouldn't have regretted but was interrupted when he saw who was at the other end of the hallway. He could sense that magick as if it was water physically filling the room with him trapped within it. Kylen turned with Althea to his chest, waltzing by her side as her scared eyes found his, pulling her so close to him that they almost toppled upon one another. Instead, they smashed into the wall, watching as the arrows of darkness flew past their heads, breaking off into multiple little shards of glass, *all aiming for them.*

Althea stopped gasping. Instead, her head turned over her shoulder. Her eyes looking as if she knew what would be there. *And she did,* because her eyes didn't so much as flinch when she looked toward her father with venom.

"Sorry to ruin such a beautiful moment," he grimaced. "But I do but believe I deserve to have a much-needed chat with my daughter." As he spoke, another ball of such horrifying magick aimed for them, and Kylen did everything in his power to get her out of the way.

A few shards of the painful magick skimmed his arm, shredding the fabric immensely before nicking at the flesh on his arms. Kylen tried not to react, but he knew just how poisonous this magick was, and he knew that he did not want to be on the other end of it.

"Kylen—" Althea gasped; her hand moved up to shelter his raw skin from her father's force.

"I'm alright," he reassured her, plastering a fake stern smile onto his lips. "I'm alright," he repeated. This time more so to convince himself.

The raw, unleashed magick within Althea's fathers' soul sent the windows rattling, the floors rattling. He could sense it; he could smell it. He turned his head, Kylen's eyes already darkened with his own magick as he begged it to rise.

It was afraid. Not answering his calls but rather ignoring them for that very reason. His magick made a mockery of himself, even as he watched the darkness rip from the king's chest like a dark, tempestuous storm cloud. Kylen looked to the King, his mind trying to calculate all the possible outcomes of this situation.

"Listen, I was willing for her sake, to put all of this in our past. I was willing to live out the rest of my days without sending army after army at you. But the moment you stepped into this castle and made *her* cry—you became my enemy again," Kylen seethed through clenched teeth as he wiped his own blood away.

The King's face lightened in colour; his hands became wrapped with a dark shadow. But then, it was as if he was frozen in time because Althea had pushed her way from behind him, heading straight into the eye of the darkness.

It was quick. Swift movements that the King knew every response to.

Kylen sent several spirals of twine like shadows toward her. All of which on an eager mission to help protect her soul.

Althea moved unpredictably quick, and despite masking her worry very well, Kylen could see the way her eyes glanced self-consciously around as her own magick swarmed from within her chest. Spiralling down her arms and already ready for war despite Althea begging for anything else.

It was so different to her father's. So light, so unexplainably clear. First, it had started with a dark afterglow mixed throughout it, presumably from the pain he knew she felt. But then, it had glowed, a raw, powerful magick filling the air that had her father's eyes widening.

Her magick met its mark, and immediately, the King's magick disintegrated, turning to dust right before his very eyes. It was murdered in such a brutal way that Kylen could not help but watch with the utmost admiration. This girl was going to reign with fire, and he was here for every second. Kylen's eyes were practically glowing in awe even as he crept toward the girl. He held his hand out with furrowed brows, begging her to flee by his side while they still could. He had left her behind once before; *he was not going to make that mistake again*.

The King had covered himself with darkness, one that hid him from their plane of sight and yet they could still both hear the frequency of the cursed magick scorching his lungs. The

King was gathering himself up, and Kylen once again beckoned Althea to take his hand.

Althea worked her magick to the best she could, moving to it as it was a dance, one she had spent all her years trapped behind the walls perfecting. Her father threw constant arrows at her, twines that twirled through the air and left blades falling.

Her moves were minimalistic, falling victim to the games it played just to give Kylen some time to go. "Run," she sneered, her head turning to his as her magick shone uncontrollably before her. Althea looked down at it then, giving Kylen a look that told him he needed to realise that his thoughts were right. She had no way to control it. She may be a master at pretending to, but she had no training for it, nowhere near enough lessons spent with Sayah learning to master it to the way she wielded life.

Althea ducked just in time to miss the shot of the shadows, but he was gaining on them, trying to force them into a trap that Kylen could feel across every inch of his skin.

His hand grabbed hers, pulling her to him right as another shadow searched for her.

"We need to go!" he demanded, trying to raise his voice over the thunderous ringing that escaped every time the King sent his dark cursed emotions after them.

Althea shook her head, a murderous calm look scraping the edges of her cheeks. "You need to go," she corrected. "I have something to finish." She turned back then, pulling out the sword, which was the one thing she had learnt with Sayah, preparing to tackle the King down with the only true skills she knew.

Althea didn't even have to think about what to do because her body just responded to it naturally, already knowing her intentions without her having a clue.

Kylen watched her, watching as she danced off his magick as

it was her opponent in a sword fight. The way she fought was the true magick within her, but now was not the time to admire that.

She wanted to kill her father; whatever plan she had evidentially been trying to make before was erased from her mind, replaced with one that involved much more blood, much more venom. "Althea, you are going to get yourself killed!" he seethed through his clenched jaw, ducking his head as the shadows skimmed his hair. "Sleep on it and if you still want to murder him in the morning, count me in; just give me time to plan!" His words were pleading.

Pleading to the only God he would ever believe in.

Kylen thrashed forward as a wave flashed past her, aiming right for him. Kylen held up his hands—his eyes, however, watched as Althea caught the magick with a flash of her blade before slicing the darkness in half. "We need to go!" He knew she would not listen, so he grabbed her wrist, pulling her towards him with such force that she almost fell. "You are going to get yourself killed!" He couldn't think straight; his mind told him to run; his instinct told him to run. But the small, quiet whispers of his heart told him to stay. And for some obscure reason that he would probably never understand, he obeyed.

"Then let me die!" she roared. "I don't care what happens to me—*just as long as he dies*." Kylen opened his mouth to speak, attempting and persuade her onto his side of things, but she had already begun to struggle against him. Her teeth grounded as tears prickled at her near glowing eyes. "He killed her, Kylen!"

Althea held her hand and blade up without even looking over her shoulder, catching the darkness that struck toward them with such ease that Kylen was questioning just whose presence he was in. "*I know*," Kylen reasoned gently, his expression softening and grip loosening. "I know he did, but you aren't going to get her back through his death."

"I *loved* her."

"I know."

There was a flick of a switch in her expression because Althea seemed to hear him for the first time tonight. His words struck right at the small part of her soul that he knew was urging her to run.

Something hit the King, and Kylen looked past Althea, watching with wide eyes as the King became surrounded. Khatri, Atticus, Zaire, Sayah and Uzziah all surrounded him, their magick on full effect. It wasn't enough to keep him down, but it was enough to give them time to run.

Sayah looked at him, meeting his stare, and she nodded; a single nod that held a message he had subconsciously been waiting to hear. Althea looked at him, her expression full of hearted questions that Kylen didn't want to answer. He couldn't, not even as he turned his back on his family for the girl he most definitely owed what was left of his life to. She saw just what he was doing, looking back over her shoulder in confusion as he began to run, his fingers intertwining with hers.

Kylen turned down the hallways with all the speed he could gather, turning every corner with such force, holding onto the little hope that they would make it.

The small door presented itself, and as if it could sense them coming, the doors flew open, inviting the two in. Kylen pulled Althea through it, guiding her before him as the very thought of her behind and in the way of danger frightened him in a way he never knew possible.

They ran down the dirt tracks, trying not to trip on the steepness that came with running down a cliffside. He just had to keep running; that's all they had to do. They had to run; they had to run for as long as it would take. "Where are we going?" Althea demanded breathlessly.

The end of the maze presented itself within minutes. Clouds presenting themselves to him as if they threatened to erupt because of the very presence His Majesty her father brought.

Kylen looked to Althea, finding her eyes on the large boats

before him. "I know you weren't too keen on the seas," he whispered lightly. "But now I'm afraid it's our only out," as he spoke, he climbed up the latter, already turning around and looking down at Althea as if his heart was in his eyes.

He took a breath before extending his hand to her. He waited, his hand floating in the air as she stared at it with a vision so determined that it looked as if she was fixating on all the mistakes of his past.

A tiny, small mumble of a cry escaped from her lips, and then Althea took his hand. An action so small and simple which made it even more confusing as to why it shaped the rest of their lives.

THE CURSED

TWENTY-NINE
ALTHEA

There were no words in any language that could describe the relief Althea saw wash over Kylen when he laid eyes on his family, cat in hand and all. Sayah led them down the docks, running through the maze that led her to wonder just how many times they had done this before.

Zaire followed behind her, Atticus and Uzziah on either side of them. Her head was small, but Althea could make out the white fur bundled within Atticus's arms. Khatri ran at the back, and to Kylen's great amusement, he was carrying a gun. Kylen laughed, a sound so fresh that Althea felt as if she might be sick. She never liked the sea, and now she didn't even truly realise that she was upon it.

Something caught her eyes, and she looked up, finding the small figure that stood on the very edge of her balcony. Althea didn't know if the others could feel it, but she could feel the crackle in the air and the way the waves began to thrash in response. A storm was brewing. One that they needed to hurry up and get away from.

She could feel it underneath her skin and in her blood. She

may not have any of that cursed magick left, but she still most definitely had the taste of it.

A large lightning strike aimed for their ship, striking down so fast that Kylen barely had time to jump out of the way. His eyes slid to hers as they had done many other countless times before. Finding hers as if he was a magnet and she was the force of it.

Althea raised her hands out of instincts, feeling as her magick listened to the pleads she wasn't aware of making. A bright white glistening magick wrapped around them before forcing its way into the air. The magick was like multiple flying hands. All striking up to clasp the lightning that was ever so dark and ever so eery.

Her magick caught it, saving the boat from her father's warpath but leaving a residue behind that she knew would take days to clean. Blood dripped from the sky, coating not only her but the others as her hands slowly and gradually moved from above her head.

Every time she used this magick, every time she beckoned it to lead her in the way of guidance, it felt as if something else had taken control of her. These weren't her movements; this was not any of her doing. She tried to toy it to her advantage, but it seemed to listen to a part of her that was not truly there.

Sayah ran over to her, placing her hands on her shoulders before wiping the splattered blood from her cheeks. "Oh, sweetheart," Sayah said, as if she could see the very pain Althea's heart was feeling. Her face softened, and she pulled her inside the cabin. "Stay here while I go work the boat. We will be out of the bay within a few minutes, and then I will come back."

Before Althea could interject, she was gone, already off and on her feet, as if being in the very same room as she was suffocating.

Althea wanted to ask what all of this would mean? She wanted to ask what would happen next? Her role in their lives had been wiped. How was she to be a Queen if there was no Kingdom to be a Queen of? She felt the ship warp with Sayah's magick, feeling as the water from under it was wielded to their advantage.

The ship moved fast, imitating the art of the sirens who lurked below.

Althea looked around, looking for something to focus on—something that would stabilise the breaths that left her lungs in panic, but everything she looked towards in seek of comfort merely floated through her. There was nothing in the world big enough to distract her; there was nothing in the world that could break away the pain that her heart was feeling.

A whimper escaped her lips, and Althea moved over to Kylen's bed, sitting down on it. Althea had never been on a boat before, and perhaps most boats looked the same—but she could tell this was Kylens. It had photos of him and his family nailed to the walls, along with maps and treasures that she knew he liked to collect stapled too. She ran her hands over her face before tucking her hair behind her ears. Althea looked up and gasped for cold fresh air, begging what was left of the Gods to save her from this misery.

She had wanted to live; she had been so eager to find a way out of this loophole that she hadn't registered the fact that she was walking right into a battlefield.

There was a knock on the door, and Althea looked up, watching as the door opened a crack before Chloe slipped through. Althea didn't think twice; she gathered the cat into her arms. Holding Chloe tightly as the sea threatened her every thought.

There was another knock on the door, and this time, Zaire floated through it. "Kylen wants everyone to meet below," they said, avoiding her eyes with everything in them. Althea wanted to remark something in response, to say something that would leave the air feeling a little lighter, but words were failing her.

How she wished that Zaire wouldn't treat her differently out of pity.

Althea didn't bother to nod; she simply rose. Holding the cat in her arms as she continued out the door. Her breaths halted as the salt air skimmed her nose. Because now the castle was hiding in the distance, and the sea surrounded them as if it was claiming their souls. Kylen's eyes were on it too, and she turned to face him. Turning towards the man who had refused to leave her just minutes ago.

Kylen stared at his castle, at his home, watching as explosion after explosion went off. His Kingdom was burning, and he hadn't chosen his people over her this time. He didn't say anything, but she could feel the pain he was feeling. It was as if the little scraps left of his magick were biting into hers, begging for hers to make him feel something—*anything*. He snapped out of his trance, shaking his head before turning away, neglecting the feelings that devastated his soul. He kept his eyes down, focussing on heading down the stairs that led below.

Althea silently followed, holding the cat to her chest tightly as if she was scared that she too would leave her… or perhaps die at the ends of her hands.

Everyone was already huddled below, a silence between them that she could not help but feel the blame for. Sayah cleared her throat, a soft sigh escaping from her lungs as her eyes moved from head to head. She went to speak and was most likely going to say something inspirational, but Atticus beat her to it.

"So, what now?" Atticus asked, looking to Kylen as if he could say something that would make it all better. "What do we do? Where do we go?"

"I don't know," Kylen admitted. "I have no idea." He looked to Althea, trying not to wince under her lifeless gaze. His voice lacked emotions; it was dry as the desserts that she read about up north-east. "Do you have any ideas, Althea?"

Did she have any ideas? That had to be a joke, right? She had no clue, none whatsoever. Her home was as good as dead, and now her new home—*Kylen's home,* had turned into a Kingdom like hers: as good as dead. There was nowhere for her to go—but she could not possibly tell them that as then they would blame it all on her.

Althea's eyes stayed on Kylen's, watching as he waited patiently for her to think. If only he could see just how painful these thoughts were. She could feel the ideas on the other side of a barrier. They were right there, but they were just out of hand's reach.

"*Wait*... there is a place—" Sayah abruptly whispered as if she was caught in a thought. "I can remember somewhere but it isn't that clear." Her eyes moved to Khatri as words flew through her head. Devastation lined her lips, but that didn't stop her from saying, "Harlia." Her expression looked as if she had choked on the word, as if she hadn't meant to say it, and yet she did.

Althea knew that word. It was a myth, a story that she used to read about.

"Harlia? The myth?" Uzziah asked through a laugh. "Yeah, as if we would make it anywhere near there."

It's a real place mother, a real, real, place.

"It's locked," Sayah confirmed, stealing Althea's attention. "It's locked, but we have the key," she corrected herself. Her attention turned towards Althea, causing her lungs to halt. There was this haze around Sayah, a colour to her aura that had Althea confused. Usually it was a subtle mix between red and orange, but now it was darker. Almost blue.

"What?" Althea questioned with a hiccup of a laugh, her voice coming out ever so broken and raw from how hard she had been trying to stop herself from crying. It had been hard to stop the sobs from erupting from her cracking soul. "I have heard rumours of Harlia being a true place… but I never thought anything of it—that it truly was true?"

"You are the key, and it is a real place." Sayah said, and once again, from the siren's own expression, she looked to be confused by what she was saying. "You are the key—you are the key—how do I know that you are the key and that it is a real place?" Sayah asked, muttering the last bit to herself.

Those four words, *you are the key,* brought back a memory that she had worked so hard on remembering, and now she wanted to forget everything about it. Althea locked eyes with Sayah as words, memories, lives that she did not remember living flashed before her eyes.

Harlia, the Kingdom of Gods. The Kingdom of those who were lost throughout the journey of battles. *It mourns.* It mourns for the lives that would forever be remembered as trapped. Althea knew the stories; she knew them all now—so how come she hadn't remembered them before. They, too, seemed to be distant memories of what her mother had told her when she was younger. Her mother was from the old lands; in fact, she had lived there, but only more recently—*it was referred to as Shinrin.*

A disguise that had been used to hide what true power hid beneath the surface of that Kingdom. *Mother is beginning to remember her past life.*

Althea used to have dreams of there; she remembered that now. She used to have such vivid dreams that some mornings she swore that she had been journeying to there across the night.

"She is the key," Kylen breathed. He looked to be intending to ask it, but he spoke it as if it was a statement. Althea looked at him, silent pleads in her eyes. He would not do what she thought he would—*no, he couldn't*. That would be absurd. Althea didn't want to be used as the key—she did not want to have that leverage hanging over her head like a noose.

"Holy Gods," Khatri beamed as he looked at Sayah. "Holy—holy Gods!"

Sayah looked at him, a look of reminiscence through her

eyes. "Yeah," she muttered. Althea looked to the siren, noting how her fingers rotated around, performing a spell that she figured helped the others realise what Althea and her were too realising. "But what I don't understand is how I didn't remember all of this until tonight. How my dreams didn't make sense until I found the scorched bodies of my guards. Y-your mother," Sayah spoke as she turned to Althea, "your mother *took away my memories.*"

Althea furrowed her brows. "Excuse me?" She gaped, although now she was slowly too remembering all that her mother had told her. *Why was she remembering all of this now that she was on the run from her father?* "But that doesn't explain why I didn't remember the land of the Gods."

"Your mother had to protect her land, so she stole the memories of my life in Harlia. She was the Ruler there, alongside her parents—although no one ever really saw them." Sayah spoke, and Althea could hear and physically feel the heartbreak within her voice. "When she went to marry your father, we had a disagreement, and I don't know if that stirred her into doing what she did, but either way, she used her abilities to wipe my memories, to make me think that I was a mere maid within her Kingdom… That is why I called you 'of Harlia' when we met, it just flowed off of my tongue."

"I—" Althea watched Sayah, no words leaving her trembling tongue.

"Okay…" Zaire gaped as they tried to make some sense of Sayah's words. "I appreciate you telling us about your revolution, but do we really think that Althea's very presence will be able to unlock a whole Kingdom that has been locked away and wiped from minds for years now—not to mention its locked under an impossible spell to break? It seems like quite a long, *long* shot."

"Well, what do you suggest we do, Z?" Kylen asked on what felt like Althea's behalf. "Are you going to just sail the seas for the next several years of your life? Until death greets you in its own beautiful and majestic way? I know it does seem like a long shot, but if Althea truly is the key—" his words stopped, choking him as he turned back to her before looking at Sayah. "Does that mean… If Althea's mother was the Princess of Harlia, that means… she is a *direct* descendant of the Gods—?"

Sayah seemed to understand what he was suggesting because her own eyebrows raised slightly, and a gasp left her tongue. "Oh my Gods, Althea, you haven't just been gifted by the Gods *you* are a direct descendant."

Her words paused and Althea looked between all of the faces staring at her. "None of this makes any sense. One, how are you all suddenly realising this. Two, why would the Gods choose me? Three, it still doesn't make sense?" Althea practically laughed.

"I know dear child, it doesn't make any sense for me either. All I know is that when I first felt the magick of your father surge threw mine… something felt off." Sayah looked to Kylen, her eyes heavy. "I think that's when I began to understand, to remember everything your mother and I found out." Althea could see the lies in her eyes, words, facts, that Sayah was prepared to keep from her.

Sayah took a deep breath before reaching for the wall. Holding onto that as her knowledge began to spill. "*Harlia* was the land of the Gods, and if your mother was from there, *which she was*, then that means your magick is directly from there too and not just a gift to your bloodline. Althea, your magick is directly from the Gods, and the rumour has always been that those with direct connections to the Gods can get through the barriers; *or even open them to the world.*" Sayah spoke so enthusiastically like she had just saved the world that Althea threatened. "Who knows what hope lays on the other side."

Kylen's hand found the pits of Althea's back, his hand like a breeze that flowed through her lungs with ease, one that she could breathe for the rest of her life.

"Althea, do you remember anything more about your mothers' home?" Kylen asked in a gentle tone that caused her to squirm uncomfortably. She hated when someone spoke to her as if she was a child, as if she was someone who needed to be tiptoed around. As if she was a ticking time bomb mere seconds away from exploding.

"No," she admitted, clenching her jaw. Her hold on the cat increased as she looked down to avoid their gazes. "I don't remember anything other than the stories that she told me. Even then, those aren't clear."

Kylen nodded, looking to Sayah about what to say next. "That's totally fine," Sayah said, a soft smile against all on her lips. "We can train your mind to reach into your mothers' soul. I can feel your mother's magick within you, so perhaps there is a way we can reach her after all. And then perhaps there is a chance that you can unlock Harlia for good."

Mother is confused. Mother doesn't understand what is happening. Harlia is meant to be a lace of myths, a place of dreamers; it cannot be real. That's absurd.

Althea shook her head, a small tight laugh leaving the darkest pits of her soul. "I don't understand. Harlia isn't real. My mother was the Queen of Shinrin but her home got wiped away with the war. I'm not a descendant of the Gods—sure I may be gifted by them but as if I would be a descendent of them." *They wouldn't treat one of their kind like this.* She turned around, leaving Kylen's touch behind as she disappeared up the stairs.

Her heart was racing, trying to catch up to the speed of her mind.

They were planning to go to the lands that Althea had come from. The lands that had been wiped from her mind too. *Why was it that the world itself had been wiped of this history?* No books mentioned anything of it; in fact, they said the opposite, whatever that may be.

They were planning to figure out just what the connection was that Althea shared with the Gods. They wanted her to train. Didn't they realise just how draining that was? Just how draining it was to train the magick that she still didn't want. She knew her mother had this magick too, and it was now her duty to protect it, but that was all too much. She had grown up thinking that this magick was bad, that all magick that was given to one through their bloodline was wild and dangerous. It felt unnatural for her to be in this position; it felt like a newfound burden that she didn't want to carry.

Althea laid back on Kylen's bed, ignoring the burning pain that wrapped its way throughout her bones.

Eloise was dead.

Her father wanted her dead.

She was a key to the Kingdom of the blessed, which was also rumoured to be dead.

And now, all the memories that had been wiped from her past were rushing back for her.

This was like a rewritten fairy-tale, and she was now put in the position of finding the deeper meaning within it.

Chloe laid at her feet, like a constant reminder that this was real. That she was now out at sea, floating in a tiny little wooden box as her father most likely prepared troops to be sent after her. He had most likely already planned her death too, preparing for the glorious impact her mythical souls' magick would make upon his horrid one.

And how powerful that truly would be.

The door opened after what felt like hours of staring at the roof as the ship rocked beneath her. Kylen appeared through it, an expression of neutral emotions holding still on his features as he pulled up a small seat by her side. He pulled over a bucket full of warm water before revealing a cloth to her. She laid still, closing her eyes with a deep painful sigh as he used the cloth to run over her face.

He was so gentle, not wanting to cause any more pain upon her quivering lips. The blood slowly turned the water brown, a murky colour that she did not look at but rather looked away from.

"I'm sorry about Eloise," he whispered in a tone that she swore she imagined. Althea stayed quiet, trying to ignore the burn of tears that threatened to erupt. After a moment, she cleared her throat, ignoring how her words quivered as she spoke, preparing herself for the burden her words held. "I'm sorry about your Kingdom."

He spent around half an hour wiping away the blood from her skin. He stayed quiet, knowing that she preferred that over talking. Was that what the next few weeks were going to look like? Her being a damsel and now a vulnerability that Kylen had to weigh his every thought over? Her dreams were full of nightmares. Visions of the night before flashing before her very eyes. As if it was cursing her for what she'd had to do. Althea was a murderer; she had always been one, so why did she now feel so different to the others? She had killed many before, taken so many lives that she had lost count, but none of them; none of them felt like this.

Althea looked over her shoulder, and once again, she found the face in the darkness that was following her like a lead. The features of Althea all made a mockery of her as she tossed and turned throughout the nightmares.

Leave me alone! She begged. Please, oh, please, just leave me alone! Don't you understand that I am tired! She screamed at the top of her lungs within her dreams, begging for anything or anyone to answer her. This wasn't fair. *It wasn't fair in any aspect.*

Althea clawed at her eyes, begging for the memories, for the stained-glass horrors of her mind to leave her be. But they just weren't listening.

Strong hands gripped her shoulders, shaking her to wake with such force that she was bound to wake up with wide eyes. Her whole body jolted up as she felt the bile rise within her throat. Her whole body burned as Kylen passed Althea the bucket.

Sobs erupted from her lungs as she threw up pure black blood. Staining not only the bucket but her lips too. Painting them a dark black that she expected Kylen to be revolted by.

His hand rubbed circles around her back, soothing her in such a way that no other had ever done before. Soothing her in such a way that just pushed her to scream. Didn't he get it? She didn't want to cry; it pained her too much to cry, and it was far too exhausting. Althea brushed his hand away, going to wipe her chin with her sleeve before his hand caught hers.

Kylen didn't so much as hesitate as he reached up with a lukewarm cloth, wiping the blood away from her decaying soul. His touch was once again gentle, and Althea turned away slowly, facing the wall of the ship as she had done for the past twenty-four hours or so. Every few minutes, she would wake. But this *—this nightmare,* this game; it was all so much better than continuing with life because she could just not do it.

The weight of the world was on her shoulders, and despite already being there for several years now, it was only just now holding full effect over her. It was only just now piercing her heart with the finest blade, urging her to crumble beneath the sheets.

Althea stared at the roof, watching as a new day began to rise through the corner of her eye. A beautiful sunrise lit up the room that Kylen had been in and out of throughout the past few days. She stayed as still as she possibly could, the confusion and anger riding her features as she thought about screaming at the world to ask why it was continuing as if nothing was happening? *Why was it continuing as if the people weren't being tortured upon these lands?*

All these 'whys' and all these questions were there, but nothing ever held the answers that she so desperately sought. Why did they not hold the answers? Didn't the Gods understand how she longed for them?

Althea didn't move.

She didn't move, and sometimes, she would even forget to breathe. Her heart was heavy, and it held her to her sheets. Holding her in such a paralysing position that nothing began to seem real.

This depression held effect over her life like nothing had ever dared to before. There had been countless reasons as to why she might have already gone through this before, but every time that idea suggested itself to her, she denied it. Focussing on something to fight for.

When Kylen betrayed her and used her own word against her, she focussed on getting revenge. And when Eloise was taken from her grasp, she planned to do anything to gain her father's forgiveness.

Because against all, she was still just a small broken soul. A child who had made a mistake and now felt forever in debt to the man who was out for her head.

Althea wouldn't say it aloud, not just yet, but she was done with that game of chasing her father's tail. She didn't need his forgiveness; she didn't want it. Because he was dead to her, he was just another victim who was going to feel her pain.

Althea didn't have a peaceful sleep on the fourth night of their days at sea, but she did have dreams of her slitting her father's throat with her dagger, watching as the dark black blood that she had run from for all these years poured out. And then, when she was finally at peace, the faces and visions came again. She saw Eloise and felt her death radiate through her entire body again as if she was drowning.

THIRTY
KYLEN

Kylen stood outside of the doors that trapped her on the other side. Althea's very heartbeat filtered through the air. Her body was so limp and so frail that he swore he was hiding a corpse from the eyes of his family. He knew her feelings; in fact, he knew them probably more so than she did. He had mourned for countless periods of times now, all of which repeating the same process that drowned any light from his rapidly beating heart. He may have mourned in a different way to Althea, but nonetheless, he mourned, and he pained for the lives that he had loved most.

He was an expert at mourning, and he wanted to help her. Still, his every touch seemed to be burning hers. She was sheering away from him as if his curse was physically burning through the delicacy of her very skin. As if she was repulsed from his very touch because of the emotions that it held.

Kylen turned away, looking towards the deck where all his people were set to work. Emotions were washing over him that seemed to feel more and more evident with every step. There was something there that made Kylen want to hold Althea and never let go.

He used to be repulsed by her very touch, but now things were different. Now he had seen a break within her walls, and he had the sudden urge to make sure that no more pain would come to her.

Kylen *hated* the Gods, and as Sayah had suggested, she had some strange, intertwined connection to them, so why didn't he hate her?

He stalked his way up the stairs, meeting Sayah, who had just gotten back from one of her many swims. Her scales were still relatively on display, even though her tail was hidden. She took a deep breath, her eyes going to her feet as if she could physically feel the pain that slipped off the Princess of Aeonia. The same princess who was now on the run by their sides.

"Any new news?" he asked to distract his mind. Holding his voice straight as his hands gripped the helm with such strength, he felt the ship rock beneath him, but it was not that that made him want to drown.

"No," Sayah mournfully admitted. "These seas have emptied because of the news that he may be setting sail over them in the next few days, so it's hard to find anything, but what I do know is that the further we head towards Harlia, the more potential threats we will face. It's most likely true that the King has figured out what we are doing." She tutted as her fingers anxiously fiddled with the wood at her side. "So, he will most likely send out ships upon ships to reach ours. All in the hope that we die."

"Not we, but she," Kylen corrected her. "You know you could all leave, right? I'm giving you the option to go and start a new life somewhere. This is my mess that I'm ready to face, but that doesn't mean that you or anyone here should be lost along the way."

Sayah tipped her head, a soft smile of pride on her lips. "It's hardly your mess."

"Oh, but it is. I started this war with her, and then I was on the verge of marrying her. She is here and in this position because of me."

"Ky, whether we had invited her to our Kingdom or not, she would have still received her Markings. She would have still been outed to be not what she is said to be." Sayah wrapped her magick around the boat, steering it slightly more to the left. "But I get what you are saying, and I have to decline. I might not speak for everyone, but I am staying. Althea needs to be trained, and I am prepared to do just that. What she just went through—what she just had to do was life-changing, which is why I'm letting her rest—"

"Rest?" Kylen asked through a laugh, one that turned heads. "S, she is killing herself! Do you not see or hear the way her soul is turning into one like mine? You may be letting her rest, and I may be allowing her this time because I don't want to be any more of a burden, but she is dragging herself to her grave. She is vomiting up black blood, for God's sake!" Kylen ran a tired hand over his face, wincing slightly as he felt the true exhaust that hid behind his features.

"The curse was a part of her soul for a long time, Kylen. It got ripped from her and basically opened a large wound. She is vomiting up black blood because the other night, when we were in her father's cursed presence, that wound got ripped open again, and now her soul is trying to survive through the yearning it has for the darkness." Sayah sighed, a tired old sound leaving her lips. "Kylen, go rest," Sayah urged her words like a pure stab to his heart.

"No, I don't need to rest!" he exclaimed. "You know what I need? I need my Kingdom—I need my people—I need just something to hold onto!" he didn't know what he meant; he couldn't make sense of it. But he knew what he was trying to say; he knew that he just wanted something that would not slip from under his clasp.

He ran both hands over his face before turning away. He

walked multiple steps to the edge of the ship, and with a deep breath, he forced himself to calm down.

Something from the corner of his eye caught his attention. It was like a rope, pulling at his throat, at his heart, beckoning for him to look her way.

Kylen looked over his shoulder, and to his great surprise, Althea stood there. She looked as if she had been visibly shot. Her eyes were full of exhaustion, her cheeks were hollowed out, and her expression told millions of stories that he would pay all of the money in the world to hear.

The worries—the pain, all the hurt that had been hanging over him slipped from his shoulders. Releasing some weight that allowed him to move. And not a second later, he was running down to her. His hands were already moving up to brush against her cheeks. "You're up?" he asked, his expression turning into one of a quizzical look.

"Really?" Even if it was a half-hearted remark of a comeback, it still brought a sly smirk to his lips. "I need to talk to Sayah." She didn't move out of his touch, and something sparked within his ill soul.

"Of course." He removed his hands from her cheeks before waving the siren over. A frail, cold, smaller hand found his, and he looked back, meeting Althea's dead stare.

"Alone," she corrected.

"Why? I'm sure that I can help."

"Kylen, I don't think you can help me with this." Althea said as her hands moved quickly to roll up her sleeves. There was a hiccup to her voice, one that sounded to hold her voice back from breaking. She revealed her wrist to him, and it was a sight that looked to be from one of her very nightmares. One that Kylen wanted to shed for her. "Oh."

The seas rocked beneath them, and Althea's whole body flinched. Her now veined with black blood hands flew out to the front of Kylen's shirt that clearly told him that if she was going down, he was going too, which was somewhat astoundingly alright with him. He moved before she could pull away, his very hand finding hers before turning it over so that he could see the black veins that ran down her arms.

Surprisingly enough, Zaire, Atticus, Uzziah, and Khatri all were keeping quiet. Their eyes were down on the tasks at hand as Kylen looked at Sayah in panic.

Sayah waved her hand before him, brushing away his worries. “It’s alright. It’s your body telling you that you need to release some of this magick you are holding,” she stated simply. “I know it’s frightening, but you did the right thing by showing us. Would you care to start training now? We can do a simple spell that will help ease the nightmares.”

Althea stared at her in a way that made her look to be planning her murder. “I’m not frightened,” she stated. Her expression, however, changed when she heard the comment about the dreams. And that seemed to persuade her whole attitude. It wasn’t enough to spark some challenge into her heart, but it strived her to ask the much-needed questions. “If I train, will that stop the nightmares—the visions?” she asked. Her voice was as quiet as a mouse. Her tone lacking any emotion whatsoever.

“No. Your nightmares will never leave you, but through training, through releasing your magick; you will find a way to lessen the darkness, to find a spark of light,” Sayah replied.

Althea looked at Kylen, and he could see millions of seas floating throughout her eyes. She waited, waiting for Kylen to do something, to act in some way. He didn’t know what it was that she needed, but he nodded. A small smile that this time wasn’t so pitiful but rather full of hope plastered onto his lips.

“Okay,” her voice was still hollow, and it was most likely him stretching the truth. But he swore he could hear a spark of hope. A spark of something more.

“Alright.” Sayah grabbed the girl’s hand, squeezing it

slightly. “Would you like to be out here or away from everyone else?” she asked.

Sayah was trying. She was trying truly incredibly hard to try with this girl. He could see it in the way she spoke. The way she suggested things. There was a pain in her eyes, pain that was left by none other than Althea’s mother. There had been a relationship between them, a pure, beautiful relationship. One that must have been heavy upon Sayah’s shoulders because she had been disappearing to the sea for long hours recently. And Kylen could always locate the new redness of her eyes every time she returned aboard.

“Away, perhaps.”

Kylen watched as Sayah guided Althea away. Disappearing through the doors that he had stood out of for several days now. “Do you think it will kill her?” Kylen asked as Khatri appeared at her side.

“Who?” Khatri questioned, “Sayah or Althea?” That was the question that had been weighing over him for days. He wanted to save Althea—he needed to find her some hope before the curse rid him of this misery, but what would it cost? His Kingdom had already been lost, and Kylen hadn’t even allowed himself to think about that yet because each time he did, the curse found another extraordinary way to weave its way into his soul. Things were going to be lost, but the question of *who* scared him more than anything. “I’m not sure.”

Kylen watched as night approached, standing about in different spots on the dock across the course of the day. He watched as the stars began to appear, and Sayah retreated from his bunker. She walked to the edge of the platform, the salty air doing wonders to the wilderness and darkness of her hair. She ran a hand through the tight, locked curls, and before Kylen could get a word to her, she dived overboard. Disappearing between the dark waves of the sea.

Kylen looked to the windows, looking to where he could see

the slight movement of Althea. He headed towards those doors, standing before them and taking a single breath before taking the wild act of opening them. He expected Althea to be in bed, the same bed that she had been in for long hours of each day every day. But for once, she was not there, and if he hadn't located her by the desk, he might have dared to say he could have been worried. Kylen exhaled as he watched her hand reach forward to the frame glued to the desk. She ran a finger over the painted faces that Sayah had gifted him for his birthday a few years ago.

"You look like your sister," she noted in a quiet voice.

"You think?" Kylen lazily replied as he tried his best to ignore the emotions that now stirred. It brought back memories of when people used to say that to him. To when he would take little Elara into town and show her the wonders of his people.

"Mhm," she mumbled as she looked toward Kylen. His eyes were already on hers, watching as a slight blush rose to her extremely pale cheeks.

"Many used to say that. They used to say Huntio looked like my mother. And that my sister and I looked like my father." he mused with a slight smile. "I know that all say that you look like your mother. And from a touch of personal experience, I can agree. You know, I don't remember much from that... *night*. But I do remember the brief few seconds of seeing you in your subconscious."

"I don't want to think about it."

Kylen nodded, understanding all too well. "Very well."

Slowly, she walked back to the bed. Sitting down on the edge of it before shuffling over to make room for him. "Tell me about them?" she questioned. "You don't have to tell me anything, but I am curious to hear about what type of people they were. Perhaps it will distract my mind."

Kylen listened, feeling slightly strangled on whether he should speak of them. It wasn't a topic he often spoke about. It wasn't a topic he would talk to anyone about. Sayah used to always overwhelm him with questions regarding them even though she knew them well. It was more so because she wanted to keep the idea of them alive in his mind. But he would always shut her down. That sparked the friendship between Zaire and him. They wouldn't ask; they wouldn't pry. They would merely continue with their life. Living it as if not a soul in the world could hurt them… and then one did.

Kylen sat on the edge of his bed, shuffling his feet slightly over as his eyes glanced anxiously around. "You really want to know?" he questioned with a furrow to his brows. Althea nodded, and Kylen sighed, figuring out where he should start. "The rumours were that they were horrible people. People who didn't even know them, may I add, spoke of them in such horrendous ways. But truthfully, they were the most kind-hearted people I knew. They were the best people I will forever know, and I am beyond grateful for having been blessed with them as my parents, even if it was for a short time only."

Althea listened, tilting her head slightly to the side as she watched the words flow from his lungs. "They cared for all. All the Kingdoms' people, all the people who visited through my Kingdom. And I believe with whatever is left of my heart that they would have adored you too."

Althea pulled her knees up to her chest, her eyes lost in thought as she moved them away. "How—how did you find out that they had died? You never told me this last time, and I never wanted to pry," she asked.

Out of all the questions she could have asked, she asked that, and oh, how strangely it had captivated him. "How did I find out that they died?" Kylen asked, repeating the very words that she had spoken.

A blush seemed to rise to Althea's cheeks, and Kylen quickly began to speak, cutting her off with the very story she had asked to hear. "I was on my way to meet with an old friend in the Realm over when I had begun to hear the whispers of the shadows. They had always been there, but these whispers were far louder than the others. I ignored them to the best that I could at first, but then I heard the whispers that were so dark and inevitably evil that I could not ignore even if I was to try. I turned on my way back home as fast as I could. Riding through the night and day, and then when I reached my Kingdom, the walls of my castle, I began to see the visions of my family. I saw my siblings playing out in the fields, playing with the cats and dogs of the wild. And then, as I walked closer to the doors, I saw my parents waiting for me. My mother was urging me to turn back; she urged me to retreat to anywhere but here. But my father—he simply said sorry." Kylen took a breath. He could feel the emotions running down his spine like running water.

"The moment I stepped inside, I could smell their blood. It was infused with the stench of the curse, and instantly I knew what had happened. My mother was outside of my siblings' quarters. Her body was devoured of emotions completely; no soul left behind. My father was found a few metres in front of my siblings, protecting them from where he was posted in the doorway. My siblings were together. My sister on the left and my brother on the right. They were all surrounded by their own blood. Dark black blood leaked from all of their eyes." He took a shuddering breath before turning back to Althea. Her features were utterly broken, with visible tears of shock filling her eyes.

"*Oh shit,* I'm sorry I did not mean to make you cry," Kylen quickly apologised. "If it was too dark, you could have said something, you know—I would have stopped—"

"No, it's not that. It's just that out of all the things I kept track of, I never found out that the curse had been the infectious thing to kill your family," Althea explained through hurried breaths. "I thought they were murdered just out of cold blood or something of the sort!" She looked to her feet, her expression emptier than before, and Kylen cursed himself for telling that awful story.

Althea looked at a loss for words as she looked at him, her eyes searching through his as if he might hold what she was searching for. "My siblings and parents did die from the curse, yes. But it wasn't *your* magick that killed them, so don't go blaming yourself or any of that self-pity shit. One, I don't need it; it will just simply make us both depressed. And two, you didn't kill them. It's as simple as that. Your father's magick killed them, and yes, the magick may have belonged to you as well, but you did not kill my family."

The expression in her eyes began to fade, and Kylen released a breath. She moved her fingers before her, and Kylen noticed that the dark veins had disappeared slightly. There were still a few visible to the eyes, but he for once tried to focus on the positives.

She inched her wrist away before laying down on the bed. "Could you please go—or at least until I am asleep?" she asked; there was self-depicted sadness in her voice. Almost as if she was longing to be taken to the depths of the seas.

Kylen looked towards her, his eyes narrowed with confusion. "Why?" he asked, catching Althea with a splash of surprise as she looked back up to him.

"Because I want to be alone," she stated with a touch of a bite that Kylen unknowingly longed for.

"But I don't want to be alone, and since I don't know if you should be either, then this is the best bet."

"Kylen, leave me be."

"No." Kylen could see how his words were slipping so easily under her skin, but it was good that it brought back some of her bite. "This is my bed, my ship. And I'm not saying that to claim it as my territory but rather instead saying that you cannot come aboard my ship and start acting like you own the place. Help out —*please*. In a few days, we will arrive at Harlia, and from beyond there, who knows what will happen." Kylen sighed as he rose to his feet. "I know that you are mourning, I know that you are in pain—"

Before he could finish what he was going to say Althea's voice of pure agony rang through the air, and Kylen's words rang dry.

THIRTY-ONE
ALTHEA

"No. Do not act like you know what I feel when you so clearly do not. *I had to kill her.* I killed her!" Althea began to move, sheering away from the sheets as if they were poisoning her flesh. Poisoning her skin and bones. "I loved her, and I killed her! Your family died, and I'm very sorry for that, but you did not have to kill them. You did not feel the life drain from their souls as your magick took over with no say. And I am so sorry for what my father did to your Kingdom, your home. I am past the point of sorry—but you will never understand." Althea was crying now, stalking towards him as her lips quivered with every breath. "I felt her die, I know that there was nothing left of her, but I still felt her die—and it should have been me!"

Something turned dark within Kylen's eyes as he shook his head and reached for her. "*Never say that again*—it should not have been you and I will thank whatever Gods that are out there that it wasn't. Do you understand me, Althea?" She turned away while holding her head in her hands, an expression of pain lining her lips. She pushed Kylen, urging him to leave the room that they were in. "Please just leave me alone!" she begged; couldn't he see the desperation on her tongue. Couldn't he see just how desperate she was?

With a swift move, Kylen grabbed at Althea's hands, turning her to him. "Sweetheart, I know you are in pain; I know you are hurting. But you must continue with your life to let her spirit live on. Don't you understand that? I've allowed you to rest and mourn for the past several days now, but enough is enough. You are killing yourself, and you need to live, and if not for yourself, then for her."

She stared at him, silent tears nicking the edge of her cheeks as her lips lay slightly parted. "But I can't," she admitted with full regret. "Because every time I take a breath, every time I look around, every time I feel the emotions that my heart carries—*I end up feeling so incredibly guilty.*"

So that's what it was. That was what was locking her to the bed and tying the ropes around her body until she was nothing more than a lost soul out at sea. Althea could see it all making sense in his head, she could see the pieces piecing together, and she wanted nothing more than to forget that she had said anything at all. "Come with me."

Althea pushed him away before turning to walk back to the bed. "Just let me feel bad for myself, please. Why aren't you thrilled? I would expect you to be joyous in a situation like this." She scoffed before tucking her messy hair back over her shoulders. The ship rocked beneath her feet, and despite how many continuous times it had done that over the past few days, Althea still flinched and grasped for the bed.

Kylen's hand found hers, and this time in a more determined and hopeful voice, he repeated, "come with me."

"Kylen, I can't be bothered by any of this. What don't you understand?"

"I'm trying—*trust me,* I am trying to understand that and be respectful of it but come with me." As he spoke, Kylen pulled her forward, his fingers linking with hers, and what a strange emotion washed over her when she felt the scars of his hands entangle with her fingers.

Althea sighed, a short, sharp, half-hearted sigh that was more for herself than anyone. She allowed Kylen to pull her along, more so because she could not find it in her heart to fight against his will.

He guided her outside, and instantly, the salty wind brushed against her nose. Pushing a breeze of fresh air down her lungs. Althea looked around, her eyes widening slightly as she took in the glorious view of the sky that was populated with millions of stars. There were so many planets, universes, and worlds out there beyond her imagination. Was there a place out there for her where she was still happy alongside her mother and Eloise? Was there a world out there where Kylen did fulfil his promise and take her away all those years ago, saving her from those years of pure misery?

Kylen tugged at her hand, and that small action spoke invisible words that guided her to continue walking. He guided her to the very front of the boat, only stopping when they reached the wooden railing. "Is this truly how you plan to kill me?" she asked as she wiped the tears away.

Kylen laughed, a breeze of music that was swept away with the wind. "Very funny. If I were to get away with your murder, I would prefer to do it in a much more glorious way. For say, spending long hours torturing your beautiful soul instead of drowning it."

Althea pulled her hand from his grip, leaving a coldness in his wake. "So, what am I doing out here other than catching a cold?"

Kylen ran his index finger along the railing, feeling as the salt-infused wood melted away against his very touch. "Stand here," he said, taking a step back, revealing a small wooden barrel she assumed he wanted her to stand atop of.

"Pardon me? Kylen, I am not standing on some wooden barrel in the middle of the sea—especially on a boat. I don't trust neither—"

"Ship," he almost automatically corrected her. "And you don't have to trust 'the boat' or the water, but rather trust *me*."

Althea dragged her eyes to him. Meeting the dark rich brown of them that she swore a softness hid within. "But that would be awfully stupid of me to trust you, don't you think?"

"Yes, but they do say whoever ends up marrying me would have to be somewhat stupid. So would it truly be such a crime?"

Althea looked down to the barrel before taking a small step forward, a small step that sent shudders of the wind down her tight spine. She sighed, a deep sigh that was one she released to hide the fear that bottled in her stomach. "Don't you dare let me fall in, Noxwell."

Kylen shook his head, brushing a hand back and through the dark mess of hair that coated his head. "I wouldn't dare."

Her left foot met with the top of the barrel before her right foot followed. She stood there with the breeze running through her hair. Her magick circled throughout it and untangled the matted locks that were a result of her not moving for several days. Her grip was white as she held onto Kylen's hands. Her breaths were harsh, mimicking the sound of her beating heart. "I'm up here, and I'm not feeling any different," she quickly said as she glanced back down at him, trying to ignore the splash of the sea that the seas greeted her with.

Kylen began to move, his hand loosening on hers, which Althea quickly disagreed with. Her nails dug into his skin, already pricking for blood as she turned on him. "Don't you dare let me go," she seethed through clenched teeth, grimacing as the salty water splashed at her skin.

"Relax." As he breathed, his hands moved to her waist, holding her steady as his eyes stayed locked with hers. "Close your eyes." She was never one to take orders from anyone. If anything, she was one to give out the orders, and Althea Evangeline always expected people to listen. But for some strange reason, her heart was beginning to trust him again, and so her eyes closed, focussing on the grip of the hands that drew circles over her hips. "I want you to picture that pain that you feel. The guilt, the mourning. All of it," he instructed, earning a frown from her. "Picture it all and pull at it. You will see a thread of magick before you, and you will want to crush it." Althea shook her head in response to his words. "You are in pain because of what you had to do to survive, and I am so proud that you are still alive to this day, but nonetheless, I want you to crush it. Crush that magick and watch it fall to its knees."

Althea's breaths began to increase, and Kylen steadied her as her legs began to tremble. "With everything in you, I want you to scream," he spoke, and this time it wasn't a suggestion, nor a statement, but rather an order.

Althea shook her head as she moved her gaze down to Kylen. "I will wake the others up. I can't." It was a weak excuse because they both knew she would be fine with waking the others up. But from what she could tell by Kylen's expression, he was set on getting her to scream.

"Scream, Althea. Let out all that extra power that you don't want. Let out all that magick that you can feel burning through your veins. You have a connection to the Gods, which means that I know you have it in you to split the world into two if that's what you wish. *Scream*."

Althea turned back to the water, feeling as it rocked and swayed beneath her. She was furious. Was that what he wanted her to feel? She was mad and upset at this cruel world because of all it had put her through. Sure, Kylen was partly to blame, but he wasn't the Gods that had ignored her all this time. He wasn't her father who had tried to kill her.

She was furious, and that was what led her to truly scream.

It burned her lungs as it erupted. It burned her lungs in half as the magick surged from her body.

Her eyes began to glow warmly, matching the glow that swarmed from beneath her skin. Her Markings burned, but it wasn't in a painful way. They spoke to her, encouraging her to keep releasing this magick that felt so unbelievably good to burn.

"Release it all. Set the world on fire. It was only ever yours to burn."

Kylen held her steady as she screamed, as fire and her magick burned his hands. He didn't sheer away, even as she sensed his pain; instead, she merely sent another string of her magick to heal the wounds she had created. Althea screamed with everything in her, and as quick as she had begun, she had stopped. Sobs replaced it, and she fell right into Kylen's arms that were ready to catch her. Althea didn't try to push him away this time; she didn't have it in her. She merely just held the buttons of his shirt, holding them close as she cried.

She wasn't aware when both pairs of legs gave way, but they did, and they both ended up on the ground. Kylen's hand ran through her hair, soothing the burn that caused her throat to ache.

"How did that feel?" Kylen whispered, his lips brushing against the touch of her hair.

Her sobs began to quieten, and she looked back out to the water that shimmered with her glow. She didn't answer him for several seconds but rather instead focussed on the feeling that was left behind. *Why had Kylen urged her to release that magick? Why did he have her well-being on his mind? Was she really that draining to be around? Was she just a walking dark cloud?* Her chest felt so much lighter, and her dark veins had completely disappeared altogether.

Althea looked up at Kylen, finding his eyes already

connected to hers. "Good," she admitted with a wobble of a smile. "That felt horribly good."

Kylen tucked the strands of hair behind her ear and nodded. "I know it did. Sayah got me to do the exact same thing in the exact same position a few months after my family passed. My magick was and is a lot darker than yours for reasons that are too long to explain, but I burned the water with all of my pain." Kylen spoke as if these memories, these experiences, didn't hurt him anymore. She envied it. She envied the feeling of how free he seemed. She wanted that. She wanted to be free and to be able to breathe again.

Kylen looked off into the distance. "You are allowed to mourn, *and my Gods, Althea*, you are more than allowed to feel bad for yourself, but you can't let that be the reason you die. I choose to look at it as Eloise dying for you, she died so that you could live, and do you know what you must do now to honour her life?"

"*Live*." Althea finished for him before sighing. She rested her head against his chest. A look of complete confusion laced her features. "How did you go on? Knowing that your family didn't get to live the life they always wanted, living with the feeling of selfishness and guilt?" Althea asked. "I don't think I can."

"You can. It's difficult. I will not lie to you; not anymore. But I will be there to help you through it as long as I live. And even when death greets me, I will still guide you through the darkness. I owe you that much."

Her eyes were glued back on his, and Althea saw a glimpse of the boy she had once wanted nothing more than to be friends with. She didn't know if it was that same magnetic force that pulled her to his lips, but either way, the seas of them found them.

The dynamic between them now was wild, and it would be a complete lie if Althea said that she was *still planning to murder him*. She had been this whole time. Whether that was by her planning through the different ways of how to take his life or how she could present his head to her father, Althea had always been fantasizing about the long hours she would spend waltzing in his blood, but now she was staring at this man's lips and wondering if they could defy the brutality of her daggers, of her power.

Althea looked back to his eyes, and her heart sunk to her stomach as she realised just where his eyes also were. She cleared her throat before rising to her feet. "Well, we should be getting some sleep before the sun rises," she whispered. "If you still want to challenge me at a game of dual tomorrow?"

The ends of his lips curled up slightly at that. "You heard my chat with Uzziah, I take it?" Kylen questioned as he walked at her side.

"I did. And I don't like him at all. Be wary. Because if he so much as crosses my invisible string, I won't hesitate to kill him. Understand?"

"Understood, my love. Glad to see that your usual self is back in shape."

"Oh, my usual self isn't anywhere near back in shape. She is gone. *Dead.* She stayed dead when I almost died. This is just me. The me who is figuring out how the Hel I am going to continue on with life after gaining my father's head on my wall."

"He has a spot on your wall?" Kylen asked, his hands unlocking the doors for her.

"Yes. Right next to yours." Althea felt a small grin threaten against her lips as she entered through the doorway, the guilt was still there, of course, but it was no longer infused with the pressure of her magick wrapping around her heart.

Kylen chuckled, running a hand through the curls on his head that had formed from the very salt air. "Well, I will leave you to it. Don't be afraid to ask any of us if you—"

Althea ignored him before pulling him through. "You can

sleep in your bed. It is yours, after all. You are the captain of this boat."

"Ship and Privateer, actually. So, am I to be blessed with your presence alongside me tonight?" he asked, slipping off his shoes as he did so.

"Perhaps. It does get rather cold in here and practically speaking, body heat is a much more reliable source than layering on unnecessary clothes."

"So, I'm only there for your practicality, or do you just miss my body?" Kylen questioned, his brow cocking up.

"Practicality."

She shrugged off the coat that she welcomed too many hours ago. Her outfit was simple, rather like his if anything. She wore one of Kylen's white shirts. A long black skirt ran down her legs. The skirt had been added today, probably instructed by Sayah when they had begun training. Other than that, she had been wearing a pair of Sayah's trousers.

Althea spun her finger around in the air. Making him turn around so he would not be blessed with the darling gaze of her bare skin. He obeyed, and not a second later, Althea had put on the new pair of trousers.

"That's enough for me," Kylen replied. Answering what she had said a few seconds ago. She had felt him get lost in his head. The way his heartbeat softened in her ears to the point where it was steady. Why was it his that she could hear so loudly? The others were all there, but they were mousey, so soft compared to the undeniable beat.

Kylen took off his top but kept his trousers on. It was cold out at sea at night, something she wasn't too fond of. He slipped into the small bed beside her, and immediately, his warmth filled hers. Neither one of them spoke but instead laid in silence. Listening to the silence of the night, the whisper of the waves, the party that lingered beneath the sea that neither one of them had been fortunate enough to be born into. The silence soothed her; his touch that she had once done everything in her power to get away from soothed her.

Althea stayed silent as his heartbeat soothed hers. She wasn't aware when she had ended up laying on his chest, but at one point, she had, and right when she fell under the spell of sleep, she felt gentle lips caress against her now untangled hair.

THIRTY-TWO

KYLEN

The sun greeted him in the kindest of ways. Brushing against his sore and aching features as he swallowed back the bitter lumps of blood that had formed in his throat overnight. It was funny how you could spend all night running from the terrors in your dreams only to wake up and find yourself in one. He moved slightly over, and that was when he heard the slight intake of air.

Kylen peaked one eye open, narrowing it against the blazing sun as he looked down and toward the girl asleep in the croak of his neck. Her breaths were soft, the bags of her eyes fading slightly after the first peaceful sleep she'd had in nights. She looked so relaxed, as if the world had finally given her a break from all the nightmares it forced her through.

Naturally, Kylen leant forward, pressing his scarred lips to the edge of her forehead before freezing. He had just done that *—he had kissed her forehead—Althea's* forehead.

He didn't know whether he should grimace or fear for his life. Kylen slipped himself out of her arms, feeling the cold eery sensation that took over his skin after her graceful presence was lost. He moved with near-silent steps over to the dresser, looking through it for a few seconds before grabbing out a nearly identical outfit to yesterday. He never realised just how handy his emergency old privateer wear would come in handy. Still, then again, he never thought he would be on the run from his own Kingdom. How strange things evolve with time.

Shutting the doors behind him, Kylen looked back out to sea, his head turning in all directions as he searched to see if the land was approaching. No land appeared itself to him, and why would it? They probably still had half a day's journey until they would see the small outline of Harlia, but even then, they had to turn left so they could get to the other side of the island, as where they were heading was far too rocky to approach on the ship. A squeak came from before him, and he felt the presence of Zaire, the fairy forming from nothing but air.

Were the in-between Realms truly more comfortable than the Realms they were journeying across? It was a question he had dwelled on for years now.

"Sleepover with the Princess?" Zaire challenged with a gleam in their eyes.

"None of that," Kylen said simply, an eyebrow raised as he swerved around them. "How is everything looking?"

"Well, your definition of good and mine are rather different. So, I say that everything is rather wonderful, but I would say it's going okay in your dictionary," Zaire blandly explained. "Atty and Uzziah are still trying to figure out how Althea can be used as a key, and apparently, by Atty's rules: sacrifice is not an option. Sayah and I—*well,* more so Sayah is in the process of searching for any news of warships controlled by his majesty himself. But really, there have been some murmurs but nothing for us to rely on."

"And you and S? How are the two of you doing?" Kylen asked casually as he shrugged on the jacket he had left out the night before. The sun burned his skin, but the wind brushed it away. Zaire looked at him with a look of suspicion on their lips.

"And what do you mean by that?" Zaire asked, tilting their head before appearing on the railing. Balancing with no worry whatsoever.

"I mean, how is everything after Khatri coming back?"

"That is none of your business, is it." Zaire snapped, crossing their arms with such force that Kylen did feel as if he was about to go for a swim. "Sayah and my relationship is strictly between us, and if you so ever dare to go and ramble about it to your little mistress on the other side of those doors, then I swear Kylen, I will have your tongue. *I will have it*, and I will staple it to the front of this ship, so it rots with salt water."

Kylen leant against the railing. A gleam of amusement lined his lips. "Mistress?" Kylen questioned. "I would hardly call her my mistress but rather instead my fiancé. You know, you two would make wonderful friends. You both have this certain spite to yourselves. Perhaps when I am gone, you two will finally bond and become… closer?"

"So, she is still your fiancé then?" Zaire asked, ignoring the rest of what Kylen had said.

"Of course, why wouldn't she be? I am still going to need a Queen when I'm gone; you do realise that, right?" Kylen asked.

He didn't want to picture their wedding; he didn't want to picture it in an overly atop church while the whole Kingdom stared. He knew he was one for attention and all, but Althea, on the other hand, seemed rather against it. If it had been his choice, he would marry her with just her present. Sure, he would need Sayah or another there to officiate the marriage, but the only person who inevitably needed to be there was Althea—and he was not one to complain about that anymore.

"Well, you don't exactly need a bride if there is no Kingdom." The words echoed through him as if he were merely Zaire, travelling throughout the Realms. They were right; if he didn't have a Kingdom, then he didn't need a bride—but what could he offer Althea now if it was not a marriage? Safety?

Protection? Training? He knew that Althea Evangeline was more than able to protect herself from the harshness of the world once she was in the correct mind space.

"I… guess you have a point there."

"I always have points; you are just too closed-minded to realise them."

"Yeah, yeah, very well. So, what's the plan for today?" Kylen asked, urging with all his will for the conversation to flow in the other direction. "Once we see the island approaching, we will guide the magick left but slowly approach at a closer angle to it and then when we are there, we just… sit until we can figure out how Althea can open the barriers?"

"Yep," Sayah said, appearing from the seas with long dark braids down her back. "I am aiming for Althea to try and reach her inner soul today. And then through the magick that will be flowing through her blood, we will establish the keys that may be needed to unlock the barriers."

Althea… always coming in to save the day. Whether she truly knew it or not. He wondered if she was frightened? Who was he kidding? She was probably exhilarated and eager to use this magick. He saw the way it radiated across her features the night before. He knew it felt good, like a burden being weighed off of her shoulders. Kylen looked back towards the door, seeing through the small planes of stained glass as her figure moved.

"Seems like she is awake, so I will begin training with her. Zaire, wake the boys, please, and when you are all out here, please try not to stare as what I'm getting Althea to do today is tricky—far trickier than anything any of you could do," Sayah tutted.

"I'm sure I could do it," Zaire echoed out as Sayah approached the doors. She turned back on her heels, a sly smile on her lips as she laughed. "I highly, highly doubt that."

Zaire scowled before turning towards the stairs that would reveal the three sleeping males. Kylen stood awkwardly in place, shuffling his feet around before turning back to the helm. As he walked, he heard the lively murmurs of Althea's voice.

☽

Kylen had seen Althea for a total of one second before being brought to the same barrel that she had stood on top of the night before. She sat on it now, cross-legged with a look of uncertainty on her lips. She held her posture straight, her chin narrowed, her eyes studying Sayah as she walked back and forth before her. Sayah was explaining what was to be done, but her attention was elsewhere, focussing on the other voices floating about.

She sensed Kylen's gaze, and her eyes slid to his, capturing the force of them with as little as a blink. Kylen cocked a brow, challenging her to focus back on Sayah, to which she rolled her eyes in response, only tightening her hold on either side of the ship.

Despite her reaction to his signals, she did listen, and her attention was once more glued onto the walking siren, who still had scales perched on her legs. Althea looked to there, and the strangest of smiles found his lips as he watched her get caught up in her mind.

Sayah snapped her fingers before the Princess, surprising all three with her swift actions. Althea blushed before answering the question she had just asked, looking back up to the siren, who apologised before hurriedly continuing. Kylen watched from afar as Althea spoke before closing her eyes; he had full confidence that she could do what Sayah was urging her to do. Still, he didn't miss the way her eyes looked around before closing.

"Hey, Uzziah, Atticus, Khatri, and Zaire. Could I speak to you all for a minute?"

All heads looked up, looking towards the King, who beckoned for their attention. Khatri and Atticus were the first to rise without questions; however, Uzziah and Zaire shared a look that outed them as suspicious. He shrugged it off merely because his chest was burning, and he wanted to sit down as well as not get in Althea's way.

They followed him, and he hopped down the steps, holding the doors open so that he would be the last to enter through. He stood there until he was physically the last one standing. Then he looked over to where Sayah was still talking, and Althea's eyes, as suspected, were on his.

He tipped his head towards her before shutting the doors, turning back to the herd of people who all looked frustrated to be there. "What is it, Kylen?" Zaire asked through a yawn.

"If it is something stupid," Uzziah interrupted, a harshness to his voice that Kylen could say that he had missed. "Then I am seriously going to be pissed off—I had just finally beaten Zaire at the card game you two made up—what's it called? Shuffle something?"

Kylen limped his way to his chair, sitting down as great relief entered through him. "I am dying." He stated with a shrug of his shoulders.

"That got morbid awfully quick," Atticus commented as he rose a hand to the back of his neck, rubbing it as if it would rub away the tension. Kylen chuckled at his comment; it was so expected that he would say something like that. He was never one for the awkward sense.

"Yes, well, what is it if not the truth?" Kylen gravely asked. "I am going to die. It's as simple as that. Hel, if I'm not in the mood to wake up tomorrow, then I may die tonight. Either way, death is going to greet us all, and I am merely probably going to be the first to leave this horrid place. There had been a course of events set into place with the original plan, but now that everything has changed, I'm afraid we will have to make some alterations. Althea is to be looked after and trained. I want her to train with Sayah so that she will be seemingly fit when it's her turn to take over my Kingdom. As for you lot, I want you to treat her as you would treat me. I know there are large differences between us, and that she is not your favourite person, especially now, but we mustn't make the mistakes that I have made. She is not just the King of Aeonias' daughter, but instead, she is the Queen of Lorundio." He paused, feeling the tension strain his back. "I have been dying for quite a while now, you three might not understand, but you, Z, do. We knew three months ago that this was starting to go severely downhill: and now we are at the bottom of the hill."

Kylen coughed once and not twice, but he felt it there, challenging his throat as if it wanted to make a mockery of him to all in this room. He couldn't stop it; as he took a breath, the cough erupted, and blood covered his hand. He was quick to move, raising his handkerchief to his lips in a hurried matter.

"Ky—" Khatri began, the worry on his face practically sending blades into his dying heart. Kylen raised his hand, shaking his head so that he would leave him alone—*please, could they just ignore all of this?* He was fine. *Kylen was fine*. He didn't need people to worry. He was merely talking about him dying to distract them from whatever it was that was causing tremors throughout the boat. They all looked up, sensing the shake of the wood that pulled at his spine.

Kylen looked up too, the distraction large enough that even he was left with a quizzical—almost terrified look on his face.

"If she is about to kill us all, I swear to the Gods—" Zaire seethed. Their eyes were glued to their hands, watching as they shook from the force in the air. Kylen could smell that scent of roses, the one she so indefinitely carried.

"Kylen!" Sayah's voice bounced off the walls, travelling right to his fearful ears, which were already full to the brim with his heartbeat. He didn't care that it wasn't a call of worry or a call of panic; he still ran, thinking of the worst outcome possible. He was light on his feet, pushing past not only Khatri but Zaire too, who were fighting their way to the door head-to-head, both in order to reach the girl whom he was not searching through the darkness for. The door flew open, and Kylen forced his way through, instantly raising a hand to block the light that Althea's soul blinded him with.

Kylen narrowed his eyes through the blinding light, looking towards what the source of all this madness of magick was. His mouth parted slightly, opening so the gasp that hurt his lungs to hold could release from the hold of his curse. His eyes lit up at the reflecting blue light that he was hypnotised by. Althea was in the air, floating a few feet above the barrel she had previously been sitting on with crossed legs. Spirals of light shone out, pink, blue, orange, and yellow, all glistening through the sky.

Kylen met Althea's ghost-like stare, watching as her eyes shone with the words she was speaking. Sayah looked over her shoulder and met Kylen's panicking stare. "What is happening to her?"

"She is contacting her inner soul," she laughed. "And Kylen, I believe that the Gods are now physically on our side," Sayah spoke as she clasped her hands over her mouth, a sound of disbelief sounding from there. "I'm not going to lie to you. I didn't think she could do it. It was an exercise her mother used to do with me when we were younger—except she didn't do it to contact the Gods but instead her inner magick—the magick that thrummed through the soil of Harlia. It was difficult—severely difficult… but my Gods, Althea is doing it."

Kylen looked from Sayah to Althea, and despite the push to laugh, he just couldn't.

Because Althea was the soul of this magick, and the last time he had been in a light like this, he had held her limp body in his arms. Waiting with everything in him for her to wake up.

THIRTY-THREE

ALTHEA

The words that flew before her eyes were mesmerising. There were thousands of voices there; all of them thrived to rejoice in her ears. Althea held up her hand, feeling as the voices brushed against her fingertips, sending spirals of chills down and throughout the veins of her arms.

Eloise spoke to her first, and Althea focussed on that sweet, rich voice so that she could hear to be louder than all the others. *Oh, my dear, dear, sweet Althea. Look at you.* There was a sadness in her voice that brought tears to her own. *Do not mourn my death because of the life that we lost. But rather live for the idea of the memories we might have made, live for the life we might have lived.* A hand met her cheek, which did not meet the eye and yet was warm with touch. "I—" how could she put it into words? How could she summarise everything she wanted to say into a sentence or two? There was too much there, too much guilt and too much anger.

Don't be mad at yourself, my love. You get to live the life I wanted to live, and I am so glad that it's you because it's always been you. Look towards the light and follow it. Connect with your magick and love it. It is a part of yourself, and you should love every part that makes you, you.

Althea smiled into the brightness around her, holding her palms up and towards the sky as her words settled into her. The new voice began to speak out; this time, it was one that sent deja-vu washing over her shoulders as if it was a tidal wave and she was its victim.

My little dove, her mother cooed into one ear and then the next. *I knew this magick would do wonders for you, and this—oh, this has just confirmed it*. Althea went to open her mouth, but her mother hushed her. *No, I do not have time. I spared a little of my magick so that I could talk to you through your soul, but my little dove, that time is weak and despite holding the power of the Gods—time is precious.*

Hush now, my dear. I need you to listen to me. I need you to apologise to Sayah on my behalf and tell her that what she remembers will come back in pieces. It will come back in pieces and tell her that if she wants to hate me, she is more than welcome to, but I need her to know that I am so grateful that she is looking after you. She has always been wonderful; look after her, Althea. Try and remember what the Gods took from you. As for you, travel to Harlia—travel there and look for—

Look for what? What was it that she needed to search for—more so, what was Sayah going to remember? Her heartbeat was racing, and yet she was not panicking. Her head turned, her eyes travelling through the brightness of her soul. Sayah said to travel deeper; the voices would be on the outside, and then on the inside, there would be more of what she needed to seek. But it wasn't clear what that was.

Althea looked up as the vision around her began changing, turning, flipping before her as colours appeared in different spots. She waited, feeling the giddiness enter through her palms and to the bottom of her stomach as what she presumed *Harlia* to look like appeared before her.

The skies were blue, the trees were green. Everything was pure, everything was natural. The scent of salt-infused air filled her senses, and the hair on her shoulders curled up into its natural curls. This vision before her was real; it felt real, so why was it located in the deepest pits of her soul? Althea reached forward; her eyes stuck to her hand not because she was mesmerised but because she could not physically drag her eyes off of her hand. They were glued to the skin, watching with such astounding horror as the sun from above began to burn the peeling flesh. Althea stepped back, tripping over something that was beyond her eyes, and when she turned around, her eyes just seemed to widen.

Harlia, which was now behind her, was burning. Fire and smoke clouded the sky, such horror washing over her as she shook her head. Her lips tightened as she looked for a way to escape from this nightmare. This was not something she wanted to see—this was not something she wanted to live through. It was horrible—it was outrageous. Althea's feet couldn't move fast enough to get her away.

She ran fast, tripping and stumbling over scattered pieces of debris. Structures fell; water washed at her feet, and she looked down, finding that a wave was crashing at her feet. Whatever this was, it was no fantasy. No inner vision.

"Grab her and go," A voice appeared from somewhere behind. "Take her back to Aeonia until it is time." Althea's face dropped as she turned over her shoulder just in time to watch as her mother pressed one last kiss to the toddler's forehead before passing her to Sayah.

Sayah nodded, not a single emotion on her face as she looked ahead at Althea's mother. "Of course, Your Majesty." She knelt down, picking up the small girl who stared back at her mother with big, blue, wavering eyes. "Say goodbye to your mother, Althea."

Lilith looked down at her daughter, and yet she did not shed a tear as the older Althea was doing now. "Goodbye, sweet dove. May the next life for you be more forgiving." Nothing seemed to register in Sayah's mind because she merely turned on her feet, already beginning to walk away as the toddler stared back at her mother through whimpers. "Oh, and Sayah?"

Sayah turned around, nodding towards the Queen, who had already wiped her memories a few months before. "Thank you for everything. You are the type of creations we aimed for when creating these Realms. Look after my daughter. Save her from the misery that I cannot prevent her from. Save her from the pain that I know is coming for her throat. You won't remember this in a minute or two, but when you do, please guide her through the realising of what she truly is. That the moment I die—*we die,* she will become the physical form *of the four Gods*—she will become the key that unlocks our home. Look after her through that, and please forgive me, old friend."

The physical form of the Gods.

Althea to her absolute and utter shock, was the physical form of the four Gods.

Lilith turned on her way, and as quick as the memories had entered through Sayah's soul, they had left through the other side. Leaving nothing in her way as Sayah turned towards the castle that she now realised was Aeonia. They appeared in Althea's room mere seconds later, skipping time and wielding it to Althea's horror. Sayah tucked Althea into her bed, pressing a picture book into her hands before pressing a kiss to her forehead. "Your mother will come to do books with you soon, honey." With that, the siren turned and left her to her bed, unknowingly aware that the magick dancing through the air was one that would make the young girl forget the last half an hour of her pure and innocent life.

Althea knew what happened next; she held a hand over her mouth and sobbed because she was staring directly into the eyes of an innocent toddler who had no clue just how much damage the next few minutes of her life would do to her. Althea turned away from this vision and found that she was back in the ruins of Harlia. She had to sit down—she had to sit down and process what she had just learned.

Oh, but her mind was elsewhere. Her mind was with the small toddler who would be now jumping out of her large bed in order to search for her mother who was already dead. Laying in pieces while her blood awaited the girl to slip in.

ALL LIES, ALL LIES. YOU HAVE BEEN TRICKED, MOTHER. NOT ONLY DID YOUR MOTHER ACCEPT HER FATE AHEAD OF TIME, BUT SHE TOO KNEW YOU WOULD HAVE TO CARRY THE BURDEN OF BEING SOMETHING THAT YOU ARE NOT!

Althea held her hands over her face as she beckoned her eyes to open and reveal the real world to her. She beckoned them to open because now she knew she had to figure out what she had to do to open the barriers that her mother had set in place.

Althea rose to her feet, her eyes stained with the red of her pain. "How could you do this to me?" she asked her soul, *the last of her mother's magick*. "How could you put me through all of that and then leave me to be some saviour that I do not want to be?" Althea screamed as the wind began to stir not only in her reality but theirs too. "I hate you! I hate you so much for leaving me here!" Althea felt the fire burn along her palms, and she called to it, she felt it as her feet began to rise from the ground, and she allowed it to. Her whole world was beginning to burn as she let out an eruption of a scream that sent the seas shaking.

Then she fell...

And a hand caught her an inch above the surface of the water. Saving her from falling in.

Kylen looked down at her, one hand connected to Sayah's and the other holding her up. His feet were on the barrel, rocking and swaying with every little jolt of the seas that were beginning to calm. "Pull me up," Althea breathed as Kylen saw the pain behind those eyes, the fear creeping down her voice like trillions of spiders in the middle of the night, creeping down their webs in search of a new shelter.

Kylen did as she begged and he pulled her to him, his hand sliding to her waist as if it was their natural dance.

She looked up at him before looking away, already in the process of getting out of his grip. Althea moved past him, holding her hand against him a second too long so that he would be forced to follow her with a fall.

"Oh my gosh—!" Sayah couldn't get the words out; she was so thrilled. So full of joy that there were tears of glee sliding down her cheeks. Little did she know that a portion of the pain flooding her chest was full of apologies for her. "You—you—did you see that?" she asked, turning to Zaire.

To Althea's surprise, Zaire nodded, holding onto Sayah's joy. "I did." She was so over the moon with what Althea had just done that the siren hadn't even noticed the way Khatri stared at her, the way his face held such pain that Althea, strangely enough, wanted to heal. He looked so lost, so confused; it physically drained her. However, Khatri wiped that expression from his face when he noticed Althea's quizzical gaze.

Sayah turned to her, grabbing for her hands with such glee that Althea knew she would feel like a monster if she pulled away like she had wanted to. All because she believed to be a sin that would drain this womens harmony. "I'm so proud of you!"

That was a new one. And how strange the words tasted. Her whole body froze—the breaths trapped in her lungs.

"I'm sorry, Sayah." Althea blurted, catching Sayah off guard as that was not the answer she had been expecting. "I'm sorry that my mother wiped your memories, and most of all, I'm sorry that she had left you just as she had left me." Sayah stared at her with such confusion, but Althea merely nodded once before pulling the siren into her arms. She was never one to hug another, but something about the situation she had been forced into left her feeling as if this was right. Althea pulled back after a moment, ignoring how all watched her with such suspicion. "I know how to unlock Harlia, but for now, I need a drink," she said before turning away.

Sayah stared at her as she pushed past, heading with her head down towards the room that she had practically made her own.

"You need a drink, aye?" Kylen questioned as he appeared at her side. "I think if anyone here needs a drink, it's me. You—you were incredible there, darling, but the sheer panic I felt when you fell towards the sea—" Kylen shook his head, grimacing as he shook the gross feeling off his shoulders.

"I wouldn't have fallen into the seas; I would have managed to save myself and you from unnecessary worrying."

"Oh, don't be mistaken, Princess, I was worried for my ears. Because I know for a fact that if I had let you fallen in, then you would not have allowed me to hear the end of it."

Althea turned to face him and pushed the door open with her back. "It's good to see you have some common courtesy."

Kylen followed in behind her, ducking his head under the doorway so that the top of his head would not meet with the daunting wood. "So, what are we drinking?" he asked. "Water? Rum?... Juice?"

Althea looked at him. A part of her did want to get wasted away on something that would ease the burden, but then again, she figured it would be wiser if she just gave it a moment. "Water," she sighed. "None of that other stuff." She began to search through his many bags, looking for the flasks he had pulled out numerous times across the past few days.

"Oh, come on, lighten up. Why not have some birthday drinks? We never did celebrate your birthday." He held his hand on his chin as if he was lost in thought. Earning a scowl from Althea as she looked back over her shoulder. *Why was he thinking of her birthday?*

"My birthday was weeks ago. I don't think drinking on

behalf of it now would do us any good. And plus, I don't feel in the mood to celebrate anything."

"Grow some balls, sweetheart. Drinking can ease all of our problems if we give it a chance—just know when to stop."

Althea looked to him again, weighing over the options of what good or bad could come from this. Only a minute later, she sighed with defeat, clicking her tongue before holding out her hand. She would admit drinking her problems away did seem like an easier way to move on than accepting them.

"What drinks do you have?"

Kylen thought about that, narrowing his eyes on her before sighing himself. "Rum?" he offered with an awkward grin on his lips that almost pushed a smile of her own to hers. "I don't even think that we have juice?"

"If that's what we have, then that's what we have," she simply replied before clicking her fingers. "I think I need a sip of anything if I want to make it through the next few days."

"Well, come with me out on the deck, then. The sunsets truly are wonderful, and because you have been wasting away behind closed doors, you are yet to see the beautiful colours of the skies."

Althea stared at him with a look of boredom on her features. She didn't really want to talk to anyone right now, but then again, it would be better than the option of wasting away with her thoughts. Althea needed a distraction. She took a step forward, and that seemed to be enough for Kylen. She looked towards him, feeling the push in her soul that told her that there was something urgent that needed to be healed.

She looked at him, studying for any wound that might be on display. Nothing revealed itself to her, however. But right as she turned away, she swore the slight pigmentation of something dark met with his sea infused lips.

Althea looked at his lips, her brows dipping slightly as she saw the blood there. "You cut your lip," she observed.

Kylen straightened up slightly, his face one of confusion. She stepped forward, and he stepped back, meeting with the wall behind him as her thumb reached up to his lips. Pressing against it as a strange gold twine of magick extended out. Wrapping down her fingers before weaving its way through his skin. Healing the little blood that alerted her to his strange pain.

There was something more below, a taste she knew with every bone in her body. But perhaps that was merely the God in her trying to devour the evil that was his soul.

Althea sighed, wiping the blood away with her thumb as the small wound healed.

Her eyes locked onto his as he slowly released the breath that formed the words, "I would have survived."

"I know." Althea did not say anything more as she exited through the doors. No, she just simply went and sat alone before Sayah silently sat at her side. She took out a bottle of rum and passed it to Atticus, who grinned brightly. He clapped his hands as he sat on Althea's other side. "Oh, how I adore parties!"

THIRTY-FOUR
KYLEN

Kylen's body felt to be chained to the wall as he slowly exhaled the muffled breaths within his lungs. He could still feel her finger on his lip. He could still taste the glorious scent of her rose-scented skin. Tingles spread across his body that were unfamiliar, so strange and foreign that it took him a pure minute to be able to catch his breath.

The thoughts he was amidst of imagining were in no way appropriate given the circumstances. But it wasn't that, that made him ashamed of them. No, it was the fact that he was here imagining these thoughts about the girl who had claimed to want to be his friend when they were both still children. It was the fact that she was a completely different person because of him, and that made everything feel so awful. But it didn't just stop at that. There was also the rude feeling of regret that hung over his shoulders. Reminding him repeatedly that he would be dead in a few days. *He would be dead, and she would live in a world where he no longer existed.*

She would be happy when he died. He was sure of it. And he should be glad that she would finally be happy. After all, he owed that much to her. But no matter how hard he tried to think of the positives that would come from his death, he just couldn't fixate on any.

Kylen released another breath before heading out the doors, his eyes noticeably avoiding hers. Kylen cleared his throat before he sat down beside Khatri and Zaire, a forced grin on his lips that Sayah had been the first to realise was a lie. Honestly, how could he say that he was surprised? She saw through all of his illusions.

"Pass the bottle, Kye," Uzziah ordered from Sayah's other side. He held one of the cups Sayah had formed, his eyebrows rising and dropping repeatedly as he eagerly waited for the liquor that he was holding.

Kylen swiftly poured himself a small glassful before passing it. To all, it looked as if he was drinking. But truthfully, he couldn't think of anything worse. Even his release had become a burden for him to hold.

Sayah eyed him down suspiciously, watching closely like she could still see through the illusions he cast. But he saw the way her expression changed when she looked towards Althea, the way Althea was trying to be kind to the siren, but her soul was too wounded otherwise.

That was how the night went on; everyone spoke, and everyone drank. He watched, joining in conversation every few minutes so that he wouldn't be outed to feeling as if he was about to die any minute. The conversation flowed around him like he was a little bird hidden beneath a nest of war.

Althea blew his mind. Speaking not only to Sayah but genuinely laughing with Atticus, and eventually, dancing with him. Something that he knew would be good for her. She whispered a question in his ear that brought a smile to Atticus's lips. For the first time, he felt jealous of his brother because he had Althea's lips graze against his ear and how he envied that position.

What was wrong with him? The last thing on his mind should be Althea's lips—Althea as a whole.

Atticus looked at her with lust in his eyes and Kylen felt just about ready to call it a night—but no, this was good for her. This was good for *him*.

Althea laid back as Sayah and Atticus spoke across her. Her eyes were now on the visible stars that swept the sky and how mesmerised Kylen was as she took each breath. How could so much power hold shelter within one body? People began to clear out, tapping out from the day as if they could have predicted the anxiety Kylen carried for the next few days ahead. Eventually, Sayah tapped his shoulder, squeezing it slightly as she mouthed the words of her departure. Perhaps she spoke them, perhaps she screamed them; either way, he didn't hear a thing. He had turned the world on mute, rather instead fixating on the sounds of the curse clawing at his lungs.

Kylen looked towards Althea, watching as she yawned before downing another drink. How she was drinking laying down was beyond him, but then again, she did seem to be able to do anything these days.

Kylen shuffled in his feet, grazing closer to her as he too turned around, laying at her side so that he could see the stars one last time. *How he would miss these stars, this scenery.*

"You know what those ones look like?" Althea asked. Breaking the silence with the royalty of her voice. She pointed to the constellation in the sky, mesmerised by how the stars created such pictures.

"What?" Kylen asked, playing along.

"They look like me putting a dagger through my father's head."

Kylen choked on a laugh of surprise before coughing abruptly. He felt the splatter of blood meet with his hand, but he ignored it, wiping it on the side of his shirt quietly before turning back to the stars. Noticing from the corner of his eyes that Althea hadn't noticed the blood. "You know what those ones look like?" Kylen asked, playing into her games.

"What?"

"You tying your father's body from your balcony so that all of the world could see the death you conquered."

Althea smiled, evidently distracting herself from the darkness within her. "Dark," she mused, turning to him as the stars caught her eyes. "I like it. You have changed your games, Noxwell."

Althea elbowed him, earning a laugh from himself as he properly laid down with a grunt of heartache. They were silent for a few minutes. Rejoicing in the peace of the sea before her eyes shut.

He looked towards her, catching the exact moment she prepared to speak. "I'm not sure I know how to unlock Harlia." He wasn't sure if it was the liquor speaking or purely her mind. Still, either way, he thanked whatever Gods that were out there for allowing him a normal conversation for once.

"I believe you will find a way."

She was quiet, no words following his as he closed his eyes. Feeling as the cold air nipped at the top of their noses. This was nice; it was settling. Quiet times like this helped his soul heal. It helped him breathe, which seemed so pathetic given that one's body should be naturally doing that.

Althea sat up, moving her knees to her chest before resting her head atop them. If he could take one snapshot of his life, it would be this, capturing the peace at sea of a girl who was finally speaking for her freedom. For a girl he knew could kill him and yet had allowed him to live for this long.

"My mother used to tell me that everything in life happened for a reason. Everything we go through is preparation for what we meet at the end of the line. I wish that to be true, but in times like this, I start to second guess." Kylen spoke as he too pushed himself up, wiping the blood from his lip.

"I used to believe that too," Althea responded. A bite to her voice that he swore there was a chance he had imagined it. "I used to think that everything happened for a reason, but then I met you. And I know that no God would have put me through what you put me through. I know that that did not happen for an intended reason but rather one of mockery." Her voice was a mere whisper, as if the fight her soul craved for was not the peace her mind longed for.

"Althea, you have to believe me when I say that I wish things had been different. You have to believe when I say that I did not want to hurt you intentionally." Althea laughed a quiet sound as she looked over at him, her stare one full of agony. Before he could think, he held a hand towards her, already rising to his feet. "Dance with me?" he asked, unsure of where this was going. "The next few days most likely will change everything. And time will no longer—*not that it ever has been*—be on our side. Dance with me while I have this chance."

She furrowed her brows, looking at the hand he extended towards her with such curiosity. "You want me to dance with you?" Her tone was soft again, and Kylen nodded.

"More than anything."

Althea studied him, her eyes grazing over his features ever so slowly.

"Dance with me. We don't have to speak; we don't have to yell nor scream. We merely just have to dance." Kylen cleared his throat and her eyes lifted to his. "I will forever be sorry for what I have put you through, Althea, but I can only hope that there is a lifetime out there where you can forgive me."

Her hand met with his, and she rose. Not saying a single word as his other hand found her hip. There was no music, no tune, no rhythm, but they danced to the silence. Because sometimes, there was nothing more intimate than finding comfort in another's breaths.

And Kylen always found that the silence was less daunting

when her head was resting against his chest, where he could feel as her every little breath skimmed across his cold and dying skin.

If he had to break every bone in his body—if he had to rip every shred of skin from his bones just to earn her forgiveness, he would. Because the greatest reward he could ever earn was a place in her heart that was not full of pain.

"Perhaps in one lifetime," she whispered, and Kylen didn't have to ask to know what she was talking about. He wanted to scream at her that they did not have time. That time wasn't one he held a forgivable friendship with.

He spun Althea out, and she watched his every breath. Her eyes were like the sea, and Kylen would happily drown within them. She swallowed, and he looked down to their feet. He watched as they waltzed across the deck as if no monsters were stretching for them. His hands held her waist, his thumbs running circles over the material that kept her from him. Althea watched him and he watched her, their eyes locked as if they were trying *for the last time* to mesmerize every feature of the others face.

He did want her forgiveness so that he could die without any heartache, but now Kylen was aware that that was not possible.

Not in this lifetime.

THIRTY-FIVE
ALTHEA

His every step had matched hers, and not once had they struck fear. Their movements were slow, steady. Almost as if they were both scared of what tomorrow may bring. Althea wanted to be mad at him; she wanted to scream at him so that he could see the pain that she felt. But her heart just wanted to breathe, it was far too tired.

Althea could still feel his hand on her hip, how that single touch had made her stiffen, how that single touch had her slowly leaning her head against his chest. Listening to the murmur that echoed below.

Every breath she took now was quick, full of anticipation as she sensed the new presence aboard. Her every step was being watched—darkness hanging over her lungs as she beckoned herself to breathe silently.

Blood—the rich scent of it coated her lips, and Althea looked around through the fog that seeped across the deck. "*Aaaaalllll-llttttttthhhhhheeeeeeeaaaaaa~*" A voice whispered, and the hairs on her arms and legs rose on end. "*Aaaaalllllttttthhhh-heeeeeaaaaaa~*" It called to her. Such agony and pain in the voice's trembling breaths. An unknown presence aboard had brought Althea out of Kylen's chambers first—she didn't understand why she had been the first one to feel it, but she had been, and now her magick was riveting beneath her fingers. Every step that she took felt as if it was being watched. She held her hands up, preparing to call to the magick that felt so majestic to use in case there was truly something there. Perhaps this magick was playing tricks on her, paying her back for not forgiving the man who didn't exactly ask for her forgiveness the night before, but either way, there was something drinking at her blood, pushing her to find the soul she could sense.

The cold wind met with her cheeks, and her eyes stayed steady. Noticing the dark sky that floated in circles above. The scenery around her seemed to flash, but to her stupidity, she ignored it, focussing on sensing the soul that was somewhere around her.

"Aaaaalllllllttttttthhhhhheeeeeeaaaaaa~"

A cold dark dagger aimed for her throat, striking her as she leant back just in time. Holding up her own sword of magick as she began to dance the dance that this stranger begged for.

Another dagger was thrown at her, and this time, it met with her shoulder, pricking against her skin until dark crimson blood appeared—her eyes furrowed for a moment, noticing that now her blood was purely red. The curse was completely gone—and her soul no longer ached for it. Althea scowled, her hands swiftly rising as she summoned all that she could to the palms of her hands. It wrapped around them, glowing brightly as she swerved around each blade. There were multiple unknown presences aboard. All of which were after her head. She could hear their thoughts, the beat of their cursed infused hearts.

She was in the war zone now, and she was the prized possession.

Althea raised her hands up with such force before screaming. It wasn't a scream of pain nor joy, but rather one of such force that pushed her magick out. Ripping the illusions out from the roots and throwing them overboard, revealing the eight cursed pirates whose boat appeared right next to theirs.

A grin appeared on her lips as Kylen appeared in the doorway, a glisten returning to her eyes. "Oh, how I missed this." She turned, her sword already slicing into a soul that had tried to take hers.

This was a game that she had invented. *This was her game*. Althea waltzed in their steps, dancing around each figure as her blades lunged out.

Kylen didn't waste any time before joining her. However, she noticed the strange aura to his soul. His steps synced with hers, and his movements matched hers perfectly.

If this was their fight, it would have been so much more fun.

But this wasn't, *and now it was a matter of life or death.*

Her feet skimmed against the wood beneath her, and she held up her blade, slicing the head off of the stolen soul that was in the midst of calling the darkness. Althea didn't bother to watch the head roll. She moved on to her next victim, using the blood that appeared beneath her to her advantage by sliding on it—moving quickly towards the cursed pirate in front of her; before trying out the magick she had loathed for so long. The light spiralled out of her, wrapping around the soul with such force that it was sliced into two.

More souls appeared off the boat, and now everyone was awake, fighting off the curse as it was spreading deathly quick. Leaping from one soul to the other that Althea could no longer ignore the giddiness that burned through her soul. This was fun. *This was glorious.* She danced this dance as Kylen appeared at her back, circling her movements so that he could defend her blindside, just as he had done multiple strange times over the past few weeks.

A man who reeked so horribly of the familiar eery curse struck for her throat, but Kylen caught it. His sword turned with such aggression that even she was shocked. He caught the man's pain and pulled on it so that he knelt before Althea.

She grinned down at him, dragging her sword across his throat before slicing it open.

Kylen covered her as she did so, yelling multiple orders over to the others. He told Uzziah and Zaire to locate the heart of the curse carrier. There had to be one person who was controlling their actions on behalf of the King, and Kylen seemingly was set on finding him.

But that was if *she didn't find them first.*

Althea jumped up onto the railing, grabbing onto the rope as another on the other side used it to their advantage. It pulled her up, and Althea flipped, her years of ballet coming into place as she landed perfectly on the other ship. Her sword rose, and she turned, pirouetting around as her sword sliced through the bodies that all lunged for her.

She could sense the message. Listening as it called to her.

Kill the girl. Kill the girl. Kill the girl. Father says kill her, so we need to kill.

Althea turned towards the helm, noticing this time: the glisten that revealed the illusion to her.

Althea wasn't sure how she knew what to do, but perhaps it was because she was quite somewhat of her own God. A deeper connection to the Realm of immortality than she had originally realised. Her actions came naturally to her, flowing so easily out of her soul that she hardly felt these deaths.

Althea jumped up, using the magick beneath her to land her behind the captain of this horrid ship. This ship was larger but in no way did it look steady. The wood and deck were covered in a darkness that reeked of blood and mould—bodies off previous victims of her father lay scattered, looking as if some had been reluctant to defy His Majesty himself. The three cursed on this ship hadn't spotted her just yet, but she could feel them sensing her. It looked as if they were multiplying, as if her father had locked them all below, and only now were they gaining access to the world. Althea had no true understanding of how she could sense these souls, but it didn't seem like the right situation to question it. So instead, she worked on plucking the dark magick from the hidden departments of her soul, beckoning it to her fingers as she darted towards the man who controlled the ship.

He revealed himself to her, or that was what she thought until she realised that he had replaced himself with another illusion of a different type. Her father appeared before her, capturing her shock for a moment too long. The darkness grabbed her from behind, wrapping around her throat as she grounded herself. She fought against it quickly, leaning right into the dreadful shadows before clasping onto the source of it. She had been tricked; there had been an illusionist pretending to be the captain as she blinded herself with the joy of finding her next victim.

A mistake she later would dwell on.

Now was not the time.

Her sword formed in her hands, and everything around her began to slow.

Her eyes glanced towards Sayah who shrieked in pain, dark crimson blood coating her hand as she stumbled a few feet back. Althea looked back to the holder before her, raising her sword up swiftly and cutting off the rope that held her to him. She had an option here; she could either continue with claiming his death, or she could swerve around, coming to Sayah's rescue as she became surrounded.

There was no thought to it. A year ago, she would have looked the siren's way and laughed as she became cornered, she would have looked away and continued on with life, but now she couldn't because this siren had been by her side through it all. This siren acted like a mother to her despite how heartbroken she truly was.

Althea slipped on the blood as she pierced through the crowd of stolen souls. Her sword waltzed through the air, new patterns of blood splattering against it as she forced the siren back. Althea rolled, kicking her leg to her left before slashing her sword to her right.

Sayah watched, and Althea didn't dare to risk her eyes in that direction. She could just imagine her expression. A mixture of horror, fear, and shock lining her features. Did she blame her? No. Not at all. This was the monster that she was. They expected her to be something great, something amazing, but she was anything but. Althea was her father's daughter, an assassin who had been wielded to her father's side. Only used or spoken to when he needed something, *anything*.

The last head rolled, and Althea released a harsh breath that pierced through the air. She braced herself for the lectures Sayah was sure to force upon her. But instead, when Althea looked over her shoulder, a deep confusion dawned upon her.

The siren didn't look at her any differently; she didn't even seem to pay attention to her. Instead, she began to use her magick to heal the gaping wound at her hip; and how mesmerised Althea was as she watched her magick nick in and out of her scaly skin.

"Are you alright?" Sayah finally asked, her voice gliding ever so graciously through the voices in her mind.

Althea stared at her before nodding. "Am I alright? Are you?" She reached up to her forehead, wiping the cold sweat away as she grinned down at the siren. "I must say, I never particularly thought fighting in the middle of the seas would be so frightening yet so enticing."

"It seems that you do have something in common with Kylen after all."

Althea shook her head, although she couldn't say she was surprised. Kylen did always speak so fondly of the sea.

She went to take a step towards the siren when something as soft as lace tingled across her skin. Weaving through the hair on her body and leaving a residue that was so awfully cold. There was a distinct sensation of worry, a feeling so dreadful that she was dreading whatever it was that she was about to see. Althea looked over her shoulder, her hands weaving with magick as the sight before her threatened death.

Kylen was surrounded. And if he were looking any differently, she might've thought that this would be exhilarating for him. There was nothing better than stealing the hearts of the dead. *Except he didn't look so sure.* His eyes and ears were dripping with black blood. Blood seeped out from his lungs as he coughed. There was no blade in his hand, but that didn't push him overboard. No, he held up his hands, prepared to fight them physically.

Althea moved before she could think. Running up to the edge of this boat and dancing over to the next. She met the wood, mere inches away from Kylen's panting body, and he had already begun to falter in his steps. "What did you do to him?" she asked through clenched teeth, the trembling in her voice far more evident than she would have liked. None of them answered, but she hadn't expected them to. Their minds were controlled by one, and that one was her father. "*What did you do to him?*" Althea yelled again, earning the stares of Kylen's family.

They all looked over, their eyes widening as if they knew something she did not.

Althea was going to murder them all; if they weren't going to answer her questions, then they were going to feel her wrath. *Her pain.*

The cursed lunged for her, but she sliced their hearts into two. The panic that filled her heart kept it beating, alerting her to the exact moment in which Atticus and Khatri had her covered. Althea turned to Kylen without a thought in her mind, her hands reaching up to his cheeks to wipe the dark blood away. Kylen looked down at her, sheering his face away as if he was ashamed for her to see him like this. His face froze as her thumb met with his skin, feeling as something heavier swarmed for her touch.

The sensation of darkness that she had never truly missed.

Her eyes were dragged away as their murmurs weaved through her mind. She had only managed to pull Kylen an inch towards her when *the cursed bomb went off.*

And oh how her body hit the cursed water.

The water was cold, icy. Althea had always imagined it to be as such, but now that she was in it, *drowning in it*—it was so much worse. Like dread as its physical being. Althea tried to fight against the current that pulled her down, but she did not know how. She had never been blessed with the lessons of the sea. She did not know how to fight this situation.

Yet even if she tried, how long would she truly try for? Wasn't this what she wanted? Didn't she want her nightmares to be washed away?

Althea never wanted to die. The idea of seeing all those that she had disappointed on the other side made her anxious, queasy. To see her mother's face—which she had already been forced to do. As well as seeing Eloise's face, which she believed to be far darker now that she had been the one to kill her.

She could already picture herself there, watching her with such anguish as the lost souls aimed for her.

Althea's body sank as the world weighed over her. Her efforts were lost to the coldness it held. Her eyes opened, narrowing against the force of the waves. The ship above was on fire. Debris filled the water as bodies sank. Naturally, her eyes searched for a familiar pair. A pair that always managed to calm her. A pair that always found her even when her darkness was too consuming.

She felt the water fill her lungs with each struggled breath. The magick within her soul stayed silent as if it was playing her into a story that she knew nothing about.

Something was swimming towards her. Perhaps it was a shark, or maybe a dragon of the sea. Either way, there was not enough air in her lungs to worry about whatever it was.

Althea had accepted her fate, no matter how painful it may be.

Her eyes had shut.

Concealing the world out as her heart began to cry.

But then two hands clasped her cheeks, begging her to open her eyes and try for a little longer.

Althea looked at Kylen, such emotions within their eyes as if they had both already watched the other's deaths. She watched with wide stammering eyes as he floated above her. She looked like his healthy insufferable self now that the water had washed away his sins.

Their eyes were locked. Trapped within the stories each pair held. Listening to the tune the others' souls sang. Althea reached her hand up to his, meeting the cold skin that she had never once truly sheered away from. It occurred to her then that she feared death. She was afraid of the beyond, what sins it may hold.

Kylen looked to be as well because as her vision began to give way, his brows tensed, reaching to the floating hair that he pushed away from her face.

Althea's eyes began to shut again, the lack of oxygen becoming too much for her drained soul to handle. She didn't want to fight it, and yet she was forcing herself to.

Sweet, sweet girl, there is not enough time in the world for this brutality. Give in to the soft darkness.

Kylen ran his thumb across her lips, beckoning for her to open her eyes. He held a stare of longing, regret, the betrayal shining heavily within his eyes. One stare so full of emotion that she didn't question his next act at all.

Kylen leant forward, his lips pressing to hers. The water that surrounded her glowed with such awe that it blurred the Hel above out. Kylen kissed her, and she kissed him back. She felt as if they were the only two that would ever matter, as if she would allow the world to burn if it meant that he was safe. How weak had she fallen? The magick Sayah had placed upon him transferred from soul to soul. Althea moved her hand up to his cheek, holding him close as if she was scared of what would come next.

Kylen kissed her gently. All the emotions over the years targeted their backs as if any of it mattered. But it didn't, not anymore. Kylen had been the one consistent thing through these weeks. He had been the one thing that she had missed, and she believed his guilt. Even if that made her stupid, Althea couldn't bring herself to care. She pulled back from him, meeting his soft stare. Kylen smiled weakly, but his smile didn't survive. His body froze over, his eyes forever trapped within his sins. Althea's eyes widened as she reached for him, a scream haunting her lungs. "Kylen—"

Her hand was an inch from his when he disappeared. Everything disappeared. Something had shot an arrow to her soul; something had turned the light within her eyes black. The magick within her soul took over, acting in favour of her—but if only it realised it was too late and that she did not need saving.

No emotions were trapped within her heart anymore. Instead, she drowned in the rhythm within, the one that kept Kylen's touch on her lips forever preserved.

☽

The bitter taste of sand ran across her lips, paining the few cuts that lay scattered. There were no wounds visible, and yet the taste of blood and the look of blood confirmed all that she needed to know. Her muscles ached, burning through her heart as she begged herself to stand.

Althea's eyes could barely open under the force of the blazing sun. She couldn't see a thing even as she finally, with much relief, pushed herself up. "Kylen?" the word didn't even leave her lips. It barely made it into the air before it landed back on her tongue, choking her out of pity and grief.

The sand under her was uncomfortable, digging into her very

flesh as she swayed in her steps. Her eyes glared through the haze of the sunshine around her, not making it easy for Althea to see where she was and what exactly had happened. “Kylen?”

She did not recognise these lands, these trees, nothing connected in her mind as she looked around. The scent in the air smelt tropical, and yet it made her head throb. Maybe that was what it was. Maybe she was still in a dream—or even better, perhaps she was dead.

Althea stepped forward, the sun-infused sand burning her toes as the panic rose in her chest. A sizzling sound filled her ears, and she looked around, looking towards the debris burning a couple of miles offshore. She looked towards the sea, finding the source of the continuous burning.

There was a barrier in the distance, one that extended over her head, except she could not see that far. The barrier she could see lined the perimeter, glistening as waves thrashed through it. Althea quickly turned on her heel, her hands dropping from her face as she realised just what sands she was running on. This wasn’t on any of Kylen’s maps because it hadn’t been explored for centuries. It was an island of untouched creatures, nature, wildlife, frozen, awake and trapped in a time that Althea knew so little about.

She was in Harlia. Harlia was around her. And just how beautiful it tasted.

Her reign of shock was short-lived as she felt the panic thrum through her fingertips. “Kylen?!” Althea screamed, her voice burning due to the internal wounds that pained her more than anything. She had hated him for so long—hated him for what he did in the past, for what he had done to her. But now, all of that felt so small as she reached for her lips, feeling the eternal kiss he had placed there. Althea hadn’t forgiven him, and now he was gone.

Most likely dead.

His lips had been on hers. He had kissed her—Kylen had

kissed her, and she hadn't skinned him alive because of it. Althea kept a hand to her lips, trying to stop the panic from surging through them. He had kissed her so that she would gain the ability to breathe beneath the seas, and yet she hadn't been able to save him. Something had knocked her out; something had been the source of all this blood on her head. Something had turned her white hair red.

Kylen, the same man she had dreamt about murdering, kissed her. Her mind was spinning, her head so full that she felt just about ready to throw up.

"Kylen!" Althea yelled. The word slipping from her tongue with so much panic that it barely made sense. She was moving on her feet, and yet no distance was made because her head was a blur, and the magick from somewhere within the forest was forcing her to follow it.

THIRTY-SIX
KYLEN

The water was a cool reminder of all that he had run from. It washed his pain away like a blanket going to a new-born child. Soothing its cries as it begged to hold onto something that wouldn't leave.

Althea looked so confused. Her face was so vulnerable, so starstruck; that Kylen wished with his whole heart that he could erase the pain he had inflicted upon her. She didn't deserve that. She didn't deserve any of it. He knew that, and he was forever paying the price for it. Althea reached for him, the feel of her lips on his still there.

He wished there was some way he could stay here, some way he could make it up to her. But hopefully, this was enough. Hopefully, this made his bad deeds seem a little less evil. The door to the afterlife opened before him, and he turned, watching and feeling like the darkness he had been pushing back for so long welcomed him. This time he couldn't prevent it. This time Kylen didn't have the will to fight against it. This time, he couldn't find the spark of light to hold him back to reality… or so he thought.

Someone was pushing down on his chest. Threatening to

break each rib within him. Kylen reached up, his hand instantly trying to stop these harsh movements. There it was there, the spark that told him to turn the other way. That same grin he knew got under Althea's skin, appearing on his lips, and he stepped for it, his hand reaching up as he felt the small warmth of it reach his soul.

"He has a heartbeat—he cannot be dead if he has something of a heartbeat—" A voice growled as Kylen searched for it.

Kylen gasped, his movements so quick that not even a second later, he was jolting up, coughing up the seawater and blood that had welcomed him to peace.

Sayah jumped back, her hands shaking before her as she stared down at him with such intent, such pain. "Sayah, you are magnificent!" Atticus cooed in utter disbelief from over his shoulder, earning a light laugh from Kylen himself, who began to cough. Zaire darted for him. Pushing past both Sayah and Khatri, who knelt at his side. They threw their hands over his aching shoulders—he didn't flinch; he didn't so much as breathe. Zaire never made contact with anyone, and here they were holding him as if they were the best of friends.

The pain that took over him showed him that he was alive and had survived.

Zaire held onto him tightly, and he knew they were refusing to cry; they were refusing to shed a single tear. Kylen held them back, a small, saddened yet insufferable smile on his lips. "I'm alive. I'm alive," he repeated, repeating the words if they held no meaning in the world.

"Of course you are. You didn't die, Kylen. I got to you before it fully gained your soul," Sayah spoke with an awfully morbid tone. She looked at him with anger, she was trying to hide it, but it was still there. Burning on her features ever so brightly. Kylen raised a hand, one that was slowly reaching over to her in caution. "How could you be so stupid!" she yelled, and for the first time, being the first to break. "How could you give away the little power you had left to save someone I was inches away from saving?"

Tears appeared on her cheeks, and his chest tightened. She was not crying. *She couldn't be.* Sayah was the strongest person here, and yet she was sobbing over the death that was about to coat her hands. "You almost died—for fucks sake, Kylen, you almost died, and I almost couldn't save you. I restored the curse within your soul by adding the magick that you stupidly yet bravely passed on. So, you are alive but only with hours to spare —unless these lands hold some miracle." The last of her words were barely audible, leaving her lips in broken whispers.

"Althea," Kylen gasped. "I passed it on to Althea, did I not?"

Sayah nodded. "You did," she confirmed, her lips quivering as she held the next load of sobs back. She didn't need to cry over his death. They all were expecting it. For God's sake, he had added it onto all of their calendars. In bright, bold letters, the words 'Kylen's predicted death date'. Of course, they had passed that date by two months, but he didn't mind. It had given him more time of living, more time of feeling the air on his skin.

"Where is she?" he asked as he pushed himself up, ignoring the physical ache in his bones. "I saved her, so where the Hel is she?"

Sayah rose as well, her hands still holding onto his. "I had to get to you first. I had to save you, so I—"

"You saved me instead of her? Sayah, I was basically already as good as dead—she still has years on her name!"

"You mean more to me! And I'm sorry if that makes me a bad person, but you are basically *my* son. You have been for years now—so if I had to choose between you and her, *I will always choose you!*" Sayah exclaimed in protest. Her expression wavering slightly as she realised what words she had just spoken. "You are basically my son Kylen Noxwell, and I don't care if you resent me for the rest of my life, but I could not let you die."

Kylen stared at her, feeling as if he was seeing this person he knew far too well for the first time ever. He had always felt like her child but never once had he said it aloud. He was afraid that it might make her… hate him.

Sayah had just brought him back from the dead, performing CPR while infusing her magick into his. Kylen had dropped her hand a second ago, but now he grabbed for it. She looked at him, her lips curling down slightly. The classic look she always held when she forced herself to be the brave one. "Thank you."

Two words that he never said enough.

"We will talk about this later, I promise, but for now, we need to find her."

"I don't think we need to look very far," Atticus advised as he turned to face them all. "Have none of you truly realised just where we are?" As he spoke, he raised a hand to the barrier that surrounded the island.

Kylen turned to it, watching as it burned. His heart sunk, and yet a strange feeling took over him. They were on Harlia, the island of the Gods, the true home to Althea. But wait—they could only access Harlia if Althea was here, which meant that she had to be here *somewhere*. Kylen was about to speak when something white caught his eyes—he wouldn't lie, he thought and hoped that it was Althea; however, it was not. It was the white cat that would always find a way to survive through wars.

Kylen pushed himself up and walked towards her, jogging slightly on his still aching feet as he picked her up swiftly. "Hey Chlo—" Chloe was covered in the scent he knew every aspect of. She smelt of roses, and that scent alone sent his heart stammering. It could have been because she had refused to leave Althea's side, or it could be because she saved Althea. "Take us to her?"

He placed Chloe back down, watching as her small little legs wobbled forward with such desperation. He felt the eyes of the others on his back, and Kylen looked over his shoulder. Sayah's stare concerned him the most, the way she didn't meet his stare even as he held hers. "We will talk about this later, I promise," he repeated, reaching for the hand that quickly found his.

Sayah nodded, sniffling back the ache that she felt. "Okay. Don't break it. *Don't break it by dying.*"

Kylen cocked a grin at her. "Wouldn't dream of it."

THIRTY-SEVEN

ALTHEA

Althea forced her way through the bush, her whole body visibly shaking.

Her mind was full of voices, voices that wanted to drown her, and this time, she could not contain their tones. The voices shouted at her in armies, all mocking the ridiculous heartbreak that filled her heart.

Kylen is dead, Kylen is dead, *Kylen has to be dead.*

Why couldn't they be quiet? Why couldn't they just shut their mouths? It wasn't fair. It wasn't right. She needed them to be quiet because the louder they got, the louder her confusion felt as to why she felt so heartbroken.

This feeling wasn't one she wanted to feel. This feeling wasn't kind to her by any means. No, it was cruel and completely unreasonable. Making a mockery of her for something she did not need to be made fun of for. It was all because she now had a heart. She had a heart and how full of aches it was.

Her steps were quick, catching up to the rhythm in her ears. She wasn't aware where her magick was pushing her to go. She only knew that if she stopped or faltered, the magick began to burn. And that was pure agony, even for her.

Perhaps by the off chance, it was leading her to Kylen.

Why was her mind making her think of him?

Why was her mind forcing her to think of the man she had spent her entire life hating only to now be thinking of him in a way that did not seem so harsh, so impractical?

No. She did not need that distraction. She couldn't handle that distraction. It led her eyes to fill with tears, practically mocking her for the way her heart was reacting. Yes, she didn't want him to be dead, but she also did not need him to be on her mind.

It was impractical.

Emotions were impractical.

They got in the way. They got in her face when she should be focussing on the task at hand instead. *Why did he have to kiss her?* Why did he have to make her feel ashamed for now feeling emotions towards him that were not negative?

Do you love him? Atticus had asked her.

And now the answer was no longer clear.

Althea stopped in her tracks as the anger began to bubble.

She was exhausted, *tired*, and still mourning for the loss of her life and the love that still held such weight over her. She dug her hands into her head, attempting to push the ache of her bone and the swell of her soul away. "*I'm tired!*" she bellowed, the words running from her lips as if they could hear the bomb within her ticking. "I am tired and sore and—*what are you making me do?* Why did you have to bring *him* back to me?" Althea panted through a cry.

Her magick tugged her forward like a little puppy trying out its new leash for the first time. And how she wished she wasn't on the other end of it.

It was exhausting, like a race she could not finish.

Althea didn't have any choice but to follow it, but if she had, she would have most definitely run the other way. She stared ahead with a blank stare, tears threatening to spill from the exhaust that held shelter on her spine, but Althea refused to cry. She was going to see what it was that was so urgently pulling her forwards, and then when she arrived there, she would dictate whether the world should burn or not.

It felt as if time was an illusion by the time the trees began to break. She had been walking for so long now that it seemed like a lie to say that she had finally appeared before some type of structure. It was small, broken pieces of what used to be an old house—she figured. But it wasn't that particular sight that caught her eye. She had caught onto an illusion now. Did the world truly want to deceive her?

Althea lifted a hand towards it, feeling the soft waves of an enchantment that shielded whatever structure that was hidden behind. She closed her eyes, summoning the magick within her to the surface. Simply saying her intention and watching as the illusion opened for her. Revealing the grand yet broken castle of Harlia to the Princess who had never found a home that felt quite right.

Althea took a step back, her eyes widening as she took in such architecture. It was large and ancient, feeling as if it was a sin to step inside—luckily, she was never one to sheer away from committing such crimes.

The magick in her chest pushed her to step forward, and yet her steps stayed frozen in place. Concealing her to the ground as she tried to decide whether she should run the other way or not.

All this time, Harlia had simply been a hidden figure of her imagination: made and turned into something beyond the eyes because she had no true facts to base it off of. It had been a forbidden safe space for her. Holding her back and securing her away from the pain that her father forced upon her. But right now, it was before her. Right now, she didn't have to pretend to be in the nameless city that she dreamed of running through.

It was as beautiful as the little legends spoke. Yes, the castle had fallen, and nature had claimed it as its throne, but that just seemed to make it all even more beautiful. As if the realms that they—*she* was scattering on were now claiming back everything that they, the world, the generations beyond it, had stolen. The surviving white walls stood tall, but pieces of the rest of it lay scattered around. Vines wrapped up the surviving walls, lopping through the windows and adding such depth as Althea looked over it. She looked over her shoulder and, in the distance, through the gaps in the trees, Althea could see other overgrown structures. Perhaps houses of the lives that once roamed these lands.

The windows—while some were bear with vines hanging down them, others had stained glass pictured in the middle, sending rainbows and such colours to dance across Althea's skin as she reached out to it. Everything was breath-taking, and Althea swore that she could feel her magick burn with excitement within her lungs.

Althea stepped over and through the small gap in the architecture, feeling as the pressure the walls held on her chest gave way, allowing her to breathe down the fresh air. The air tasted different here, not only compared to Aeonia because of all the pollution: but in Lorundio too. Lorundio held the air of the seas, infused with the goodness that the people of *his* Kingdom created.

Harlia smelt fresh. There was no rot in the air as you would see and smell in other Kingdoms. No humans, mortals, or even immortals were sensed to be here, so everything within these walls was truly pure. The trees, as scientists spoke, said that they were diffusers for nature, taking whatever pollution that may be in the air and running it through the filters of the leaves until the air was to their standards. It worked here, and from the lack of souls that lurked across these islands, the air, the nature, all of the above was pure. And Althea's magick was practically doing flips with every step she took. It was as if her magick of the Gods knew that this was where she belonged. And despite all the pain, heartbreak, and wounds, all of it seemed to be pardoned because of the feelings that she was feeling now. Althea even dared to say that she felt at ease here, like there was a chance of something more to bring joy to her life.

But then she remembered Kylen, *and she couldn't shake the lost feelings and emotions off of her shoulders*.

She stepped within the walls that sent a strange sense of deja-vu over her shoulders. Her eyes glided from one wall to the other and slowly up the roof that revealed the clear blue sky through broken cracks. There was a snap of a twig, and Althea halted, catching sight of a deer prancing away after having seen Althea's figure.

How weird that must be for an animal, to see someone after centuries of silence.

Everything was broken. Pieces of history were scattered across the ground as if it was preserving history forever.

It was a good distraction, but it didn't push the tears from her eyes. It led her to wonder what Kylen may do if he were here and how he might act if he was truly by her side. And how *damn reckless* she felt for thinking of him.

Althea entered through the old hallways of the Harlian Palace, revealing herself to be in a large room that was still full to the brim with books. *How had they stayed intact all these years?* The nature had not once gotten to them. If anything, it had just heightened their state of security. The books were truly beautiful and ancient, but it was not that that caught her mind. It was not that that made her magick sparkle within her blood.

Althea approached the altar, looking towards the book that was spread out there. There was a glisten around it, a ripple within the illusion that surrounded it. Althea slowly began to extend her hand out to it. She felt this illusion loud and clear; it was stronger than the others, a stronger force spreading atop it.

The words on the page were jumbled. All mixed up so that the words in this book were not readable. Althea's hand may have stopped, but she took a breath and extended it out further.

Her fingers met with a force, and just like that, everything around her *began to shake*, and everything began to tremor with such magick that she could feel every inch. Her head dropped to her feet; her stomach followed as she heard the cracks beneath her.

The floor gave away, and Althea felt herself fall through the air. This was it. She had prevented death for this long; she was bound to meet up with it at some point. A scream erupted from her lungs, and Althea searched through her soul. She seemed to have magick for nearly everything, so where the fuck was the magick for this?

Althea hit the ground before she could do anything, however. No magick, no abilities, no *nothing* could've prepared her for that fall.

The pain was waiting for her, and yet as she was left waiting for it in return. There was something almost scaly—squishy, beneath her. Something so cold, slimy that her mind was distracted of any potential pain.

Althea's whole body froze, her breaths halting as she turned her head to look at whatever it was that was beneath her. An eye stared back at her, and then two. Althea pushed herself back, another scream burning her lungs as she stared into the eyes of a dragon.

And this time, she was not exaggerating,

"Oh, Hel *no-no-no-no-no-no*." Althea began to whimper. Pushing herself back with all the force she could gather. Her eyes stayed trained on the dragons' watching as it turned to her, slowly moving to follow Althea as she did her best to scramble away.

"*HELP*!" she knew her screams were useless and mindless, but they were the only thing that she could think to do. "Oh my

Gods—!" Althea looked to the dragon as it dawned on her with a wicked smile; she had magick—*she could survive this*. She would find some miraculous way to get out of whatever mess she had just caused and survive.

Her hands quickly crossed the front of her, slicing the realities in half and summoning her magick through its cracks. It glistened before her, and she prepared herself to strike. Rising her hands up and pulling back when a figure of another mortal being quickly ran out. Stealing the last of the air from her shielded airways.

A man with dark skin and curly looking hair similar to Atticus's appeared before her. His face holding such panic. "*Okay-okay-okay-okay-okay*—just breathe, just breathe," he beckoned her through his unfamiliar accent. "He isn't going to hurt you; he is most definitely not going to hurt *you*."

"He is a dragon! And as fantastic as they sound they kill people!" Althea exclaimed as if it wasn't obvious enough. "Get behind me," she ordered, not taking a second to think about how he just might be here.

"Yeah, not happening. You need to put those hands down and just—" As he spoke, Althea stepped forward, the light from above radiating onto her features as if she was glass and the world around her was hers to burn. "Althea—*Althea Evangeline*."

That was not what she was expecting to hear. Althea tilted her head as her magick grew brighter. She knew people knew her name and features, but this island had been untouched for years. "How do you know my name?" She asked rather quickly. "Better question yet—how are you even here?"

"I..." the boy before her seemed to be at a loss for words. He just stared at her, slowly rubbing the back of his neck as she took a step forward. Althea cocked her head to the side, a blade extending from her wrist as she sized the boy up.

"How do you know who I am?" Althea repeated, this time with such force. "How are you on this island. My mother—"

"Your mother saved me. She allowed me to live out my days here with Adreasteia so that when you finally made your way back home, I could help you; guide you through your mothers' footsteps," the man explained as if he was making any sense. Althea watched him carefully, her eyes keeping track of his and the so-called Adreasteia behind him.

She didn't believe him.

She wasn't even meant to come back to these islands any time soon.

"I don't believe you," Althea stated. "Why would my mother trust you and not tell me the truth about all of this? It doesn't make sense. My magick has led me here, and if you don't be clear with me, I will kill you," Althea stated, the deadliness carving its way into his posture.

"I believe you," the male quickly rebutted. "But answers will come if you just give me time."

"You don't have time."

"*Okay*, okay, my name is Adonis." Althea screwed her brows. She didn't care for his name. That held no power or meaning over her. "*I am your brother.*" Now that did, that sparked something horrible.

"What?" Althea asked, clearly puzzled. She looked down to his arms, noting how his skin was far darker than hers. And neither one of her parents had had dark skin. "No offence, but I don't see how you could be my brother. My mother and father are both—"

"Yes, I know." Adonis finished for her. "Your mother had a lover here, and she got pregnant with me just weeks before she left to marry your father, and… *boom*… a child."

"I don't believe you," Althea stated, this time a feistier bite to her tongue. "My mother wouldn't do that to my father. She loved him. She was in love with him."

"Don't lie to yourself, Althea. I know that you've been questioning it too. Our mother is dead, she is dead, and who killed her? Ever since you received your Markings, your life has changed dreadfully. You have been welcomed into this new world that you know nothing about, and that led to questions which led to mistrust," Adonis cooed. His tone didn't separate the two tones it held. He sounded to be mocking her as well as feeling bad for her. And she wouldn't stand for either.

Althea knew that what he was saying was the truth; she had been asking a lot of questions recently, ones she did not know the answer to. But nonetheless, she did not need some teenager looking, overgrown male to be questioning her on her life. "My father did not kill my mother—and even if he did, she had brought that fate to herself. My mother knew she was going to die before she did. and yet she did not do anything about it." Althea spoke with such force as if it was not breaking her heart to even think about it. "What do you know about me?" Althea asked, taking a step closer towards him.

Adreasteia shuffled from behind him, the black dragons' eyes reflecting the power that she so dangerously held. Her dark scales lightened with blues and purples as she reflected the sun. "It's okay," Adonis whispered over his shoulder. "I know that you lost your mother when you were three years old. Then after that, you were tricked by the King of Lorundio and then fell in love with the girl in your castle. You have been trained into this figure that your father wants people to fear. A makeshift ballerina who is also a murderer. I know almost everything about you, Althea. I've been keeping tabs—the cursed in your castle, the crows in the wind, I have my ways of protecting you and not once have you ever been alone."

"*That is horrifyingly creepy.*"

There it was, the voice that had been following her around all day in her mind. However, this time it echoed through the room, alerting his presence to her across every piece of old furniture. Alerting her brain and soul that she was not dreaming at all.

Althea looked up quickly, her expression blank as she looked towards the hole that she had fallen from. She lifted her hand to block the blazing sun from her vision. Squeezing her eyes to make out the figure that stood above, and oh how joyously mad it made her heart to see him.

This had to be a cruel dream, but for once, *she was not complaining.*

Yes, she had been in denial that Kylen had even died, but she was also sure of it. She had been daydreaming of this day for so long now that she was sure everything would feel so exceptionally good.

That was *not* the case.

His lips had touched hers, and suddenly, all these new pushed down emotions had swarmed through her. Causing her to deny everything she should accept.

Kylen jumped down by Sayah's side, her magick wrapping around his so that the landing wouldn't be so harsh. He looked at Adonis, his glare full of an emotion she could no longer read. "I suggest you back up, mate." His voice was like ice, slipping into Adonis's with a deadliness that she had only ever seen a very rare number of times.

"Kylen Noxwell, King of Lorundio, future King of Harlia, that is if you don't die."

Kylen seemed to turn pale, his eyes slipping to Sayah's as they spoke inaudible words. But no matter the fact that Adonis's words had gotten to him, Kylen kept his expression.

"Oh, come on, tell them, Miss Linix!" Adonis exclaimed, focussing his full attention on Sayah, who stared at him with furrowed eyes. Althea looked at them, something like shock rising within her heart. "You know who I am; you trained me after all."

"I'm afraid I lost my memories, boy," Sayah spoke gravely, her voice holding no light.

"*Oh, of course*, because mother took them away from you."

"She is not your mother!" Althea exclaimed as the clouds above began to appear. "She is not your mother, so for the Gods' sake, stop referring to her as one!"

Adonis stared at her, "I will admit I had this going a lot better in my head." The dragon huffed from behind him, and Kylen took a quick step back, extending a hand across Althea as if that made any difference.

"*Holy shit—*" Kylen gasped, his eyes turning wide. He looked over his shoulder at Althea, and she noticed that his frightened expression softened at hers. He stood right before her, his lips inches away from hers. *Could he see the uncertainty on her features?*

None of this felt real. It all felt like a mess that she was trapped within.

"*He's telling the truth*, I—I think," Sayah spoke, interrupting both of their thoughts. "I remember her son of dragons, *mind you*, I cannot remember if he is him, but I remember the myth."

Althea looked at him, her eyes full of even more uncertainty than before. She stepped forward, but Kylen stopped her with a gentle touch. She looked at him, a small smile lining her lips, one that felt so unnatural and yet so right. "I can look after myself."

"I know."

She could see the option he was giving her. He was giving her the ability to turn back and let him deal with it. But her magick brought her here, and she was going to figure out just what all of this meant.

Althea continued past Kylen and Sayah before arriving inches before her proclaimed brother. *Reach to him, reach to him, reach to him.*

She didn't give him a second to pull back. No. She just

quickly raised her hands to his cheeks as her mother's voice instructed her to. "W-what is she doing?" Adonis asked as he attempted to break free. She felt the little yet powerful magick he held surge through her, and within seconds Althea stumbled back, no words or expression on her furrowed face.

Kylen was quick to tug her back and away from the dragon that looked about ready to butcher them all. He guided her so that his back was on the others and that she was out of harm's way. Althea wasn't looking at him, however, her eyes were plastered on the ground.

His cold hand met her cheek, and she looked up; her eyes full of such fear that she begged to drown in. "*He's telling the truth.*" This couldn't be real; this couldn't be true. Her mother had had another child, and she did not know?

Did her father even know?

THIRTY-EIGHT
KYLEN

It wasn't clear whether those few words caused relief within him or concern. Either way, he wasn't happy with the male and his little pet behind him.

Althea stared at him with eyes full of worry. Inaudible concern that he knew that if she even tried to speak on it, no words would depart. The look on her face told him that she did, in fact, want to discuss the fact that he had just returned from what felt like the dead—*he even dared to think that she may even want to talk about the kiss.* Still, he knew her well enough to know that he would be speaking with blood dripping from his lips if he even dared to speak anything of it.

Althea turned back on the man before her, pulling out a sword of her own being. "So, tell me," she began with a turn of her head. "Tell me everything important that you know about me."

This wasn't fair. He had been sitting on that broken throne for minutes now, and not once had he said anything useful. He was completely just going on about everything he pridefully knew about Althea and partially Kylen too. Sayah stared at him with a blank stare. Khatri and Zaire on her tail as if she was drowning.

"Okay, so congratulations that you know about my life. But quite frankly, I don't care that you know about all my 'trauma'," Althea said, dragging her words on. "No one gives two shits if you know my birthday or not. I just want to know why my mother didn't tell my father about what all of this means!"

Kylen watched as Adonis flinched under Althea's words. He watched with a hidden grin as Adonis tried to hold his quivering posture. He knew what this position was like; he knew what it was like to try and not give way under Althea's harsh force. Adonis leant forward, his hand meeting Althea's wrist, and she scowled as she flinched away, her magick pushing him back; saving the boy from Kylen's sudden anger.

Kylen extended his sword forward. "Touch her again, and I will rip your eyes from their sockets. I will cut your hands off and shove all of it down your wretched throat."

Adonis stared at Kylen with such fear that he heard Althea snicker with delight. A sound that he would happily get drunk on for the last of his hours. "Oh, he does know," Adonis said, causing Althea's own confidence to drain as he turned back to him. "He does know, and he doesn't quite seem to care if we are being honest."

"That's a lie. My father would tell me if I had a brother."

"He doesn't consider me to be one, however." Adonis turned to Kylen eyeing him slyly. "That is where the story thickens, my friends. You see, your father doesn't care for my existence. In fact, he doesn't even realise that I am still alive."

Althea leant back on the debris of the roof that had overgrown with thorns. Not flinching whatsoever as Kylen turned his piercing eyes off of Adonis and over to her. "What do you mean by still alive?" Kylen questioned. "Did he try to send someone off to kill you or something?"

"Bingo. Dear old Althea's father sent out several assassins, and after they failed to deliver my head, he came for me himself. What a pity that he was met with the barriers instead of my army. I would have loved to see his face when he realised dragons were still existing. But *blah, blah, blah,* your father wanted me dead because he believed I was the heir to the Gods, just how glorious it will be when he realises it is the other way around."

"My father knows?" Althea asked, her eyes faltering. She tried to hide the fact that she stumbled back slightly, but Kylen saw the way her feet slipped. "My father knew about the magick with the Gods—*no, he wouldn't lie to me.*"

"It isn't called a lie if you never asked."

Kylen was getting sick of this game. He was sick of the fact that every question Adonis was asked was answered with a question of his own. Or it might not have been a question he would answer with. It was also words that did not make any sense. Placed on his tongue to rather make a mockery of them.

"I—" Althea couldn't get whatever it was that she was saying out of her mouth. She instead just shook her head, the disbelief dripping away as she turned on her feet. "I need air."

"You have air; this whole castle is full of air! You cannot run away from the truth any longer, Althea. You are the physical form of the Gods—*accept it and save us all!* You became it when you so selfishly forced mother to give up her eternal being for you."

Althea's eyes widened, but no words left her lungs. She looked to Kylen, who looked back, slowly shaking her head before rushing through the doors. Ignoring the curse of Kylen's gaze as he ran for her hand.

"Oh, so *they* don't know. Why don't we tell them, then? Why don't we tell them what you've been keeping from their precious little ears?"

Althea stopped, her eyes meeting with darker ones. "I don't know what you are talking about—or what drugs you are on, but I want nothing of it."

"What are you going to do? Are you going to threaten me if I say something? Are you going to be the little assassin your daddy has raised you to be when you could be the Gods your mother had once been?"

A tear dripped down Althea's cheek, and Kylen turned to Sayah with eyes of disbelief. What Adonis was saying was true. Althea was the—*Gods?*

Kylen looked to Althea and found her eyes faltering as she shook her head at the boy who was said to be her brother. "I'm not a God," she whispered through a laugh. "It's insane! I don't want to be a God—I've never believed in them before, so why start now?"

Adonis took a step forward, and Kylen extended his blade out, earning a scowl from the dragon, but this time he did not flinch. "Back away."

Adonis looked at him; his brows furrowed. "Don't you see how insane she is acting? Don't you realise what harm she is doing for this world if she doesn't take up the role mother has left for her? She is our only chance at survival—we need to jump onto it. Althea, you aren't a God; you are the Gods."

"*No, if anything*, you are the one acting insane," Kylen swiftly answered him as if his mind wasn't not making sense. "I believe that she is acting rather reasonable given the circumstances and all. If I had just found out that I was a fucking God, I would be pissed—beyond pissed. So, if anything, I say that you are handling this rather well, sweetheart."

Althea looked to him as she bit down on the insides of her cheeks, her eyes threatening to allow the lost Kingdom to burn. She still had that look on her face that showed him how truly shocked she was. How even the truth was harsher than the lies.

"Plus, you need to stop with all of that guilt-tripping. You need to realise that our worlds are already doomed. The Gods would've done something by now if they were anything good."

"But don't you see, there are no Gods. She has the power of all four Goddesses. Because her mother—"

"Was the physical form of them all," Sayah finished for the boy. "I—I remember that now. That was why I tried to stop Lilith from marrying your father." Kylen looked at her, the same shock on his face that laced Altheas. "She died, which meant it got passed onto Althea—that's why everything always felt so surreal when I trained her." She choked on a sob as she looked to Althea, her expression damned.

"But I don't want to have this magick let alone be the hope for these fucking worlds. I don't know what to do, and anyway, I'm not God-like. I'm not pure nor innocent. Why would I be the one gifted with this power?" Althea shook her head as she fiddled with her hair. "It's not right. It doesn't make any sense. I kill people. All I have done during my years of living and breathing is torture my people's lives—their souls. No soul would want me as their God. I wouldn't be able to give them what they ask."

"Althea, you need to accept the fact that you have no choice!" Adonis yelled, and before Kylen could interrupt, he went off again. "You have no choice as your life has already been written for you. You just need to shut up about it and do what you've been set with doing."

Althea stared at Adonis as if she had just been shot. "Watch it." Kylen sneered as he stepped forward, turning his sword under the sunlight so that Adonis could see the magick wielded by Sayah there. "Do not speak to her in such a tone."

"Or what?" Adonis exclaimed through a laugh. "You are going to kill me? We are all going to die anyway if Althea doesn't accept her fate."

"Yes, I will kill you, and I will be glad of it because you are one horrible, manipulative man." Kylen retorted with such aggression. "Althea is—...*Althea?*" He looked around, his eyes searching for the figure that he could no longer sense.

"She fled," Khatri answered for him. "The moment we entered, she ran, and Atticus went with her."

Adonis looked to the dragon that stood outside of the walls. "Find her."

Kylen didn't wait to hear what happened next; instead, he began to run. He watched as Sayah, Uzziah, Khatri and Zaire all pulled out weapons on the dragon and its boy.

"Althea!" Kylen shouted through the empty halls as he ran. "Althea, where are you—" he heard her panicked breaths—the way Atticus was so desperately asking her what he could do, what she needed, *who* he needed to get.

Kylen entered through the room, his eyes instantly finding Atticus's before looking down to the ground where Althea had her hands clasped over her ears as magick began to stir in the air around her. She was on her knees, trying not to fall from the tremors that echoed with her magick. "I don't know what to do—I don't know how to calm her." Atticus exhaled swiftly, his hands shaking before him as if he was the one hurt.

"I will take care of it. Just go help S with fending off the boy and his pet."

Atticus nodded, and instantly he ran, disappearing through the doors.

Kylen approached Althea not even a second later, slowly kneeling before her as he tried not to let the sound of her sobs break through his walls.

"Leave me alone," Althea snarled as she looked up at him, and when he didn't leave, she reacted again. "Leave me alone!" Her words sent the walls rattling, threatening even more of the structure to crumble. Althea looked to that, her eyes wide in not only fear but pain too. She clasped her hands over her ears as if the voices were far too heavy upon her crumbling heart. *"I don't want this. I don't want this. I don't want this."* She sobbed, her hands shaking against the ground as thunder began to brew. "Kylen, I cannot be a God. I don't want to be a God.

Why does no one get that? Queen I can live with but God —*God I cannot*."

"I know," Kylen reached forward to touch her hair, and Althea pulled away from his touch.

"Don't you dare touch me. Don't you realise that I know what happens next? That I know after I allow you into my life, you will once again tear everything down! My God—does nothing *ever fucking work out?"* Her nails were practically digging wounds into her scalp, beckoning whatever she heard to steer away.

"No, Althea, I wouldn't do that again. I wouldn't hurt you—*I never wanted to*."

"You say that and then you go and do!" Althea turned around on him, rising to her feet as her eyes stared through his. "I want to trust you, and I hate myself that I want that. But I cannot allow myself to, not again, not anymore."

Kylen took a step forward as he too, rose to his feet. "Althea, let's just breathe. We will figure out a loophole to this all."

"Tell me, Kylen," Althea began as she turned to him with her brows furrowed. "Have you lied to me since all of this began again? Have you lied to me at all? Because my magick is screaming at me and telling me that you have. This magick that is filling my head with voices is telling me that everything you say has a double meaning to it. One that I'm not going to like."

Kylen stared at her. How was he going to answer this? He had been doing exactly that, but not intentionally—*never intentionally*. Kylen reached for her hand when they both saw it, the dark black veins that covered the hands of a dead man. "*Yes*." His voice was near quiet, ever so faint to the ones that he too, was hearing. "Althea, the reason you are becoming Queen is because I'm dying."

THIRTY-NINE
ALTHEA

Althea knew this nightmare far too well, she knew her role in it, and she knew the emotions that would flow with the arrows to her heart. She knew it all, and yet not once did it make it easier for her to breathe and look at Kylen and see the man she had trusted.

"You—*you were going to leave me as Queen?"* Althea took a step back as everything froze, as the rain began to drip from the clouds above as if they were crying on her behalf. "You were going to leave me as Queen…" That was what she had wanted. To kill him and the crown become hers—so why did it feel as if her heart had been torn into two?

Kylen reached for her, and she pulled her hand back, her eyes furrowing with such pain. "Well yeah, I figured that I owed you that much."

"*No,* stop it." Althea pulled her hand from his grip. Turning her head away from his as Kylen's eyes found hers. She wished that she could find a piece of the ruins to hide beneath. Her head was within her heart, her gaze full of such agony that she felt as if she was going to be sick. Why didn't the Gods or her own mother understand? Why didn't they realise that she was tired of constantly being thrown comets of new information regarding the life of lies that she lived? Althea fell a few steps back; her eyes trembled across the patterns of the weeds and roots that covered the last of the marble on the ground. "Just stop it."

They all begged her to *forgive him;* they all begged her to give him another chance, just as they had been tricking her into doing this the whole time. Kylen quickly followed, and she scolded beneath her breaths, her eyes cast over to him as if physical flames would shoot from them. Althea muttered words of such death that the weather began to wield itself to her, allowing her to get some release through that because apparently, that was all the world could offer its God.

He grabbed at her hand, and she turned around to him, her actions so quick that he barely saw her hand coming, and yet he still caught it as if he knew every move. Something that fuelled even more anger within her. "Althea, stop," he ordered, and Althea laughed at the harshness of his words.

"How are you to give me orders when you have lied to me once again?" Althea howled, her magick sending the very walls trembling. "How are you going to seriously give me orders when I have just found out that you have been manipulating me this entire time?"

"Althea—"

"No! I never wanted to be Queen. I never wanted to marry you, and yet I still became trapped within your walls, only to find out that you are dying and leaving the weight of your Kingdom on my shoulders." Althea scowled, her gaze icy. She didn't understand how this was different from her plans; she didn't understand why it hurt her soul as if she had been physically wounded. There was just something to it that whispered to the magick within her blood. Begging for it to kill him, what a change of pace that was considering that just a day ago, it had been urging her to forgive him.

"Althea, I'm sorry, truly. But you were basically going to do the same to me, so I don't see what the problem is—"

"*I hate you.*" She held her chin up high, playing the role of the hateful enemy once again. She took a breath as her lips trembled, beckoning her to cry. "I hate you with everything in my soul, and I will *always* hate you." Althea watched as her words met with their target, splitting his soul into two and returning the other half of it to her. She was waiting for that feeling of satisfaction, the one that confirmed for her that what she was doing was right.

But that feeling never came, and the voices for once were quiet.

"*No, please, Althea, just listen—*"

"What? You are going to beg for my forgiveness again? You are going to expect me to get on my hands and knees all so you can die with no burden on your chest?" Althea laughed, rolling her eyes with such aggression before pushing him back with such force. Althea saw the darkness there within her veins, hearing the ever so familiar calls and oh, how it made her lips quiver. "You haven't changed a bit."

Mother is mad.

Mother is angry.

How long have you known this boy? This liar?

Mother have you known him for twenty seconds or twenty years?

"Althea, I'm so sorry."

"I hate you," Althea repeated through a laugh, trying to rid her grip of his but instead only tightening his hand on hers. "Let go of me and just leave me alone." *Why wasn't he accepting the truth?* Why was he being so infuriating and neglecting the truth that was meant to stab beneath his flesh? Her whole head was screaming, getting to the point where it was unbearably loud, and all she could do was cower under it.

Althea gained on him, her eyes locking with Kylen's. A blade was extending from her hand and pressing against the flesh of his chest. "Why don't I do you a favour here and now? Why don't I take your life from your hands and leave you with the burden of becoming one of my victims?"

"That would never be a burden on my behalf. I would rather die at your hands in every lifetime if I could."

Althea shook her head, a sneer leaving her chapped lips. "I hate you with everything in me—*how is that not affecting you?"* she cried with no tears, her restraint echoing off of the cracked walls and striving straight for her own heart.

"Because I know that no matter what I do, I will never have enough time in the world to make it up to you. I know that in every lifetime if I die at the ends of your hands, it will never be enough. You did not deserve what I put you through. You did not deserve the pain that I have caused you—and that breaks my heart in ways that are unexplainable."

With one swift movement, she tried to escape his clasp, but her efforts were short-lived when her body was pulled to his, her face mere inches from his. "I hate you…" Her words didn't escape her lungs as words, but rather sobs took their place. She looked to him in search, her eyes dancing through his, remembering how his movements always synced with hers. Althea sighed such a deep, heavy sigh that sent thunder brewing in the storm above. "Why—*why* don't I hate you?" Althea questioned through a breaking exhale.

"I don't know; perhaps it's the same reasoning to why I could never hate you."

Althea held both of her hands to her chest as she stared up at him with soft eyes. "I want to hate you, and yet I cannot—*why*—why can I not hate you? It has never been this difficult before." Althea spoke as she kept her piercing gaze on Kylen. "I never wanted emotions, a heart—they do far worse than any good."

"And yet you have one." Kylen's hands reached down to Althea's cheeks. His thumb slowly dragging across her bruised flesh, a mourning expression plastering his skin for the time they both knew they would not have. "But do not be ashamed of your mortal heart, be wary of it and protect it, but you should learn to wear it with pride, as that is what will make you the hope our world needs."

Althea moved her hand up to his, her magick spiralling out in an attempt to soothe his, but his magick was no longer answering any of its calls. Tears dripped from her cheeks that she would have once been ashamed of, but now she could not find it in her to worry about herself when the man she felt to *love* was dying before her. "Kylen, I don't want to be the hero. I cannot be what they deserve."

Althea realised it then, just how she had evolved from that small assassin at her father's side. She had a heart, and without realising it, she had been wearing it with pride.

"Don't be the hero, never be the hero. Because then you will have to join me in the afterlife far sooner than I would like, and you need to live. You need to fall in love, meet the other half of your soul."

Althea looked up at him as her breathing evened out. She wondered what he would think if he was within her mind. Would he be frightened of her thoughts? Or would he be surprised that she was questioning whether his soul was the lost part of hers?

"Kylen…" the word died on her tongue as everything began to louden. Her whole world stopped as she watched the black veins on Kylen's throat swarm to his eyes. He took two steps back, confusion splattering onto her as if she was the one falling to the ground beneath them.

Althea fell with Kylen, her hands immediately going to his cheeks, her fingers shaking as she tried to summon anything that would help him. Yet, Althea knew the magick that she needed was not one that she still had. She most likely had the magick to heal him and extract the curse from his soul, but she had been so reluctant to learn, that that didn't matter. "*What is it?* Kylen, what is it?" His whole body was convulsing, dark black blood beginning to drip from not only his nose but mouth too.

Kylen's breaths began to quicken, his hands trembling as he wiped the blood away. "*No*. I-I don't want to die." His words were soft, and yet they were loud enough to hang over her for the rest of her days. He shook his head, his hands staying pressed against his face as if he could stop it—she met those hands with hands of her own, gently holding the trembling fingers as she held a brave face.

Althea nodded, trying her best not to act as heartbroken as the ruthless assassin of the night truly was. "You aren't going to die. You will be fine," Althea promised as her voice threatened to break.

Kylen nodded, his face full of despair as he began to believe her empty promises. "I don't want to die, Althea."

The way her name left his tongue caused all the hair on her arms to rise. Althea whimpered as her thumbs ran circles over his cheeks, listening as his heartbeat began to slow beneath. "I won't let you die—I can't let you die. *Somebody—help!*" Althea breathed, screaming the last two words as if they were the last that she would ever speak.

It was funny how that when she had died, *almost died*, her soul didn't burn the way it was burning now. Her conscience wasn't putting her through misery as it was now. Why did she have to grow one? Why did she have to find the heart that Kylen had preserved for her all these torturous years?

No soul answered her, and Althea looked back down at him, the man who she had been so young and blindly in love with at a young age. Now she was not so young, and yet the love aspect had never changed. It had merely gone into hibernation to allow her soul to heal, a treasure not many were gifted with these days.

Tears ran down her cheeks, and Althea leaned into Kylen's touch as he raised a very weak hand towards her. "Don't cry, sweetheart. I will be okay—right?" Althea heard the attempt at keeping his words positive, but she too heard as he choked on them. Blood splattered onto her throat as he slowly yet tiredly moved his hand to wipe there. "It was enchanting to meet you, Althea Evangeline."

Althea saw it then, the rope of the invisible curse that dragged along the ground. She looked up, following it with an expression so dull that she looked just about ready to execute the world if it meant saving him. Her heart challenged to break every bone in her body as she bared her eyes on her father, who was grinning at her with his head tilted in the doorway. "What a truly, truly, inspiring sight." He clapped his hands, no emotion whatsoever on his features as he watched them. "*Daughter, daughter, daughter*, haven't you learned?"

Kylen's hand had dropped to hers as he heard that voice. He tried squeezing them, but his chest convulsed with the curse as the darkness began to pool into his eyes. "*No*—stop!" Althea begged, feeling so weak now that she was pleading with the devil.

"I cannot, child. I'm simply just removing an obstacle that was bound to leave us sooner than later. I'm speeding up the process. Can you really blame me for getting impatient?"

Althea shook her head as her hands hovered over his chest. She tried to focus on calling her magick, the magick she loathed, but her heart was too full and afraid that she was distracted from the task at hand. "*Stop*—please! I know you can stop this; I have seen you do it to me—please just take this curse from his soul, and I will go willingly with you."

"*Althea*—no." Kylen's words didn't sound like his words.

They were tiny, breaking down.

"How weak have you become, child? I thought that I raised you to be better than this?" The King shook his head as he held his hand up. "I guess we will have to get a move on with your death too."

She watched it as if her death was about to occur in a tiring dream. He raised his hand, the darkness circling it like eels swimming in a pool of blood. Althea didn't even try to react as his magick aimed for her. She felt too lost. Too scared. She had turned into the exact person that she used to laugh at. The exact mortal she made such unfair judgments about. Althea turned her head down to Kylen, her hair brushing over his body as she increased her hold on his hand. "It will—*it will be okay*."

She leant down, pressing a kiss to his forehead as she squeezed her eyes shut.

Althea had a heart, and she was now prepared to follow it into the afterlife.

She could feel the magick coming for her, and yet it never reached her because something—*someone* had stopped it. Althea looked up hurriedly, her eyes locking with Atticus as he stood by Sayah and Khatri's side.

"For love, right?" A muffled and restrained sob escaped from Atticus' lips as he laid sight on the boy in her arms.

"For love," Althea agreed, the words challenging her to a death by a thousand cuts.

"*I—I am going to kill you*," Sayah sneered with anger as her voice broke. Althea began to cry harder as she watched the siren look over at her son, such heartbreak in those golden eyes. "I am going to kill you for everything you did to my family. First Kylen, his parents—my friends, my boys, Khatri, my baby, Lilith and now Althea. I am going to send your soul right down to the pits of Hel, and you are going to suffer greatly for it all." For such words leaving her lips, Althea noticed the moment Khatri had realised what she had said.

Baby.

His face flattened, and he looked back to her father, such inevitable rage within those respectful eyes that she would have never noticed it if she had not seen his next moves.

Sayah's magick spiralled out as her arms laced with scales. She looked to the King as both Khatri and Atticus, as well as

Uzziah and Zaire, forged their magick with her. Althea knew that she had been alive for centuries now, but she never quite fully expected just what type of spells one would learn along the way.

Kylen's hand began to loosen on hers, and she looked back down as colours began to spiral out in the room before her. Althea felt terribly weak, *terribly weak, and vulnerable*, which were two feelings she hated most in this world. "—Forgive me, my love."

Althea had to lean down to hear him, but almost instantly, she nodded, her hand moving back to the hair that she gently brushed back. "Of course I do. I was just too stubborn before to tell you so." There were small speckles of light bursting from her fingertips, but it wasn't enough to end him of this misery. Death almost seemed like mercy.

Perhaps in this Realm, it was.

Kylen smiled weakly, a weak smile to his lips that brought one to hers, yet hers froze as she heard the final beat of his heart echo throughout her soul. "*Kylen?*" she gasped and began to shake him—the world freezing around her. "*No, this isn't funny* —Kylen?" His body did not react the way hers did as she began to push for him to wake up.

No, it just stayed limp beneath her very touch, and Althea let out a cry like no other. A wail that damned her mother for forcing two children to play the ruthless roles as heirs when all they wanted was to be friends.

"*No-no-NO!*" she leant over Kylen, holding him to her chest as her tears soaked into his shirt. Althea rocked the corpse back and forth, pleading with everything in her for him to open his eyes. She just wanted him to say one word. He could call her darling, love, beloved, anything. She didn't care—she just needed to hear his voice again. "Wake up, wake up, please, *I will do anything.*"

Mother is sad. Mother is hurt. Why aren't you helping me? Althea wanted to scream.

She damned her father for forcing the friendship to end. She damned him for killing the girl she loved and lost. Her whole world was full of pain—all pain that was directed to break her… and yet it was not that that broke her.

No, it was watching the people she loved suffer around her that truly tore her soul into two.

Althea's Markings began to glow, a burn to them as she forced herself to her feet. Her eyes moved to her father's, barely paying notice to her so-called brother, who watched in the doorway. Her father met her stare and Althea's dropped of emotion—of heartbreak.

She lifted her sleeves up, allowing her father to lay eyes upon the Markings she loathed. But now, she hated them for different reasons. Althea hated them because they had allowed Kylen to die. They had allowed him to leave her alone, and for the first time ever, that was not what she wanted.

The ground began to tremor beneath her, and the clouds radiated with lightning.

Althea Evangeline was a God, and she was going to kill him —s*he was going to kill them all.*

That wasn't a question nor a statement. It was a fact. Althea was going to burn the world for what *HE* had done to her. For what *HE* had put them all through.

Althea held out her hands before her as lighting met with them, and right as everyone began to stop fighting, she threw the menacing power at her father, watching as fear shone throughout his eyes.

Sayah, Zaire, Uzziah and Atticus all jumped out of her way, their eyes going straight to the body as sobs began to emerge through the air. Uzziah—to her shock was the first to rise to his feet, nodding towards her as if he was prepared to follow her into death.

"You cannot beat me, Althea. Do not even bother wasting your breath!"

Althea allowed his words to flow through her as if they were meaningless. She closed her eyes, feeling the curse that stunk so heavily on either side of the room. Althea didn't care what would happen to her—*she didn't care what would come of her name*. She was far past caring, and now destroying her father, and everything he loved seemed like a far grander plan.

Trails of twine extended from her chest, meeting both her father's soul and Kylen's at once. She felt the curse beneath it and how her father struggled to break free as he sent such horrible shadows her way. Sayah caught each one on her behalf. Her face was grief-stricken as she had just lost the boy she had practically raised.

Althea grabbed at the curse that murdered them both. The only difference was that Kylen didn't let the evil change him. He welcomed it and closed his eyes as his soul moved on. Her father, *he had become it*. And now, she was forcing it from his chest and into her own. She erupted with a scream that sent the Realms shattering beneath her and Althea felt the curse begin to seek comfort within her soul. She felt the darkness cloud her vision with her screams. She felt it make itself comfortable, and yet Althea did not allow herself to cower.

She was a God. She was a God. She was a God.

Mother was a God.

They say that all great Gods make a sacrifice for their people, and perhaps this was hers.

FORTY
KYLEN

He wanted nothing more than to believe the rumours. He wanted to believe Sayah when she said that death would be as easy as falling asleep, but now he knew the truth. Death was not as soft as it seemed; no, it was rather horrible if anything else.

Yet it had not been as bad when Althea had held him until his very last breath. Her precious tears wasted upon him despite all. What a twist of fate that truly was. The only burden he carried on his shoulders now was that they did not have time to make up for everything that he had put her through. He knew that he kept repeating those words and thinking them, but they were the words he had worked so hard on forming.

Because out of all twenty six letters in the alphabet, none of them was enough to make up for what he had done to her. It was going to follow him around with every step through the afterlife as he longed for a love that would never be gifted to him.

Kylen felt as if he was falling, his head meeting with the hard ground as the last few seconds of his sight searched for the girl who had managed to make everything feel far less daunting. Kylen looked to her as death met with him, as the gates to the afterlife opened and welcomed him with open cold arms. He saw his parents waiting with smiles, his two biological siblings in their forever young bodies standing by their sides.

How truly captivating that sight was.

None moved, all staying in the same place before his mother, at last, stepped forward. She approached him, her hand meeting with his heart. “She’s fighting for you. After all you did, she is fighting for you. Don’t betray her again by allowing yourself to die before your time.”

What she said made no sense to him. He was too fixated on the shape of her face to notice just what she was saying. Her face was changing, going from his mother smiling to Althea screaming. It was strange, truly strange. But he didn’t question it, not even as a hand-pulled him harshly into the opposite direction.

FORTY-ONE
ALTHEA

Althea felt as the darkness made a home within her soul. She felt the light within drain away ever so quickly. Her long, proud hair began to turn black, her nails, lips, eyes, all drained of colour as she begged the purity of her heart to flee with it.

Her father screamed and screamed as the others watched with such fear. Sayah watched as Zaire and Khatri held her back, holding her upright as she begged for Althea to stop. Repeating the same words repeatedly. "She's just a kid—She's just a kid." What a pity it was that she felt so devoted to Althea's life. *Didn't she realise that it had been doomed from the start?* That she had never truly been a child? Didn't they all realise that it had only been wasted time until Althea found her true self—*and what a glorious weapon that would be.*

Althea dragged her heavy head over her shoulder, finding Kylen's body as it flooded out with all the impurities that was *her* curse. He looked so frozen in time as if the future historians couldn't wait to get their hands on him, he who just had to be carved by the Gods themselves. His eyes dripped with the curse as it ran from his soul, and within seconds she saw the brown of them there again, a hand reaching out to her that welcomed her to the other side.

Althea noted every feature across his skin as the magick settled within. She noted the scars, the bruises, the wounds, the slight bump of his nose that appeared clearer on some days than others. She looked to his hair that she remembered braiding when they were twelve, and she vowed to him that she would be an extraordinary friend, what wasted potential that was.

She smiled as she thought over all those moments, reliving every moment that defined them today. And it was strange because she not only looked back at that and cried for revenge, but this time she looked back at it and almost purely smiled through her sobs.

Because fate had brought them back together again, and her soul was no longer wounded because of him.

She didn't want to die. She never had, but Althea supposed that if she was going to, she would make a moment of it. She was going to make the world remember her name.

Everything began to fade around her, and Althea allowed her head to fall back as ethereal silence greeted her for once in her life. But despite waiting for it, Althea didn't meet with the floor; instead, the same dragon that brought an outlandish feeling over her caught her swiftly, wrapping her into its arms as the roof above dared to crumble.

Althea fell as her eyes rolled back, feeling like the weight atop of her shoulders finally gained access to crushing her.

Her head hit the small, still standing ice-cold floor as everything went silent and the dragon surrounded her. The voices died. The magick that begged to be used died. And as Althea laid there with her dark hair surrounding her, she couldn't help but hold the thought that there was something more waiting for her the next time she opened her eyes.

The next time she dared to defy the world.

So, this was how it was going to end. Everything in her life had led to this moment; everything in her life had led her to death *herself*. Althea had tried to save Kylen's life from being washed away in the last few seconds of hers, but she never heard the beat of his heart return to him.

So perhaps in the next lifetime, things would be easier. Perhaps in the next life, she would be raised to be a killer instead of a lover. Because they always did say that love was the one thing that would bring the world to its knees, and it seems like just that was about to happen.

FORTY-TWO
KYLEN

Even as a little boy Kylen Noxwell had asked Zaire Esteria what it was like to be placed in the Realms of the in-between. He wondered if it was far less daunting than the Realms he had been born into. But now that he was there, he could see everything that was happening and yet not do anything about it—he realised that it was pure torture. He was in Hel.

A flash of lightning that rained from the storms above flashed down, and within a second, he could hear the lost beat of his heart again.

He opened his eyes against the world, steering away as it all became far too bright for him to handle. Kylen pushed himself up, leaning on his side as he coughed away the blood from his healing lungs. It dawned on him then just how quiet everything was. How there weren't any voices begging him to let the darkness win.

As quick as ever, his eyes moved to the body his family was all crowded around on the floor, and oh, how quick his heart sunk.

There Althea was, and her forever enchanting eyes were on him.

She looked so different, and yet she was still as beautiful as ever. Her features had changed, and now he carried the burden of not knowing what to do, how to react. What was one meant to do when they saw the soul whom they love, overcome with a darkness they knew everything about? What was he meant to do now that he realised that this pain in his chest was love?

True *fucking* love.

Althea's hair was still long. Except it was curled and black. Her lips had a dark red tint to them, the bags under her eyes hollower than they had been minutes before. Kylen noticed her hands as Sayah's tears hung over her, begging for the girl to awaken with the magick she pushed into her soul. Her hands were covered in dark veins, like a wildfire spreading to her soul.

He caught the flicker of movement over his shoulder, and he looked the other way, watching as the King he knew and wanted dead began to rise. Althea was going to be furious—*when she woke up*, which Kylen was sure she would. She would be furious that she hadn't been able to kill him.

Sayah's eyes slipped to his as he watched his movements of failure radiate from him as he struggled to his feet. Her face dropped of colour, and her eyes widened. His name was on her lips as a mere whisper, and yet she could not speak it because of the fear that consumed her body and soul.

Kylen couldn't seem to get the words out either, but Sayah could see what he was trying to say because her head too looked over her shoulder at the figure there, her eyebrows narrowed so finely as she planned his death in her mind.

The King no longer reeked of the curse; he had no magick within him whatsoever. His eyes went down to his hands before moving to Althea. He rose to his feet with such effort that Kylen was sure that the rest of Harlia was left to be doomed.

He snarled something under his breath, and Kylen quickly moved, pushing his weight from under him to try and reach them in time. But his body was still waking up; his soul was still healing. Kylen had to move quickly; he had to dance on his feet if he wanted to save them—*except his soul was covered in bruises*.

But then, miraculously, a figure took his place, and Kylen looked up and over from the pile of his blood to Uzziah, who held his sword of the Realms before him. "*Oh, I don't think so,*" he cooed. "You aren't going to lay a finger near my King nor my Queen, understand?"

Althea's father laughed. "They are both as good as dead, boy. Let me reach my daughter so that I can bring her back home."

It was Adonis who appeared out of the darkness that spoke this time, his eyes full of such power that he truly did look like a son of the Gods. "She is home."

The King had no chance to fight back, and to Kylen's satisfaction, he watched his breaths waste away as the dragon and Adonis captured him. Kylen slowly returned to the state of his body, and instantly, with the help of his brothers, Khatri and Atticus, he was moving towards Althea.

She laid in Sayah's arms like an angel laying upon the clouds of the next lifetime. Her face was so delicately placed that she looked to be wearing a mask. He couldn't believe what he was seeing. He couldn't believe that this girl here, the one that was so set on killing him, had healed *his* soul. *Kylen didn't want to believe it.*

Kylen always liked to say that he believed in the Gods. But truth be told, he stopped the moment he realised just how cruel the Realms were that he was born into.

He stopped believing in them the moment he had to leave Althea's presence behind on the other side of those wooden doors seven years ago.

Yet as Kylen laid eyes on Althea and his hands found her ice-cold cheeks, he knew that he had been in the presence of a God this whole time, and for once, there wasn't a minute where he didn't believe in her. No matter how he had claimed to do the opposite of just that.

"I'm afraid she's dead," Adonis whispered mournfully over his shoulders.

"But she's cold," Atticus whispered as his chest heaved. "You cannot be truly dead unless you are warm and dead." He was shaking his head, trying to wipe away the tears so that Kylen would not see them, and yet he did. Kylen realised then that the task he had given the boy had gone to use, and perhaps he had made Althea feel less alone in the last of her days—Gods knew that Kylen should have been the one to do that, and yet he had failed to even do that.

"I'm afraid her soul within has rotted, meaning that there is no longer warmth within there." Again, Adonis spoke about her as if *he* was in pain—as if *he* hadn't been objectifying her this whole time. Kylen turned up at him with such disgust, such distaste.

Kylen went to spit venom at the man, but Zaire beat him to it, and their question made Kylen want to crawl back into his grave and allow the vultures to pick at his soul as if that would be easier to undergo than this.

"Will she find the afterlife?"

Sayah's lips trembled now, and she looked up from Althea with an expression that echoed silence. "No. She will not." Sayah choked on a sob, and for the first time since he had returned, she didn't flinch out of Khatri's touch. "Her soul has rotted, and we are now left in a world without the Gods—*I failed.*" Sayah began to weep, her tears burning through the soil around her. "I'm sorry Kye, I'm so—*so* sorry."

Kylen wished never to hear again.

He wished never to see again.

Unless he was to lay his eyes upon her grace, the tone of her.

Or he was to hear the villainous melodies that escaped her lungs. How ungrateful he had been.

How was this the game that he was playing fair? That Althea was dead in a world that was meant to be hers, and he was alive in a world that wanted him dead. Now he was left to carry the guilt that he could already predict would drag him to her grave.

Sayah placed her hand on his shoulder, whimpering back the tears and letting go of Althea's limp hand that he swiftly swam for. How cold her beloved skin was. Kylen felt as if time had stopped—what was time when all you wanted to do was hide? How does time play a part in the world, then? It would keep going, and that was going to be the worst for Kylen. Because he did not think he could survive in a world where she was a mere memory. "Kylen, it's time. If we don't part with her soon, then the curse will escape from her chest, and the Kingdoms will burn."

"Let them burn."

"Kye, Althea is dead. She is *gone*."

EPILOGUE
THE DANCE OF DEATH AND THE REBIRTH OF NEW BEGINNINGS

"We mourn the loss of Queen Althea Noxwell, a true hero among all. She died saving us all from the curse, a true leader indeed. Her actions, her *choices*, will be remembered by all."

Those were the only words Kylen Noxwell had heard throughout the entire service. He couldn't bear to open his ears any longer after those lies. It was an injustice like no other. Didn't they realise that Althea hadn't had any choice over any of it? If she had, there might have been a chance that her heart would be still beating that glorious rhythm—standing tall and wearing her beauty with such true pride. Althea has—*had* that grace about her, and now he was wishing to be able to tell her that. That he saw how she wore her beauty as a shield—how truly inspiring that had been to witness first-hand.

How he had taken it for granted.

Kylen looked over his shoulder to the throne that sat cold at his side. His dull brown eyes scraping over it as if he had been the one to personally slice the dagger through her heart, watching as her eyes connected with his for the last time. But he hadn't been… he swore to never hurt her heart again, and yet she was no longer walking among these Realms. Leaving him to feel as if he had committed that treacherous act.

If only she knew how distraught his dreams had been, how he woke up every time his eyes fell cold in tears, throbbing sweat shielding his body as he reached for the body that was meant to be at his side.

She was meant to be holding his hands, giving him that look that made him feel like a child again. A type of giddiness that was far too far to reach, how his arms felt tired.

Zaire had commented the other day that he should be an expert by now at grief and dealing with it all; he always did manage to find the other end of it one way or another. Yet, he was anything but an expert; if anything, he felt as with time, he had gotten worse at coping.

Time always deceived him, tricking his mind and doing pirouettes before the browns of them. He always found himself forgetting just how hard it was. He forgot how consuming the waves were over his frail soul—yes, his soul had been freed now, but to what extent?

An extent he was not willing to make.

How could he have been so foolish? To fall in love with the girl he knew he could never have. The Gods had deemed them as rivals, enemies because of his own doing. She was Juliet and he was Romeo, going so far to hold a knife before his very heart in an attempt to rid himself of this pain, how it was insufferable. His dreams were full of her.

Those eyes, the oceans of them. Kylen had found peace amongst the seas, he had found himself after each loss, and for some obscure reason that was beyond his understanding, she had been born with the very eyes that resonated him with that feeling. That grounding that he felt each time he had been blessed to stare into them.

His days blended into one exhausting breath, each challenging him in unexplainable ways. Kylen didn't feel this way because he had the curse—no, he felt this way because he was mourning a life that he did not want to mourn for, and yet with every insufferable breath, he found his soul burning, his heart alight.

Did that make him cruel?

Did that make Kylen Noxwell a horrible human for not wanting to mourn any longer?

He felt as if his whole childhood had been one long, gigantic session of mourning. He felt as if it was never-ending. As if he was in a never-ending story.

First, his parents, how blinding his life had been. His siblings, how lonely his life had been. Then his brothers, how quiet his life had been. Then his Kingdom, how confronting his life had been. And now Althea—*why did this death seem to ache the most?*

He didn't want it to because he knew he didn't deserve her, not after he put his Kingdom before her.

Kylen was so blind back then; now he was prepared to sacrifice every life roaming this Realm if it meant that she would still be by his side, smiling as if they were both kids again, sitting silently on his bed, staring up at the stars and wishing for a beyond.

Kylen quietly entered his quarters, silently shutting the wooden doors behind him so that Sayah would not be alerted of his broken presence. He turned around, looking towards the stained glass that lay scattered across his floors. Trying to piece together the puzzle that had been floating through his hollow mind since arriving back at the docks of Lorundio, finding his Kingdom rebuilding themselves in the hope that their leaders would return unharmed. How he would never forget the way the people looked at him to see if Althea was there too.

The last day they had spent on the island of Harlia, he had spent doing anything in his power to distract himself from the tomb that laid below the very caste he stalked across. He went from room to room, searching and searching for the inevitable. Because what he was genuinely looking for was something —*someone* that was no longer in his grasp.

How trapped he felt.

That was how he found the crumbled church, laying surrounded by trees and wildlife, something so surreal that made it even more twisted to stand within. Kylen had entered through the church, and immediately, his eyes had caught onto those Harlian blue eyes. His heart had leapt a beat or two, and for a glimpse of a moment, his whole world stopped—and all he could do was stare. *However, then he realised that he was staring into the eyes of the stained-glass mural of Althea.*

And despite how the Gods had tried to convince him otherwise, he knew it was her, because he could see that gleam in her eyes. How the oceans reflected her inner wickedness.

Kylen approached the stained glass that leaned against the wall. Sometime across the decades, it had fallen, and yet it had not smashed, saved by the magick that Kylen could feel as he reached for Althea's cheek.

Only a few of the panels had smashed, but the ones with *him* too within the murals… had been saved.

There were two sheets of glass. The first being tinier murals of different scenes from her life.

Her birth.
Her mother's death.
The tests that assured her of no Elemental Magick… *how they had fibbed.*
Kylen's betrayal—his *darn* betrayal.
Eloise's 'death'.

Sneaking through Kylen's Kingdom, to being turned away by Erwin.

Althea's outburst—bringing his brothers back.

Kylen and Althea sharing a bed while her father lingered about.

Eloise's true death and fleeing to Harlia.

Their kiss.

How he had forced himself to forget that.

Kylen arriving at where Althea laid limp.

She had wanted more time. He had seen it in those frozen eyes and how he would never forget the single tears that ran down her cheek.

Then the after effects of her death. The darkness embraced her as if it was him; *how cruel could it be.*

From the left side of the room, his hand had been reaching for hers, and from the right side of the room, her hand had been reaching for his.

Because even in death, their souls knew that they were one. As if he was a new moon and she was the full moon that made him glow.

Then there was one last tile, one last picture that showed her sea glazed eyes full of a depth of darkness—something he was familiar with.

And how a part of him was grateful that she didn't have to fight against that evil.

Kylen looked down to the rest of the stained glass, all of which were smashed to pieces, leaving him unaware of what was to happen next in her apparent scripted life.

That made his stomach turn, knowing that the girl who should be here now, exploring the Kingdom where she could be happy, had been merely playing a role in a play for the mere amusement of the Gods, *Althea's mother.*

Besides the pictures, one large mural took up a large portion of his rug. Althea was pictured in the middle with her arms extended. The four goddesses surrounded her as their power drained into her slowly. If only he had figured it out sooner, if only he had realised her fate, perhaps he would have been able to find a loophole. There always had to be a loophole to things as dangerous as this… *so why wasn't there?*

Kylen ran his hands over his tense flesh as he sat on the edge of the sofa. Pushing away the thin woven blanket his mother had made him lifetimes ago.

He could feel that his family knew of his suffering. But not one of them said anything; *not one of them mourned the way his heart did.* Sure, Atticus left fresh flowers at her memorial every day. Khatri made sure to keep her room untouched. Chloe followed Kylen around in fear that he would do something reckless. Zaire and Uzziah stayed quiet, and Sayah… Sayah was often found in that same room Khatri protected, holding onto one of the girls' dresses and silently crying because time was not in their favour.

Not anymore.

How could he explain this feeling?

Kylen Noxwell, King of Lorundio, had his heart longing for the daughter of the man that he had vowed to kill the moment he became aware that *his* curse—the curse he had stolen from Erwin and his brother (who were both still missing) had killed his parents. Althea wondered why he did what he did, and yes, he could have told her that, but it wasn't just that that affected him so immensely. It was all the evil he had done that made the words trapped in his throat ache with every breath. He could have told her, but then how different was he from *him*—her father? He had left Althea for dead, had he not? The only difference was that that burden followed him like an old cat, the same white cat that slept on Althea's side every night.

Kylen's eyes were buried in the depths of his palms, rubbing away the exhaust that stretched behind. He stayed like that for the rest of the night, sheltering himself from the rain that mourned for the loss he knew would drive him to insanity.

It was around sunrise when a knock at his door had his eyes meeting with the head that appeared there. Uzziah stood tall, his eyes away from the darkness as he cleared his throat. "The King is in the throne room; he demands to talk to you, Kye."

"Why is he out of his cell?" Kylen bared, a rumble of a dark sneer coating his lips.

"He demanded it to be urgent… *and well*, we had to keep him away from Sayah who was prepared to skin him of his flesh." Uzziah explained, still noticeably avoiding his gaze.

Kylen studied him for a moment, his eyes curving over every bone in his body before sighing a deep, *heavy* sigh. "Very well, *I do owe him a visit today."*

The air was cold as he crept through it; a smell so dark that he had stupidly assumed that it was the King who reeked of *death.* Kylen approached where *her* father stood, eyeing him down before Atticus threatened the old King to spit his words out. A push of his blade at his backside.

"I want to offer you a bargain."

Such humour erupted through his heart and Kylen looked to the floor with a shake of his head. But of course, he couldn't help but drag his eyes back up to the King with a groan so sour. "You… *want to offer me*… a bargain?" It was ignorant, arrogant, and awfully obnoxious. How Kylen was going to enjoy ripping his eyes from their sockets tonight. "*What in your fucking stupid mind thinks that I*—the man you have done everything to destroy, is going to make a bargain with *you*?" Kylen asked as the man held his stare unblinking. "*You are fucking insane.*"

"Your Kingdom has gone through *so* much within these past few weeks. You owe it hope, *you owe it*—"

"Yeah, and I wonder who ripped it of it in the first place. You crushed my Kingdom's hope when you decided to throw a bloody tantrum." Kylen growled back in response, his words slicing through the air and sending the very windows rattling. Kylen looked to them, looking to the storm that hadn't stopped pouring since *her* death. He could feel the other presences on either side of him, Uzziah, Sayah, Khatri, Atticus and Zaire, all watching the King down as if they could feel his every thought.

"I did what I had to. That's what a war is, son. Now, I want to make you a bargain. If you agree to let my Kingdom reign in peace and free me *now* of your ways: I will fight with you against the King of the East."

The way the old man's voice travelled its way around his every bone had Kylen laughing. It was pathetic, *truly*. He turned his tiring old gaze back onto him, grief-stricken humour to his voice as he spoke, "The King hasn't even declared war yet."

"Oh, but he will. The moment he learns that the curse is gone he will come for us all—it was the only thing holding him back." The King watched Kylen with such determination in his eyes, noting down every emotion Kylen no longer cared to keep hidden. His heart had been ripped apart and skinned, and now his mind was far past caring about anything as pathetic as that.

Kylen looked to be thinking as he dragged his gaze over his shoulder, barely paying any attention to all of the eyes on his. "If war is declared, then I do say that we could make a rather good team," Kylen trailed on, slowly raising his hand towards the male before him. Sayah made a sound of shock, however Zaire held her back. "As I do need—"

"Yes, I agree, son." The King answered almost immediately, meeting Kylen's hand halfway. His flesh was cold, the bones of his hands poking into the blood of Kylen's. The air seemed to freeze around him, but Kylen paid no notice to that.

If only he had looked towards the doorway and met with those troubled, pained, yet ocean like eyes that stared through the crack of the entry. If only he listened to the way the wind feared for the girl's life which was now on the line.

Althea Evangeline, the girl who was fighting away the curse that lived in her lungs with every breath, took two steps back, her eyes dark with something of a feeling she had grown to know all too well over these fatal years. *Kylen Noxwell was not doing this to her again.* She had defied death for him—travelled across seas and used all these new abilities just so that she could reach him again; *and now he was punishing her with this?*

Mother should learn to listen.

It hadn't made sense to her to why she was alive. Not until she decided to listen to what the voices were saying, to truly hear what their whispers carried. They never intended to kill her; they were just preparing her physical body to claim as their own as her magick was all that they wanted. All that Adonis Evermore had wanted.

But Althea was never someone to allow another to get their own way.

Adonis' scent had been seeping across every wall within that old cruel room, and yet Althea had not been blessed to claim his death as her own as he had already fled. Leaving her to drown in the darkness that the chains kept her within.

She had found his pet and whether it was this dark, cruel magick that wielded itself to her every touch, or whether it was her change of heart, Adreasteia had flown her across the seas, searching for the boy she was now going to give another chance to.

However now her heart was frozen, slowly sealing over with a villainous curse as her emotions drew a noose around her throat.

Kylen had betrayed her,

and that betrayal had allowed her heart to be vulnerable for a second too long.

Every little splinter of her spine became trapped behind bars as the spirits of the cursed danced across her bones. This was what they needed to claim her body as their own, they had needed her heart to break; and now it had.

Her soul drifted into the cold wind as Althea blinked and her eyes became a darkness beyond the night. Her hair had always been black since she had awoken again, but now there were shadows to it, seeping around every curl.

The spirits smiled and a large smile crept onto Althea's cheeks as she turned away. If only Althea—*the true, real, Althea,* who was now trapped in a tiny cage, hidden away in the depths of her cursed soul, had seen what Kylen had done next.

"If war is declared then I do say that we could make a rather good team… as I do need something pathetic enough to use as bait to feed to the other side." And with that, Kylen had pulled on the King's hand and tugged him forward. His other hand had balled into a fist, and he had punched him across the face, feeling as his cheek bone threatened to shatter beneath his eternal pain. Kylen had taken multiple steps back before he kicked the old King in the gut, watching with cruel eyes as blood coated his dark tiles. "Take him away, *now*."

☽

There was a new presence on the grounds that Sayah Linix had felt through the wind of the night. She had been following it the moment she felt the blade on her throat slice its way through her flesh as she fought the pains of her dreams. Sayah had felt and held onto the presence of the *Queen of Gods*, holding it so tightly as she opened her eyes and found blood pooling at her sides.

Sayah sat up quickly, choking while swallowing down the fear and blood in pure crimson panic. Her eyes widened and yet furrowed as she knew not to present herself to be so scared in front of such a force. *The curse was practically dripping off of the girl she wanted to reach to.*

The girl that stood before her didn't look like the girl she remembered. She wore dark hair and darker eyes. Dark black veins seeping through her throat as she stared down at her. She didn't look like the girl Sayah remembered, but she wasn't about to assume that Althea Evangeline had allowed the darkness to win.

Althea flexed the blade along Sayah's jaw, watching as the blood danced across her quivering skin. Her eyes watching as her shadows extended up to Sayah's bare throat, a hint of amusement to them as the girl of many voices chuckled softly.

"Hello," Althea forced herself to say. "Long time, no see."

Sayah tried to speak, but only blood met her tongue. "Don't waste your breath." As the words left her lips Althea closed her eyes for a moment, flinching to something or someone that Sayah could not see, *not hear*. "She's sorry." Althea blurted as she opened her eyes again, revealing the dark blue of them which was screaming for help from the siren whose magick was no longer hers to command. "She tried to argue against us, but we wouldn't listen—*we wouldn't hear what she had to say.*"

Althea turned on her heel, running a hand through her dark black hair and Sayah knew that whoever it was that was speaking to her was not the girl that she had wished to raise. "Don't take this death personally, woman of the sea, it is merely to send a message towards the King who is burying his nose in a hole that is already doomed."

Sayah shook her head, and her vision wavered; however, she forced it away. She needed to help this girl—*the girl that made her silently cry with relief as blood stained her clothes.* "Al—"

Althea whose soul reeked of the curse turned back to her and shook her head, wiping at her blood as she tried to take a step forward to reach her—*to save her*. But then something shot throughout her soul—*Sayah could feel the energy,* but it was gone as quick as it was there. And now, the immortal siren was staring into the eyes of a dead girl.

A girl who had the cursed spirits living in her.

"We will find a good resting place for you in the afterlife, woman of the sea; you, and your daughter—*it will be sweet indeed*. We are not that much of a monster."

She guided the siren down, patting her head as her vision turned to darkness, meeting the bright light with the laugh of a child who had Sayah's eyes and Khatri's smile. Althea, who was trapped somewhere within her soul, fell against the bars of the cell of her mind; listening to the halt of the siren's heartbeat as the curse took over hers. Tears dripped down her cheeks, and yet she did not flinch, she did not falter, no, instead she watched as her body began its journey to Aeonia, the Kingdom the spirits were going to burn.

The girl that looked to be Althea looked over her shoulder as she fled Lorundio's grounds, gazing over towards the memories *she* had once begged to forget and yet now held onto because everything was a mere blur. Her body wasn't physical and her magick didn't respond to her calls: but Althea knew that she was alive. She had to be. The curse and the spirits that roamed within the darkness had control of her physical body, trapping her to the cell of her mind, *her soul*.

The spirits wanted her to forget everything. They did all that they could to get her to forget *everything*. And perhaps she had forgotten some things—such as the whisper of his name, the memories of her life, the world that she had been forced to burn through at such a young age... But now, she held onto everything that *mattered*. The curse that traced every inch of her body had failed to wipe the memories of her heart, the one cage within her body that could not wipe the trace of *his love*.

Althea, the true Althea who was a prisoner within her own body stared at the same spot on the prison wall, planning a revenge that would have the curse and all of its spirits begging for mercy. Her heart was full and yet it was not weak, *Althea would not allow herself to be as such*. There was a boy who her heart whispered of. However, his name was not clear to her, and his words were not loud enough to hear.

Yet there was one realisation that came with the trace of his jaw, the bump of his nose, and that was that death do us apart wasn't a promise.

It was a curse.

Acknowledgments

Let me begin by saying to you, to whoever is reading this, I acknowledge you, and I am forever grateful that you are reading my work. This story has consumed me for the past several years. It is a story I have been desperate to tell, and I am thrilled to be able to finally share it. This book is going to be a part of a series, and I hope that throughout it, you find peace, love, hope, and strength in the characters. I hope this book gives you what you are searching for.

Firstly, I must thank those of you who bought my vision to life; my editor Alex Halverson, your eyes are truly 'magick' and I don't know what I would have done without you. To my cover artist, Miriam Schwardt, I thank you endlessly for creating the cover of my dreams.

I am eternally grateful to my family and friends who have been by my side from the beginning. You have put up with my endless book talk (everyone knows that is all I talk about), and I am so appreciative. To my parents who have supported me through it all and always believed in my abilities, thank you for giving me the courage to follow my dreams and confidence to take the chance. To my siblings who are mostly too young to read this book, I can't wait to read it to you when you are older, and I hope you share my passion for reading and writing. To my friends from school, I appreciate you all acting as if you knew what I was talking about when I constantly spoke about Gods, Elemental Realms, Souls and Magick in class. I will forever be grateful for your encouragement.

Now, to some special acknowledgments. This book is dedicated to my grandparents, John and Glenda Schubert. I will forever be grateful for the love and support you have given me throughout my life. You have been nothing but encouraging and supportive in everything I have ever done, and I love you both beyond words. Your interest in my book (and future books) motivated me and kept me going, even when at times, the end seemed so far away. You will never know how much it meant to me when you both told me how proud you were and how you could not wait to read my book. You have always been my biggest supporters. Pa, I love that I share your love for reading and writing and I hope to be half the writer you are. Nana, one of my fondest memories is growing up listening to you read to me. You both have had such a strong influence on my life, and I hope to always make you proud.

To my mum, I am so grateful that you have always believed in me and encouraged me to reach for the stars. You are so important to me and will always be my best friend. Thank you for all that you do for me. I love you forever and always.

To Ian Campbell, for always sending me the sweetest messages and showering me with love and support throughout it all. I love you.

To Sofia Alonso, you were there in that tiny classroom in year nine, where I randomly decided to try my hand at writing. I had so many crazy ideas and I had no idea if I could bring them to life, but you believed in me. Our friendship means the world to me, and I love you so much. I can't wait for our future adventures together, where we travel the world.

To Steph Pinwill, my friend since the beginning. Thank you for all the early morning chats and for listening to my long painful book talk rants. Whether I was happy or sad, anxious or excited, you always knew what to say and how to make me feel better. I will forever value our friendship.

To Chloe, my darling cat that passed away during the writing of this book. You spent 18 years on this earth, but may you forever live on through this series.

While writing this book there were a few artists I would listen to on repeat. These artists included: Taylor Swift, the God herself. Gracie Abrams, an Angel on earth. Phoebe Bridgers, a beautiful Soul. And lastly, Conan Gray and Olivia Rodrigo, who made the long nights a little less lonely. Thank you for the inspiration.

Finally to my readers, never could I have imagined a nicer and more supportive group of people. Many of you I have spoken to over the years on social media and your excitement and encouragement was next level. I often floated ideas online, never expecting in a million years to get the response I got. You made me so excited to bring these characters to life and I knew you would love them just as much as I did. To my beta readers, I hope you know that your comments and annotations made my day. You input was much appreciated.

I have so many worlds in my mind; some bought to life in this book, and some yet to be bought to life. I can't wait to travel this journey with you.

Thank you, Sienna xoxo

www.ingramcontent.com/pod-product-compliance
Lightning Source LLC
Chambersburg PA
CBHW020245120726
47904CB00001B/102

* 9 7 8 0 6 4 5 4 5 2 2 0 4 *